THE RIGHT GUARD

A Novel

by

ALEXANDRA HAMLET

Foxboro Press LLC
Annapolis

This is a work of fiction.
Only the articles at the lead of chapters 1-38, 72 (with references at the back of the book) are from actual events. Otherwise, all names, characters, places and incidents in the body of the book either are the product of the author's imagination or are used fictitiously, and any resemblance to actual persons, living or dead, business establishments, events or locales is entirely coincidental.

Foxboro Press LLC
1997 Annapolis Exchange Parkway, Suite 300
Annapolis, Maryland 21401

Published in 2012

Library of Congress Cataloging in Publication Data
Hamlet, Alexandra E
The Right Guard
Includes references.
LCCN: 2011931721
ISBN: 978-0-9846493-0-3 (Original Edition)
ISBN: 978-0-9846493-3-4 (Special Edition)

Printed in the United States of America

Acknowledgments

Few authors are solely responsible for the content and publication of a book. It takes legions of talented people editing, contributing, making suggestions, being supportive when you think you just are not going to get there. It also takes friends and family who keep your spirits up and the prize of a finished product, in sight. There are too many to mention and thank here. If your name is not here, I did not forget you, I merely honored your request to remain in the background or stay anonymous. For some of you, please know how deeply I appreciate your service to our country and your insight throughout my pages.

I met Rowena Farrar too many years ago to remember. She was my first editor for novel and article writing. She was the founder and President of the Richmond, Virginia Branch of the National League of American Pen Women, accomplished women in arts, letters and music. An accomplished short story writer and novelist herself and also the wife of a USAF Colonel, we shared a great deal of similarities in later life. 'Ro,' was a fabulous friend, editor, mentor and teacher of writing. Though long passed away, she greatly influenced the beginning of this effort.

Virginia "Ginny" Barnes Price and I met over 22 years ago. She traveled with me internationally when I lectured throughout the world on business and culture. She was my "nanny" when I entered Harvard's graduate school in Anthropology, as a rather mature adult. She loves to remind me of that hot summer day some years ago when I asked if she could help me type the 'final draft.' What started out as business became a great friendship. We became fun co-conspirators on life's journey and it remains to this day.

John Sano, former Deputy Director of the National Clandestine Service, CIA was of tremendous assistance and kept me in line with the validity of my material. With his help and strong guiding hand, I will be forever grateful to him for his professionalism, patience and humor throughout my feeble attempts at appearing knowledgeable and trying to ask poignant questions.

Brigadier General Donald Streater, USAF Ret. with whom I worked alongside in defense and respect to the utmost, offered his expertise in technical editing with ammunitions and firearms. Colonel Robert M. Johnston, USAF Ret. was one of the first to read Right Guard and he offered excellent suggestions and encouragement when the work was in its infancy.

My own family, brothers Walter, Richard, Thomas and Joel; the wonderful help from my sister-in-law, Suzette Bradley and my step children Jon-David, Jessica, and Andrea—my thanks for their loving support. My husband, David, lent support and encouragement when there was little. David, [retired USAF Colonel and a United States Air Force Academy graduate] tirelessly went through more edits that any spouse should have to. He gave support, suggestions and constant loving reassurance to a wife struggling to get a book into print. I can never thank him enough.

Mother taught me to think out of the box and to follow my dreams. My father launched me into the world to seek answers to satisfy an insatiable curiosity. I asked him once, "Papa, what do you want me to be?" He answered, "Honey, I don't care *what* you do in life . . . whatever it is, just *do it damn well.*"

I wish he could be here to help celebrate this effort and my first novel. I still miss him terribly.

AH

DEDICATION

This book is dedicated to all those, known and unknown, who are now serving or have served in the service and/or protection, of the United States of America.
My deepest appreciation and thanks for your service and sacrifices.
May you always find safe passage home, be secure in the knowledge that your sacrifice was not in vain and find peace.

AH

"There is hardly an instance of an intact army giving rise to a religious, revolutionary or nationalist movement. On the other hand, a disintegrating army—whether by orderly process of demobilization or by desertion due to demoralization—is fertile ground for a proselytizing movement."

Eric Hoffer,
THE TRUE BELIEVER

CHAPTER 1

[Rip-offs From U.S. Arms Stockpiles: Will It Be An A-Bomb Next?—. . . American military bases are being plundered of thousands of weapons and explosives, despite increasingly tough security measures. Losses from U.S. bases worldwide include rifles, pistols, grenade launchers and even surface-to-air missiles and antitank rockets. . . . All told, more than 11,000 military weapons have been reported officially as stolen in the last six years. Thousands more have simply vanished, but theft cannot be proved. Conventional ammunition may be disappearing faster yet – at the rate of 1 million or more rounds a year. Defense security officials say they have no reliable estimate because of a lack of precise record keeping. . . . The Defense Department has 6.2 million small arms spread around the world today, ranging from .22-caliber pistols to 81-mm mortars. The Army alone has more than 19,000 separate stockpiles of guns and ammunition. . . . Congressman Herbert [Louisiana] recently asked, "What can we think when the Pentagon tries to wipe out a loss of 450 machine guns as a bookkeeping mistake?" . . . Who steals the weapons? . . .—U. S. News & World Report] [1]

April 12, 1978

The rape always came back in Eric's nightmares. It tormented and haunted him in those early morning hours when it's hazy about what is real and what is an hallucination. The terrible dream was always the same. Eric was a young boy again, living with his family

1

in a retention camp Quonset hut in southern Germany. Something called "war" is over. His father, Field Marshall Adjutant Count Frederick vonErhenrich, is serving his time along with other German officers, rebuilding a devastated Europe under the direction of the allied forces. Eric tries to eat a meager dinner of some starchy substance he can't identify or remember. His father slowly rises to answer the loud pounding on the door of their cold, sparse quarters. The door is thrown open and a drunk, unshaven American captain pistol whips his father and throws him out into bitterly cold deep snow, made even more miserable by the freezing rain. An equally slovenly American sergeant points a gun at the shivering man's pale temple then kicks him in the stomach repeatedly as he struggles to get up. His father cries out in pain then yells to them in German, "Eric, Hans, help your mother. Protect her. Anna, run!!"

Even with the drab, loose-fitting gray woolen clothes and the misery of the camp, Countess Alexia vonErhenrich has maintained her poise and appeal, a lush-figured, golden-haired beauty still striking. Her proud, thin face streaked with tears as her slender fingers scratch at the gunman's jacket, trying to pull him away from her husband. The captain slaps her hard across her face and throws the elegant woman back inside.

Eric is only four, his brother thirteen and his sister ten, but the three bite and punch at the obscene intruder now groping for their mother and yelling words in English they don't understand. The sergeant pulls them away from their mother and forces them outside. His mother's screams from the hut tear at Eric's heart. Finally, the noise has summoned three other weary German captives of the allied retention camp.

Struggling through the deep snow from their personal cramped huts, in nightclothes and without protection from the fierce cold, the three ex-German officers yell and move swiftly to overpower the drunken American sergeant then enter the hut and jerk the grunting captain off his mother. She tries to cover her breasts, bruised and bloody from the attack. Her vacant eyes follow the rapist as she slowly covers herself then struggles outside to help her battered husband, her torn dress flapping in the bitter cold wind.

Eric can taste the salty blood in his mouth from biting the raging man's leg.

He gazes out the Quonset door where the heat escapes and the winter gusts whip through the cramped un-insulated hut. He stares at the man standing, hiding in the shadows smoking a cigarette, silently watching everything. As the silhouette draws in air and the hot cigarette ash glows, a shimmer of light reveals for an instant the man's face.

Wolfgang Shumacher, one of the German officers frantically hailed by Eric's father, also turns toward the figure in the shadows. Eric strains over and over again to see the figure's eyes and the shape of his face, but he only sees wisps of smoke then the man melts away.

His sister, Anna, sobs. His brother Hans holds a silent, resentful rage; his own boyish face purple with anger.

His recurring dream of the rape now shifts . . . . Still deep in his trance-like reverie, Eric sees a silver plane carrying the family from Germany to snow-covered Greenland then to the United States. The rutted fields of the retention camp near Munich transform into lush green Virginia mountains, replacing a little boy's bleak memory of wooden barracks squatting in mud holes. His new simplified last name, Brent, sounds strange and so short. He asks his father why they are going to live in the land of their enemy. His father, quiet and taciturn, doesn't answer.

The dream erupts and fast-forwards again. Eric sees a note roughly tied around a stone, amid scattered glass in the family's living room. "Nazi go home," it says in a primitive mountain scrawl.

The loud sound in his head of more smashing glass suddenly awakens him. Eric bolts upright, breathing heavily until finally his heart slows and he sits up on the side of the bed, motionless. It was a nightmare that was far more memory than dream, but that was not the worst of it. Every time he got a "personal and immediate" message from the Central Intelligence Agency in Langley, Virginia—it triggered the nightmare's return.

CHAPTER 2

[Big Cache of Guns, Ammo Stolen from Guard Armory, Enough weapons and ammunition to outfit a full Army company have been stolen from a National Guard armory in Suburban Compton, authorities reported today. "It's frightening to think that this (arsenal) would fall into the wrong hands," said Compton Police Sgt. W.H. Williams. "It appears that the theft was a highly organized thing . . ."—Charleston Daily Mail, West Virginia] [2]

Richmond, Virginia's summer heat—a vast humid veil—hung over the city and reflected early waves of misery from the hot pavement. Eric felt the heat through the soles of his shoes as he left the law office and walked along Main Street, the "Wall Street" of Virginia's southern capital city. This was a freak day for April, one usually cool and rainy. The old people of Richmond knew these freak days to be predictors for summer. Coming was 'hell's furnace' with plenty of hot Sunday afternoon sermons and stifling picnics where people prayed for afternoon showers to "cool things down."

The messenger's face had been a blank slate—no memorable features. He was as nondescript and bland as cardboard; the way CIA headquarters at Langley liked them. Dressed in a grey suit and carrying a black brief case, he bumped into Eric Brent in front of 'Bradfords on Main', an expensive stationery store for Richmond's elite. With a weak apology, he mumbled, "Langley, *now*," . . . the words for Eric were like ragged fingernails drawn across a blackboard: irritating and too familiar.

Eric's hand shot up to his injured shoulder. The "bump" was intentional and hard. Eric gazed into the store window and searched the reflecting glass panes scanning for someone watching, suspicious glances, and odd movements of someone in a crowd. He reached inside his jacket and felt something wet and sticky. Damn . . . his wound was bleeding again.

Though he had little time for most lawyers, Eric's visit to the attorney was fruitful. They were necessary for the mire of legalities if he had even the slightest chance of hanging on to his invention. Carrying the drafts of his first gun prototype under one arm, his normally cautious nature was further rubbed raw by the unwanted summons from the Agency. Three blocks away he found a pay phone in a small coffee shop.

John Ross, CIA's Chief of the Special Operations Group (SOG), an elite paramilitary element in the agency's Special Activities Division, (SAD) wanted to see him *immediately*. It was his third attempt to reach Eric in two days. Since Eric made himself *unavailable*, a "foot soldier" was sent out to find him. "Let's do it right, shall we?" Ross said. "Come in on the back side."

As a member of SOG, the SAD also displayed the group's strengths of agility, adaptability and lethality. While some of the others he worked with came from military or paramilitary backgrounds, Eric was drawn from within the ranks of the CIA's Directorate of Operations. The Special Operations Group, and particularly its Special Activities Division, were considered to be some of the most skilled and lethal forces in the world. Even so, answering a direct call from a Chief at Langley was the type of call that still makes a case officer's guts churn: simple, immediate and to the point. Worse yet, it was at Langley instead of a local office or a prearranged meeting location. Eric's familiar nightmare was a premonition of the meeting with Ross at the agency.

CHAPTER 3

[Gigantic Theft Of Weapons From Armory, LOS ANGELES (AP)-Enough weapons and ammunition to outfit a full Army company were stolen from a National Guard armory in suburban Compton, and authorities feared that the theft was the work of terrorists, a chief investigator in the case said today . . . . Missing items included 96 M16 rifles, seven M60 machine guns, eight M79 grenade launchers, one .45-caliber automatic pistol, 15 bayonets, 3,360 rounds of .50-caliber bullets, 1,000 rounds of 7.62-caliber bullets, 45 rounds of .45-caliber ammunition, 40 grenades, 16 smoke grenades and 100 riot grenades. Authorities said 75 gas masks also were missing. An FBI agent said the quantity of weapons and ammunition could fully equip an Army combat company.

Investigators said entry to the armory was through a side door and a vacuum drill was used to pierce the weapons vault, which an armory sergeant recalled locking at 10 a.m. Wednesday. An Army official said that the firing pins had been removed before the weapons were placed in storage in a vault. The pins were kept in another vault, which apparently was not entered. Lt. Col. Andrew Wolf, public relations officer for the Military Department in Sacramento, said in a telephone interview that this is standard practice when armories are left unattended. "Unless they find replacement pins, the guns would be useless without the firing pins in them," Wolf said. However, Compton police officials said acquiring replacement firing pins would not be much of a problem . . . .—Oakland Tribune, California] [3]

April 14th

An aging, thick-necked ex-case officer assigned to chauffeur Eric to Ross' office at CIA headquarters wheeled hard past the back gate at the intelligence complex in Langley. Eric wanted to drive himself, but Ross wouldn't hear of it. The wind rustling Eric's blondish hair irritated him as it blew across his ruggedly handsome face.

His ice-blue eyes were unflinching, as they reflected the late morning sun slipping behind an overcast sky.

The driver's overhanging belly jostled at each quick turn. Then he swore, hunting for an open slot to park. Twice he came upon what looked like a good spot only to find a small sports car or motorcycle nestled deep in the parking place.

Eric was shot on his last assignment with the Agency. Leaving his buddy and fellow case officer face down in the mud and running was unthinkable and the next slug got him. No matter what they taught him at The Farm, CIA's operative training school in Eastern Virginia, he could not leave his partner behind. He moved fast and if he had taken a second slower than the eternity that it took to crouch and drag his colleague over to a dry ditch, a third round would have ended Eric's 38 years.

As it was, the piercing pain radiating from his twice-festered right shoulder reminded him that a case officer's worst enemy is bad timing. The constant even-paced throbbing challenged his breakfast again and he tried to think of something else. When the driver made two sharp turns around the lot, Eric bobbed about the seat like a Bozo doll. His injury had made him more aware of his second weakness, an old intestinal hit in Viet Nam, and Eric hated it.

Had his father been shot during the Second World War? He couldn't remember. What few treasured war stories that survived his growing up lacked details. What stayed with him was the tall, proudly upright image of his father. Even in Hitler's army, he had no master. He once sent a trainload of hungry, freezing Jews in the wrong direction, away from the camps and certain death. On too many other occasions he disobeyed orders for humanitarian reasons. He protested to Hitler's henchmen that he misunderstood the orders, but his disobedience finally caught up with him. Two of his father's young soldiers ordered to shoot him on sight could not carry it out. The war was ending and the two young men refused to be part of one more insane dictate. Once they confided the orders to Count vonErhenrich, he helped them escape to the allies. The man's honor and the respect he commanded from his junior officers saved him once more from doom.

The sour ex-case officer gave up and delivered his "cargo" at the back entrance, where he jerked the car door open. Eric placed one unsteady foot on the asphalt. He grabbed his drafts and waited for his stomach to catch up. The other leg out, he held the door handle and slowly rose. Eric glanced back at the irritated driver to make sure he would wait, then scanned the front of the complex that always reminded case officers of a shining experimental data lab—a sort of governmental house of horrors. He did not want to come. On the outside, the Central Intelligence Agency's buildings were neat and trim. Inside, life was sterile. Langley was polished brass and tiles with information too organized and people too efficient—it always rubbed him the wrong way. For strays like him, to be called into Langley made most C/Os [case officer] skin crawl, watching their "caged" bureaucratic counterparts amble about the hallways with computer statistics and meeting plans carried in spa-tanned hands.

Langley was like any other large and powerful corporation. There were power players, bright young achievers on their way up, and manipulating supervisors. Some hid in crevices waiting retirement while others were on their way out—outcasts who overstepped some unnamed boundary. Their stock in trade was information and control. Instead of mergers and acquisitions they dealt in over-throws, takeovers, influence and arrangements of elimination. Eric understood the intelligence games so clearly. His father taught him well about survival in a mad system.

Eric slowly, apprehensively, made his way onto the second floor, finally entering his boss' office. Ross' secretary, Amanda, a long-time veteran of the bureaucratic wars, waved him through the door.

Muscular and still lean, approaching his mid-forties, Ross' short, steel-gray hair tapered close around his taut, tanned face. The deep creases bordering his thin lips rarely gave way to a smile. His grayish-blue eyes always appeared to Eric as if he were holding back some great secret . . . and Ross had spent 15 years cultivating that impression. The Chief reached out and slapped Eric's back. A gesture of affectionate welcome? No. Catching Ross' expression, Eric suspected it was part of some typically sadistic test. He could not help flinching but managed a nervous smile and a deep breath before collapsing in the nearest chair. *Ross knew about the shoulder.*

" 'Oh, I'm doing just fine,' " the Chief coolly mimicked an earlier phone call with Eric. He drew his arms close to his chest and leaned against his desk. Its smooth lines and uncluttered modern walnut design lent an air of "strictly business." The plush blue carpet and four signed western-styled prints of horses were Ross' way of reminding Eric of his position with the Agency.

Eric knew what was coming next; another in the long series of bitches about his shoulder.

"This is the second time it's opened to drain. You can't blame that on an inept surgeon." Ross' voice was superficially calm, like a dam holding back a crested river. "If you had stopped working you'd be healed." Ross found his pipe, and lit it, flicking the match into the ashtray. It was another of those annoying little mementos from a former agency director that Ross loved to point out, to anyone who would listen. Settling back down behind his desk, he puffed little gray clouds of brandy-scented smoke, fixing his eyes on the wounded shoulder.

Ross anchored his foot on an opened lower desk drawer. It was the same drawer where everyone knew his ex-wife's picture lay, face up. She probably knew it, too. Ross never talked about Miriam, not even when she flew in from California to carve on his heart again and wheedle out more money. What could he say? It was hard to create illusions when you worked in a place where people's training and passion were in the unveiling of lies and secrets.

"You still working on that private project of yours?" asked Ross, his creased face expressionless.

Eric nodded.

"How does that gun concept work again? What is it you're doing with it?"

"It's a liquid fuel-injected gun," Eric answered. Somehow it was better to never volunteer more than they ask for.

Chief Ross continued digging. His pipe held too tightly between his teeth, re-lighting the rough-cut tobacco. It took three tries to light the pipe's bowl. "Got a Hollywood name for it?" asked Ross. "Must have some glitz if you want it to be popular." He glared at Eric through the flame.

It was more information than Eric wanted to give, but finally he said, "Yeah, H-PAR."

"Meaning . . .?" Ross just wasn't going to let him off easy.

"Hypergolic-Propulsion Actuated Round," said Eric, cringing at what he felt was going to be a barrage of questions that he did not want to answer. Ross surprised him and just asked, "Does it work?"

The man can really be a pain in the ass, thought Eric, but then replied evenly. "Brannen Technology doesn't lend out its best metallurgist and seals experts if it thinks something isn't going to make it."

"Well," Ross replied, "you seem to have the big boys interested."

"So it seems." *So, Ross had heard the gossip at the complex.* Eric reached in his pocket and pulled out a folded envelope. He threw it across the desk.

Ross picked up the envelope and glanced at the return address. "Wolfgang Shumacher . . . he was a friend of your father's, wasn't he?"

Eric said nothing.

"He still at NASA?"

"He's in their propulsion lab now."

"You going to see him?"

"Only to discuss possibilities. No money, no R & D. I need his contacts."

Ross studied the wrinkled envelope, and then pulled out the two-page letter. He scanned it with casual interest as though it was his *second* time reading the information. He sat back in his chair and loosened his tie, laying the letter down too quickly. "We can help with research and development, *too*," he said deliberately.

"So what is it going to cost me?" Eric asked.

"No cost. Just a little cooperation."

"I don't like it already. Besides, if you want a piece of the action—it may never come. In the computer simulations, the concept works fine, but . . . ."

"Eric, it's not *that* type of interest. We don't care if it works or not . . . we have a problem. Your project might be of some help in a situation coming up. Maybe could use it as bait." Ross took off his jacket, threw it across a chair and rolled up his shirtsleeves.

Eric knew this was his body language ploy learned at some seminar. It was his "let's get down to work" stance.

"Shumacher invited you down," Ross stated. "Why don't you see him? If he can help, whatever we can add would be gravy. Providing of course you agreed to let us use the project as cover."

"What part would I play?" Eric asked.

"You'd play yourself."

"Excuse me? No cover?"

Pause. "Not this time."

The dam broke for Eric. "What the hell does that mean?"

"We need you to be who you are to make it go. All except the part about you being one of us."

Eric sat back in his chair and repositioned his aching shoulder. "Ross, I've got other people to consider, men who want in with me financially and otherwise. I'm not about to jeopardize my chances over some company scheme. Besides, I'm almost out. I've just got a few months to go."

Ross paced about the room avoiding his glance. Not looking at Eric, he said in a sudden emotional burst, "We *need* you this time." He was at his best when he imitated sincerity and he knew what Eric knew—no one was ever totally *out*.

"You need H-PAR," Eric corrected him.

"Absolutely not, goddamn it, it's not that. Your background in the military service and your marksmanship ability are valuable. You're also known as a hard-on conservative. We need a man like that, but we also need one who's a decent operator."

Eric silently studied Ross as the Chief stretched his arms and moved about his office. He knew the Chief was tactically organizing his next move.

"You're bright, Eric, just like your father. That's why the Pentagon brought him here after the war. Europe's post-war "brain drain" fed us tremendous technical and scientific talent. I know you're leaving us and going on to your own endeavors. It's in your blood. Science and high tech are our lifeblood, too. We can help you get there faster. You're a man of many talents—we're willing *to pay* for using those talents."

"Ross, let's get one thing straight between us. My father came here because they gave him a choice. Get turned over to the Russians, rot in a cell, or work for the Americans—same as Shumacher. Cut the crap. Don't shovel up the motherhood and apple-pie speech."

Ross retreated temporarily. *Time to regroup.*

Eric worked and played hard alongside John Ross, got stupefyingly drunk and railed at the bureaucracy with him, but Ross was still a master at manipulation games. Once a case officer joined an investigation there *was* no leaving until it was over.

CHAPTER 4

[**Missing Rifle Truck Just Lagging Behind,** *An Army National Guard truck loaded with 40 M-16 automatic rifles that was reported missing last night was located today with all the weapons accounted for, state police said. Troopers from the LaFayette substation said the 2 1/ 2 ton signal truck was discovered missing by military officials from a convoy that had stopped for the night near LaFayette.*

*According to troopers, the vehicle caught up with the rest of the 100-vehicle convoy early today after developing mechanical problems on the road. The convoy was traveling on Route 81 from Binghamton to Fort Drum near Watertown for military maneuvers. The vehicle was part of Company C, 242nd Signal Battalion.—***Syracuse Herald Journal,** *Syracuse, New York [4]*

Ross slumped back down in his leather chair. His right hand stroked a stainless steel pyramid paperweight. He appeared annoyed that Eric was not accepting his act at face value. Absently, he kicked the bottom desk drawer back into place. "We'll need you to have a strong back for this one."

Eric stared down at the plush carpet. Ross could help him, he thought. No doubt Agency contacts could open doors and provide financial help in return. "Difficult?" he asked after a long calculated silence.

15

"Could be for the wrong man," Ross answered.

"I'm keeping both paychecks."

Ross' face surrendered a discreet grin. "You always have before."

"The rest?" Eric sighed. With that simple statement, he was in.

Ross hesitated, obviously sorting through the bits and pieces cluttering his otherwise orderly mind. His face and manner changed quickly from irritation to his assured, arrogant self. *That is his strength*, Eric thought. He is whatever he needs to be to get the job done: glib, clever . . . *convincing*.

The supervisor dialed a few digits on his desk phone. "I'm in a meeting. No calls." The heavy scent of his pipe disappeared and he began re-lighting. He didn't look at Eric, his eyes focusing on the emerging smoke. "The military reduced Fort Bryson, in Texas, to half strength some months ago. It's on the chopping block. Various National Guard units asked for their equipment, some new vehicles and other items across the country. The United States Property and Fiscal Office, through Guard Bureau logistics, put inventories in motion across the country to see what the different units had . . . you know, like what they needed most. When the tallied audit sheets returned"—Ross' voice dropped—"Defense Intelligence revealed a little surprise." Ross stopped and puffed out thick white, pungent smoke. He spoke emphatically, pointing his forefinger and thumb at Eric like a cocked pistol. "Over one million items, everything from tanks, jeeps and planes to rounds and automatic weapons were missing throughout the country. Just . . . gone . . . ."

Eric felt an uneasy tightening in his chest. The briefing was making him temporarily forget the pain in his shoulder. He watched John Ross lean back in his chair. His supervisor's thin face reflected a momentary glimpse of his own disbelief. There was more and when Eric braced suddenly, the pain in his shoulder returned.

"No one could believe the audit sheets. Some of them used civilians in the inventory instead of using military technicians, so they called another audit." Ross pulled the pipe away from between his teeth. "Every god-damn thing was back! Near Little Rock, Arkansas, so much disappeared and reappeared at the National Guard headquarters that some of 'em thought they had a phantom army somewhere."

Eric's gaze was impassively fixed on the plush blue carpet. His breathing quickened as the details unfolded giving away his concern. He knew Ross noticed the change: tradecraft.

"That's not all," Ross added and he leaned toward Eric, his hands clasped around the pipe's sculptured bowl. "Defense Intelligence planned another surprise audit two weeks ago. The equipment is slowly disappearing again."

"Christ!" Eric said under his breath. He shook his head then stared at Ross. "Where's all that stuff going? Who's hiding it? And where?"

"Some place where no one would think to look for it."

"Go on."

"We suspect it might be right under the government's nose," Ross said wryly.

"You have confirmation?"

"Suspicion," Ross added.

"So, what's the deal?" Eric asked.

"Who the hell knows for sure, besides, that's why you're here." Ross pulled a box from his desk drawer and lifted out a black vinyl-covered wrist weight, the kind competition shooters use to build strength. "How long will it be before you'll be in shape to practice shooting with this?" Ross threw the black padded five-pound wrist weight across the desk into Eric's lap.

It startled Eric into changing the subject. Typical of Ross, but Eric was used to the game and knew he had to be patient.

"Why do you want me to increase my arm strength? What's the target?"

"How long?" Ross persisted.

"Six weeks or so." Eric examined the wrist weight and read its label. "You know I qualified years ago."

Ross maintained a patient, silent stare; he'd heard it all before.

"And, I'm better than those clowns downstairs." But Eric still knew that his shoulder wound would be a handicap.

Ross peered at him with one eye shut: a habit that surfaced when he already knew the answers. "When was the last time you were in a pistol competition?"

Eric looked up and caught the man's cold stare. "In the Air Force. Some time ago."

"Are you still breaking 2600?"

"Ross, you're being a pain in the ass, you already know that."

He leaned closer to Eric, raised his eyebrows and lowered his voice. "You can't be just a good shot, Eric. This time your shooting has to be perfect."

Eric twirled the ends of his mustache. His shooting *was almost perfect*. "Why the practice?"

"You're going back into competition."

"And?" Eric coaxed.

Ross smiled then rested against his comfortable chair. He was being patronizing again. "We'll let you know, *what* you need to know, *when* you need to know it."

"Very funny," Eric said following the familiar comment from agency supervisors.

Eric repositioned his body. The pressure of the overstuffed chair against his shoulder hurt.

"When you heal and start practicing, we'll need you here in Virginia. There's an area in Richmond called Bel Air. We'll set you up there. It's an old Victorian resort village that's turned into sub-urbia." Ross handed him a piece of paper scratched with a name and address. "It's the carriage house of one of the old village homes, belongs to Matt and Fran Watson. He's done some work for us in the past, but only knows that we need a place for someone to stay."

Eric's pain squeezed him again when he lifted himself from the chair and turned to leave. He flushed and was suddenly light-headed. He waited a few seconds to stabilize himself, breathing deeply again.

Ross would say no more until he needed to know. "We'll keep you up on how things are going," Ross said.

Eric grasped the doorknob; he could feel his supervisor's calculated stare burning between his shoulder blades.

"Better tend to that shoulder, I'll need you soon."

Eric turned back and caught the man's glance. A pencil replaced the pipe in Ross' mouth and he shuffled a few papers underneath the steel paperweight.

Ross was unbearable when anything went wrong, or when any of his men made his group look bad. His instincts from command in the military made him jump to their defense when someone criticized his people, although more out of design than really caring. Defending a subordinate, particularly one who was clearly in the right, afforded him two unusual opportunities: an ego power play against the superior accuser, and instant loyalty from his people.

To Eric, Ross sold out to the bureaucracy at Langley long ago. Ross was a known game master whose allegiance no one questioned. But, like others, he was beginning to trade his principles for security in a job where there was none.

Eric wondered how long it would take before the bureaucracy would get to Ross, dangle a promotion before his eyes in trade for a tidying up of some operation gone sour or some unexpected change of events. How long would it be before Ross would sell out one of his own to appease another deal brewing? When would he use one of his veteran case officers as chum for the sharks dealing in agency life as a bureaucratic commodity?

As in any negotiation, something of value is given up for something perceived as having a greater value. Only too often, a bad deal was made. Bad deals in the company were expensive in human terms. Eric and the others knew they often lost their best veteran players in the negotiated ins and outs of the intelligence and clandestine trades. Ross was not giving up a lot of information. Eric didn't think it was possible, but he left in more discomfort than when he came.

CHAPTER 5

*[District Police Chase Down Stolen Weapons Carrier, Washington, D.C.—A man stole a weapons carrier from an Army National Guard Armory in Annapolis, drove it nearly 50 miles undetected to the District and led D.C. police on a chase . . . officer's attention was that the suspect didn't have the headlights on, . . . When the driver of the military vehicle saw the police officer, he sped off, . . . charged with two counts of assault on a police officer and unauthorized use of a vehicle. No estimate of damage to the military and police vehicles was available . . . he was taken to D.C. General Hospital and treated for minor injuries that police said he received during the . . . . The reason for the vehicle's theft and its trip to Washington was not known. Local, state and federal authorities were investigating.—*The Washington Post*] [5]*

April 25th

At first glance, Airmont Foundation's houses appeared more like small mansions nestled together on a Virginia plantation than the meeting lodges of a conference center. Few people outside high-level government knew that Airmont rented out the lodges only to provide a front. The rentals gave the lodges legitimacy and maintained the Agency's cover. It didn't hurt to keep the coffers full of "unappropriated" money. The intelligence community and the military often held secret meetings there. Its Northern Virginia location made it conveniently near to Washington. The grazing cattle near the elegant houses were a sufficiently authentic addition to ward off the curious. To a trained eye, the overall effect was a center too lush and elegant to be government-owned, but too postcard-perfectly manicured not to be.

John Ross had insisted that Eric come to the high-level meeting. He scrutinized his driver, Patrick, as the man maneuvered the car around the ruts in the sandy road. Twice, Patrick had jumped out to remove a large limb lying across what seemed like a farmer's tractor trail. Ross wondered if others had found another clear road into the area. In the back seat Eric and former Director of Central Intelligence (DCI) Stuart Jason tried to maintain their composure. The Lincoln passed acres of farmland and slowly lumbered through a wooded area to an unexpected clearing where the road suddenly became paved and smooth.

The Lincoln's passengers watched as Army and Navy helicopters hovered in the dark sky, their blades swirling above the blue lights on the landing pad. Some of the craft had unloaded their passengers; others seemed to be searching for a spot of their own. Amid the flashing lights and excitement, one large Navy chopper landed, and current Director of Central Intelligence [DCI] James Oldfield, ducked away from the blades with two protective aides running alongside. Eric watched until the group was out of his sight. It was surreal: helicopters swirling, shadows in business suits and military uniforms running clear of noisy, beating blades, and Black Angus cattle mooing and huddling with curiosity in little groups at the far edge of the clearing.

Eric knew how unusual it was to be invited to such a high-level meeting. Oldfield made sure that Jason and Ross knew he disapproved. It hardly mattered to Jason, since he had left the bureaucracy and no longer had to please anyone. He rallied those to the meeting as he saw fit. Stuart Jason came back as a special advisor for this particular assignment and made it known he would bend this time for no one.

Oldfield, a neat, physically handsome man resembled a retired, celebrity sports figure. He had attended the right schools and university; he'd married into the right family and had received early promotions during his military career. He headed a federal agency for two years and gained recognition by resolving a crisis between a national union and a two-month-old strike that threatened to cripple industry. No one ever doubted his courage or bravery in his military career but if asked, those close to him remembered him as political from the very beginning. He was fearless and steadfast but structured and well rehearsed. The right people who could pull the right strings admired him. Unfortunately, there were some who interpreted all this as just the right criteria to head the fortress at Langley.

Eric did not approve of Oldfield, but then no one asked him. He knew Oldfield never really understood the "company's backbone"; those who had the real power and loyalties within the Agency were surprisingly well hidden. To Eric it was the ultimate in ironies: the real CIA hidden from its appointed leadership within its own sanctuary. If given enough time, Oldfield would also wash out of their system and cast his bid into the political arena where some thought he really belonged.

By the time the Lincoln approached the sparsely lit private drive in front of the third mansion, military staff cars and other vehicles already lined the narrow road. Military guards were on the outside and, Eric was sure, in the woods nearby. The two entered the baronial-styled house, with Eric close behind Jason. Ross casually followed some of the military brass into a small reception and conference area where coffee and sandwiches on blue and gold porcelain plates lay on a broad buffet table in the light blue tapestried room. The carefully tended plants and exquisite blue and white flowered Chinese porcelain gave the impression of vast estate holdings, and certainly not the typical government meeting house.

Jason and Secretary of Defense Kurt Hoffman, an outwardly pleasant man thickening from too much middle age and too many gourmet receptions, immediately found each other. They began talking quietly and Eric could hear Secretary Hoffman's Germanic-accented English answer Jason's soft, yet direct, questions. For a long time now, an American citizen, Hoffman's childhood in Germany left an imprint on his English. Generally noted for his sartorial style, Secretary Hoffman's expensive but badly wrinkled suit evidenced his long flight in.

Both men sat in overstuffed green striped chairs near the center of the room. Eric watched Jason speaking intently, creases forming on his forehead above plain, gold-colored wire-rimmed glasses, the gray streaks in his black hair adding a dignified air. Jason was not as physically imposing as Oldfield, yet his demeanor and his concentration on whomever he was speaking with, gave him a presence far greater than his physical stature. Eric's respect for the former DCI, Stuart Jason, was shared both in this complex and throughout the government.

Jason was in intelligence since the age of twenty. After WWII, at twenty-two years old, the allies dropped Jason into East Germany to begin an almost impossible information-gathering assignment against the communists. The enemy captured two of the five-man team and killed another. Jason returned carrying the last man across his back, although suffering with a chest wound that would have put most men on their knees. At twenty-five, he received the CIA's Intelligence Medal for Valor.

Twenty-six years later Eric Brent received the same medal with Jason standing nearby smiling his approval. Dropped behind the Laotian border, Eric managed to stay alive for three weeks in an enemy-filled jungle and return to safety with a delicate, secret instrument in his pocket, and a wounded young captain across his shoulders. He managed this, despite the shell that had torn into his abdomen, an injury, which later claimed a third of his intestines. When Eric received his citation, the President, placed his arm around Eric's shoulder and said his escapades read like the action in a Batman comic book. Unfortunately, the remark made it back to the Agency and Eric had to endure the "Batman" handle for the rest of his career.

Eric knew that the Agency granted few of the awards but the name of one recipient was still secret—his deed still highly classified. Only the upper echelon of the high-level staff knew who he was and so far, it was one commendation not filtered through to those outside the intelligence complex. Maybe it belonged to one of the anonymous "stars" on the entrance wall at Langley Headquarters. As far as most in the Agency knew, Eric and Jason were among the few recipients.

CHAPTER 6

*[**Mass, Armory Secured,** —BOSTON (AP)—Added precautions were being taken at National Guard armories throughout the state following the theft of weapons from the armory in Danvers, a National Guard Spokesman said Tuesday. Capt.Chip Hoar said he was not at liberty to detail what the extra precautions are. He also said an inventory had been completed and that in addition to the weapons stole, 10 pieces of body armor, known as flak jackets and three binoculars were missing. Officials said 100 weapons were taken in the theft, . . . Capt. Hal Duttoh of the National Guard said burglaries by militant revolutionary groups in the early 1970s led to such security precautions as storing firing mechanisms separately from weapons. . . . "We can't turn our backs on it," [Richard Bates, special agent in charge of the FBI office] but there are a "number of people who might be considered capable" of such a theft as well as a number authorities don't know about . . . .—**Kennebec Journal, Augusta, Maine**] [6]*

Oldfield entered the conference room abruptly like a storm blowing into the room. His body language implied agitation, but for no specific reason other than to create attention. His two aides scurried close beside him. Secretary Hoffman, his large blue eyes set beneath his broad forehead, glanced at Oldfield through his heavy-lensed, tortoise-rimmed glasses. He continued his conversation with Jason without even a nod acknowledging

Oldfield's arrival. Oldfield made a point of going to the Secretary's chair first, extending his hand.

It was Oldfield's standard power move, but Secretary Hoffman got up slowly skirting his chair and touched the current DCI on his back first. It took the wind out of Oldfield's approach. "James," he said, "we've been waiting for you." Jason sat quietly in the comfortable chair. His legs crossed and his hands in his lap, he merely looked up into Oldfield's face. A faint smile touched the corners of Jason's mouth, as he took in Hoffman's greeting. The clash of personalities and style was obvious among the men, but then again, they were there for reasons other than social.

When the three men exited the room, Eric followed. Hoffman still avoided Oldfield's handshake. Eric saw the Secretary's tactic too, and was amused. Eric's father had taught him that a man's handshake was a sign of his personal bond. Hoffman, the son of German immigrants, obviously thought the same. Oldfield was going to have to work hard. It was pretty obvious that he was not a favorite with one of the administration's most powerful men.

At eight-thirty, the men gathered around a large oval table in the center of the room. Eric sat with Ross, "sidelining" away from the table, nearer the wall where brass lamps gracefully arched away from the brocade wallpaper. One white middle-aged butler served coffee from a large silver service while another placed glasses and pitchers of water beside each place then both men left.

A security man from inside the room locked the door and nodded to Secretary Hoffman. Eric felt like an impatient child at a religious confirmation service. Although he knew most of the information, Jason reminded him: "You should get to know the scope of the session and see first-hand some of the problems." Having to deal with the administrative slug work and the people who thrived on it always made Eric edgy.

Hoffman rose first to address the group. The Secretary cleared his throat and began his accented monotone voice filling the room. "Gentlemen, I'm taking the opportunity to speak first here. After a meeting with the President and some of the staff of your commands, we've come up with some information I believe you will find most enlightening. Some of this may seem trivial at first, but I ask for your patience, as I believe you will see the point." He removed his thick glasses, rubbed out a spot on the lens with his handkerchief, and walked around one end of the table before adding, "I'm afraid a most disconcerting point at that."

Hoffman motioned to a security guard. From an adjoining room two men brought in a large cardboard box filled with blue bound books of computer rips. The guards handed one book to each of the eleven men around the table. Present were the Directors of the National Security Agency, the National Guard Bureau, Flag officers from all the active Military Services, as well as Reserve Components while Oldfield and Jason represented the CIA. As Oldfield looked around, he noted the Director of the FBI, Michael Halstead, was also there. Halstead seemed the perfect Washington political hard case, who only looked out for his interests and was extremely difficult to read. He always made Oldfield uncomfortable.

"Before you, gentlemen, is a long list of numbers gathered from a computer room two weeks ago. The figures correspond mainly to the equipment assigned to the Guard Bureau, but it affects the rest of you as well." Secretary Hoffman walked around the table with one hand in his pocket and the other occasionally flipping his glasses around his wrist. "Part of an exercise the Guard Bureau has been carrying out for some months has been to categorize, relocate, and move some equipment around the country. All this was done for a reduction in forces the President called for at Fort Bryson. As you know, Bryson is one of many bases recently closed out. The original purpose was to ascertain logistics and equipment needs in the Reserve and Guard components."

"We also did another audit on aircraft," Hoffman continued, "small naval surface craft and vehicles, most of it 'mothball' fleet items. When the compiled figures of inventories were brought into the accounting office," Secretary Hoffman paused, his glance encompassing the entire room of men; "some million or so defense items were missing. Everything from handguns and rifles, to tanks, planes, and service vehicles—and it is just the tip of the iceberg."

"Before notifying anyone about this, the Guard Bureau couldn't believe their figures and took another inventory."

Expressions from stunned disbelief to troubled concern ranged throughout the room on the men's faces. Some, like Oldfield, began taking notes.

The stout Secretary of Defense stopped to pour himself a glass of water and dab his handkerchief over his sweating forehead. "After the second count, the Bureau's figures showed almost every missing item was accounted for, complete with serials . . . everything. We evaluated all this. Shortly after that evaluation, the report you'll find in the front of the books before you—Guard Bureau sent to me. In essence it states that from the Bureau's investigation and re-evaluation of their inventories across the country, over one million items relating to warfare and the defense of this country disappeared, then *reappeared— one million items*, gentlemen—all in a matter of twenty days. The missing mothball fleet items, however, are completely gone."

The men in the room looked silently at one another, and then they began thumbing through the computer lists.

"What you have here are comparison totals of two inventories. They're listed by state and company. This involves the National Guard armories around the country." Hoffman stopped again to take some water. "However, it ultimately involves everyone. My first reaction was that some of the weapons were surplus or transferred to other Services for training. But we have no record. I'm hoping that, if this is the case, some of you will shed some light on the subject."

Secretary Hoffman sat down on the edge of his chair. "Before planning this meeting tonight, Army CID made an unannounced inventory. This time they ordered only a partial inventory. They took a no-notice sampling of only a few states. This morning I received some of those figures. The arms and vehicles are slowly disappearing again. *We know this for sure.*"

CHAPTER 7

*[**Armory Burglars Had Inside Data?** LOS ANGELES (AP)—Authorities were investigating the possibility today that inside information was available to burglars who took more than 100 weapons and thousands of rounds of ammunition from a California Army National Guard armory in suburban Compton. "I've been a cop 10 years and I worked in burglary for three years and I've never seen a more professional job," Compton police Sgt. Cliff Smith said. "They had that place covered like a blanket. They knew exactly what to do, where to go and what to take. There was no wasted effort. He said the burglars appeared to have just the right equipment to accomplish their job. Nothing inside the armory was used to get where they were going," Smith told a reporter last night . . . .—**The Chronicle Telegram, Elyria, Ohio**] [7]*

Hoffman dropped himself into his chair, pushed his glasses back on the ridge of his pronounced nose, and clasped his pudgy fingers in front of him waiting for a response.

Several people began talking at once, mostly wanting to know if this mainly involved the National Guard or were their particular branches fingered, too. Hoffman held his hand up to quiet the crowd. "From all available information and indications, it is the Guard and the Reserves, with indications pointing to small groups from other branches."

Taking in a labored breath, Hoffman looked around the table. "There's more, gentlemen. We are continuing our investigations. What I do have to tell you is **not** preposterous." Secretary Hoffman glanced at the former Director of Central Intelligence, Stuart Jason. Jason quietly observed the men around the table as Hoffman continued. "We have supporting evidence from the field that there's a secret, self-contained military movement in the making, involving large numbers of National Guardsmen and Reservists among others in government. We also think there are many who will be involved without ever knowing it. What we don't know is who the top participants are, and what their final objective is going to be."

In stunned silence the men looked at each other. One uneasy Army general asked again, "Why the National Guard and Reserves?"

Hoffman answered, "These are men who have their own businesses, professional jobs, highly trained technical people, all have a desire to remain part of a strong military but decided for a variety of reasons to be part-timers. They have access and mobility to one of the largest weapons arsenals in the world—the National Guard and Reserve components. I believe they are frustrated and angered over what's happening not only socially and economically to this country, but also politically and in foreign policies."

"Mr. Secretary," another general interrupted, "I know myself of many instances where arms were issued and the paperwork lagged behind." He motioned around the table "We all do . . . but a secret movement?"

"Over the past few months we've come up with a picture which seems to defy logic, but is becoming more plausible every day. It's obvious we must act and soon." Secretary Hoffman turned to current Director of Central Intelligence, Oldfield who was sitting silently, his hands clasped into a fist. "James, please take it from here."

The current DCI finished writing on his pad and stood up. Oldfield had a fetish for note taking and was a real stickler for the complete picture in the finest of detail. Although his abrupt personality lacked refinement, those present grudgingly appreciated his thoroughness: the only grace that saved him in many tough intel situations.

Without preamble, DCI Oldfield said, "The action we'll take will be called Project Warrior. You all know Stuart Jason. He will temporarily command the administration of this project. I believe his experience and familiarity with most of the players will be an invaluable asset." Oldfield introduced Ross to the group as the CIA Chief of the Special Operations Group, in charge of those in the field tracking the guardsmen and the search for all weapons missing. Under Jason's instructions, they did not introduce Eric.

Oldfield brusquely went on. "There is always the possibility of computer error. But, after three checks in the mainframes and in the sub-terminals, we ruled that out. There's no mistake, gentlemen, the arms are coming and going and the Agency has been monitoring it for some time to see how deeply this thing reaches."

Michael Halstead, Director of the FBI, surveyed the room with his intense brown eyes. In his late forties, he was still athletic. A slight ridge on his nose, a college football injury added an interesting flaw to his face. But the hawkish nose and a weak chin gave him a predatory look that was not far from his personality. Casting an irritated glance first in Secretary Hoffman's direction, he said suddenly, "From what I've seen here, Oldfield, it's obvious that you knew about this long before I did. And I'd like to know why before this goes any further."

Oldfield continued walking around the table while FBI Director Halstead, in his standard irritatingly loud voice, complained. "This is an internal U.S. problem! Why weren't we notified sooner; why are you in on this before the FBI and why is the CIA involved at all? Need I remind you that you are only responsible for actions taken outside the U.S.? You are way out of your charter and you know it."

Oldfield stepped to the silver coffee service and poured another cup, ignoring Halstead.

Jason rose from the table and interrupted. "I can explain, Mike," he said to the FBI Director. "Initially this information didn't come from domestic sources."

Oldfield turned to Director Halstead and broke in on Jason. "You ought to know that disinformation much like this is fed constantly to us to tie up staff, money and efforts tracing bad leads all over creation. That shouldn't be news to the FBI or to any of you. The game is to keep us busy and looking the wrong way."

Stuart Jason took back control. "We received foreign information that the U.S. has a problem with its own military stockpiling arms internally. We thought it was another red herring, just another chase in the dark, but we did check it out. Of course, our only resource for investigating these kinds of things is through internal military intelligence. As you all know they report up the line to intelligence agencies, not the FBI." Jason added, "At the same time news about the shortages was coming in. We made the decision to prepare a report for the FBI, but then that cache of arms was found hidden in a California desert. Mike, you came in at that point."

Oldfield chimed in, "The serial numbers from that cache matched with the missing inventories. We thought it was best to hold our report to see where your own investigation of that went, rather than risking leaks when you had independent knowledge of the facts."

"Later," added Secretary Hoffman, "another cache was found in New Mexico, and then some were stolen from an arsenal in Massachusetts. The name 'Right Guard' emerged: a name that we think has some significance to this group."

"Mike," Jason added before sitting down, "things were becoming so sensitive here, and with the possible foreign connection, we couldn't risk going ahead and turning this information over to you for arrests until we knew what else was involved."

"Besides," said DCI Oldfield, "most of those we came across here in the U.S. were definitely the Indians and not the chiefs anyway. If we arrested them we would drive the rest underground. We can't risk that until we know more."

FBI Director Halstead sat silently with an acidic flush to his face. Jason and Oldfield knew Halstead had to swallow it because the FBI's investigation led nowhere. The Right Guard information came through an unexpected foreign source, one treasured and protected by the agency and one definitely not to be given over to the FBI. That normally made both men a little pleased, but not today. This trusted "source" had also given over information about a potential secret Right Guard installation within the U.S. This was the most troubling piece of information. Jason's questions centered around, do they trust the source and look for it? Is it a red herring—a false clue? If it was a red herring then what was the hidden agenda of the trusted source?

Eric remembered Ross telling him, "I am afraid that I just can't trust Mike. He is looking out for his own interests and leads a team that's so damn arrest-oriented. We have to keep them at bay until we know everything. If we let them in on it now, and some Elliot Ness gets hold of a few names, it will all be tubed."

"Are there any foreign connections?" Eric recalled having asked Ross days earlier.

"Not as far as we know, but whether there is or isn't, that's the explanation we give Halstead . . . and the *rest* of the FBI."

CHAPTER 8

[*Reuters—A government employee union said today that the theft of small arms and plastic explosives from U.S. military bases had become so serious that the military has been forced to adopt new security measures . . . . losses of small arms and plastic explosives have reached "epidemic proportions," . . . However, an army spokesman in Washington denied the union's charges and said the increased security measures were part of an eight-month-old program . . . the government is being spurred by large-scale theft to initiate "stringent new security measures." . . . missing weapons included M-16 rifles, grenade and rocket launchers, machine guns and ammunition . . . singled out were the Red River Arsenal in Arkansas, Fort Bliss, Texas and installations at Rock Island and Joliet, Illinois as among those affected . . .—Reuters Ltd]* [8]*

Well past midnight, they compared the numbers on the computer sheets. After much argument, Jason's fears over the recent reports were more than justified. They gave no other rational explanation of the arms disappearing and reappearing. All agreed they wanted an in-depth investigation and they swore to secrecy. Project Warrior and the Right Guard would now consume much more of their lives than any of them imagined.

Oldfield gathered up the bound computer rips and carried them out in a cardboard box. Only Stuart Jason kept his and returned it to a pocket divider inside his briefcase. Hoffman, Jason,

Ross, and Eric were the last to leave. When they walked outside together, security was nearby but out of earshot.

"Do you think Mike is going to play?" Hoffman asked.

"I don't know." Jason sighed from fatigue. "I just don't know." Nodding to the driver who stopped near them, Jason lifted himself into the car then collapsed into the comfortable leather backseat. "I have enough troubles without playing nursemaid between the two agencies. The President is on my back for an explanation of all this, and frankly I need them both on one side—*mine*—and not playing some goddamn political game."

"Yes, I know." Secretary Hoffman pulled off his thick glasses and rubbed his eyes, now red from the smoke that had filled the meeting room. "I can understand why it had to be done." Hoffman replaced his tortoise frames. "Stuart, let's try not to ram it too much down Halstead's throat. We may need his *unofficial* as well as his official cooperation before it's all over. It'll be a lot more palatable to him if he can look like a player."

Jason's eyes looked tired. He nodded to his old friend, as the Secretary of Defense moved toward his own chauffeured car back to Washington, D.C.

Ross and Eric joined Jason in the Lincoln. Beginning the long guard-chauffeured ride back, Eric's mind wandered to the article Jason handed him earlier in the day. "Army Misplaces Launchers" headed up the short news story. Buried in the back pages of a local newspaper, it explained that three Hawk air defense missile launchers were missing from a fort in Texas. A Defense Department spokesman assured reporters that the launchers were "not dangerous" as there were no missiles on them. The spokesman added that although they "appeared to be misplaced," it was probably an "error in the paperwork."

Eric's eyes scanned the last visible light of Airmont's buildings from the Lincoln's car window before the road led them through the woods again and into complete darkness.

Eric massaged the bridge of his nose, and glanced at Stuart Jason sitting in the darkened car's back seat.

Jason stared into the black night; his unfocused eyes and tensed mouth accentuated his growing concern and disbelief. Then former DCI Jason sat back against the car seat. He leaned against the head rest and closed his eyes. "Fools," Jason murmured.

CHAPTER 9

[UPI—Investigators looking into the theft of military vehicles and equipment from two California National Guard armories in Fresno believe the items may be in the hands of marijuana plantation operators or a survivalist paramilitary group.

Some of the equipment was actually mislocated and has since been found, authorities said.

But three jeeps and four trailers reported stolen from the Chance Avenue armory and some communications, camping and camouflage equipment reported missing from another NG facility near the Fresno Air Terminal are still missing . . . . .—UPI] [9]

April 30th

Drake Cochran's in-town house parties were a great place to pick up the occasional piece of valuable gossip. Eric accepted his invitations more to gather information than to satisfy his social needs. He worked with Drake on the campus newspaper at the University of Richmond. When Drake came to Washington to work for the United States Information Agency, they kept in touch. Press secretaries and advance teams paraded through his bashes between trips and it took only a few drinks and an experienced ear to pick up on political strategies and other dirt from Washington, Maryland and

Virginia. Newcomers to Washington's bizarre brand of journalism would often ramble on about their latest assignment, and then gracelessly sidestep when no one recognized their name from the papers or the talk shows.

Young socialites occasionally sashayed through wearing the exceptional in fashion although not necessarily the best taste for the season. Expensive and professionally designed makeup across surgically enhanced and rehearsed smiles gave some of them illusions of culture and depth. For most, though, the finery and the role-playing could not camouflage hawkish eyes searching for prey—a well-known name to be seen with, good marriage material and a well hung male for an evening. Well, there were a few things that Eric felt he could oblige . . . .

A sea captain at the end of the Civil War built Drake's home in Georgetown. Close to the narrow street, it sported a mellow-pink brick front, double entrance doors of stained oak and a large, well-polished doorknocker. His living room and library had retained its original dark walnut paneling. It was there that the fifty or so guests, some that Drake even knew, mixed, drank, gossiped and eavesdropped.

Eric saw Jill Warren before she saw him. Leaning against the wood paneling in the front hallway, he watched her sip from her glass, her rich dark brown hair cascaded to her shoulders framing her porcelain-colored, perfectly oval face. Physically she had changed little since their college days. Eric noticed the thin line at the corners of her full, sensitive lips and thought it made her look even sexier. She was talking to one of the local studs, who obviously thought he was getting lucky. Eric knew he would change that misperception.

A brassy middle-aged woman standing beside Eric laughed loudly at some joke then slouched to treat him to a full view of her cleavage. Jill turned at the laughter and caught the chunky blonde as she impetuously reached over to Eric and playfully flicked the edge of his mustache. Abruptly turning away, Jill escaped into another room. He followed her and the closer he came the stronger he could smell the citrus and roses—her trademark perfume.

As his hand touched her shoulder, she whirled around. He sensed her losing composure. After nine years it was obvious she still remembered some pretty spectacular times they shared . . . both in and out of bed. For Eric, many others since Jill were like holding on to a soggy towel.

"Hello, Jill." He pulled out his best little-boy smile and hoped for a positive response despite the slight quiver at the corners of her mouth. The moisture in her intense hazel-brown and green eyes reflected the light from the antique chandelier overhead.

"It's been some time." His hand brushed her sleeve. "Drake told me some interesting people were coming here tonight." He had known for weeks she was invited.

"Eric, well . . ." Her words came with no warmth. Quickly placing her drink on a nearby table, she moved away from him toward the front door. "I've got to go. It's great seeing you." He followed, protecting his shoulder against the well-lubricated crowd. Despite his precautions, the cheesy blonde spied him and again tried to corral him, managing to trip into him, splashing her drink on his suit. His face showed the pain as his left hand shot up to his throbbing shoulder following Jill and escaping through Drake's front door.

Outside, Jill turned to him with all her grudges suddenly forgotten. "You're hurt."

"It's all right," he lied. Casting nervous glances at the people suddenly streaming through the front door, he took her by the arm, guiding her further out into the quiet street. "Look," he said, "I'm hungry. Let's go get something." His body felt drawn and his eyes irritated from cigarette smoke. He thought about the lunch he had thrown up and wondered if he could keep his next meal down. The aching wound was nauseating him again.

Jill glanced uneasily at his shoulder. They walked away from Drake's home and the noise and laughter faded. "What happened to you, Eric?"

"Car accident," he shrugged, adding quickly, "How about a drink? The Ebb Tide Grill isn't too far away and we could talk about old times."

"What *old times?*" she said, mouthing each word meticulously. He struck the nerve. "You mean the time I loved you and you left without saying so much as adios?"

She was true Sagittarian—quick, honest, but often more direct than was comfortable for Eric. He liked holding the control button. Though Jill's questions and moves were unpredictable, it excited him; it kept him alert.

Her eyes flashed with anger. "Look, Eric, this is just great seeing you, but I've maneuvered myself out of a relationship with someone who wouldn't grow up. Now, I have a steady man in my life and no intention of changing that."

Eric smiled. He placed his left hand on the back of Jill's neck, and she jumped as if he had shocked her . . . then she settled against his hand. He parted her long dark hair and brought her closer. Jill just stood there holding her breath, letting it happen. As Eric bent over to kiss her, his mouth twitched from the pain in his shoulder. Tasting once more the soft, full mouth he remembered, it brought back a flood of memories he'd never managed to forget.

She turned, stiff at first . . . but slowly softened to his kiss without protest then urgently pressed her lips to his.

"You *remember*, don't you," he whispered. "We *were* the best."

CHAPTER 10

[Fence, Trucks, Damaged,—Newark Police Report,—. . . damage to a fence and two Ohio National Guard trucks at the Ohio National Guard Armory, Hollar Lane and 35th Street. One truck was driven through a fence, which separates Hollar Lane from the armory parking lot, into a second truck parked outside of the fence along Hollar Lane. Both trucks sustained front-end damage. The incident, which occurred prior to 1p.m. Wednesday, is thought to be the result of vandalism. Estimated loss is $900 . . . .—The Advocate, Newark] [10]

Neatly tucked away in downtown Washington, The Ebb Tide Grill was not far from the White House. The dark mahogany tables, white tablecloths, and muted browns of the old restaurant hinted that it was more a man's establishment. Famous customers from the past frequented the Grill like Presidents Grant, Johnson, Cleveland, McKinley, Theodore Roosevelt, and Harding. Rumors floated that occasionally modern American Presidents came there, leaned against the antique bar in the darkness, and put down a few under the large stuffed animal heads hanging on the walls. Secret Service Agents often drifted in and blended into the woodwork whenever the nation's chief executive was nearby. A huge oil of a beautiful nude woman hung over the more private back bar and it lent a certain distinction to the masculine decor of the narrow, dimly lit restaurant at night.

They both ordered bourbon on the rocks and spinach omelets, usually a Sunday morning brunch specialty of the house. Eric's stomach, still delicate from his Viet Nam wounds, gave him fits if he took any heartier fare.

He studied Jill, silently taking in the minute changes since they were last together; longer hair, refined eyebrows, and full lips. The few extra pounds were a positive addition, rounding out what he remembered to be a feminine but too taut athletic body.

"You look good, Jill," he said as he followed her neckline down. "Why are you working for a jerk-off like Bailor Moorehead?"

"Long story." She ruefully shook her head. "I'm not too sure I want to talk about it."

"I've got all evening and all night." When the drinks came, he downed his quickly and ordered another. "The last I heard, you were working for the Examiner. What happened?"

"One minute I was working on a series of articles about pollution in the James River; then poof, fledgling reporter Jill Warren was out on her ass." She looked away and was embarrassed.

Eric continued to study her, patiently waiting for a better answer.

"I researched the industrial end of the story. You know, visiting large industries in the area and asking questions about what they dump into the water. I arrived mostly unannounced and took a few pictures of the disposal areas complete with some weird looking floating suds and orange and purple water. I was good enough that a television reporter wanted to team up with me on a nuclear waste spill being covered up on the coast. The managing editor walked in one day and invited me into his office, told me I wasn't doing well in my reporting, you know, like not getting enough information or the facts straight? Oh, then he says, maybe I should consider writing obituaries for a while. He took all of my film and relieved me of my assignment."

"Does he have that film now?"

"I'm afraid so. An upsetting scene . . ." she mimicked. "I returned and threw it at him."

"Bad move."

"I was confused. First time being fired," she said and raised her glass.

Eric listened attentively but he began to lose his concentration as citrus and roses delicately drifted across the table. "Your hair . . . it always looked like sable on an autumn day."

"Ah, that wonderful silver tongue. Bourbon talking?" she asked.

He smiled. "No, but the bourbon has helped my shoulder."

"How did you get hurt? *The truth*," she insisted.

"Got shot."

"Is that all you can tell?"

He nodded, "Just about. Now, let's get back to Moorehead. Why did you go work for him?"

"He was my best way back to the ranks of the employed at the time. Actually Drake called one day and said he heard Moorehead needed a press secretary."

"You accepted a job with a Northern Virginia Democrat!" There was derision in his voice at her choice of political company. Most Virginians had tagged the Democrats from the northern part of the state as being conservative and not like their more liberal comrades in Congress. *But to good old archconservative Eric,* Jill thought, *Virginia Democrats reminded him of the inmates at Lorton Prison—Washington, D.C. criminals living on Virginia soil.*

"The reality of the situation, Eric, was I became jobless. Apartments in Georgetown do not come gratis."

Eric held up his glass and toasted: "Well, here's to that moron Bailor Moorehead, with hopes he's *not* re-elected to the U.S. Senate. With the Senate we have now, it's too bad being a moron isn't an Olympic sport." Eager for relief, he drank the bourbon and gently repositioned his elbow. His shoulder joint ached so much it felt like it was rotting. He could eat little food until more drinks came.

Okay Eric, time to fess up, he thought. He said that he had not "just left" her after college but the words were too clumsy. He reminded her that the Agency could pull him away without notice. He explained that he was called for an assignment but couldn't tell her that he was with the Agency's controversial domestic intelligence group. His job that summer involved infiltrating a group of foreign student radicals. Because of the nature of the assignment, he hadn't been able to contact her. After the long unexplained separation, she had every reason to think the relationship was over. Then their lives took other paths.

"I didn't know what I was getting into," he said. "I had no right to involve you until I knew for sure what life with them was going to be like." He looked away at the other late night diners seated in the classic rounded, caned chairs. No one was close enough to hear them. The pain was easing and he was enjoying himself with a woman for the first time in many years—no sloppy sexual innuendoes, no feminine games, and a little depth to a conversation. Not much to ask but often hard for him to find in Washington, D.C.

He jostled three ice cubes in the bottom of his glass. As they melted, his "front" also began to lose its chill. His voice lowered. "I wasn't ready for you, Jill. It was happening too fast."

She quickly changed the subject. "What's it like behind the hallowed walls of Langley?" She asked, folding her arms tight across her chest and sitting back in her chair.

Eric looked down at his melting cubes in the glass. He smiled to himself then moved gently back in his chair. *All right,* he thought, *I won't press it . . . for now.* He changed the subject along with her. "I spend so little time there; I don't think I'm the one to ask."

"Like your work?" she asked.

"It's still interesting, but some of the decision-makers often rub me the wrong way."

"Disillusioned?"

"No, not so much that. They have good people, Jill; people who stand on their principles and know what the true nature of what intelligence should be. I suppose *they* are responsible for my staying in this long."

Eric nodded at the young male waiter for bourbon. "Double," he ordered. The waiter nodded then returned quickly. Most of the other patrons left the restaurant, but the candles still flickered on the empty tables. Thanks to the bourbon, he was temporarily at ease again. Still, he felt a gnawing sensation in his guts. The wound in his shoulder didn't help his anxiety over his work. It was all happening like before . . . love found, love snatched away. This time the Agency would use him for a dangerous assignment because he was seasoned bait. He knew Jill wanted answers, but he couldn't accommodate. Instead it was a time to ask if he could see her again or find out if she wanted the past left in place. "When there's no right or wrong decision," Ross once told him, "make a sane one."

"Let's go," he said softly and leaned forward. At that moment, he hoped she would go with him, despite her alarm over his being shot or the uneasiness of a lost love appearing on a doorstep. He wanted to fondle her firm, round breasts like before . . . feel her straddle him . . . plummet between soft thighs and feel her shudder, anxiously inviting him in. He wanted to taste her and ride her until there was no more urgency—then hold her gently in his arms and soothe away the tempest.

But when he stood up from his chair the pain returned with a sharp jab. It reminded him that for the time being all he could do was look at her, fantasize, and breathe in the delicate, expensive scent of citrus and roses.

CHAPTER 11

[Combat Units Roam Nation, Washington—Recently an electronics plant in Ciudad Juarez, just south of the border down Mexico way, was hijacked. Four Marxist-Leninists, three heavily armed men with automatic weapons accompanied by a woman comrade, raced through the door onto the production floor. They waved their guns. They delivered a get-rid-of-your oppressors oration to hundreds of workers. And they shot an angry 24-year old maintenance manager "right in the forehead. Dead. The Sept 23 Communist League orders had been carried out.

Can't happen here—North of the border? Yesr it can' . . . .—Herald Times Reporter, Manitowoc, Wisconsin] [11]

May 9th

Deacon Malway spun the covert plans like a menacing web repeatedly in his mind. His grand plan for subversion and takeover, so tantalizingly close. Restless, he roamed most of the night from room to room throughout his red-brick mansion running his blue-veined hands across his forehead. The peace he sought evaded him.

Brushed straight back, his stark-white hair was a most remarkable feature, framing his ruddy face. Deacon carried an almost grandfatherly countenance, deceptively giving the impression of the utmost concern and kindness. His heavy eyebrows hung over two deep-set dark eyes. Deacon knew his gaze was unnerving, even spellbinding. An old friend compared the famous Deacon stare to Merlin's . . . as if he needed any wizardry. Deacon found humor in the Arthurian comparison, but arrogantly accepted it as a matter of fact. His personality was as faceted as the large diamond ring he wore on his right hand but his dominant persona was tightly controlled, able to change demeanor and disposition in a heartbeat to suit his purpose and ambition.

Seated in his library and resting his stocky frame in a large leather chair, Deacon poured bourbon into a blue-flowered porcelain cup half-filled with hot tea. He stared across the vast neatly trimmed moonlit lawns from the library's bay window. Sleep did not come easily these days. Despite his sixty-eight years, his mind teemed with facts, figures and surreptitious plans, all competing for precious little available time. Sometimes his ill health concerned him more than anyone knew. His fear of dying before the dream of takeover reached promise sent nightmares to accompany his fitful sleep.

His acumen at handling big business as well as government was legendary. He revived a flagging high-tech research and development firm responsible for vital government and industry contracts. His uncle left him a foundering company nearly ruined fifteen years earlier and under his control the firm had blossomed, then thrived. Well known for his ruthless handling of investors, lawyers, government officials he ridiculed and fought them, and anyone else who refused to accept the merits of 'his way or the highway' and his accompanying plans.

When it suited him and his interests, he championed charities and espoused fair play—especially in the presence of those he wished to impress. Despite his reputation, he was gifted at persuading those he needed to convince. His gifts of persuasion were so refined they were, almost sociopathic in intensity as he could convince even the best judges of character of his sincerity. He could raise and lower the emotions of his following with all the calculated skill of a teary-eyed, chin-quivering television evangelist. Deacon could excite them, lead them, and then take them apart while smiling into their believing eyes. He hated anyone who stood in his way, and had a special revulsion for lawyers, whom he viewed as law's whores, bellying up for anyone's dollar. "The rule-mongers" he called them. Many of them disgusted him for what he saw as leeching and control. Even those who hated Deacon often cited his disdain for lawyers as his one redeeming feature.

A prodigious worker, Deacon often worked alongside his techies and other workers, putting in longer and more intense hours than anyone. A driven man at work and a tyrant at home, he had little respect for women, particularly those in the workplace. At best, Deacon viewed women as ornamental property, fair game and fodder.

Those who knew him well said he could name only a few he thought worthy of his confidences. "Friends," a word still in his lexicon, applied only to few. Deacon molded this loose band of people into a cadre of conspirators. As leader, he displayed an air of absolute authority while remaining calm, being aloof and ultimately displaying that he was very much in charge.

A bumper sticker displayed the official motto of one local Guard unit: "Get Your Guard Right, Join the National Guard." Deacon chose it to name his group, and the thought of turning this phrase, just as he was to turn the people involved, appealed to him. He labeled the group "Right Guard," and the name immediately stuck with the others. Quickly signifying the shadow movement they had become, the *Right Guard* would soon shake the American government and many of its people at its highest echelons.

CHAPTER 12

[The State,—Thieves cut through the roof and concrete arms vault of a U.S. Army Reserve armory in Chico over the weekend and stole an undisclosed number of weapons; the Butte County Sheriff's Department reported. Sheriff's Capt. Mick Grey said the thieves "were selective in what they took, primarily automatic weapons," but that the armory's weapons supply also included grenade and rocket launchers as well as mortars. The thieves left behind "quite a few weapons," Grey said, adding that he did not know how much ammunition, if any was taken.

The Army refused to comment, and the FBI, which sealed off the armory in preparation for an inventory, declined immediate comment. Grey said there were no messages or slogans left at the armory to indicate who the thieves were. In San Francisco, a 6th Army Presidio spokeswoman said the Chico armory, which is a base for about 80 reservists, was not fitted with a burglar alarm. —The Times Mirror, Los Angeles Time.] [12]

Earlier in the day, Deacon heaved his aching, tired body into his silver Jeep and visited Lieutenant Colonel Robert Kendall at a special installation Right Guard had set up for their use outside Richmond, Virginia. Slightly built and baby-faced, Kendall's jumpy nerves appeared to idle in high gear. Despite Kendall's inherent uneasiness, Deacon needed the man's logistics brilliance in working with numbers and laborious organizational details.

Once inside the unfinished installation, Deacon noticed Kendall's nervous hands and his inability to look into his eyes more than a few seconds. "The report . . . Bob?" Deacon asked, filling his pipe. Despite his doctor's repeated "no smoking" order he was not going to quit. Deacon didn't have much use for doctors either.

"I know it's due for the meeting coming up, but I . . . I'm just having a hard time finishing it."

Deacon suspected Kendall's words couldn't find their way from his uneasy mind to paper. "You having trouble with this?" Deacon asked. He closely scrutinized the man's expression for telltale stress signs signaling some perilous weakness in the man which could threaten their cause. It was there but Deacon missed it.

"Pressure of the work is pretty intense. There's a lot coming at once, and it's all happening so quickly," Kendall replied.

Both of the men surveyed the area where the carpenter's tools and huge spindles of wire lay scattered near the gate. The civilian workmen finished one tall fence then left for the weekend. The two stood alone amid the rubble and stray pieces of wire and dust.

"You think you're the only one who feels this way?"

"Of course not," Kendall snapped back. He caught himself, retreating into a more respectful manner. "It's the retraining centers. Deacon, are you sure we're doing the right thing with them?"

Deacon's head dropped with a nod. He attempted a fatherly reply. "You have to understand Bob, those who are brought here will not be kept here indefinitely. Once they learn a trade or service of some sort, or show they're capable of going on to higher learning, or prove they can be self-supporting some other way, they can leave." He paused and watched Lt. Col. Kendall staring at the opened doors of the empty barracks-like buildings. "Bob, this is not a punishment for them," Deacon added.

Kendall's fixed gaze was as though he expected someone to appear there.

The mounting mid-day sun glazed the metal of the twelve-foot-high fence and glistened on the surfaces of the new barbed wire mesh stacked in rolls on the ground. Deacon recalled the other sixty detainment and retraining centers like this one he had inspected across the country over the past year. With a side-glance he watched Kendall treading past the gates and the empty guard posts at the entrances of each of the buildings. Kendall didn't enter any of them. Deacon followed him, listening . . . observing. Kendall acted as if some invisible force were keeping him from crossing each threshold. When Kendall stopped, Deacon paused too and observed him nervously working his slender fingers through the tall, secure wire fence. Like a small child, he peered half filled with curiosity and fear at the same time. Appearing detached for a few moments, Kendall became trance-like.

Images flashed quickly through Deacon's mind, vivid black and white scenes of detention camps from the Second World War. One in particular was of a Quonset hut in southern Germany. He felt frozen in time, as if he were a speck crawling on top of a huge image of history. When Kendall left the fence, Deacon's reverie vanished, and only the familiar uneasy sensation in his chest made him realize that he was indeed there, and his view from outside the fence was real. The hottest part of the day was beating down on them. Deacon felt exhausted already and the heat annoyed him.

Kendall slid his hands back into his pants pockets as he pulled his elbows close to his side. His voice was low and strained. "Why are *you* doing this?"

Deacon blotted his perspiring brow. He said nothing and continued observing Kendall.

"You have everything," Kendall went on, "money, prestige, power. You nod your head and government offices and corporations panic. You already dine and golf with all the bigwigs in Washington; your wife is a top-drawer socialite, your son's a prominent surgeon. Why are you risking all of that?" Kendall looked genuinely puzzled.

"There's a cancer in our society, Bob," Deacon replied. "Whatever you, I, or others have will trickle away if we don't excise that cancer. No one has too much or too little to risk. It's something that must be done or there's nothing left for this country but a long downhill slide!"

Someone more observant would have noticed Deacon taking a deep, labored breath. He would have seen his hesitation before speaking and that momentary faraway look in his dark blue eyes before folding his arms too tightly against his chest and hiding his hands. But, Kendall was uneasy himself and his powers of observation never were much anyway. He had missed a deeper truth about Deacon Malway.

Only a few knew that Deacon didn't live in the same household with his own family. Any personal life could not survive his rigid demand for perfection. His wife rarely resided in their mansion, preferring the river home and a fair distance between them. His son avoided his phone calls since long before his medical school days. He enjoyed the academic freedom his father's money provided him but despised how it was earned and the driven father who earned it. Slicing up struggling corporations, selling off holdings and picking their bones and settling out the assets didn't interest him as it did his father. Deacon's public life was a far cry from his self-inflicted solitude.

Kendall leaned against a metal post that was not yet hung with barbed wire. "Are there many others like me?" Kendall asked.

"Of course," Deacon threw his hands up. "Intelligent men always question orders and plans when they seem contrary to their beliefs. But it's not us you should be questioning. It's the other side. Come on, Bob," Deacon suddenly spoke softly and placed his hand on the man's shoulder, and Kendall seemed to relax. "This isn't the place to talk." He wanted to get out of the heat, and he could see that Kendall might need more bolstering.

The two men left the dusty camp construction site together. The lonely visit took only twenty minutes but seemed much longer to Deacon. Kendall's strange behavior required no explaining. This was the third incident in the past month where at the requests of some of the commanders, Deacon had personally rallied and calmed someone's frayed nerves. For the monumental task they sought, it amazed him that only a few hesitated in their commitments.

It hung heavily over everyone's head; if successful, they would be national American heroes; if they lost, they would be traitors on their own soil.

CHAPTER 13

[Armory Burglars Steal Firearms, Danvers, Mass. (AP)—Burglars broke into the National Guard Armory here and stole more than a hundred firearms—but authorities said Monday the thieves could not find the firing pins that make them work. Seven M-60 machines guns. 92 M-16 semi-automatic rifles and a .45—caliber Colt pistol were taken, along with two M-203 grenade launchers used to fire grenades, sometime over the weekend, a guard spokesman said. A final inventory of the theft was under way. The armory was unstaffed from 5 p.m. Friday until Monday morning when the theft was discovered. "It had to be a professional (job)." said Sgt. Roger Cyr of the Danvers Police Department . . . Holes were found in four places in the fence, probably to provide alternative escape routes, he said. The burglars then entered the building by jimmying the rear door—the only door that wasn't wired to the second alarm system . . . .—Kennebec Journal, Augusta, Maine] [13]

May 16th

The flight to Arkansas was easier this time. Deacon's ankles didn't swell, and the sensation in his chest was subsiding, so the medication was obviously working. The flight gave him a chance to catch up on some much-needed rest. Since sundown he'd been perched in a Land Rover beside Major William Adkins, a thin long-legged man in his fifties who headed up Right Guard's secret Arkansas installation. When night fell, they approached their destination with only their parking lights leading the way. Their vehicle led the way as they slowly waded through the darkness on their second haul in four months to the secret place.

Adkins' deep creases around a hard mouth gave his face an uncompromising, no-nonsense expression as he inspected the installation's front. Straight black hair framed his high cheekbones and swarthy face emphasizing his American Indian heritage.

Adkins strong, dependable reputation fingered him by the men as one of the best they had. Many had similar credentials, but Adkins was different. Adkins not only labored tirelessly in their struggle, Deacon thought Adkins *believed* they were right.

A young soldier at the gatehouse stood at attention when Adkins and Deacon appeared. It was so dark the two could barely see his shadowed face. Adkins casually returned the young soldier's snapped salute.

"Is Captain Benson here?" he asked.

"No, sir," the young soldier replied, "just Staff Sergeant Peterson and me. We've checked out everything, sir, and it's all quiet here. Captain Benson gave us instructions to proceed if he couldn't come."

Adkins listened and bit his lower lip, a habit he had when tackling problems. "Did Benson call before you left?" Adkins asked.

"No, sir. But this came for you, sir," as he handed the major an envelope. "Courier brought it this evening."

Adkins returned to the Land Rover with Deacon at his side. He lifted a battery lamp from the floorboard to read.

"Is everything okay?" Deacon asked.

"Yes sir," answered Adkins.

"Where's Rake Benson?"

"That's what this is about." Adkins crumpled the telegram. "Rake can't make it. Some last minute emergency in Virginia. He and the General had some extra equipment come in at the arsenal and they couldn't leave. Also, according to this," Adkins held up the paper wad then stuffed it in his shirt pocket, "Guard Bureau wanted to take a count of weapons in the arsenals, and they had to rush some things back at the last minute."

"Maybe I should have stayed in Virginia on this one."

"No," said Adkins. "It's fine. These checks happen all the time."

"I had no word of any 'check' from my other sources," said Deacon.

"If Rake Benson needed help or thought something didn't smell right, he'd say so. You know the General. If it was bad he'd be on Rake like white on rice. It's fine."

Deacon slipped some medication under his tongue.

Adkins glanced at Deacon's hands maneuvering the white plastic cap back on his medicine bottle. "Rake Benson is a good man. He knows what he's doing."

From his driver's seat Adkins signaled with a red light to the waiting convoy of vehicles behind him. The staff sergeant and the young corporal opened the gates, allowing Adkins to enter. After passing the barbed wire gate, he pulled over alongside the fence then hopped out of the vehicle.

Deacon tediously followed and both men held up red-coned flashlights, marking the way for the others. After the waiting vans, trucks, and cars entered, parked, and the dust cleared they gathered around Deacon and Adkins. The group, toting gas lamps and large battery pack flashlights, was remarkably similar to the previous assemblage who guarded Number Seventeen before their arrival. They appeared committed to their tasks yet casual and un-regimented despite their military uniforms.

Deacon studied the group. They were not hardened mercenaries. On the contrary, some faces were soft and without color from lives spent in offices; while other weathered faces belonged to athletic types used to jogging through upper middle class neighborhoods trying to toughen aging muscles into submission. A few others had given up the battle and were thickening into middle age. Some were of young faces that had lost their innocence.

Ten years earlier no one, not even Deacon would guess that such a disparate mixture could come to common ground with so dangerous a mission and one that could be kept secret for so long.

CHAPTER 14

[Ohio Armory Safe by Electronics, (UPI)—Ohio National Guard officers say they are not worried about thefts of weapons and ammunition from Ohio Guard armories because of a massive system of electronic burglar alarms and watchmen. Guard officials made the statement Friday after a report of the theft of machine guns, grenade launchers, bayonets and thousands of rounds of ammunition from a Guard armory at Compton, Calif . . . . "Ohio is probably better protected than most states," Wilson said, [CW04 William Wilson, armory maintenance officer] "We had a rash of thefts from our armories back about 1969 and decided then to install the burglar alarm systems." . . . The Coshocton Tribune, East North Central Ohio] [14]

Adkins stood amidst them with one hand on his hip and the other holding his battery lamp. The lights threw eerie shadows about the unusual assembly. "You have your directions," he said. "We have this weekend to finish setting up the last of our installations. Everything should be in final working order by the end of this month. At daybreak we begin working in shifts while some of you sleep, then switch every four hours. It shouldn't take long." He paused, bit his lower lip again and walked around the inner circle with his light casting contoured shadows on the men's faces. "Next weekend we'll have a drill for some of you Guardsmen and

Reservists. I suggest you let the duty officer here know the weekends you'll be able to join us. The rest of you—from out of town or out of state—we'll have a separate duty roster for you. But for now, just let us know your free weekends. We'll be in touch. Everyone wears BDUs gentlemen; we've all got to look the same. It will be our universal uniform for now." Adkins grinned.

Subdued laughter emerged from the group.

"Take care of the gear we've issued you. More comes later."

Deacon quietly strolled about the group near Adkins. He studied the alert faces of civilians in camouflage uniforms who became soldiers on weekends and two weeks in the summer each year. They knew military life; men who still felt the call to serve yet lived and struggled to keep businesses afloat in a world where too many gave too much away at their expense. He gazed into the eyes of men who had high school educations, masters and doctorates; some were technicians and professionals, while others had small businesses or were in managerial positions in private companies or in the government.

Adkins paused, then glanced at Deacon and gave him a slight nod.

"We're all working for the same thing." Immediately all eyes centered on Deacon. He was their mentor and their supreme commander; the aging white-haired man was now the balance between those who would be in power and their military. "We're closer to our goal than ever before, but it'll be difficult throughout this last phase. Security here must be tighter than you ever thought possible. You're going to help shape the future of the greatest nation on earth. Honor will be on your shoulders as we work to help make our people self-sufficient and proud again." Deacon paused to cough. While clearing his throat, he waved his hand for Adkins to carry on.

Adkins examined the circle. "Miller's going to pass out location sheets for the supplies. Follow these orders. We have two days to get everything put up. I don't need to explain the urgency or the need for secrecy and speed in all this."

In the lamplight, Adkins' thin face showed the strain and fatigue, images not lost on Deacon.

"That's all, gentlemen," Adkins said. He helped pass out directions where each packed vehicle was to unload. The directions would be gathered back and burned before the weekend was over. The men hustled to their respective duties and in muted but determined voices carried out their orders amid the shadows.

Adkins set down his lamp on the tailgate of someone's civilian station wagon and watched the men scramble in the darkness. He pulled a wrinkled piece of paper from his pocket and secured it on a clipboard filled with inventory sheets and sat beside the light on the tailgate to take a closer look. Deacon watched as he scratched off the last line on the paper reading, "Arkansas, Number 17, Headquarters: Adkins." They looked at each other and for a moment shared all the pride, anxieties and fears of their accomplishments over the last six months.

The installation they called Number Seventeen was non-operational for three years. A former secret testing ground for experimental aircraft, it closed when the Air Force decided to drop the project. In recent years the base fell into a caretaker status. A panel studied possible future uses, but delayed their findings for six months. Amid reams of paper that flowed from the Pentagon it was lost. Suddenly the military higher-ups requested more urgent matters to tend to like congressional decisions on the Defense Department budget. "They just put it in moth balls," as one General expressed it later. Number Seventeen's facilities were big enough to hold no more than a few battalions and all their equipment. These facilities, the curved-top, metal Quonset huts and cement block and wooden barracks dotted the American landscape from one coast to the other. Of no more use to the military, the Pentagon ignored them until someone could think of something better to do with them. Someone had.

CHAPTER 15

[Last Taps for Fort Ord, By David H. Hackworth,—. . . Long considered the crown jewel of army posts, Fort Ord will shut down over the next two years. The army estimates it will save between $150 million and $200 million annually . . . . Fort Ord is just one of the 121 U.S. military bases to get the ax . . . Dozens more have been partially closed or reduced . . . It's never easy to close unneeded bases. Bases mean jobs, and jobs mean votes . . . . Newsweek] [15]

The military was a customer again and it delighted the nearby townspeople. They *looked* like soldiers; they were *secretive* like the previous military occupants, and the town scrambled to provide their supplies, equipment and business needs.

Similar to the former tenants, as one gas station owner noticed, they seemed most active on weekends. Convoys crawled in long lines, moving in the darkness from late night to the early morning weekend hours. The Great Eats Bakery Shoppe owner noticed the groups' unusual hours as she opened her shop at 3 a.m. to begin the town's only supply of freshly baked bread.

Grocer, Jeff Bowles, witnessed first-hand large military equipment and weapons coming and going at unusual hours. However, on delivering his food and produce orders to the mess hall, quantities ordered did not quite seem to match up to the bodies needed to run the installation.

From outward appearances with the "government" back in town, most of the small businesses were curious but gearing up for a good year. None of the locals wanted to question the best thing coming their way in a long time.

CHAPTER 16

[Thefts of U.S. Weapons Said to Benefit Terrorists, LONDON (Reuters)—The United States is the world's largest supplier of arms to terrorists through thefts from its armories, according to a report published here today.

The report issued by the Center for Contemporary Studies, an independent group that reviews social and political trends, said that guns stolen in raids on the United States Army depots in Europe had ended up in such places as Northern Ireland, Bangladesh and El Salvador.

The Army had acknowledged that enough arms to equip 8,000 men had been stolen from the United States depots between 1971 and 1974, the report said . . . .—New York Times, London] [16]

May 27th

Lunches were easy to pull off. Most women are comfortable with "just lunch." Dinner could be something more serious, so Eric worked extra hard at letting Jill know it was a simple good-bye token of affection.

"Let's have dinner," Eric suggested to her. "Say good-bye, one last hurrah between friends." However, he used the same excuse two weeks earlier when he wanted to see Jill and four days later when he drove in the area and stopped by her office to see how the campaign was going.

71

The Ebb Tide Grill was home turf for Eric. He wanted to be with her in a familiar place where he had a history. He wanted to take her there again. It was comfortable in one sense, but he was about to go *undercover* again and Ross would say maybe *stupid* . . . then *dangerous*.

They were unpretentious in each other's company and after dinner, they quietly left like two lovers: talking in hushed tones, lightly touching one another, and quietly walking arm in arm out the door. The warm rain started drizzling when they arrived, and by the time they left, it stopped.

Heading back to Georgetown and finding parking was always an adventure in itself along the lettered streets as the historic area was perpetually cluttered with tourists and local shoppers. As usual, the closest parking space available was three blocks away. The puddles on the uneven brick sidewalks in this historic section of Washington, D.C. glistened ahead of their path as they occasionally passed an old iron street lamp in the darkness.

"They want you again, don't they?" Jill asked Eric as they walked up a slight hill on their way back to her apartment.

"Who?" he asked.

"Eric, you're jumpy tonight." She stopped walking for a moment and stared at him. "You're physically better and they *want* you for another assignment." There was a soft quality to her voice. "I'm right, *aren't* I?" She maneuvered her arm in his and continued walking.

"I told you that I may be leaving town soon. Just a short trip." She was guessing, but either he was showing his nerves or she was a mind reader. Either way, it wasn't good.

They neared her apartment and climbed a gracefully curving black iron stairway to the front door.

"Jill, you're spooked too easily. I think . . ." but before he could finish they *both* heard the faint ringing and she quickly hunted for her key in the darkness. She forgot to leave the front porch light on when they left for dinner and now she groped in the folds of her purse rummaging for the house key. Eric dutifully held her bag open for her to continue when she suddenly reached in her dress pocket and exclaimed, "Oh, what an idiot. It was *here* all the time." Pushing the large key into the old brass lock, she opened the door and ran, only to hear the phone shake off its last ring just as she picked up the receiver.

She said nothing, but from her expression Eric guessed she knew the caller. His picture was neatly framed in silver and placed on a small side table in the living room. A dark-haired thirtyish man, smiling, sat on an old split rail fence in a rural setting with folded arms. By his expression he seemed pretty pleased with himself.

Eric thought the face in the silver frame was P. Scott Barren. Away at a Dental Association Convention in New Orleans, it was probably good old P. Scott calling on the phone. Luckily he was invited in when the phone rang. Eric smiled, leaning against her mantle, wanting an invitation to stay even if it was *just to talk.*

"Want me to make some coffee?" she asked, walking toward him. Her ice blue silk dress gently followed the soft curves of her body, and when she stopped in front of him the delicate scent of her perfume flooded his senses. *Citrus and roses.*

"Jill," he spoke softly and reached out to her. She stood motionless in front of him. With one arm around her waist he pulled her firmly to him. He could feel her chest rise taking in an extended breath. When she tried to whisper, "Eric . . . I don't think so," he covered her mouth with his, kissing her gently. He could feel her subtle protest: her palms pushing him back then giving way to his gentle pressure. He kissed her neck then lightly nibbled her ear, breathing in warm air. His lips slowly traced the arching lines of her neck down to the top button of her silk dress.

Jill gently stopped him. Her slender fingers softly caressed his face then delicately nudged him away. Running a nervous hand through her dark hair, she turned away from him. Eric didn't want to give her a second chance to refuse him. Eric knew she well remembered the lost weekends and the heated, unstoppable lovemaking that consumed them. Slowly he approached her again. His head lowered, he turned slightly, concentrating on her lips.

"It's *not* going to happen, Eric." Jill said softly. "This is *my* fault." She seemed to fumble for excuses. "I didn't expect to invite you in." Jill looked at him then turned away. It was obvious that she was uncomfortable now looking into his face.

Eric glanced at the silver frame. He nodded toward it. "You two really that serious?" he asked.

"*He* is. He says he wants to marry me."

"And?"

"He's a fine man. Stable, well . . . somewhat. And I don't expect I'll have to worry about his disappearing for some unheard of country in the middle of the night."

"Is that what you want? A station wagon, a dog and two kids in the suburbs?" Eric placed one hand on his hip. He waited for an answer but she hesitated too long. He knew she was still searching for one.

"It may be what I want. At least it was before you came back. It'll be the same again after you leave."

The phone rang again—a jarring interruption. Jill waited until she had taken in two deep breaths before lifting the receiver and slowly placing it to her ear. After some delay, she spoke, "Hello, darling."

Eric turned away and gazed outside a large bay window at the passersby. It was raining again. His thoughts began to drift just for a few seconds to his assignment, the danger, and now a former lover entering and complicating his playing field.

Eric emerged from his private thoughts with Jill still hanging on the phone with *good old* P. Scott. He tried not to listen at first then watched as Jill withdrew like a reprimanded child. It irked him to see it.

"No, I haven't gotten your mail today," she said still on the phone. "Tomorrow I won't have as many strategy meetings. I plan to pick it all up then." She hesitated, and then her forehead wrinkled. "Scott, I'm sorry. If you remember, I *work* also. I'll do the best I can . . . tomorrow. I did get your suit to the cleaners and they said ready on Tuesday." There was a long pause. "Good. I'm glad you're having a good time. Be careful driving back to the hotel. Yes, of course, let Ben drive," she said referring to Scott's brother, also a dentist. "Yes . . . well brothers are like that, let him drive, Scott," she repeated. Eric heard her voice lower. She hesitated again then turned her back to him. "I love you, too." Another long pause. "Tonight? Nothing special. Dinner with a girlfriend. School chum. Yes, of course I will, Tuesday, I'll be there. Okay. Good night." She hung up. The force with which she laid the receiver into its cradle told him she was more than irritated. Jill pulled open a drawer. She found some notepaper and scratched down a few notes.

Eric saw the small Colt .25 caliber automatic lying between some bills and a pamphlet, 'Physicians Against Handguns'. He reached for the Colt. "*Yours?*" he asked.

"Yes. It makes me feel better knowing it's there at night if I need it," Jill said.

"Physicians Against Handguns?" he questioned her but, he already knew about P. Scott.

"Eric, it's Scott's. He has a right to do and believe in what he wants."

"You're selling out, Jill. It's not you. You won't have the stomach for what's ahead of you."

Jill took the gun from him and shoved it deep into the desk drawer, and slammed it closed. "Eric, please leave now."

"Just a friend, a *girlfriend*?" he asked her, his light blue eyes penetrating her facade. "You don't lie to the one you *love*, Jill." He pulled his hands from his pockets and deliberately walked in front of her. He grabbed her shoulders. "What do you do in bed with him? 'Yes, Scott, I love this, Scott, oh—keep it up, you're the best, Scott,' " he emulated.

Tears flooded her hazel colored eyes but he kept up the pressure. As he cupped his hands tenderly around her face, he took in her tears and her quivering lips. Before she could reply, he lifted her chin and placed his mouth on hers once more. First, he was gentle, then firm. He held her tightly against his body feeling her unyielding breasts press into him. He wanted her to feel his own frustration and to remember those lost Saturday afternoons when they learned to play, excite and ignite each other.

Jill didn't try to free herself from his grip. But when he broke the embrace to look at her again and caress her breast, she hung her head down then buried it into his chest. "Your leaving was *terrible* for me, Eric. It's not at all easy, you coming back this way." Jill went limp then walked away from him. She slumped to the sofa facing the large windows and curled her feet beneath her. "We were so innocent then. One minute I had everything: you, an upcoming grant for graduate school, and my sanity. In one week it vanished. Not even Drake knew where you were. I won't risk myself for that again. I don't feel the *same way* now."

He listened to her quietly and felt the same turmoil going on inside him. There was so much he couldn't share with her. The summer after their graduation she went to England, then Germany, for special studies in political science. If the Agency knew of their involvement, they would have chosen someone else for the assignment Eric so badly wanted. A loved one overseas meant too much vulnerability.

"I know you're going off on some assignment again, Eric. No, don't lie to me. Let's just say, I *feel* it coming. I thought a few days back I could walk away from Scott and back to where we left off but now I don't think so."

"Don't think about it now. No decisions. We'll handle it later," he too quickly spoke out.

Jill left the sofa and walked to the front window to look out. Eric stood behind her and gently maneuvered his arm around her tapered waist. She pulled away from him and sat on the arm of a large overstuffed chair. "Eric it was all a different perspective then. Love found, love lost. Drake was the only one who could console the empty hole in my chest. You want me to do this *again*?"

"Later," he insisted and took control, stopping her from surrendering to a line of reason he did not want to hear. He took her hand and held it between his, then kissed the delicate freckles across her slender fingers. "I don't want to leave it like this, but there's no more time. Let's save it for the Shore." The Eastern Shore of Maryland was a special place for them. Both of them felt a special sense of freedom that came from being near and on the Chesapeake Bay. It had been their escape and what they sought together when life closed in.

"How long?" she asked, her sad eyes remembering.

"It's only a short one. This time I *promise*."

Jill momentarily regained her composure. "Eric, I can't promise you anything. I may be with Scott when you come back."

He didn't answer.

"Not like before, is it?" she asked, looking up at him. "Promises of love and devotion. Seducing each other so skillfully that . . . ."

"*Don't* do this." He walked to the big chair and pulled her up to him. He hugged her gently and rocked her like a small child. He could not tell her that despite others he still dreamt of her like a schoolboy fantasizing. Occasional nights when he lay awake and alone for hours he drifted to thoughts about being inside her . . . so close that he could feel her heart beating wildly then yielding to a quiet, rhythmic tremble. *Jill, don't do this now,* he thought.

It was a long three blocks back to his car. The rain started again but the wet drizzle didn't bother him. Summer was coming and the gentle warm Washington rain reflected his mood. He re-thought her phone conversation with her drunken dentist boyfriend. It amused Eric that she could not be honest with Scott about their dinner engagement. Had she told Scott about *him*? In her private moments with Scott, did she think of *him*? Was Scott a man she could share her soul with or did she have to hide her past like a hurt child? Did Scott know *her* cravings and needs? Could he fill them and revel in them late at night when passion would not let *her* sleep?

"Damn it," Eric muttered to himself. If she can't be herself with P. Scott Barren on the phone, how could he *know* her at all; how could he help satisfy her insatiable curiosity about the world or soothe her complex woman's soul when she was low or better still—how could he know what really set her on fire in bed?

CHAPTER 17

[Abstract: NYC police probe possibility that M-16 rifles and ammunition stolen from Yonkers National Guard armory were used in a hold-up of Harlem Savings Bank—The New York Times, New York Times, New York] [17]

"She's been floundering about since you two broke up," Drake told Eric two days ago. They chatted while running around the inside track at the Capital Sports Club. "P. Scott's a pretty unsophisticated boor: a drag, really. Tries to fit into D.C. *society*. A *dentist*, for God's sake." Drake was playing "informer" with Eric, and he obviously enjoyed putting down the man he labeled an "arrogant asshole" at his parties. "Scott Barren is always on the make for whatever will roll over for him," he told Eric. "Political pull, financial status, women and whomever . . . *whatever*—doesn't matter with him."

Drake's unruly carrot-colored hair—boyishly styled, his interest tended more toward his own athletic prowess with the crew team at the D.C. boathouse, his ability to throw a successful party, and keeping up with his friends in Georgetown than in climbing the capital's social ladder. He liked working for the United States Information Agency but it was not his only means of support. The Cochran family amassed substantial real estate holdings in Northern Virginia, and Drake's grandmother practically single-handedly ran the *real* social strata of Washington, D.C.—a Blue Book-Blue Blood. There was no need for him to put out the effort; he was well vested by birth.

"Is he going into politics?" Eric asked.

"Don't think so. He's more a political groupie. He holds some office in his professional association and he formed a chapter of Physicians Against Handguns for this region. Likes to be in the papers. Katherine just bought one of the old homes to renovate down at Logan Circle. You should buy something on the Circle; the area's coming back. Anyway, she saw him late one night down there . . . seems he may have an occasional weakness for the *ladies* down at 13th and P Streets. That sort of jerk . . . you know?"

Eric *did* know. He had known most of it for a long time.

When the two stopped jogging, they walked another lap at the club to cool down. "He may be a real dickhead, but I think he's really got the hots for Jill. Seems serious. That bother you?" Drake asked.

"No. Just wanted to know what the attraction was, that's all."

Drake knew it was not '*all*', but he was a good enough friend not to say so.

CHAPTER 18

[Security devices Hinder Thefts At Many Armories, Lincoln, (AP)—A spot check of National Guard armories on Sunday showed that most are unguarded by humans but many have electronic security devices designed to prevent the kind of break-in and arms theft that occurred last week in Compton, Calif.

The FBI has said that enough weapons were stolen from the California facility between Wednesday and Thursday night to equip an Army combat company. The armory in the Los Angeles suburb was unguarded at the time of the theft. Officials said they were in the process of installing an electronic security system.

The National Guard armory at Muskogee, Okla., Was burglarized on June 27 and authorities said five pistols and three machine guns were taken. The case is still unsolved . . . .—The Lincoln Star, Lincoln, Nebraska.] [18]

June 28th

Matt Watson's decisive mind controlled his body movements. He was courteous, steady and intentional. His intense eyes always searching, his pale skin and thinning brownish-gray hair gave him the appearance of a man who had spent a great part of his life seated at an obscure desk. However, Watson carefully cultivated this studied, suburban-Joe look. Underneath loose-fitting, comfortable clothes his thinness could be mistaken for a man slight of figure with delicate bone structure. However, the casual khakis and faded

81

yellow sweater camouflaged taut, lean muscles dense from heavy exercise. Operatives who worked in darkness, boarded ships, and jumped from aircraft were rarely the heavily muscled, baby-oiled glistening Hollywood version. They were hard and lean, quick and fluid—and they often looked a lot like Matt Watson, Eric's contact man.

"My wife will show you around," Watson said speaking to Eric with a faint smile lifting the corners of his mouth. "I don't usually go to the county committee meetings, but they're trying to dam up the creek behind the house," Watson explained. "I don't want a swamp back there."

There was the smell of fresh coffee in the house and lemon cake. Yes, lemon cake with ginger, Eric guessed. The couple expected Eric's evening arrival. Watson smoothly excused himself and firmly shook Eric's hand. Again, Watson produced that thin, half-twist smile that seemed so familiar, but Eric just couldn't place it. His face was otherwise unremarkable; except for his eyes, something there pinged Eric's memory. Outwardly, Watson was good-natured and very composed. He enjoyed a pipe, gripping it tightly between his teeth and talking at the same time. His firm handshake felt like that of a man who could be counted on—apparently Langley trusted him.

Ross supplied Eric with the usual details but little about Watson's background. He and his wife fit comfortably into the quaint Victorian Bel Air community, southwest of Richmond. Watson had few financial worries as a senior partner in a Virginia computer company. He only rented out the carriage house next to his large home to help pay taxes for the convenience of having it there. His wife's family and their friends used the little apartment in the summer. In winter, University of Richmond students were the usual tenants. However, this year it needed renovating and they turned down prospective student renters until next fall.

Fran Watson, a brown-haired, large, buxom woman with a delicate, beautiful face and a lilting voice led Eric on a tour of the carriage house. "We usually don't rent this out in the summer," she said, "But we're not going to have much family in and it's a waste to just let it sit. Needs life in here."

"Have you lived here long?" Eric asked her.

"Nine years or so. It seems longer, I tend to forget. When we came, people in this area began to restore these old homes." She nodded to her own home. "Ours was a small resort inn built at the turn of the century. Can you imagine that?" She smiled, and opened the ground level door to show him inside. "Richmond's wealthy took the train here when the area was their summer playground. Now we're an annexed part of the city. I guess that happens a lot, wouldn't you say?"

Eric agreed, smiling. He thought she would be a knockout if she lost thirty pounds. With her husband on the thin side, Eric found the match amusing.

The Watson's built the little carriage house apartment on two levels. Inside there was a wide dirt floor where carriages and touring cars once parked. Now a storage place, Watson's lawn equipment and tools hung in neat, straight rows on peg-board paneled walls. On entering Eric could smell lawnmower oil and fresh cut grass and damp woven straw. An inside stair clung to the wall and led up to the second level and a small apartment.

Eric liked the apartment living room. It appeared larger than its actual size because she redecorated with mirrors and replaced the small windows facing the woods with larger ones. The room bore a slight oriental appearance with woven beige wallpaper, black furniture, and a pleasing use of red, yellow and gold. Despite the strong colors, Fran Watson made good use of silk prints and oriental vases—mementos from having lived in Asia.

"Do you have pets?" he asked her, opening a closet inside the small bathroom.

"An old Irish setter, 'Micky.' He's really Matt's. He's ancient . . . our best friend. You?"

"Springador. Jager. Means 'hunter' in German. He's a great dog."

"You speak German?" she asked.

"I used to. But you lose it when you don't speak it."

"You're right about that. Matt's adequately fluent in a couple of languages, but he's always claiming he's lost them, too."

"About Jager," Eric continued, "Can I have him here? Do you mind?"

"No, I don't think there'll be problems with that. The county has laws about keeping dogs collared and chained, but you can use the run we have for Micky. He used it before he got arthritis." Fran handed Eric his keys. "Where is Jager?"

"In Georgetown now. A friend is keeping him for me." Eric smiled at the woman. He hid his hands in his pockets.

"Looks like we have a deal," Fran commented, offering a soft, Southern hand. "Coffee and cake, Mr. Brent?"

CHAPTER 19

[No Ties suspected in Weapons Theft, Fresno, Calif (AP)—. . . Thieves stole 97 MM rifles and a very large quantity of military supplies from an armory at nearby Clovis on July 31, 1972.

Investigators sought, meanwhile, to determine how the Fresno area armory was entered for the most recent theft. The building's sophisticated intrusion detection device was undisturbed and appeared to be in working order, a spokesman said Thursday. There were no guards on duty at the time.— **Charleston Daily Mail, West Virginia]** *[19]*

Pete, one of Eric's few Agency buddies, promised Eric he would do the deed. Wrap one friendly black Springador in yellow ribbons and place him on Jill's top brick step. Then pin a note on his leather leash; tie it to the winding black iron railing leading to her Georgetown apartment in Washington, D.C. Ring the bell and disappear.

Alone, Jill opened the door, searched for a face, then looked down and saw only the black Springador. Resembling a black Irish setter, he whined, and then wagged his tail as if he expected his master to be inside. When he was not immediately coaxed in, his expression changed. His ears moved forward, he closed his mouth and his black eyes fixed on her. Quickly she scanned the street.

No one was in sight. Yellow ribbons dangled all over the poor dog. No woman's handiwork here. The amateurish bows drooped in varying lengths of ribbon, some falling apart. With a sigh, she led the four-footed black and yellow spectacle into the house.

The dog sat in front of her sofa, the leash still dangling from his neck. The pathetic yellow ribbons fell and curled up on her carpet. Ears up and head cocked to one side . . . he seemed as surprised as she was at being there.

"Jager," she said aloud, reading from the note. The dog's ears perked up again and he came toward her, licking her hands and wagging his tail. Jill finished reading the note. She blew out a heavy sigh. "How am I going to explain you?" she said suddenly laughing and clearing the ribbons from his muzzle. Jill rubbed his head and led him back to the kitchen. He seemed perfectly at home, and when she opened the refrigerator door, he sat in front of her holding up his right paw, expecting a treat.

Laughing, she watched him try to pick up a slice of Danish ham from the paper towel on her kitchen floor. She pulled out a pair of scissors from a kitchen drawer and sat on the floor in front of him cutting away the yellow curls. Jager gulped down the meat. "I bet Eric doesn't feed you this well." He squatted down in front of her and licked her face, unaware that the salty taste was coming from Jill's tears.

She knew in a short time that Jager would rejoin Eric. Exactly where and what he was doing, she didn't know. She wasn't sure she wanted to know.

CHAPTER 20

*[Most Armories Unguarded, Some Have Security Alarms, (AP)—. . .
Officials said there was no sign of forcible entry and theorized that someone
hid inside the armory during the day, waited until it was deserted and then
stole the weapons.*

*The armories in the state are unguarded and officials said they had no
plans for any new security. They said the locks and gun vaults are sufficient
protection. National Guard units elsewhere said they already had special security systems. In Massachusetts, officials said the Boston armory is guarded 24
hours a day; the other 69 armories in the state have "intrusion detection sys
tems" hooked up to state or local police offices . . . .—Warren Times Observer,
Warren Pennsylvania] [20]*

Eric's first weeks in Richmond were endless days of visits to lawyers, meetings with other inventors and phone calls from Brannen Technology. If the investment money showed up, they said they
could start research the next month.

Establishing himself was always the tedious part of the job,
as he made the rounds, visiting gun shops, getting the word on
the latest weapons, and spreading the word that he spent a lot
of time touring around and shooting in various matches and
championships.

According to three gun stores, Chesterfield County's Pinehill Shooting Club was the best around. There were Stoney Glen and Peterson's Point Gun clubs, but everyone generally agreed, Pinehill was still the best. Besides, it was near Bel Air where Eric was staying in the converted carriage house. Pinehill's members had "a little more money," one man confided in Eric, "and time to fix it up right." He found that true.

Although Pinehill was plain on the outside, a square cement building on three sides with a rustic barn board front and a dirt parking lot, the lounge was more upscale, with leather chairs instead of patched vinyl castoffs. The range could hold twenty shooters at one time with ten on either side of a podium serving the presiding range official.

The Club closed early on Mondays, and Eric had arrived late. All day he worked on his design with a metallurgist in Richmond. They both had become so involved in the design, the day got away from them.

He placed his membership key in the lock and entered the side door. The wooden gun box weighed heavily on his still healing shoulder. He entered the range and dropped two quarters in the slot to keep the air conditioning running for a few more hours. The club automated its use to save money. The system made a rattling noise, and then toned down to a mild whining sound pumping out the cool air. He didn't mind the resonance; it kept him company on the solitary range.

For three hours, he kept firing away at the targets with his .45 and .22 caliber match pistols. The automatically retrievable targets were the same he used on CIA and Quantico ranges near Langley. He stayed concentrated on the black and white circled target until it blurred from fatigue. He tired from the weight of the guns, something he would have to correct immediately: endurance was part of competition.

Brass casings lay everywhere around his position at the firing line, another reminder of how much an improvement his caseless lightweight weapon concept will be. He pressed the button to retrieve his target, changed to another design, and then sent it down range. He exercised at his position on the line before firing again, moving his arms in circles. Stretching out his hands and fingers, he flinched as a dull pain ran through his shoulder muscle. He exercised again, more slowly this time.

Alone on the range with only the machine's whining and darkness already outside, Eric's thoughts wandered. An old friend from his past ragged him about psyching out his opponents when they both shot for the Air Force Pistol Team. Eric was good at it. His friend died in Vietnam, along with more than Eric wanted to remember.

As Eric loaded the .22 caliber pistol, he thought about his choices in life, particularly in joining the Agency. *Had it been a mistake?* He loaded another magazine in his .45 automatic, and thought about Ross and Jason, who had been a Master Shooter. He began firing the .45 again, getting into the rhythm of the recoil. The loud crack of the shots echoed throughout the range, seemingly magnifying their sound and strangely amplifying his loneliness. Eric remembered his father's "shooting days" and could almost see him pointing his pistol downrange, eyeing his target and striking it with incredible accuracy. When his father could break away from his job at the Pentagon, Eric sometimes tagged along with him to the pistol range at nearby Quantico Marine Base. As a boy of ten, he thought his father was the finest shot in the world.

His shoulder aching again, he shot off the final round of the .45, unloaded it and packed it away. The .22 would go easier on him now.

The air conditioning unit at the range suddenly swallowed the quarters, belched, then cut off, startling Eric. Because of the squeaks and creaks of the machine, he missed hearing a key being inserted into the club's side door. Without warning the range door suddenly jerked open behind him. *Damn, the .45 was packed up.* He didn't turn around but grabbed his .22, instantly slamming a magazine into the butt. He held it close to his chest, point up. Alarmed but still controlled, he spun around toward the intruders . . . his gun pointed at them. Two men dressed in business suits entered casually, both smiling.

"Well, well," said Eric, looking up. He slowly lowered the gun to his side. "What brings the almighty down from the mount?" He grinned at Pete Miller who was bringing in an ammunition can and placing it at his spot on the range. Eric meant his comment for Ross. His supervisor remained stoic and silent.

Ross strolled around looking at the range and then at Eric's gun box sitting on the platform. His tie loosened, the cuffs of his shirt showed wear. He appeared as fatigued as his wrinkled gray suit.

Pete, his one-time partner on a long assignment, was smiling one of his sarcastic grins at Eric. Pete seemed to enjoy the verbal shots between Ross and Eric—whom he jokingly called "Batman" or the "hairy-lip hero."

"How's it going?" asked Pete. "Hardware looks pretty good."

"Not bad. Like riding a bike, you just don't forget. Check these out." Eric handed Pete three of the targets he had shot during his early hours on the range. Ross sometimes was comical when he played the *man in charge*. He quietly strutted about with his hands in his pockets just as arrogant as always.

Pete handed a target to Ross who closely inspected the hits. "What's this?" he asked, pointing to one shot that strayed to the eight ring although the others were in a tight group between the ten and the x-ring.

"Every so often I throw one. My trigger pull is not right yet, but it's damn good for not seriously competing in ten years," Eric said.

Ross nodded pensively, and then reached for the other targets.

"We brought you this," said Pete. He handed Eric a new Army Premium Grade Wadcutter .45. "It's been specially accurized by the Marksmanship Training Unit. That's for you, too," Pete added, pointing to the ammunition can. "We thought you could use the extra."

Ross said nothing. He threw the targets on a bench then leaned against a shooter's stand and checked out the contents of Eric's gun box.

Pete shuffled to a nearby drink machine and dropped some change into the slot. He waited for the can to slide and clank down the shaft before continuing the conversation.

"There's a private league match coming up soon that *we* want you to enter. There's someone there you're to meet. He's in the army guard, but he'll be there shooting as a civilian . . . name is Rake Benson." Pete lifted the soda and drank from the metal can, eyes still on Eric.

Ross silently peered into the scope mounted on the open lid of Eric's gun box. He refocused at Eric's target down range.

"What do I need to know about him?" asked Eric.

"Nothing now," said Pete.

Ross broke in. "We'll let you know . . . ."

". . . Okay, okay, I know," Eric said, finishing the sentence . . . "what I need to know when I need to know it."

"The match is an invitational in Bristol," Ross said, still looking through the scope. "There'll be a few shooters there from out of state. Just make a few right wing comments and be your glorious conservative self." Ross turned and faced him. "Just drop a few lines here and there and see who picks up on them."

"Your name is on the match invitation list," Pete added. "You should be getting registration forms any day."

"Anything else?" Brent turned around to finish closing up his gun box.

"Yes," Pete replied. "We arranged a small front page article about your invention for the Bristol paper for that weekend. We need to get a black and white head and shoulders shot. There's none in the file that we can use."

Ross added, "Eric, you need to know that Rake's father, Taylor Benson, may be a point of interest to us too. Rake is your target.

But, whatever else you bring in surrounding Taylor Benson would be gravy."

"Why the interest in his father?" Eric asked Ross.

"We know at one time Taylor Benson did some research in weapon systems. He worked with a guy named Joseph Halsey. Halsey is also of interest to us right now. It would be interesting to know if there is a connection between them and the Right Guard."

Eric looked back at his position on the range and caught Ross unpacking the last of the guns from his black box. He set two weapons on top of Eric's gun stand and two boxes of bullets beside each.

"What the hell are you doing?" Eric blurted out.

"You can't be 'almost perfect' this time," Ross told him." He glanced at Eric then looked down the range through the scope.

"Yes, I know, *dead perfect*," Eric said. "I practiced all afternoon, Ross. These are not bad scores for the first time in ten years. I'm tired, my shoulder aches and it's getting hot in here. Besides, I can come back tomorrow."

Ross tossed him a gun. "You get your paycheck this week?"

"Yes."

"It covers that." Ross strolled to the air conditioning unit and dropped in two quarters. The machine rattled and started again. He slapped Eric on the back echoing, "Practice, practice, practice."

Eric winced from the ache in his shoulder. The two men slipped out, leaving him fuming . . . but he was reloading to fire again.

CHAPTER 21

[Arms Stolen at Armor, Los Angeles (AP . . .—Investigators said entry to the armory was through a side door and a vacuum drill was used to pierce the weapons vault, which an armory sergeant recalled locking at 10 a.m. Wednesday. A Compton police spokesman said a motive for the theft was not known immediately.—The Newport Daily News, Newport, Rhode Island] [21]

July 10th

"It was odd, those twelve fighter aircraft . . . detailed out far longer than normal," Captain Johnston thought, as he prepared Moony Air Force base's monthly readiness report. Damnedest thing about it was their exercises concluded two weeks ago.

When he tried to bring it to the Colonel's attention, someone told him they were on an unscheduled special exercise and that he was to report them as "accounted for." Even stranger still, all of the wartime munitions and reserve spares were gone too. However, Johnston's senior officer was adamant about the unscheduled special exercise.

Captain Johnston had no way of knowing that 45 other Air Force units that month also had similar problems accounting for all of their combat helicopters and fighters.

Shortly after he brought it to the Colonel's attention a second time, Johnston was suddenly reassigned to a special duty concerning base clean up and beautification.

CHAPTER 22

[Rip-offs From U.S. Arms Stockpiles: Will It Be An A-Bomb Next?—...
Because of the big wallop of today's military weapons, even one loss is consid-
ered serious. Says a Defense official: "When one man armed with an M-16
automatic rifle opposes five cops with pistols, the odds favor the M-16."...
—U. S. News & World Report] [22]

The pistol club in Bristol was much like other clubs around rural Virginia. The partially finished inside had only two paneled walls. Hand-scrawled and photocopied notes about upcoming matches stuck to the fake walnut paneling with staples and tape. Naked wires against pink insulation ran through the rest of the framework like large exposed veins.

The solitary sportsmen arriving to compete in the match seemed almost to be clones. Dressed in denim and military-colored cotton greens and tans, each toted his own gun box as if he were carrying the secrets of the sport inside.

Eric sat down on a wooden folding chair near the registration table and ate a rubbery hot dog smothered under jalapeno mustard and burnt onions, a specialty of the club president's wife. Annoyed about the *tube steak*, it reminded him of his own mother's household that ran more to gourmet cuisine. She never allowed "hot dogs" in the home even when they moved to America. She once dismissed a cook for serving sauerkraut with Wiener Schnitzel. "Peasant food," she had explained in her soft upper-class Germanic style, "is not served at our dining table." It was remnants of a past that she clung to when little else could console her. However, the elegant world she wanted to remember was forever lost to her.

Between bites, Eric watched the "rabbit foot" rituals of the men getting ready for the match. Some of it was showmanship, some was a psych-out, and the rest was pure superstition.

Eric watched a top-heavy woman helping to register the shooters. She rolled her eyes and horse-laughed at one man's answers. The other registrants tried to shut her out so they could concentrate on the forms, but her howls became louder and more irritating. Oblivious to how she was affecting the shooters, she cackled on. Eric could see it was upsetting some of the contestants' pre-match routines and he listened to the antics of *one* shooter still having fun with the obnoxious woman. Her laugh could be heard above the twenty or so shooters preparing for the day.

As Eric watched, a sandy-haired man stepped up to the adjacent registrar. "Here's your blood money," the man said.

The registrar in front of him grinned, revealing a space between his two front teeth. "Benson, you and your daddy own half of Grasmere County. Don't you come in here crying poor-mouth."

Eric watched as the gap-toothed man called out the name, "*Rake Benson*. His name is on the second list there." Eric poked the last of his tube steak in his mouth and casually glanced around the clubhouse.

"Any new shooters?" Benson asked the registrar.

"Mostly regulars. But we do have a new fella we haven't seen before," the man nodded to Eric. "Name's Brent. He's from Richmond."

Rake Benson stepped close to where Eric was sitting and carefully set his gun box on the floor. He peered at the match information sheet. It was mimeographed like a country church bulletin and was just as tough to decipher.

Eric toted his box to the firing line in the next room. Rake followed. "Looks like we're firing side by side. I've been firing in these matches since I was twelve and I'm not any better . . . Rake Benson," he said, extending his hand.

"Eric Brent." Eric laughed and grasped his hand. Benson's hair was almost as blond as his own was and his blue eyes were clear and lively. When he smiled, the muscles in his left cheek jumped before his mouth opened. Benson's eyes drew Eric in. Eric's father's quips about life had always served his son well, especially the one about the eyes being the barometer of the soul—it was so with Rake Benson.

There was tautness to Rake's face that was rugged. His broad shoulders met a slim waist and his agile, graceful movements suggested moneyed Southern refinement. He delivered a handshake with authority like a Virginia gentleman honoring a bargain; a type of 'handshake' that still permeated Virginia's legal system as well as the local culture.

Both men set their black boxes at their positions on the firing tables, lifted the lids, and focused their scopes down range. Eric wanted Rake to make the next move. He didn't have to wait long.

"What do you do in Richmond?" Rake asked.

"I'm working on a new gun concept half the time and shooting in matches the other half."

"Sounds like a *rough* life." Rake pulled out a box of ammunition. "This gun concept—yours or someone else's?"

"Mine." Reaching into his box, Eric wiped his hands on one of Fran Watson's worn kitchen towels-turned oil rag.

"What exactly is it?"

"A new concept in propulsion." Eric pulled out his gun tray and boxes of ammunition.

"Tom," Rake turned and yelled at the referee, "are we going to get sighters before this match?" When a nod came from the other side of the range, he responded, "Damn, I'm glad about that. I'm not sighted in for this range," he confessed to Eric. Using a small screwdriver, he turned a screw on top of his .22 until it clicked a few times. "Tell me more about it. You going to be the new Sam Colt?"

"Colt would turn in his grave," Eric said with a half smile, "if he knew what I had on the drawing boards." *Throw out bits and pieces*, Ross told him.

"Well, now. Sounds like this boy might have *something*. You know, my dad would be interested in talking to you about this. He experimented with new arms designs in his day." Rake checked the sights on his gun. "When's the unveiling of this marvelous new toy. What do you call it?"

"Call it H-PAR, Hypergolic Propulsion Actuated Round," Eric said. "Well, I really shouldn't be giving away the farm. Legal work still needs to be hammered out."

The referee shouted out, "Quiet on the line," and looked at the two men. The other shooters took him seriously. Stillness fell over the range. The only definable sounds left were of men repositioning their boots on the grainy cement floor, the creaking of a gun box lid being clipped back more securely and throats clearing.

"We'll talk later," Rake whispered. "I want to hear more."

I'm in . . . Eric thought.

Both men pulled their ear protectors down and the match began with a deafening volley of rounds.

CHAPTER 23

[Patrols Too Costly, Alarm Systems Protect Armories, (AP)—Most National Guard armories have antiburglary systems, but an informal survey shows many are unguarded by humans mainly because officials say security patrols are too costly . . . . Thieves in recent years have broken into other armories in California and storage facilities in a number of other states, including Pennsylvania, Florida, Massachusetts, Kansas and Oklahoma. "The Guard just doesn't have enough people to have them sit in an armory all the time," said Lt. Rick Roberts, a Guard spokesman in Philadelphia . . . . .—Syracuse Herald Journal, Syracuse, New York.] [23]

Eric rolled his car into the carriage house driveway in Bel Air at one-thirty in the morning. Dragging himself up the stairs, he lumbered in and collapsed on the sofa. The match ran two hours over and afterward they celebrated hard. When time came to eat, a greasy hamburger followed the second jalapeno hot dog. What was left of his intestines from the Vietnam injury did not digest mayonnaise, eggs, or red meat well. The hamburger grease didn't help either and occasionally when chased by too much alcohol it caused hellacious pains and he would bleed in the morning. The humid air was also making his shoulder ache. *Damn, he thought.*

When the telephone rang, he quickly woke up instantly alert.

John Ross' voice sounded too calm and almost tired. "Where've you been? I've been calling for three hours."

"We celebrated after the match. Some of us went to a local tavern."

"How'd you do?"

"I managed third place in the open." He knew Ross would be pleased. "I met our 'friend' at the match," Eric continued. "Interesting man."

Ross still said nothing. He waited patiently at the phone for Eric to continue.

Eric came back in a slow, deliberate voice. "You knew all along this was going to involve my getting back into the damn military and you didn't once mention it."

"So, he talked about the Guard?" asked Ross.

"He wants me on their pistol team."

"Good group. What's the matter, getting too old for it?" Then quickly Ross added before Eric could answer, "Well, got anything else?"

"He said there were some slots open in Richmond. He's checking. So, now I have to join? Damn it!"

"I don't know." Ross remained noncommittal. "If that's what it takes. You can handle that, can't you?" Ross laughed. It was out of character for him. "Anything more?"

"No," said Eric.

"Now, let him call you back. If he tries to get you to join, just say you'll think about it. Stall a little. When you do join, tell them your main reason for coming in would be to shoot on the team and to get back on flying status. Let's get in there legitimately. No suspicions. Just make it neat and clean."

Eric was too tired to argue. He shouldered the receiver to his ear and tossed his shoes across the room.

"Keep in touch," said Ross.

"Yeah." Eric fell back on the sofa, too tired to make it to the bedroom yet too bothered to sleep.

CHAPTER 24

[Large Arms Supply Stolen From Guard, Fresno, California (AP)—. . . Missing from the San Joaquin Valley weapons dump were 58 automatic M16 rifles, two .45-caliber pistols, four .38-caliber pistols, four .38-caliber revolvers, two M60 machine guns and three 40mm grenade launchers. In addition, thieves stole almost 2,000 rounds of ammunition for the weapons, along with 40 riot-control chemical grenades . . . On July 31, 1972, thieves invaded the armory here and escaped with 97 M14 rifles and a large quantity of military supplies, including a three-quarter ton truck which apparently was used to haul the arms away.—The Charleston Gazette, Charleston, West Virginia] [24]

July 11th

"I thought you said there were thirty-five planes," Captain Rake Benson, in civilian clothes, nervously paced about Major William Adkins' amply furnished office at Installation Seventeen outside Little Rock. "I only counted twenty on the flight line."

Adkins bit his bottom lip. His ruddy-colored face, chiseled like a cigar store Indian, broke into a grin. He leaned back and tilted his desk chair. "The rest are in those camouflaged buildings on the other side of the runway."

Adkins studied Rake's face and watched him pace about. "How's everything in Virginia?" he asked Rake.

"General Randolph wants to see you later in the week. He's flying out to the San Joaquin Valley soon and later is going to bring some new inventory sheets with him. He's really loaded up with gear," said Rake.

"We all are." Adkins walked to a window and looked out over the bustling installation. "Those two men there," Adkins pointed through the blinds, "are congressmen." He turned back and watched Rake still pacing with his hands in his pockets.

Rake stopped for a moment and peered through the blinds with Adkins. "Was it wise to bring 'em here?" asked Rake, one hand now fidgeting with the back of his neck.

"For those two, yes." Adkins again intently studied his guest. "They're our pipeline to the President. They will be having a meeting with the 'Chief' when he's notified of the state of his government. Those two will handle things for us from that end."

"How much do they know?" asked Rake.

"Just about everything." Adkins saw the tiny sweat beads underneath Rake's eyes. He waited. Whatever was triggering Rake's anxiety, he knew it would eventually surface. The man wore his emotions on his sleeves. "Don't worry," Adkins answered. "We can trust them."

"How do you know?"

Adkins grinned. "We have enough on them and, besides, they don't have a prayer of being re-elected."

Rake walked to the window and watched the two suited up and stiff-postured congressmen being led off the airfield. "Let's take a walk outside. I feel closed-in, in here. You mind?"

"Come on," Adkins agreed. "I want to show you two new helicopters we've just got in."

From a distance, no one could tell there was any age difference between the two men. Adkins glided on jogger's legs, his quick movements like those of a much younger man.

"Who'll be calling the final showdown?" Rake asked. He shoved his hands in his pockets again.

"Some say it'll be a group decision between our man in the Pentagon, two in the White House and one in the Justice Department."

"It's close. I can feel it," Rake said.

They reached the edge of the pavement where the airstrip began. The pebbles and sand, swept to the far edge of the tarmac and away from helicopters, crackled underneath their shoes.

Adkins asked matter-of-factly, "Nervous?"

"Not over this part of it. I have something on my mind but I don't know what it means," said Rake.

"Want to talk?"

"Bill, it's my old man. We had it out some days ago. He *knows*. He thinks the same way we do but he's still waving the flag from the forties." Rake Benson bent over and picked up a small rock from his path. He threw it far away from the tarmac and into some scrub brush. "It's not important that he knows, but he's innocently caught up in all this. When I drove to the farm the other night he just stared out into the darkness. You know, like old people do when they're thinking about dying."

Major Adkins' arms crossed his chest, "Come on . . . I want to show you something" and they turned to the center of the tarmac. "What do you mean about getting caught up? What did Taylor say?"

"He isn't a fool. He knows that I've been traveling all over the country, and some of *his* cronies are pretty well plugged in. I think someone either told him or hinted strongly enough for him to figure it out. It worries me," Rake pulled at his bottom lip. "I just hope he stays out of it."

They approached the two newly arrived Cobra helicopters on the center of the airstrip. Major Adkins stepped up to inspect the new choppers, rubbing his hand across the metal rivets, almost caressing the exterior.

"Bill," Rake said, "these airframes are a good haul but I'm in no mood to take one out today." He skirted around the belly of the helicopter. "But I'll take this baby out on a run before I leave here tomorrow."

"Don't let your father get to you, Rake. His generation would've done the same in its time. He'll come around. Taylor Benson is a businessman; Rake, your father knows what's happening out there!" Adkins glanced at his watch. "I've got to meet with those congressmen before they go back to Washington."

The two hustled back.

The welcomed breeze suddenly stopped and the midday heat began slowly draining them. "What was all this on the phone about some new man?" Adkins asked on the way back, removing his cap and wiping a damp brow as he walked. "We've got many good men like that. What makes *him* so special?"

"If what he says he's developing is for real, it could make a difference . . . give us a little more edge when the time comes for us to move out and later on," Rake said.

Adkins grinned and replied emphatically, "We already *have* our 'edge.' "

CHAPTER 25

[Security Standards Vary at National Guard Armories, Lima, Ohio (AP)—. . . . A spot check was made Sunday in the wake of last week's looting of an armory in Compton, California, in which the FBI said thieves stole enough sophisticated weaponry to equip more than 150 soldiers for combat. . . . A spokesman said when stolen arms are recovered they often go unclaimed because the Guard doesn't want to admit its security was breeched. Guard spokesman have denied the charge . . . .—The Lima News, Lima, Ohio] [25]

July 15th

From the road's entrance it was hard to tell how many men were arriving onto the grounds and parking behind the ten-foot high, ivy-covered brick wall. They staggered the late evening arrival times by ten minutes so each man could pull in discreetly and lower the profile of a group meeting in the exclusive Richmond residential area. High shrubs and trees lined the long winding ribbon of gray cobblestones leading to Deacon Malway's mansion. One plain-clothes security guard ushered most in through a side door, not seen from the huge home's colonial front. Two other well-dressed plainclothes guardsmen checked names from a list as the guests emerged into a side foyer.

Newcomers to the mansion ambled and gawked their way to Deacon's second floor library where small groups of men clustered near a massive rectangular mahogany table so polished it mirrored the chandelier above it. Some sat in comfortable dark brown leather chairs while others browsed through the worn, cloth-bound original volumes neatly arranged on the shelves. House staff moved quietly from one group of men to the next with trays of drinks and fried scallops wrapped in bacon. Deacon sat down at one end of the large table—a subtle signal to start. It brought the meeting to a relaxed order as everyone hunted for a seat.

"We have a new member tonight," Deacon said. "He's new to our organization, but he's not new to our way of thinking." Mr. Davenport is in television and communications and will help us with media strategy. We decided that when we move we want to keep the public informed of exactly what's happening and why. Any of you who watch network news credits may recognize Robert Davenport's name."

Amused faces nodded recognition throughout the library. Most there knew of Davenport in the television industry and in the public eye and he was another prize in Deacon's pocket.

Deacon gloated as he held himself ramrod-straight and gloated over their new catch. "The day we set the government right, is code-named 'Wings' Day." The men present accepted the new name in silence.

"You'll know the actual date within several weeks, maybe sooner if things go well. The precise time . . . 'Flight' Hour." The names are functional so we can communicate with relatively little suspicion." Deacon pulled at his glass of bourbon and shot a penetrating glance at each man present as if gauging his commitment. He continued as though he were a professor lecturing his students.

"Gentlemen, we're all here tonight to accomplish several things. One task is to play devil's advocate. These past few months we shared our doubts and fears, each in our own way. This is not unusual for a group embarking on drastic steps to save a nation.

If our 'Right Guard' doesn't move like clockwork, so the average American citizen can get up, feel as if things are still normal and go to work the next morning, this country could be paralyzed, even *collapse* overnight." His voice rang like a tower bell on the word "collapse." He was a minister tending his flock, and he knew just how to covet them into his fold.

Lt.Col. Kendall sat uneasily beside Major Adkins at the highly polished table. Kendall felt an uncomfortable dry mouth despite constantly drinking from his water glass. Placing his hand over his mouth, he wrinkled his forehead and appeared intensely absorbed with Deacon's conversation.

Deacon continued lecturing. Beneath his protruding bushy eyebrows his eyes swept across his audience. "Some of you have never met the man sitting next to you," he said, and began walking about the library, pointing a finger in their direction. "But, except for Mr. Davenport, I've personally met with everyone in this room—many times. That, indeed, was intentional."

He strode to the end of the long table, picked up an envelope and held it up like an offering from believers. "I can tell you that those who are financing our plans are pleased with our progress." Deacon paused and waved the envelope in the air, "A week ago, we received a large final amount—the last installments from investors that we needed to finish this initial phase."

"The equipment at our installations is now all in place and the plans are laid out. Tonight we finalize the last piece, the headquarters. Our people are from the White House, Media, Congress, the Pentagon, the Justice Department and even the Secret Service. All our final plans must be put to rest and sealed tonight before we leave. May I remind you that not everyone will be interacting with the military Right Guardsmen. Some of you will be working alone."

Deacon stopped and turned to the two U.S. Congressmen sitting near the head of the table. "Joe, you and George will still take custody of the President on Wings Day."

One of the men around the table lifted an eyebrow. "Easier said than done. Only the Secret Service's Director, Deputy Director and the head of the White House detail have immediate access to the President. At least two secret service agents always guard him. They would never allow anyone within spitting distance of the President whom they did not know or had previously vetted."

Congressman George Bailey spoke up. "We've made it a point that the President and those who protect him do *know us* well. My wife is a close friend and confidante of the First Lady. They go back to university days. Why do you think *we* were chosen?"

Ignoring both remarks, Deacon went on. "Our high level Secret Service insider will join you for the President's house arrest; move him along quickly. Be congenial until he's inside the confinement room and out of sight. Tell him what you damn well please, but *get him into that room!*"

"And after that?" Congressman Joe Calliman asked.

Deacon smiled. "When your Secret Service inside collaborator arrives, he will probably have the Deputy Director of the Secret Service with him. We've arranged for the Deputy to be called away. You'll have a particularly tough job because there'll be only the three of you. There'll be no armed Guardsmen around to help until later."

Deacon sipped his bourbon then added as an afterthought, "Congress will be informed that their powers are nullified until further notice and held incommunicado. Those congressmen who are stateside will be arrested or put under house arrest by *our* guardsmen. At the Flight Hour, those on junkets or other travel status nationally or internationally, will be grounded immediately or held up where they are for *national security reasons*." Deacon paused just a moment for another sip of bourbon, and then stared back into their faces. "Let's see how well the 'servants of the people' do when they can't spend any more of our money."

The group laughed. Then retired general, Cyrus Randolph asked Deacon, "We're worried about containing only the biggies at this point. Who should that be?"

Without a moment's hesitation, Deacon responded. "Permanent Select Committee on Intelligence, Speaker of the House, Chairman of the Senate Select Committee on Intelligence, House Appropriations Committee, Senate Appropriations Committee, Senate Armed Forces Committee members, Majority Leader, Minority Leader . . . any more questions?" Gripping his drink glass in one hand and placing the other hand in his pocket, he slowly paced around the table, his practiced eye examining gestures and body language. He was talented at observing people so casually that most would not believe he could sense and detect their smallest flaws and 'tells'.

Kendall's back had been to Deacon through most of his soliloquy. Had Deacon been facing Kendall, he would have noticed how Kendall squirmed uneasily in his seat, hardly able to focus his attention on the "mentor" longer than a few minutes. When the meeting recessed for a break, Kendall excused himself then slipped into a bathroom adjoining a guestroom and vomited, nearly collapsing from the tension.

Twenty minutes later, Deacon resumed his place at the head of the table and asked for the latest status.

"The last Right Guard unit was recently set up in Arkansas," announced a man from the Pentagon. He held a wad of reports in his hand and read statistics from them. "Equipment is flowing well from Unit 456 back again into the supplier units, with no hitches, and no apparent suspicion. This last one, along with other units across the country, will be operational within fourteen days of your go-ahead." The man sat down.

"Major Adkins," Deacon asked, "anything to add about your Arkansas installation?"

"There's been no mention of the numbers of weapons and aircraft we now have on hand, that information is here," Adkins pointed to a folder in front of him on the table.

"I, too, have that information," said General Cyrus Randolph, suddenly speaking up. "I have here figures and inventories of equipment from our Virginia operations that have already been reported to Deacon." He pointed to a large black folder on the table with a twisted, arthritic finger.

Lt.Col. Robert Kendall entered the library, and quietly sat back down. "Bob . . . your reports?" Deacon asked looking up at him.

Except for Kendall, the men at the meeting seemed calm. But there was an earth tremor in Kendall's soul and in his stomach that kept him from the reassurance of the gathering. No one considered him a farsighted man, and though he chose to be conservative, his principles were more liberal—he had a penchant for going along with the crowd then becoming exorcised at the first sign of real or perceived injustice; however he lacked the guts or endurance to continue the scuffle he would start. Deacon thought Kendall should have gone into politics but the man's value in helping to organize details kept him with the Right Guard's top echelon.

Kendall slowly stood up and reached for the folder in front of him. Although his voice was slightly off-key he managed to keep his composure. "The detainment and retraining centers are almost finished," he began. "Most have beds, running toilets. We're organizing for sufficient security until the Right Guardsmen can come back and man the installations. The wire and fencing arrived for the last one in Virginia. We will install it soon. The last major installation of the detainment centers came about a week ago." Kendall cleared his throat. "From the transfer points—that is any rioters and those who are looting in the streets—they'll be sent to the centers. More vehicle installation details are here but I'm sure everyone knows how they will operate. Excessive violence will not be tolerated." Kendall tried to come off as authoritative and self-confident. "As you know, the centers are mainly to retrain detainees who need work skills. In the centers they'll be taught trades and services, and they'll be released." Kendall's voice became faint and he felt that sickly roll of fluid from his stomach making a second effort to go back up his throat. The first attempt made him leave the room. He delicately slid back into his chair. When the others began to give their reports, he again left quietly but no one knew it was to lose the rest of his supper.

Burt Collins, campaign manager for Bailor Moorehead, raised a manicured hand. He was almost pretty and sported an arrogant, prissy nature to match. "My campaign is beginning to get hot and I'm starting to draw attention in Moorehead's camp. The extensive media coverage we're getting is becoming too risky. I'll be at the next meeting, but after that I'll have to hide in the political cloisters until Flight Hour."

"What does Moorehead know?" Deacon asked the campaign manager.

"Neither Moorehead nor his closest cronies have the slightest clue. They're too busy setting up their bullshit giveaway programs at our expense. They won't know what the hell's going on until it's all over. Others in Congress who have a hint of this are waiting to see which way the wind will blow before they officially 'come out of the closet.' "

Deacon nodded.

"This is my last political campaign, gentlemen." The young man looked at the head of the table. "Over the last six years, I've been a professional campaign manager, press secretary, and aide to many different politicians across the country. I can tell you where the regional political power structures are, especially in the smaller campaigns. It's knowledge of those power havens and how those involved think and react, that'll aid the Right Guard later."

"What the hell are you doing in Moorehead's camp and a way lefty one at that?" a congressman asked. "These days he has about as much clout as fish bait. And he's only a local boy."

"I agree." Burt Collins smiled. His eyes shifted in Deacon's direction. "Really, it's just a base of operations. I'm working with General Randolph on some projects and it keeps me near the pulse of our operation."

Deacon nodded his approval at Collins.

A man in his sixties from the Justice Department raised a liver-spotted hand. "Deacon, I think we should also consider another potential problem. What about a safety valve for a delay in plans or an emergency stop order for Wings Day?"

"Yes, Martin. We're working on that. We'll have that in place by our next meeting."

They discussed contacts inside cable and broadcast firms, especially those with up-link capabilities and their access to special frequencies used throughout the country. High security bases could now be jammed at the precise time. They asked Deacon about the special plainclothes troops on Wings Day who would visit Senator's and Congressional Representatives' homes and round them up for temporary house arrest for briefings and "re-orientation." Deacon hinted that Wings Day would fall on an uneventful holiday.

The contact from the Department of Defense announced that the Special Forces assigned to seize the headquarters of the large mechanized military installations on Wings Day finished their training. Aided by high-ranking military and civilians, the commander told the troops that their training was for "taking down terrorists."

There was some talk about arranging support and backing with another country, once *Wings* activated. This was not a point of contention but still needed addressing. Deacon, Randolph and Adkins previously discussed this along with the rest of the Right Guard upper echelon. Finally, the debate ended with Deacon's satisfaction over the matter. There would be no foreign intervention or foreign help taken. The takeover was strictly to stay within the Right Guard. Everyone feared that once a foreign entity gained any foothold they would want more control. They were *still* Americans. They wanted no other nation taking part in what they all considered a patriotic act of saving the Constitution on their own soil.

IT WAS LATE. The house staff returned, but this time few touched the liquor. Kendall was among those who did again and again on his now empty stomach, and somehow managed to hide it from Deacon.

Breaking up into informal clusters, the men now seemed no different from any other cocktail party group. The vital planning meeting that was to decide the future of the most powerful country on earth gave way to personal conversations about business, family and the political state of the country.

General Randolph took Deacon aside. "Rake couldn't be here. He's taking care of some aircraft that's just arrived into inventory. He's also looking over a recruit who has come up with a very interesting weapon concept that Brannen Technologies is interested in. This boy sounds pretty smart. I know it's late in the game but we can use all of the help we can get and he seems to be the type of man we need in the organization."

"Background?" Deacon asked with a raised brow. "They're working on it," replied Randolph.

"Have them speed it up," said Deacon. Although it was not critical now, the new information interested him.

"When Wings becomes reality, we'll need people who can bring us new technology to keep us on top," General Randolph added.

Deacon glanced at General Cyrus Randolph. "You'll see Rake before the rest of us will. Tell him we'll see what we can do about him. What's his name?

"Eric Brent," replied Randolph.

"I want to see security reports first. Then I'll decide."

Kendall steadied himself by holding on to a nearby chair as he struggled to answer calmly. He threw down his fourth drink. Once again he avoided Deacon's glance by turning his back just as their leader walked by.

Deacon's attention shifted to a conversation about some old cronies from North Carolina who approached Rake's father. Deacon learned that the men mentioned uncertain rumors about unrest in the "civilian military." Deacon knew that leaks were inevitable but it was vital to follow up and quash all of them until after Wings Day. Deacon's interest focused on hearing about the cronies who knew too much. "Should we take care of it?" General Randolph whispered as he brushed by Deacon.

"In due time, Cyrus. In due time," Deacon responded. "I'm working it."

CHAPTER 26

[F-14 Brake Parts Stolen in Norfolk, Norfolk Virginia (AP)—More than $20,000 worth of F-14 Tomcat fighter jet brake parts have been reported stolen from the Naval Air Rework Facility here. The theft occurred Saturday night from a security cage in one of NARF's buildings at Norfolk Naval Air Station... the building housing the cage was patrolled by security officers....—The Richmond News Leader, Virginia.] [26]

Two days later, Kendall heard the radio news story while he was in Florida on an emergency call to re-inspect another detainment center. A taxi driver fought his way through a torrential rainstorm as Kendall listened on the taxi's radio to the story of two men, in their sixties, North Carolinians from their drivers' licenses. They were shot and found floating in the Chesapeake Bay near Tilghman Island. The radio announcer mentioned no names and gave few details except that "authorities were investigating."

"Drugs, I bet," the taxi driver piped up. "Two old boys into selling that crap, sure as hell."

Kendall didn't respond. Did Deacon decide to take out the old codgers who approached Rake's father? Kendall remembered overhearing Deacon telling Adkins to use force only if the situation called for it. Adkins' choice was obvious.

Kendall asked the driver for some music. He wanted to dismiss the news from his thoughts. He stared blankly through the windshield, and then studied the taxi driver concentrating on the road. Kendall could barely see the road's dividing lines through the downpour. He sat back against the seat and then escaped into his own thoughts. He could not relax. There was too much to think about now. He slapped his pocket then shut his eyes. The tranquilizers were in his suitcase. He breathed deep repeatedly and tried to force himself to drift and relax.

Minutes later Kendall stopped the driver and flung open the door. Half out of the taxi he heaved his last meal alongside the highway. The hard-hitting rain was saturating his clothes but it could not extinguish the boiler fire in his guts.

CHAPTER 27

[Abstract: New York, . . . Government witness scheduled to testify in case involving theft of 30 automatic rifles from Rhode Island National Guard Armory, dies from injuries suffered when home is ripped by explosion . . . police report that bomb had been deliberately set . . . . The New York Times] [27]

July 20th

A summer cloudburst pelted the area from Central Virginia to Maryland with the hardest hitting weather of the season. The rain fell like a transparent, humid veil hanging over Washington, D.C. and on to Interstate 95 toward Richmond, causing temporary flooding in some of the lower counties. It was early evening before Eric could leave Richmond, weaving around the large hauling trucks, the heavy rain, and the highway construction that constantly surrounds Washington. He stopped at a prearranged fast food restaurant just off the major route and met up with a security officer. Too risky for him to be seen anywhere near the intelligence complex now, special arrangements made it easier to keep him protected.

Eric was driven directly to the lower basement of the Headquarters building at Langley. Secreted in the backseat of the vehicle, they came in the Route 123 entrance and whirled past a large guard gate with armed security guards and went in the direction of the underground garage. They were not inspected but waved quickly through the security checkpoint. Security already had the car's license plate number and knew the vehicle would be coming through fast. They held out a separate badge then barricades lifted and a heavy metal steel door began to roll up. They parked among the armored vehicles and vans with tinted windows.

Eric was escorted to the lower basement private elevator, key and badge activated. The elevator went directly to the second floor and to the Director of Security's office and his highly secured conference room.

Passing the Director of Security's plaques and citations, Eric followed the beige carpet past a mahogany desk and into a conference room off to the side. Ross' formality over his arrival at CIA was annoying. The Chief was busy thumbing through files and reports. Two others in the room were also rooting through green-lined computer sheets haphazardly laid about the Langley office.

"Eric," he began, "you know Pete and Patrick and Mr. Jason. The other case officers here will be helping out later."

Eric joined Stuart Jason seated quietly at a long fold-up table where computer sheets and boxes of military gray vinyl binders lay scattered. The two fought the same enemy at different times and places and both succeeded. Though never expressed, they shared mutual admiration and understanding.

In his private thoughts, Eric wondered how Oldfield was taking Jason's stint of "administrative field supervision." He envisioned Oldfield stomping about his office, raising hell because someone called a former Director of Central Intelligence in for a job he thought *he* could handle alone. What really filtered back down the line was that Oldfield said precious little about Jason coming on temporarily. His only comment was, "I know everyone will remember who's *ultimately* running the show."

Oldfield was having enough problems with a congressional watchdog committee now attacking the Agency for past deeds. It was his job now to hold off the posse while the sensitive investigative picture behind the scenes could continue without congressional interruption. That's what they told everyone. But through the communications crevices and down hallways where inside intel information occasionally surfaced, word was that unless Oldfield called in someone who knew what he was doing, an Agency "in-house" group would do it their own way.

"We'll have more space to look at the reports in the conference room," Ross said, eyeing the masses of paper that were coming out of the boxes. The men grabbed what they could and filed out of the office. Eric lagged behind long enough to extend his hand to Jason.

The former DCI responded in his calm, unassuming manner. "You're doing some good work. You know it will get ugly before it's all over. You prepared for that?"

"Yes, sir. I think we all are." Both men left Ross' office to join the others. There was not a lot of love lost at the Agency for their new DCI Oldfield. Eric heard about the derisive jokes and scorn they liberally heaped on Oldfield at every opportunity, particularly by the ops officers. Some of it Oldfield deserved; some he didn't. It got pretty embarrassing at times, even for the hard core old-timers.

Stuart Jason was extremely popular as a most fair and honorable man. He was a tough act to follow, and Jason only commented that Oldfield deserved a personal and professional opportunity to bring the Agency along and that he was here to help. The difference between the men's styles was more emphasized by Jason's calm courtliness.

"What's happening out there?" Ross asked, once all the men found their way to the conference room. Two other case officers and another chief sat quietly away from the table, their yellow and blue-lined tablets lay ready on their laps.

"I met Rake Benson," Eric reported. "We had a few beers together . . . talked a little politics. He's interested in my invention. Not only that, but he's mentioned my joining a Guard unit."

Ross stared at Jason, then back at Eric. "Anything else?" he asked, fidgeting with a pencil.

"He's in business with his father, half mining information, half import-export; and he hates non-productive people who are taking his money via the government." Eric added, "I'm not too far off that mark myself." Ross let the comment drift by.

Jason was skimming a report; he looked up and grinned.

"He's a Southern gentleman with a degree in engineering," Eric continued. "He's smart . . . too bright to be doing what he's doing."

"What do you mean?" asked Ross.

"Someone like Rake should be more heavily involved in the family business or in mineral research. He could earn ten times more money. He toys with the business and heads up the pistol team playing military on weekends."

Jason spoke without looking up from the reports. "The Reserves have many smart and talented men and women who just like to keep a hand in what's going on. It's not that unusual." Jason slowly laid the report down and turned to Eric. "One might say Eric Brent joined the Guard for the same reason." The former DCI's gaze lingered.

Eric took in a deep breath. "How soon do I have to move in?"

"Yesterday," Ross responded and he motioned Patrick and Pete out of the room. The other case officers quietly remained.

"I want to know more," Eric said matter-of-factly. "I think it's about time."

From his expression, Jason and Ross knew it was not a request.

"You going to keep me in the dark?" Eric prodded.

Ross became anxious. He nervously reached for his pipe. No doubt he remembered a previous assignment where Eric stopped his end of the investigation after learning what they wanted him to do would have violated any sane man's principles.

For that defiant act, some at Langley wanted to crucify Eric, but Jason stepped in. Whether for personal reasons or because Jason recognized a similarity between them, no one knew. All that had surfaced outside Langley was a simple, respectful relationship between a fair-haired stray and a former Director of Central Intelligence. Both men knew that case officers meet up with few strict principles in a world where diverse cultures, deception, and headquarters' authority collide. However, those who survive and are good, develop a particular type of private autonomy. They usually don't cross those final *personal* and moral boundaries they set for themselves. Throughout their "career" it is often the only fragment of private sanity that makes sense when the rest of the world falls around them.

"I want to know the rest," Eric snapped, repeating himself. Ross looked at Jason. Jason nodded to go ahead.

"You know already that arms are moving in and out of arsenals. Something's happening in the military," Ross stated, pulling his pipe away. "We think it mainly involves the Guard and the Reserve components. Planes and other equipment stolen from units are now showing up in isolated sections of the country. The numbers are unbelievable!" Ross left his chair. "We think the Guard is spearheading a planned military conspiracy . . . civilians who have their hands on one of the largest arsenals in the world."

"And Rake?" Eric asked.

"We suspect Rake and others like him are involved up to their necks."

"What's the bottom line?"

"Eric, we're only guessing," Jason spoke up.

"What could they do?" asked Eric incredulously.

Ross straightened and stated with a grim expression, "Take over the U.S. and put it under martial law until certain criteria are met within the government."

"No way. Too massive a job. How can this happen without a hint until now?" Eric fought back.

Ross sat on the end of the conference table, his arms folded. "Eric, you wouldn't believe how tight the information has been. We couldn't get a decent trace on anyone. Not one of ours in the military could get as much as a hint . . . until now."

"Now?"

"Just a streak of dumb luck. We have an informant although he's not giving us much. All we know is that he's a 'detail' man for their installation setups. He's so jumpy he can hardly talk. The guy can hardly keep food in his gut."

Jason added, "We can't push him now. He doesn't trust us enough to know if we are real or another branch of their movement."

Ross paced again in front of the conference table. "How soon can you join?"

"I'm not sure Rake or the others trust me. It may be too soon now. If I push it, he may get suspicious."

Jason threw a stack of papers on the polished table. "It *has* to be now," he said. "We don't know how much time *we've* got."

"If it's a bad placement, I'm dead meat," Eric told them.

Ross jumped back in. "The case is top priority. Whatever you need, you'll be covered, big time."

Everyone waited.

Jason tried again. "Eric, of course we have other talent but your background and present circumstances are a natural. We can't set a man in place any better than where you are now. We have to move quickly and get inside."

"Too much for you, Eric?" Ross pumped him. It was what he always asked when he wanted to push someone near the edge, his normal goading. In the field they joked about Chief Ross' occasional patronizing and tiresome humor. It didn't deserve an answer.

"Now what?" Eric asked.

The other case officers left the room as if on cue. Only Jason, Ross and Eric remained.

Former DCI Jason stood up to stretch his legs. Jason took a few deep breaths then, sliding his hands into his pants pocket, he strolled to the large window. The shades formed shadowed lines across his face, blocking out the strong parking lot lights. "Eric," he said, "your briefing begins tomorrow and will go for a few days. There'll be a handful of men with you. We have a list of suspected Right Guard people in your section, some you know already and the rest you'll know in due time."

"The next few days you'll have a lot to read," said Ross. "The information is still hot. We're also compiling military records and psychological profiles."

"Who's the informant?" Eric asked.

"A close insider, Eric," Ross said. "He was one of several involved with the installation kept most secret for this whole operation."

"How'd you get hold of him?" Eric asked.

"He contacted us," Ross responded. "He heads up some aspect of the Virginia operation. The guy's name is Kendall. He's completely out of it; his nerves are shot. We're temporarily hiding him in a medical ward in Baltimore."

"Is he going back?"

"We hope so, Eric," Jason added. "*If* we can turn him and *if* he can handle it."

"Can you trust his information?" Eric propped his feet on a nearby leather chair.

"Everything he told us checked out," said Jason, "to the last detail. Names, locales, everything. You'll get all the back-up you need and more, but you've got to move now." Jason lowered his voice. "Ross is the only one you're to report to. Is that understood?" All of the calm and confidence left Jason's face. His normally gleaming eyes and self-assured calm faded. "There are some here who're waiting it out to see which way this will go down. I don't care who or what shows up out there, you're only to give Ross or me your reports." He went to the window and stood staring through the blinds.

"Once in the Guard," Ross suddenly jumped into the conversation, "you'll compete in the Wilson Matches in Little Rock,

Arkansas, as a member of the Virginia Guard Team. Everything is set up."

"But you have to be competing in the Guard months before you even can go to the Wilson Matches," Eric snapped. "It's too soon."

"Rake already knows you're good." Ross reached for his pipe and started to fill it with heavy tobacco. "We're trying to fix it so that one of Rake's men can't make it and you'll be an alternate. You've got to get closer to him."

Jason sat back down placing his arms on the chair, surveying his charges. He opened a file and threw some black and white photos on the desk taken by a KH-11 satellite. "You'll be on your own for one segment of this. Preferably by Rake's invitation or your own design, an installation outside Little Rock must be checked out."

Ross broke in, "We got this yesterday on Installation Seventeen." He pointed to the photos scattered on the table. "The vertical aerials show little about what's really down there. Our new *Director*," he added with a sarcastic scorn to his voice, "thinks these are fantastic—all the newest technology available. They don't show us a damn thing!" He held a bright flame over his pipe's bowl and sucked in the acrid smoke. Ross shook the match flame out and threw it in an ashtray. "We need more," he said to Eric.

"Should be easy," said Eric. His mind raced, remembering previous stunts he pulled to get inside military operations.

"Don't count on it," said Ross. "It may take you a week to get in there." He leaned forward. "Eric, this is no joke, they are serious. Their system is very closely held and tough to penetrate. Plus, they have insiders well placed in many of the agencies. If you can't get in on Rake's invitation, you'll have to work a way in yourself."

"But why go to all this pistol team stuff just to get me to Arkansas?"

"Once you're down there with the pistol team," Ross answered, "it'll be a lot easier to break you away from Rake. There's a lot of activity at the matches. You'll have a good excuse to hide in uniform.

Also we can arrange it so you and Rake will be shooting on different relays that will give you a lot of time apart."

"Eric, you've got to be careful on this one. Already they've been keying files on you," Jason said. "Our computers sent up a flag when one of their bases in Arkansas tried to get information through our terminals. We sent back a clean bill of health on you, but it bothers me that they're looking *to us* for that information."

"What's interesting, Eric," Ross said, "is that the base isn't supposed to exist. It was put on caretaker status three years ago. These men slipped in and carried on like they were part of the regular military."

"Slick, wouldn't you say?" Jason stated. "When the computer system here picked up their signature, that's when we did some checking." Jason paused to glance at his watch. "Gents, I've got to go."

Eric glanced at his suit lapel and said, "You're not wearing your pin," referring to a miniature of the Agency's Intelligence Medal for Valor. "You're not wearing yours," Jason responded.

"The secret recipient ever get to wear his miniature?"

"I don't know." Jason's mouth curled into a curious smile. "I never asked him, but then everyone would know who he is, wouldn't they?" He gave a little salute to Ross and pulled the conference room door quietly behind him.

"You getting your money all right?" Ross asked, collecting the scattered papers on the table.

"Fine. Why's Jason in on this? Have they finally figured out Oldfield just looks good in the shower?"

Ross shook his head. "Don't go getting yourself out on a limb too far. Just remember that Oldfield has to give his approval for any Special Activities Division mobile or static surveillance out there to cover your ass. When this starts cooking if those Guardsmen follow through on this goddamn thing, there's going to be hell to pay. Oldfield won't forget something like you blowing off your mouth, particularly since you are one of his own." Ross studied Eric and broke out another flame for the pipe.

"Did you ever burn one of yours, Ross?" Eric asked.

Ross studied the young man's face. There was an alien tone in Eric's voice. Still trying to light his pipe, Ross was otherwise motionless. "No. It's one reason I'm still a Division Chief instead of upstairs. I never did hammer one of mine out there, no matter how bad it was or which way it was going. *That* man didn't either," said Ross, nodding toward the door where Jason had just left.

The two silently walked back to Ross' office. After closing the door, Ross handed Eric another check in an envelope. "You may need this until the rest arrives. Look, Eric, Mike Halstead is frothing at the mouth to get an arrest. Some asshole passed the FBI information about that informant, Kendall. The bureau has been crawling all over us for the past week. For chrissake, don't give anything away to those guys—I don't care who you like over there. All Halstead wants is to be a goddamn hero ever since the media made Hoover look so bad. We want 'em just looking for the weapons and out of our act until we can see if there's a foreign connection."

Eric nodded, agreeing.

The Chief looked away and jerked the pipe from his mouth. "If they succeed, you'll be in the middle of it and it won't be pretty. Lines will be drawn not only throughout the military, but *here*, too."

"Whose side will you be on?" Eric asked.

Ross paused for a moment. "The side of the angels, you know that."

"You know, sounds like some of the plans are for a sensible government . . . better than the one we know. The more I learn about it, the better it sounds," Eric told Ross.

Ross took in a labored breath then looked into Eric's face. "At times it does sound good Eric, but you can't cut people off overnight. There has to be something better than just giving money away, but it has to be done gradually and legally—not like what Rake Benson and company have in mind. Giveaway government programs that have gradually increased over the years have to disappear the same way, a little at a time. The Right Guard motives may be okay but if they take over forcibly tomorrow it'll be a blood bath and unquestionably—treason."

"It may come to that anyway," Eric said.

Ross nervously shuffled computer papers from one side of his desk to the other. He studied Eric intently this time. *Did Eric know about Deacon yet?* he thought to himself.

Eric's voice lowered on leaving Chief Ross' office. "I wonder how we all manage to sleep at night."

"Some of us *haven't* since day one," Ross calmly quipped back at him without looking up.

Eric left the headquarters building and was taken to a safe house for the evening. He left the same way he entered: secreted, escorted, cover protected.

CHAPTER 28

[Abstract: Compton, California (New York Times—. . . National Guard spokesman say although firing pins and bolt assemblies had been removed from guns, it might be possible, though difficult, to secure replacements. FBI and police are investigating the possibility that terrorist group engineered heist . . .—The New York Times] [28]

July 22nd

The updated briefing at the Langley Complex in Virginia lasted four days. Eric and fifteen other case officers read reams of paper on the beginnings of the Right Guard movement. They studied profiles, personal histories, and military records. Because of the wide usage of the Social Security numbers, they read mountains of information on each of their subjects, including income tax returns, spending habits, job habits, driving records, voting registration records, magazine subscriptions, donations, club affiliations, bank accounts, credit ratings—to name only a few.

Each of the profiles was critiqued and summarized by three different psychiatrists. Each man wrote a separate summary from their specialized fields, one from the humanist approach, another from the trait and factor approach, and the last from the behaviorist approach. The three reports gave a highly dynamic view of each subject's personality.

When Eric came to Rake Benson's file he sifted through the papers twice. A mention of his childhood psychiatric therapy after his brother drowned, found its way into a report when Rake applied for flight training in the military. Eric thought it was amazing what the Agency had access to, pulled from the reams of information gathered on individuals over the years.

The fair-haired child in Rake's family was Stonefield "Beau" Benson, Rake's older brother and would-be poet, who took after their mother. Because Beau shared her interests, he had also received more of her affection and praise. As youngsters, Beau was always smarter and faster than Rake, and had proven to be overwhelmingly tough competition. Beau's good-natured and confident personality often gave way to showing off at the wrong time. Eric thought that daring confidence probably contributed to the events surrounding Beau's drowning while Rake froze and helplessly stood watching.

An excellent student at Georgia Tech, and a veteran of two tours in Vietnam, Rake emerged through the report's pages and personality profiles as pro-military. He was a man not afraid of competition—a good businessman, definitely heterosexual. The brutal, senseless murders of his wife and son by a midnight intruder, identified only as a young white male, had almost destroyed him.

Eric read two and three times the masses of notes they gave him. None of it changed his opinion of his new acquaintance. He couldn't help it; he liked the man.

On the last day of the briefing, a senior analyst and a case officer scurried through the door and handed out "tailored" research packets. Some were compiled for case officers who would be in special situations. Eric's packet included up-to-the-hour material on people he would be meeting, more information about the geographical areas where they would be operating and types of arsenal items they could expect to see.

Charles Anders, the fortyish case officer in charge had a square face and light gray eyes that matched the color of his suit. His ruddy tanned complexion, tailored suit, and obvious physical fitness led

Eric to suspect that he played often on country club tennis courts: a typical upstairs intelligence case officer. A budding Ross, he thought.

"Good morning, gentlemen," Anders began. "You should be well-briefed on all potential contacts. Each of you has your pre-arranged *in*. Your efforts will be the key to providing the information we need to counter this. By now you know there's a high probability that an overthrow of the government is in the planning. It's centered primarily in the National Guard and Reserves. It also involves some full-time military, and some civilian government employees, particularly in the Department of Defense who are posted in military bases throughout the U.S. Also we know of high ranking officers who have jobs in the civil-military complexes that are involved." After watching with interest until the last special packet went out, Anders spread wide his suit jacket and placed his hands on his hips. "We still have only sketchy information about those involved or even all the circumstances. We need you to infiltrate. Before we go in to put this conspiracy down, we want to know as much as possible about the Right Guard. Clearly, once this is over, there'll be massive changes in policy and accountability. At this point, we have no idea whether we'll go throughout the military cleaning house, or just push those involved out of the Guard and the Reserves."

The officer's assured tone amused Eric. He sounded so certain that the military would not succeed in their revolt. Eric knew no one could be sure at this point, not even after Langley collected and analyzed all the pieces to the puzzle.

Anders introduced a senior analyst and the analyst carried on with the remainder of the information. "My summary will be a short overview," the senior analyst continued. "A detailed outline of the beginnings of what we know of the 'Right Guard' is in the top folder in your packet."

The analyst's personal summary interested the men more than the massive pile of paperwork before them.

"At the end of World War II, the huge numbers of high ranking military officers and civilian employees, particularly dealing in war products, was no longer needed. Layoffs and reduced forces created an overflow of socially mobile, relatively highly educated ex-officers. The big fortune 500 corporations, their subsidiaries, and the companies they control enjoyed their war-time prosperity, and a number of them selectively employed some of those officers or saw to it that someone else did."

"Politicians and political favors were bought and sold. Sometimes, corporations got these men elected to some office or appointed staff. Since many of them wanted to keep their fingers in the military, the only way was to get into the National Guard or Reserves. Corporate policies involving veterans and time-off pay for Guard and Reserve duty motivated a large number to get back in."

"Also, it meant a great deal to them to hold on to their rank. With the war over, the corporations looked to the political arena to help assure the most favorable economical climate for their businesses. When they wanted regulatory controls, they would create them. When the controls no longer served their purposes they dismantled them."

The senior analyst stopped for a moment and took a drink of ice water from a tray on the table in front of the room. He glanced around to make sure he had everyone's attention before going on. He looked at Anders and got the nod to continue with the briefing session.

"The end result of corporate buying and selling of political candidates and broad government agency influence was that big business created a very one-sided economic environment in the U.S. The ex-military men continued in the reserve forces, and the privilege extended as their sons came along. When the fathers' military commitments ended, they were replaced by their sons in the Guard, Reserves and high state positions."

"In the sixties and throughout the Viet Nam War, military spending pumped the major corporations' finances up. Unfortunately, for those corporations, the result politically was a wrenching power shift. The military and the corporations closely associated with them lost much of their political power and influence and the economic picture began a downward spiral. The result of so much of their political manipulation had come home to roost."

"In the early seventies, the oil debacle and our weakened economic position made it appear to many of the corporate heads that there well could be a collapse of the American dollar. Politically, the laws being created were so full of social legislation bullshit, and there were so many clowns in Congress, the legislative body could do nothing but pass popular giveaway programs. The people who held power and economic clout for so long started to believe that they must make a move to bypass the Congress, and an impotent President and regain economic viability."

Eric noted the expressions of the other case officers in the room. For some, it was as if light bulbs had suddenly clicked on, while for others it was disbelief . . . but all understood.

The senior analyst paused to take another drink and tried to remember if he covered all the bases. "So," he continued, "they turned to their civilian military. They didn't have to worry about the standing army, there would be no beach landing; they would attack from within."

"Right Guard had no apparent deliberate design until recently. It emerged as an alternative method of action. With their backs against the wall, these men recognized that their military connections had other uses. And they had their hands in some of the country's biggest arsenals with little accountability. Gaining immediate support of those with a like mind was simple. They were already in their camps." Anders stopped again and thumbed through a packet. "The details, you'll find in your folder. Items like civilian and military communications jamming, riot control, media influencing, everything we've learned about them up to now is here. There's some serious reading ahead of you today," Anders added.

The rustle of turning pages began and continued for eight difficult hours. The men read, they became uncomfortable and they disbelieved.

CHAPTER 29

[Abstract: Four gunman dressed in military clothing rob New York's National Guard Armory in Yonkers, New York of eight M-16 rifles and 3,000 rounds of ammunition.—The New York Times, New York] [29]

Four demanding days of information, research and reading finally ended. After the two hour drive back to the carriage house in Bel Air, Eric felt a fatigue only another case officer could know—a desire to seek some warm, quiet place where he could rest a clouded mind and relax from sheer endurance and find a temporary peace.

Jager rested at Eric's feet and watched his master's every movement. It was Jill's warmth and her candid uncompromising smile that he yearned for now. He sipped his beer and dialed her number. It was late but he hoped she would still pick up the phone.

"Hi, there," he began. "I'm Jack Worthy for the Northern Virginia Telegraph. Is it true that your candidate was out last night poking everything that walked and popping supporters' panty hose waistbands at a local reception?"

A dead silence hung briefly at the other end of the line. "What do you . . . damn it, Eric, is that you? Do you have to say such things? Wait a minute. Let me sit up in bed and get a grip on myself." She came back on the line after he heard some ruffling of pillows. "For all I know," she said, laughing, "that's exactly where he is."

"The thought should keep color in your cheeks."

"Well, I've got enough color in my cheeks now to keep me warm for a long time, thank you very much," she said.

"What's happening?"

"Nothing major. Lots of little things to drive me insane. They hired an errand boy for us after I convinced them that much of my time was going to 'do nothing' tasks. The guy they hired is Moorehead's nephew. The poor guy can't make it around the corner to the copy center without getting lost, or coming back with the wrong batch of releases."

"Hm-mm," he laughed. "Sounds like fun."

"Tell me, just tell me, how can someone enter a copier's shop to get a batch of press releases run off, stand there and wait for them, then come back with another candidate's releases?"

"That boy's got real *talent*."

"Oh, he's got *talent*, all right." Jill responded. "Word has it that he's the main stud for three other political campaigns at the same time. You wouldn't believe, what marches in the office panting for him around 5 o'clock."

"I told you about working for the Democrats," he chided.

"Well, at this rate, I'm ready to believe anything."

"How's everything else?" His voice was sympathetic.

"Fine, except a few hundred other things going wrong on the campaign. Moorehead has no idea how the state is doing economically. Tonight I've got to finish a draft for him to read to farmers in a depressed area tomorrow. And get this—he's donning overalls for the occasion. He's never worn a pair in his life." She paused. Her spirits sounded low. "I suppose I'm surviving. I miss you."

"I miss you, too," he responded.

"Any chance of your coming to D.C., or any place nearby?"

"We'll see," he said. "I just wanted to call you. See how things were going."

She asked solemnly, "How dangerous is it, Eric?"

"It's not going to be bad."

"You don't lie well," she told him.

Eric laughed. "I hope the Chief doesn't hear that. He thinks I'm a star."

"You're crazy."

"Yep, that's why you love me so much," he said then he waited for an answer. There was none. Maybe it was too soon to expect one. "I'll be in touch again soon. Get some sleep. You'll need it to push that broken-down candidate of yours." Eric gently placed the receiver back in its cradle.

His insides hurt again. Lunch had included red meat and it rarely agreed with him now. He wanted some white rice. It always seemed to soothe the acid in his guts.

With the air conditioner off and the windows up, he stood over his small gas stove, lifted the lid on a copper pan and stirred the rice once. He heard a siren shrieking in the distance and he hoped that the investigation would soon be over and that there wouldn't be a white van flickering red and racing for him.

Across the wooded yard, he saw a light in the Watson's attic. At first he thought it was just a street lamp glaring off one of the small windowpanes that fanned out from the top of the walk-in attic. No. It was definitely a light. Probably Fran Watson searching for the straw mat rugs she mentioned the other day. She said she wanted to lay them out for the rest of the summer: old, arthritic Micky had gotten fleas in the cotton rugs.

However, Fran Watson had been in bed for hours. A summer cold was taking its toll on her and she told her husband that she needed the rest.

CHAPTER 30

[The State, Thieves cut through the roof and concrete arms vault of a U.S. Army Reserve armory in Chico over the weekend and stole an undisclosed number of weapons, the Butte County Sheriff's Department reported . . . . the thieves were "selective in what they took, primarily automatic weapons," but that the armory's weapons supply also included grenade and rocket launchers as well as mortars. The Thieves left behind "quite a few weapons," . . . . he did not know how much ammunition, if any, was taken. The Army refused to comment, and the FBI, which sealed off the armory in preparation for an inventory, declined immediate comment . . . . —The Tmes Mirror, Los Angeles] [30]

July 30th

Earlier in the day Eric and Rake drove to the Falcon Street Armory in Richmond. The recruiting officer officially welcomed Eric into the National Guard. "You'll be a warrant officer until a flight slot opens. You'll be putting in stick time with an instructor to be made current again. When you qualify on your last STAN-EVAL ride, you'll be on flying status and assigned with the air ambulance unit out at the airport." He read the enlistment papers aloud then they crossed the hall for the swearing in and oath signing ceremony. When the ritual was over, Rake smiled "How do you feel?"

"Just as lousy as the last time I went through it."

"Come on home with me. We need a drink to celebrate. It's not too far away."

Eric accepted.

Rake never said much about his family's wealth. Bellevue, the Benson family home, surpassed any expectations Eric may have had of the sprawling white Greek-columned home. Perched on top of a hill in the lush, green countryside of Virginia's Grasmere County, there were tennis courts, a pond and a swimming pool surrounded by a fruit grove.

Louise, a small black woman with a confident wide smile, ushered them into the drawing room. While Eric drank bourbon, Rake showered and returned in beige kakis, a light blue shirt and loafers—an unspoken Southern aristocratic uniform.

"How about a tour?" Eric asked.

The request obviously pleased Rake, who showed Eric around with emphatic enthusiasm. They went from room to room; each filled with the Benson family history. The rooms were lush with heavy silk drapes, tapestry walls and family portraits posing with favorite pets. During the grand tour, Rake pointed through a large bay window to a stretch of woods. "There's a hunting lodge on the other side of those pine trees where we stay during the autumn deer drives." Eric could see why Rake was so proud of Bellevue. It was an estate where a man had the upper hand: elegant *and functional.*

The house tour ended when Louise's high-pitched voice called out that dinner was ready. Though the rest of the home was open to the clean country air, the dining room was air-conditioned. The dining room was right out of an ante-bellum novel. Rose-colored draperies hung in voluminous folds framing a dark mahogany sideboard. The antique silver service on the old sideboard gleamed when the light from an 18th Century chandelier reflected throughout the room.

Both men joined Rake's parents, already seated in the room. The elder Benson's gaze was spirited, despite a milky white cataract that was prominent in his left eye. Broken bluish veins ran through his lower cheeks. Callused hands, the sign of a gentleman farmer who was not afraid of physical work, waved them to their seats.

Verdie Benson, Rake's mother, although a little overbearing at times, was likable enough. She dominated the conversation, and Eric thought it unusual for a man of Taylor Benson's power and obvious wealth to play second fiddle to his wife.

After dinner she declined dessert and excused herself. The three men enjoyed the momentary silence. Eric sensed that Rake was waiting for the old man to speak first. He was in the South— the men would take their coffee and maybe smoke or drink, talk about their women's latest adventures or tell a light hearted joke before getting serious.

Finally, Taylor Benson said, somewhat casually, "Rake tells me you have an interesting invention."

"Yes, sir. I do."

"Liquid propellant systems have been around for some time, you know. What makes yours so special?"

Something about the old man's expression warned Eric not to underestimate him. With his wife away, the elder Benson's personality and presence was suddenly much stronger and Eric realized the *man's hand* on the estate. "Never underestimate a Southern gentleman who gives real courtesy to his woman in public," Eric remembered his father saying. "It is bred into them. Do not mistake it for weakness."

"Not only is it liquid propellant, it is caseless as well," Eric explained. "No brass. Chemical reactive operation with very little residue."

Taylor Benson motioned to Louise with his hand that he needed pencil and paper. The three men remained at the table mulling over Eric's quickly drawn sketches.

"No brass," the old man repeated aloud. "Gawd, wouldn't the government get excited over that! Ammunition would be so light a soldier in the field could carry almost four times the amount he's carrying now. Jus' think of aircraft and how much more they'd be able to haul. The theory is good, but there are a lot of inherent problems." Benson sipped his coffee. "I was interested in something like this back in the fifties, Eric. Friend of mine, Joe Halsey, was doing nearly the same thing."

"I know that name, Halsey," said Eric.

"Well, you should. He almost succeeded. I was with Halsey when he checked his liquid propellant idea at Aberdeen testing ground. The damn thing exploded . . . man lost his right hand. Of course, that's not anything you'd have picked up in the Defense Documentation Center Progress Report. No one's going to describe failures to the DDC when they're hungry for another lump of project money."

"But this one *will* work," said Eric.

"Whether it will or won't, Eric, you do have one hell of a good firm doing technological backup work for you. Brannen Technologies is just about the best around."

"It works in the computer. That much we do know, sir."

"Well, let me see some more. The next time you come, bring an offering memorandum with you and we'll talk." Rake's father extended his hand. "You come back and see us real soon. Next time I'll look a little deeper into the subject with you. I'm afraid I'm not feeling my best tonight. Age does that to you sometimes, boy."

"Yes, sir." He left the room and Eric turned to Rake. "What do you think?"

"I think he wants to see more. If he weren't interested he would not waste his breath on it. He keeps to himself, even when he gets sick. You know the type." He got up suddenly. "Come on, man. It's too pleasant an evening to waste sitting inside. Let's go down to the pond. I used to skip school all the time and go down there."

They left the house and strolled across the deep green lawn toward the pond as a soft breeze began to kick up. Streaks of red and gold blazed across the early evening sky. The sun had almost set, lending a warm, welcoming cast to Bellevue.

"My teachers would call Daddy and say I wasn't in school. He would come down to the pond and tan my hide 'til I could hardly sit down."

Eric followed Rake, wondering how the "approach" would come. "I think you have a good thing going there," Rake began, "but with the type of government we have, man, you might as well kiss any good enterprise good-bye. Those boys in Washington, Eric, are not going to let you enjoy any of the fruits of your labor. When the first prototype is made, if it shows promise they'll slap a secrecy order on it. They almost succeeded in conning Americans into believing that it's wrong to be able to defend their own homes. Hell, the bastards have even managed to cut the Navy, the Coast Guard, and the Air Force Pistol Teams." *It's funny*, Eric thought, *Rake really lives for the team.*

"Yes, but those pistol teams had little to do with the member's military job assignment except for the infantry and military police. When Congress gets in the cutting mode, things like the pistol teams take it in the shorts. Maybe they thought it wasn't useful especially when they don't fire on men in the field."

"Eric. That's just great. I'm sure it delights our enemies. If we go to war again, we'd better have as many damn good shots as we can muster. If the next war isn't nuclear, and I don't think it will be, it'll come to ground combat. Don't you see, man? Military arts like the pistol teams were not only incentives to be a good shot, they were also good recruiting tools."

"It was probably a matter of economics."

"Economics, my ass." Rake answered. "While they were cutting back on the shooting teams they were pumping money into politically correct crap."

Eric was silent.

"You keep destroying incentives, people don't strive for anything and quality goes to hell," Rake said. "When you get a little past that, Eric, you might as well open your gates and let socialism and communism in, because they've got you by the balls already."

Rake picked up a handful of small rocks and began skipping them across the top of the still water. Eric joined in and each tried to out-skip the other.

Pointing at a pole in the water, Rake said, "Try and hit that." Rake's throw was smooth and accurate. The pebbles made a ringing sound bouncing off the brown crusting metal pole and into the dark water. Five more times he hit it, the stones clanging hard off the pole.

"Hey, no fair," Eric said. "You've practiced."

Rake didn't respond but continued hurling stones, harder and harder, until he was almost coming out of his shoes. Abruptly, Rake stopped. "My brother Beau drowned out there when he was eighteen," he said, his voice unsteady. "It happened pretty near that pole. I was only eleven then. All I could do was stand here and watch him go down."

"Man, I'm sorry. Didn't know. Must have been tough on you." Eric put his hand on Rake's shoulder, not knowing what to say. His brother and then his wife and child. There seemed no end to the cruel tragedy in Rake's life.

"It was pretty painful when I was a kid. I used to have nightmares about it all of the time. Doesn't happen much any more, but you never forget. He was my hero," Rake said. "Honest to God, Beau was a real champion—I loved him."

Walking back to the house, Eric tried to change the somber tone. "What's a rich boy like you doing in the military?"

"I like the people and I like flying. It doesn't take up all that much time and we're not really that regimented. The full-time regulars, those guys have such an unrealistic view of us."

They reached the porch and Eric sat in the swing. Rake plopped down on the bright yellow and white striped porch sofa and rested his feet on the arms.

"Isn't it interesting," he said, placing his hands behind his head, "that our government has overlooked the amount of firepower the civilians have in the Reserves and Guard?" He stretched out.

"Middle and upper classes never revolt—why should they worry." said Eric, trying to draw him out.

"Just think about it for a minute, Eric. Take a look at the National Guard and the Reserves. They are middle class Joe America types and definitely not the loyal palace Guard."

"I never really thought about it." Eric listened and remembered what Jason had preached about the Right Guard recruitment approach.

Rake continued. "Not only do we live in the communities and see all the government giveaways to people who don't deserve it, but we've got to pay for it. This is unusual in history. Never before has there been a civilian soldier of the type we have now. Most of us are conservative, independent, and politically to the right. We have a 'leave me alone and let live my own life' attitude, and have our hands on a tremendous amount of firepower. Another thing, Eric, why do you think the average American is so sensitive about gun legislation?"

"Well, the right to bear arms does have a lot of emotional draw." Eric replied.

"If you ask a conservative, he knows damn well why the left wants the guns taken away. He'll tell you it's because there can't be severe taxation and confiscation of property and forcing people against their will to accept laws that only the left wing politicians want, unless all the guns are collected and no one can forcibly resist. Think, Eric. You get the guns off the streets and what can the people do when things start getting really bad?"

Louise came through the porch door and set a tray of glasses and liqueur on a table in front of Rake, then left.

Eric asked, "Do you think a comfortable middle class would ever revolt?"

"It would have to be a select group of individuals who are really attuned to what's going on in this country." Rake said. He served Eric the cordial then held his up in front of his face, watching the light from the house shine through the crystal.

"They would have to build a large, powerful enough force to handle the economic and social problems of this country."

"Security risks would be phenomenal!" Eric exclaimed.

"Eric," Rake laughed, "that's the thorn in the rose." Rake played with him. "These days, news travels so fast, the media would catch on before it could get off the ground." Glancing at Eric, he took another sip.

Eric responded, "It would have to be a select group of people building all this carefully. But someone would leak it to the press, some gutless wonder who wants to sell out cheap. Funny thing about such people. They're usually not against what's going on, it's because they have inadequate personalities. Most come from leaks on the inside." Eric leaned over to refill his glass, and then changed his position in the swing. "I wonder if there ever could be a way to ensure enough secrecy at the beginning to allow it to work."

"You'd have to hand pick everyone involved and screen the hell out of them, then strike before anyone has time to change his mind. There would also have to be that absolute certainty of knowing what would happen to you if you decided to betray it." Rake responded. He stroked a large orange Tabby cat purring next to him on the sofa.

"Rake, you know what one Cobra unit and one mechanized infantry battalion could do to a city."

"I hate the idea of that kind of destruction," Rake said. "It disgusts me and there's a way to avoid it. One way is don't allow social conditions to exist where you're feeding and raising parasites and letting them multiply only to have them turn around and fight you or out-vote you when you say 'no more.' "

The cat nudged for more attention until Rake gently pushed its head aside. "Why is it that people can't see what happens time and again? Why can't they realize that these programs with their offer of meaningless jobs destroy the character of people? Hell, man, even some government workers have meaningless jobs. No matter what you give people unwilling to work, it's never enough."

"Sometimes I think the people's revolution has already begun," said Eric.

"It's been in the making for some time in this country, and no lefty is going to have the guts or the intelligence to admit they were wrong. When this country is controlled by mob rule, and when these have-nots multiply even more, come election time they're going to vote in their man. He'll point his finger in our direction and say, 'There is the problem. I'll take from them what they owe you and see that you get yours.'" Again, Rake stroked the head of the cat. "Suppose the middle class did see it. At this point what could they do?"

Eric sipped the last of the liqueur. "Without force, the only way is a tax revolt. If the government doesn't have the money, it can't spend it."

"Oh, hell, Eric!" Rake sat up suddenly. "You know no politician is going to let anyone get away with that. If people like us didn't pay taxes in this country or if it looked like a run to get personal money out of the banks, the IRS or somebody would interfere. Even if the people were successful in revolting against taxes, the politicians would get back by making cuts in areas that are vital. Then the bastards would get back at you by voting in another tax. Hell, they aren't going to cut their own throats." Rake folded his arms and sat back. The cat, satisfied with all of the attention, jumped down. "But there's one other thing, Eric. Let's suppose we could control where the cuts are to be made, and how much. Knowing where you and I would want these cuts, do you really think there wouldn't be violence? Some people would go on a rampage of looting, stealing and killing to get what they wanted."

Louise appeared again. "Mr. Rake, anything else? Kitchen's closing down."

"No. Everything's fine. Thank you for this evening."

"Good night," she said and carried the tray back inside.

Eric waited until she was back in the house. "What about someone like *her*?" he asked.

"What about *her?*" Rake countered.

"What do you think should happen to people like Louise?"

"*Nothing*, Eric. Louise and her husband *are* productive people. Why would anyone want to change that?" Rake leaned forward. "Look, Eric, I'm not a racist. This is *not* a black and white issue. None of my views on this developed out of any bigotry. No harm would come to people like Louise and her man. They're **not** who we're after here."

The two men watched a faded gray '65 Pontiac come rolling up the driveway and stop for Louise. The door swung open and her husband's smile could be seen from the porch.

Rake looked away at the old car leaving the driveway, then back at Eric. "Whatever suffering there would be, don't forget there are always charitable organizations and people, and there are two inherent advantages of charity over welfare. It's the only moral way of getting money, and those people contributing voluntarily for benevolent reasons can have a more direct say into how that money is to be used. Any contributor to a charity who doesn't like the way the program is being handled can do something about it. What could be more moral than that?"

There was a long pause. Rake's words came hard and then the silence was heavy with his political and social ideals. "Eric," he finally said, "let's suppose there's a group of people who are trying to head off just what I am talking about. Let's also suppose they think the same as you and me and that some politicians, businessmen and others have met from time to time to discuss which way this country is going. You like to meet them?"

Eric asked as casually as possible, "Maybe. What's in it for me?"

"They might want to support your invention. It's going to be people with thoughts similar to yours and mine who can appreciate what you've done so far to get those creative ideas off the ground."

Eric nodded. "Where and when?"

"For now, you'll have to leave that up to me. It may be soon. An evening next week?"

"I could be there. Just let me know."

They firmly shook hands. *I'm in* Eric thought.

ERIC DROVE HIS yellow sports car through the Bensons' gate. Still pumped from his meeting with Rake, he was now just relaxing. The little sports car spun out onto the highway and he was looking forward to the flight of freedom that comes on a long stretch of rural road, late on a summer night.

When he finally opened the door to the carriage house, Jager jumped up, placing his paws on Eric's chest. "No more Danish ham for you," Eric laughed. "Here you get dog food."

After a brisk walk in the woods behind the apartment, master and dog returned to the little carriage house. Eric dropped on top of the bed, exhausted, as Jager sprawled at his feet. His last thoughts before sleep drifted to Rake's firm handshake. He understood now why those in the Agency were drawing battle lines. It made sense why Ross did not tell him the whole story before the assignment. It was all beginning to look different.

Eric knew that soon Ross would want to know where *he* stood. He would have to make the ultimate decision for himself. *Which way would he go?*

CHAPTER 31

[Keyword: Weapons, Boston (Reuters)—A government employees union said today that the theft of small arms and plastic explosives of U.S. military bases had become so serious that the military has been forced to adopt new security measures. . . . He said the government is being spurred by large-scale theft to initiate "stringent new security measures". . . .—Reuters Limited] [31]

August 6th

"Are you sure there's a meeting here?" Eric asked, puzzled that only one automobile was in sight. Rake turned into the long paved driveway, climbed to the top of the darkened hill, and parked. At night, Retired General Cyrus Randolph's Civil War Beloin arsenal looked like a medieval gray brick fortress without a moat. It sat on a huge man-made hill just outside Richmond, with only a battered station wagon standing sentry at the hill's crest, reminding Eric of an old, worn-out hunting dog.

"The best way to attract attention is to have Lincolns and Cadillacs lined from the drive to the door," Rake said.

They entered the house and met the guards. Eric's awareness of everything around him alerted his senses. One of the plain-clothes guards closely scrutinized him while the other checked a written list. Eric could hear male laughter coming from a nearby room. The

151

two young men were led to a large room facing Richmond's James River. That side of the arsenal was hidden from the road where they entered but open to the river view. The main floor was a military museum. The lower floors of the arsenal were still in use holding arms and weapons but this time, illegally.

General Randolph renovated the old arsenal's top floor into a private home. Decorated with originals and exquisite reproductions of Virginia's colonial collections, the inside reminded Eric of the old Virginia plantations along the shores farther down the James River. Two plain-clothes guards entered the room. One asked them to wait.

In another spacious room just down a narrow hallway, Eric sensed Deacon and the others were waiting. He guessed Deacon decided to invite him after all computer checks and service records came back clean. Ross saw to that.

When the two young men entered the room, all eyes focused on Eric.

Some watched him closely, noting, his confident relaxed manner. When they introduced him to each man, although casually dressed, they nodded formally, their body postures rigid. He was conscious of Deacon's shrewd eyes and commanding presence long before he saw the snow-white hair and the inconspicuous chair Deacon chose where he could remain relatively unobtrusive.

Deacon fascinated him yet Eric felt uncomfortable in his presence. He was one of those men who can make it known immediately by their carriage that they are the captains and the kings.

They passed out reports of Eric's invention. After a few moments looking over the diagrams, Deacon nodded to Rake, who then signaled to Eric. Eric paused long enough to get their attention then launched into a brief lecture. His system was superior to the others the government had tried some twenty years ago. He covered every angle both positive and negative of his work. Dr. Malcolm Potter, a leader in research and development for high tech projects, was Deacon's guest at the meeting and appeared impressed. After a half-hour Eric finished, and sat down.

The group quieted. Everyone knew that Deacon and Potter would pass their approval before anyone else.

Deacon spoke first. "As much as we are interested in your concept, Brent, the political climate in this country has destroyed the incentive to invest capital in such a high-risk venture."

"I understand that, sir. But if the government seizes the concept there'll be nothing in it for me, or for anyone else. I may have a little difficulty getting my first seed money but once that's done, I'll be all right."

"No, Brent. Not even then. But that's something for you, me and Potter here, to discuss over good whiskey some other time. Do you suppose the current crop of politicians in this country have ever realized that they created a monster by demanding all these government regulations to limit competition?"

"I think some of them do."

With a disgruntled "humpf" Deacon said, "On certain issues, maybe. But what I'm asking is do you think the bastards realize their actions are causing the economic and moral decline of this country?"

"You make a good point." Eric said.

"Eric, the only responses you're seeing from the politicians in this country is self-serving, pandering for votes. What are they doing for the people who actually produce things in this country? They are so good at mouthing pious social catchwords and making hard-working people feel guilty so they can push their giveaway social programs. Eric, it is killing us."

Eric remained quiet, his mouth partly open, breathing erratically. He was trying to follow Deacon's logic. Deacon was beginning to make sense but Eric knew there was so much more he didn't know.

Deacon waited a few moments then responded, "I thought you *wouldn't* have an answer." Government never reduces its power on its own. Suppose, Brent, there could be a reinterpreted Constitution based on the economic concerns of our forefathers, whereby the federal government would be generally dismantled except for the police, the judiciary, and the military? There would be room for public works like highways and airports, but those infrastructure things would be supported as well. Suppose there would be no federal income tax ever again?" Deacon's voice fell softly over the group like snowflakes. His skill was incredible and it always drew the attention he sought.

"Suppose there were men who were willing to try for a goal like that, knowing there would never be a personal financial gain, but many personal losses?" Deacon asked.

The man's words affected Eric almost as if someone slapped him in the face. He struggled for composure. "It would take a powerful group to organize themselves to affect this country politically and economically," Eric said.

"You think it could ever be done?" Deacon asked. His face was turning pink from the blood rushing to the surface. His blood pressure was up again.

"I'm not sure, but I'm not the man to ask," Eric told him.

"Brent, if I know Rake Benson I know he's laid on you his political philosophy."

"Yes, sir."

"Would you call that radical thinking? Fanaticism?"

"No. But I still favor a tax revolt," Eric blurted back. If it comes to bloodshed, at least we'd be defending ourselves. The others—their acts would be the immoral ones." Eric noticed Adkins' quick glance at Deacon. The two shared a point of interest.

"I respect your acute awareness of morality, Mr. Brent," said the white-haired man. "But, let me appeal to your good sense. Do you really think it's the nature of the average American to instigate a major tax revolt? Really? The ones who watch the soaps and buy the amazing potato peeler off the television—do you think they're going to mastermind a tax revolt? Those people? A revolt as complicated as one needing such focused, intelligent action. Do you think it could get through Congress without compromises changing it beyond recognition?" Deacon was straining, and he coughed.

"No, I don't think so." Eric's answer came naturally, with no hesitation. It was a strange sensation, passing through his body and mind, and he noted the sincerity of their interests in his ideas. The electricity in the air and the magnetism of Deacon made him think the meeting was much more significant than just a sterile discussion of an invention.

Eric began experiencing an odd feeling of accomplishment. The Agency had gone to great lengths to get him before these men, but it was his own personal creativity that had brought him here. Ross knew scarcely anything about his work and invention. To Ross it was only another avenue to get where he wanted to go—a man on the inside. It was at once exciting and frightening to know that people of this caliber appreciated what he accomplished and believed in his work enough to let him inside their confidences. This was no ordinary penetration of a fringe group. Without Eric and the strength of his own accomplishments, the Agency would never have anyone inside in time.

Deacon began grandstanding. Eric guessed that it was what he knew best. He was magnificent. His skill in accenting the precise word with just the right tone made every ear perk up. But even more important, he was making it sound sensible.

Eric continued to listen in thoughtful silence as Deacon closed it all out.

"In all societies, in spite of all efforts to equalize everything and everybody, there will always be some who suffer more than others. We can talk about this until we're blue in the face, but until people with the capabilities to really change things do something, then all we're engaging in, is intellectual and philosophical masturbation."

Eric felt a sudden surge of energy, and he knew that Deacon's words electrified every man in the room.

"Brent," Deacon continued, his voice lowered, "you'll never realize anything from your invention without the proper backing.

I know you don't have the money. If you really want to succeed you're going to have to put something into changing the world. You have come here to ask us to take all the risks, hassles, and expenses of this project." Deacon paused to sip from his drink. "I ask you why should we? What risks are you willing to take? What investment would you be willing to make to ensure it's being worth our time to help you?"

Deacon was studying him. Eric realized it and was uncomfortable. He sensed the man's strange ability to look into his soul and extract its essence. He suddenly felt anxious. What could Deacon read in him? The older man's glance seemed eerily to convey a father-to-son look. The sensation made him feel uneasy.

With glistening eyes and a faint smile, Deacon walked toward Eric and asked softly, "Want to buy a little stock in *changing the world?*"

"What are my options?" Eric asked his heart pounding. For a moment Deacon seemed set back by his question. He glanced about the room at the others then took another slow deliberate drink from his water glass. He leaned closer and spoke softly. "Do you even know what I'm *asking* of you, man?"

"I think I do," Eric struggled to keep his voice calm. "But I need to know more."

Pushing his glass away, Deacon accepted the challenge. "In your presentation you asked that we be open-minded. We ask the same of you. We don't have a clear and concise portfolio that's iron-clad. Our ideas are not a Wall Street show and tell. It's more a matter of orientation, and that takes a little time. Interested?"

"I think so. But it's hard to say without knowing exactly what's involved. What's my first step?"

Deacon looked at Adkins then back at Eric. "Your first step is to understand the absolute certainty of what will happen to you if anything said here is leaked. If you decide at some point to withdraw, you withdraw in silence."

Eric nodded.

"We need to create the right conditions so it's worth investing in you. Rake will be your mentor."

Deacon seemed to pull back into himself. He turned away and cleared his throat. He wiped a perspiring brow, then faced Eric and pronounced curtly, "Thank you for coming." Deacon smiled, "We'll meet again *soon*."

Rake had been silent during most of the ordeal, as if watching a brother go through an initiation. Eric turned to him and whispered, "What's next?"

Rake met Deacon's eyes for instructions, then he nodded and the two left the room.

Eric turned around just long enough to catch Deacon's look of approval and his words of encouragement spoken to Rake. Deacon called out, "Brent, we'll let you know . . . ." In his mind, he repeated the words as he had done so often with Ross, ". . . *what you need to know, when you need to know it.*" Eric's heart felt as if it might jump into his throat and choke him. He was afraid to look again into the man's face. He thought he was far enough away so that any change of expression would go unrecognized, but he was unsure. The man's words unnerved him.

On his way home, Eric's tired eyes scanned the rear view mirror. He thought he saw a car with only its parking lights on climbing the hills behind him, but when he slowed down—it disappeared.

CHAPTER 32

[Keyword: Weapons, Boston (Reuters)—. . . Mr. Sullivan said the missing weapons included M-16 rifles, grenade and rocket launchers, machine guns and ammunition. He singled out the Red River Arsenal in Arkansas, Fort Bliss, Texas and installations at Rock Island and Joliet, Illinois, as among those affected. The army spokesman confirmed that large weapon caches were stolen from National Guard armories in Ohio and Florida. Most of the 84 weapons stolen in Ohio were recovered, he said. The Boston-based union based its allegations on reports from its local officers at installations across the country . . . .—Reuters Limited] [32]

After Eric left, the men at the arsenal broke up into small clusters then visited the three bars set up around the room. For some, the evening ended quietly.

"It's not necessary to jump on this," Deacon had told them. All that's necessary is that you explore his potential."

"Why do we need a new man?" one of the men asked after they reassembled more casually. "I thought we agreed—no new men this close to the final hours. Bringing in Brent makes me nervous."

"We're being careful," Deacon said. "We can use him in some minor job for the time being. All of you heard the technology reports from Potter. Don't fool yourself. This man has a brilliant

159

mind. I don't think even *he* can appreciate what he's accomplished. He could change the entire weaponry system of the U.S. and modern warfare." The thought excited him. "However, I'm not foolish," Deacon said to them. "None of us is."

"I don't think he should see any of the installations." Major Adkins' abrupt entrance into the conversation was grating. He sat with elbows on his chair holding his second drink. "We have nothing on him to assure his secrecy. If any word leaks out about what we have at even one base, the entire operation will be destroyed. Deacon, I don't like it." Major William Adkins' stern voice filtered through the other conversations. "I've got to get back to Arkansas this week, and I'll go back with more peace of mind if I know we haven't broken security."

Only Deacon knew how uneasy he was. "William, there's a reason for all this. You know that I am not accustomed to explaining myself, but Kendall's got much catching up to do when he returns. He'll need the help that Brent may be able to give." Deacon pointed to a man who seemed a slightly younger version of himself. "Martin, before I forget, make sure Rake tells Brent about working with Kendall when he comes back. I don't want Rake promising him too much."

"Has anyone heard from Kendall?" Adkins asked.

"No. I don't know what he's doing," Cyrus Randolph said. "Bob's letter said something about promotion review and he would get back in touch shortly." With his crooked fingers, the retired General lifted his whiskey glass to a tired, drawn mouth.

"Let us know if anything develops, will you, Cyrus?" Deacon noticed the time and motioned that he was leaving. He had rested earlier in the day, but was exhausted again.

Before he could gather the contents of his briefcase, Adkins sidestepped and hustled Deacon privately out to the balcony overlooking the James River. He closed the sliding glass door to keep the cooled air from escaping the room. "Got something, William?" he asked as he lit a cigar. He held the flame a little longer to view Adkins' worried face, then Deacon relaxed and looked at the evening's calm on the river where the moonlight reflected across the ripples.

In a rare outburst, Adkins broke the quiet mood. "I don't want anything to upset our plans. Damn it, there's been so much of our lives poured into this, I don't want it ruined at the eleventh hour over someone or something we're not sure of."

Deacon was surprised to see him lose his composure. He leaned back against the guardrail. Puffing on his cigar, he asked, "Is there anything wrong at Number Seventeen?"

"No. Seventeen's fine. We completed our requirements for air-powers and the rest will come in soon."

"Good," Deacon grasped the cigar with two fingers and pulled it from his mouth. "William, you and I go back a long way. I absolutely trust your judgment. Whatever it is that's bothering you, would it have anything to do with your old man not making it through with *his* invention? Is it eating you a little to watch someone, who could be your *younger brother*, walk in with it in his hand?" Adkins' eyes suddenly grew large with question. Deacon added, "William, I was at Aberdeen on the day your step-father blew his hand away. I know how much it must have hurt you to see him laughed at by the top brass on that testing ground. He was a real man, William. He never gave up and he got rich for his efforts, but you shouldn't have any animosity toward that kid. Halsey upset a few men in his day. You'd better believe it."

"It's not that," Major William Adkins responded, shoving his hands deep in his pockets.

"I don't know. But if it is you shouldn't feel that way. We all respect what Halsey did to advance his ideas. Without his efforts Brent might never have succeeded."

"Does he know who I am?" asked Adkins.

"Doesn't appear to know."

"Let's keep it that way, Deacon."

Deacon puffed on the long cigar and strained one eye on Adkins. "I agree. But only if you want it that way." He slapped

Adkins on his back. "You're a good man. God knows we couldn't have set up these installations without you. That's the truth." Deacon accepted on the surface that Adkins had temporarily buried his frustration; but he also wanted to believe that Adkins was no longer upset.

CHAPTER 33

[Abstract: Newburyport, Massachusetts,—Armory heavily damaged by fire and explosion; ammunition and truck stolen; later recovered.—The New York Times.] [33]

August 10th

Breakfast wasn't sitting well in his stomach when Eric drove to the James River Park. He felt as if his guts were trying to digest raw cardboard. He parked at the huge modern concrete park monolith, a solemn, gray structure donated and built by Richmond's founding fathers. Eric took the stairs two at a time up to the third story deck.

Eric stared out over the marshes alongside the murky, spinning water then back up at Richmond's skyline. It brought back memories of his father and the first time he saw the tall buildings across the river jutting up tall against a sunny sky. His first ride across the bridge joining the south side of Richmond to the main city core was in a black, polished military staff car. He was still wearing short leather pants with long socks. His father, with his strong East Prussian accent, announced to Eric that this was to be his new home.

His father brought Eric closer to him so he could gaze out the tinted window at the tree-covered islands in the middle of the James

163

River. Eric started to speak in German, but his father held up his hand, gently stopping his son in mid-sentence, "This is not the land of your enemies, Eric," he said in English. "There are good people here. Same as your own. You must speak English now."

A man sitting in the rear seat riding with them smiled. His father turned to the man and nodded his way. "Herr Shumacher here thinks the same. Isn't that so?"

Eric remembered looking up into Wolfgang Schumacher's creased smile and kindly eyes nodding, yes. As Herr Shumacher turned his face toward the river Eric noticed the man's grin falling away as he began saying in German, "I hope they have honor and good sense here. I pray it never gets out of hand."

Taking in the view of the bridge from where he now stood, Eric could see that it badly needed repair and renovation. Its four narrow lanes had been covered with cement patches and looked like a worn-out pair of jeans.

A firm hand suddenly rested on his shoulder. He counted to three before turning around. Eric gave no flinch, no flighty tension, at least none that Ross could see.

Eric had learned his lessons well from those early days at Camp Peary in Williamsburg, Virginia, the CIA's Special Activities Division's officer training base. Eric called it "Camp Swampy" but otherwise known as "the Farm" they had taught him well the tricks of the trade that would keep a man alive when he's undercover.

Ross was typically dressed in his gray suit and spit shined black boots. The gray suit was pressed and his shirt matched well. Ross was most meticulous when Miriam was back in town, he thought.

Ross explained that he had another meeting in Norfolk. He seemed more serious than usual, although he made it clear that their meeting in the park was happenstance. Eric wished he could believe him, but his queasy stomach never lied.

"How's it going?" Ross asked, pulling out the familiar pipe.

"I have some interesting notes to turn in," Eric said.

"Good, good," Ross responded. Both men grew silent and glanced around for anyone who could be within earshot.

"I think I met the head men. Rake got me in on the premise that they wanted to hear more about my invention. They offered to invest in it, but with a kicker. They expect me to help create the right conditions to make it worth their time." Eric seemed worried and looked away from Ross.

Puffing on his pipe, the Chief coolly listened. "What are the right conditions? I would think they already exist—if they're as big as we think they are."

"They're big, all right. These guys are out to change the system. They will make the case that they are working within the framework of a strict interpretation of the Constitution."

Ross collected his pipe. His voice grew cold and strained. "Do you have anything other than *philosophy* to report?"

His frustration was so obvious, Eric thought. Langley must be having a hard time coming up with anything solid. "Philosophy is mostly what I've gotten so far. I have a few names to check out." He handed Ross a folded piece of paper. "The big meeting was at General Cyrus Randolph's Beloin Arsenal. They just wanted to meet me and ask me a few questions."

"Military presence?"

"They were there, all right, but I couldn't tell how many. Everyone was in civilian dress. Judging from their mannerisms, though, the room was full of some heavy-hitter military. That's hard to hide."

"Any weapons?" Ross asked.

"Hints of it. I haven't seen anything, but I haven't pushed for it. I'm afraid to move until they give an okay. I get the feeling that many of them aren't happy with someone new suddenly on the scene." Eric added, "One other complication, I think they want me to work under Kendall."

"Kendall?!"

"Yes. Rake told me about it this morning. Kendall was supposed to be working close to General Randolph on their takeover period. They're beginning to wonder what the army is doing with him."

"That guy can't even brush his own teeth," Ross sighed. A worry crease appeared on his forehead. "Another damn unpredictable twist. We've written a few 'letters from home' to ward off suspicions until we could figure out what to do. We're thinking about a letter going back to the Guard that he's had an accident and is comatose in an out-of-the-way civilian hospital.

Eric nervously stared at Ross. "Damn it, I wish you guys would hurry up and arrange something. When he doesn't come back, I may need a new slot. I'd prefer to be placed in one work detail now so I can burrow in."

"We're working it. Any hint of foreign involvement?"

"Not that I can tell. Rake hasn't mentioned it and I haven't seen anything."

Ross shrugged. "If military other than ours is involved, they'd keep a low profile until the Right Guard makes their move." Ross squinted at Eric out of one eye. He spoke the words like he was trying to jab Eric with a hot poker. "What did you think about *Deacon*?"

Eric turned his head quickly toward the Chief. "You know about him?"

"I didn't know, I suspected. Now I know"

Eric stared out over the city. "I'm not too sure, other than Deacon, who has the real power; the rules seem to be fairly open.

"I know, but the word for now is to hold tight and keep your fingers on the pulse. No decisions yet."

"Who *is* Deacon?" Eric asked.

Ross looked up. "You meet him?"

"*Who* is Deacon?" Eric repeated.

"A former case officer. He made you and me look like boy scouts compared to what he did in his day. He's World War II and Korean War vintage. You had to be a little crazy to do what men like him did, and it was obvious that Deacon fit the mold well. I worked with him once when I was a rookie. He got out when his father died and left him a large conglomerate." Then he added quietly, "I knew Deacon was involved. He had to be. Jason was Deacon's deputy some years back."

Eric's disbelief froze the expression on his face.

"It's true," Ross added. "Deacon's involvement is part of the reason Jason was called back in. No one at the complex knows him better, and no one has the kind of minds those two have. It would take one to out-guess the other and to predict what moves they'd make."

"Do you think Deacon has ties with the old-timers in the company?"

"As far as we know, Deacon has plenty of admirers but he's not contacted anyone. At least anyone who's talking." A faint smirk passed Chief Ross' face then disappeared. "We think you're still safe."

"Damn," snapped Eric, "I hope so."

The young case officer shifted away from the city's view and crossed his arms in front of him.

Ross scrutinized the parking lot where there was an inconspicuous late model dark blue Ford and a driver waited patiently for his return. He emptied the contents of the pipe against the outer side of the gray cement wall. The two watched as the burnt flakes floated gently to the ground. "By the way," he said, "has Halstead or any of his FBI crew tried to get anything from you?"

"While I'm undercover?" Eric asked.

"Yes. A new FBI agent looked up one of ours in Toledo for an 'interview'. He blew our man's cover and that compromised some hard-to-get information we were hot to bag. It's amazing . . . you just can't make this stuff up."

"Ross, if one of those guys pulls that crap, I'll hammer him," Eric told him. "Can't you do something about it?"

"I can't, but Jason is looking into it."

"Analysts come up with anything solid?" Eric asked.

Ross stuffed the pipe back into his jacket pocket. "No, it's almost the same as before. Bits and pieces of information indicate that this is so big we can hardly believe it. The file looks like a set of encyclopedias. I've listened to miles of taped conversations and still, we have only a general understanding of their network, but it seems one center is at Beloin Arsenal. That makes it all the more important that you get closer and take a look at what's in that old Civil War arsenal." He paused and looked toward the car. "I've got to head out for Norfolk. I'll be in touch. Other than keeping an eye open for those weapons, don't surface again until you hear from me."

"Got it."

Ross retrieved his wire-rimmed, aviator's sunglasses from his shirt pocket and placed them over his grayish-blue eyes. "Wolfgang Shumacher wants to see you. I can arrange for you to go to NASA if you want."

Eric nodded yes.

"I'll be seeing you soon." He walked quickly toward the car. Before entering, he turned back to look at Eric. As Jason so often did, Ross gave a subtle salute. Eric nodded and let it pass.

CHAPTER 34

[New York Times Abstract: National Guard units in Illinois and several other states have been instructed to remove firing devices from weapons stored in armories in case weapons are stolen.—The New York Times] [34]

August 13th

Boxes of specially meshed masks, sticks, vests and other riot training gear lay in a neat row on a paved square. The platoon leader at Arkansas' Seventeen Headquarters divided the group in half. Some were to play rioters while the others practiced the art of keeping an unruly crowd in line.

Deacon walked briskly outside the Arkansas headquarters office. Hurrying, he wanted to reach the training area and deliver what he considered crucial instructions. He hustled to the far side of the airfield where the pavement and grass met and where Major William Adkins was training men in another phase of Wings Day.

The platoon leader saluted. Deacon snapped a return, then faced the assemblage to deliver the message that scores of other National Guard and Reserve commanders were delivering across the United States. "Stand at ease. This won't take long," he ordered.

Some of the men were dressed in jeans and T-shirts, others in uniforms. They all waited attentively for his message.

Deacon folded his arms against his chest. "What the major is teaching you may be the most important phase of our project. Your behavior will convince the rest of the country that we're here not to destroy, but to serve as a temporary means of control until order is established again."

There was no wind. The arid field carried his voice clear to the other side.

"If any of you get a thrill out of seeing confused people hurt, you don't belong here. None of this is an excuse to injure people. If this collective effort is handled right, the result will be the utmost in satisfaction for all of us and will go down peacefully."

Deacon watched as Major Adkins and three other men, who were training the platoon, checked faces, hands and body language and sought out potential problems. Deacon had made it clear, if one man makes a violent spectacle of himself, they'll all look bad. "In every state and at every installation, we've got to have the most disciplined group of men ever assembled to carry out a plan. You must truly know and understand the principle as well as the methods," Deacon told them.

"Gentlemen," Deacon continued, "your job is to hold down the violence in the streets, not to create it. Once it's known that the federal giveaways and other bureaucratic monstrosities financed by the taxpayer's money will be stopped, there will be some unhappy people. Some may take to the streets to save their right 'not to work'. Members of federal enforcement organizations, and all state and municipal police will be of help to us, up to a point, on Wings Day, until they find out they're being manipulated. There will be mass confusion. Commands will be handed down to them from our people within the system. Remember all their lives they've been used to taking orders through the system. Most of them will only follow orders and never realize they're being used in the first few hours of the takeover. When they figure out what's happening, some will enthusiastically join and others will turn on you. You'll have to disarm the ones who may turn on you, before they know what's happening. You're going to have to be good enough to deal with men who've had the same training as you."

Adkins looked around at the expectant faces and added, "We're hoping our plan will be such an overwhelming force, they won't try," he added. Some of the men glanced at each other, confirming that they were becoming involved in a potential revolution. "We don't want martial law," Adkins said. He began to move among the men. "This is not to be a permanent military takeover. It's a temporary changing of the caretakers of the Constitution."

With a tired but thorough gaze into each man's face, Deacon drew a long labored breath. "I want you to remember this, too" Deacon said, "if after Wings Day the cornerstones of this country, corporations, big business, and other productive segments of our society refuse to support us, we may have to step down quickly. We've talked about this all along, and it is all the more reason to keep our own house in order." There was a pause for questions. There were none.

He repeated the words that had become a battle cry to those who had been involved in the project for many years. "It's time to say 'No more.'" His last words left ringing in everyone's ears, Deacon surveyed the now pumped assembly, turned on his heel, and walked off to cheers.

In another of Seventeen's stark but functional conference rooms, a group had come from many Right Guard installations and arsenals, gathered there for a training session of a different nature. They patiently waited for Deacon.

Deacon sorted through papers in Adkins' office, searching through the stack of manila folders on his desk, trying to locate the one he needed. As he lifted and tossed each aside, a creased newspaper clipping drifted from one of the folders to the floor like a dead leaf. Yellowed with age, slightly torn and curled at its edges, it caught his attention and, curious, he picked up the clipping and examined it.

The article was an account of Joseph Halsey, a former military commander and inventor, whose concept of a liquid propellant weapon was tested at Aberdeen. It described the explosion and Halsey's injuries. Because of the apparent failure of the invention, the U.S. Government had stopped the funding on any liquid propellant concept.

Deacon returned the clipping to the folder, thick with other yellowed media accounts about the invention's concept and its inventor. Late for his conference room meeting, he moved quickly through the corridor to reach the men who would help bring to fruition the Right Guard movement: his dream and the ultimate plan of many—known and unknown.

CHAPTER 35

*[Keyord: Weapons, Honolulu (UPI)—Machine guns, .45-caliber pistols and other weapons stolen from the armory at Kaneohe Marine Corps Air Station have been recovered, authorities reported . . . . The FBI said it was investigating a civilian suspect. The names of those in custody were not disclosed . . .
—United Press International] [35]*

August 18th

It felt good to be back at the carriage house in Bel Air and have some time alone. Eric had spent most of the day with Rake, explaining in depth what H-PAR could mean for the Right Guard. He produced drawings of the proposed model and interpreted its concept in detail. Rake was impressed. He mentioned a business dinner meeting he wanted Eric to attend in the middle of the week.

"The locations for these get-togethers are kept quiet until just before. Deacon's been riding us about security. You'll know when I pick you up."

He slumped down in a chair in his living room, drank a beer and watched the sunset. He dialed Jill's number several times but after each series of long rings with no answer he felt emptier. He could see Jager from his window. The dog cornered a squirrel against some bushes and stood motionless. His nose lowered to get a good sniff and with one paw lifted, his shoulder muscles protruded into a frozen stance. The squirrel suddenly scampered up a nearby tree. Jager leaped and began to chase him, barking loudly at the frightened animal until the line pulled taut. Setting his beer down, Eric joined the fun. When he unhooked the line, the ecstatic dog ran through the underbrush and sped back to the tree where the squirrel had escaped. Then he ran to Eric, jumping up against his chest, then off again through the brush.

The setting sun gleamed through the trees like spun gold and in the depth of the woods the temperature was cooling down. Eric heard the dog as he ran a good distance ahead along Micky's old run barking at everything that moved.

He thought about Jill again and wondered if a meeting with her somewhere away from Richmond could be arranged. Ross had gotten word to him, "We think she's not seeing P. Scott anymore. Could be just a lovers spat but her D.C. shadow thinks it's ended."

The faint, disappearing sunlight reminded him of the sun peeking through the windows of her Georgetown apartment, speckling the walls. He conjured up an image of her nude body stretched beneath the bed covers and his hands exploring and massaging her. He remembered a tempestuous discussion they had shared over pizza about the government's involvement in Southeast Asia. He had strongly disagreed with her but Jill relentlessly kept pursuing the issue for fun, then playfully threw a piece of pizza at him; he retaliated and held her to the floor, tickling her into fits of laughter until she screamed "uncle" in utter defeat. He missed her.

Jager unexpectedly stopped barking in the woods. Eric called the dog's name, but got no response. He called again in another direction and still no sound from the animal. Quickening his pace down the path, he rounded a slight curve. Matt Watson was bending down on one knee rubbing the dog's head and scratching his back. "Good boy, that's a good boy," he was saying softly. Then he looked up at Eric. "My brother used to raise Springadors; the new lines are good animals."

Eric extended his hand. "How's it going? Looks like I've missed seeing you and your wife a lot lately."

Watson rose and gave a firm handshake. "Fran's mother has been ill, and we've been making the trip to Charlottesville almost four times a week to check her until we can get a full-time nurse."

"I'm sorry to hear that."

"Well, I'd be sorry too if she were a younger woman but she's done everything and has traveled everywhere. She's had the fullest life of anyone I've ever met. She's dying, she knows it; her only request is to go comfortably. I want to see that it happens that way." Watson spoke the words without emotion. He seemed to manifest an inner strength forming calmness and sobriety. Most people usually misjudged this as shyness. "I've let Jager off the line a few times to walk with me in the woods. Hope you don't mind?" Watson asked.

"I appreciate it, and I know Jager does," Eric said, rubbing the dog's head.

"Anytime, anytime."

"Been practicing?" Eric nodded toward the leather satchel Watson just picked up before they started walking back to the house.

"Just test firing some ammo. Last year I had the prettiest buck you've ever seen in my sights. I pulled on him and nothing happened but 'click.' The buck ran and I tried to get off another shot, and got another dud. The rest of my rounds were bad, too, and when I got back to the lodge, so was the whole damn box. Bad primers."

"I used to go with my father. I'm not sure I can remember what a good deer drive is like anymore." As Eric spoke, he noticed Watson shifting the long narrow case around behind him, away from Eric's view. The lessons from the farm: the subtle telltale signs of body language were still with Eric. It had become a part of him now like breathing. Eric was alerted to the gun's weight resting against the bottom of the sack as it made an impression forming a definite outline of the top of the gun, revealing what he thought was the telescopic sight of a rifle.

"Where do you hunt?" Eric asked.

Watson paused on the trail. He pulled out a pipe and began to stuff the bowl.

The ritual reminded Eric of Chief Ross.

"I usually wind up around the Chickahominy River. There's good game in that area," Watson said. He held the pipe between his teeth as he spoke.

As the two continued their walk back, the conversation changed to dogs and it ended with remarks about Jager, who was running around their feet playfully biting at their shoes. Watson walked toward his home and nodded good-bye with his pipe still firmly between his teeth.

Eric hooked the Springador back to the line, and went upstairs to make coffee. Filling the pot from the tap, he thought back to his hunting days with his father. Watson's conversation struck a note. Using rifles for deer hunting east of the Blue Ridge Mountains, in all but a very few counties, was unlawful, he suddenly remembered, you had to use shotguns. Eric thought the law had not changed.

When steam burst from the pot's spout in little gusts, he removed it from the stove. He stared out of his window at the Watson home and at the small-paned third story windows where Watson's workshop occasionally showed a light during late hours. He thought about his friendly neighbor, a man who said he hunted with his rifle in an area where Eric felt sure it was not lawful. A man who had a computer company at his disposal. That fleshy hint of Watson's smile kept prodding his memory, making the hair at the back of his neck stand up. He couldn't place the man. Was all this friendliness sincere? Could he be trusted? Apparently Ross and Langley thought so.

CHAPTER 36

[Keyword: Valleybriefs, Fresno, California (UPI)—Investigators looking into the theft of military vehicles and equipment from two California National Guard armories in Fresno believe the items may be in the hands of marijuana plantation operators or a survivalist paramilitary group . . . .—United Press International] [36]

August 15th

The men around the table at the dinner meeting knew retired General Cyrus Randolph as a legendary old warrior. Deacon's carefully selected guests stood and applauded Cyrus, despite his late arrival. The General, a wiry, tanned man with arthritic hands and a thin ribbon of flesh for a mouth, smiled a modest acknowledgment. The group then climbed the stairs to Deacon's huge library and laid their portfolios on the table in front of their places.

Deacon's eyes were on General Cyrus Randolph, still a relative newcomer to the top echelon, despite being an old friend of Deacon's and a long-time supporter of his ideas. "Our plans," Deacon began, "called for General Randolph to be active only after Wings Day. Because of his vast background in detainment centers, he was slated to help Kendall. You may know that some time ago we asked him to take what became Kendall's job, but he declined because he felt we needed a younger man. Since Kendall's injury, we're pleased that Cyrus is now going to take charge of that area. He'll be in his arsenal on Wings Day, and then transferred as the new commander of the detainment centers." The men applauded Randolph again.

"We delayed Wings Day for a short while," Deacon told them, "so that Cyrus can familiarize himself with the new detainment centers. That's a key point for the southeast portion of this operation. Your reports, please."

Each man in turn reported that his area was ready. Deacon noted each, with a "Well done," and turned to the industrialists assigned to evaluate Eric's H-PAR. "We checked Eric Brent's military background all the way back to his teens, when he joined the Air Force." He laced his praise of Eric with information of his military past, but only those facts that those at Langley chose to leave in. "Brent will be invaluable to us," Deacon continued, "but we'll use him on a limited basis. He can help Cyrus for now, and then later take a position on Wings Day in the arsenal. That's all I want him to do until we're in control."

Deacon motioned to the door, and Eric and Rake were invited in.

At the end of the day Jill made a last stop at a Moorehead satellite office in downtown Richmond. She had been in town most of the day helping the local campaign staff visit small county newspaper offices and make appointments for Candidate Moorehead's interviews. Moorehead phoned from his Northern Virginia headquarters fuming.

"Have you seen this morning's Times Dispatch?" he yelled into the phone.

"Not yet," she said. "I haven't had time."

"Well, get a goddamn copy and read it."

"I've just walked in, Bailor. Hold on for a second." She motioned frantically to one of the campaign workers for a paper. She scanned the pages until she saw the State section.

The press picked up on a little known fact that the opposition just released. Moorehead was trying to woo blacks, claiming he was the candidate for the minority, yet he belonged to several private clubs with no apparent black membership. The article reminded the public that when he was a young representative in the state legislature, he had voted against the integration of public schools. The press was beginning to have a holiday with the inconsistencies of Bailor Moorehead, the "people's candidate" for the U.S. Senate.

"Yes, Bailor, I see it."

"Jill, I've tried to reach Burt Collins all day long. I can't find anybody when I need him. I've got to be at a dinner tonight, and Burt's in Richmond. Find him and get a release out, pronto. My notes on this thing are on my desk. Burt will give you the strategy from there to follow. You got that?"

"Bailor, where is Burt? Is he here?"

"How the hell do I know where? You two should keep in touch with each other. I don't know why I hired a *woman* to do a man's job anyway."

"Bailor, calm down. This is not new material."

"Woman, if this costs me the campaign, it's your ass."

"Wait a minute," she bristled. "Transfer me to one of the staff members there. He must have left a message or something."

"I'm busy," the candidate yelled before hanging up the phone. "That's your damn problem."

Jill threw the receiver down in disgust. "That stupid jerk," she said aloud. She scanned her personal telephone book for Burt Collins' Alexandria phone number.

"Wait a minute," Burt Collins' wife said, and when she returned to the phone she gave Jill a Richmond address that he had scribbled in a calendar book on his desk. The Colin Street Road address had "fund-raiser dinner, 8 o'clock," written beside it. There was also a note, "*See Deacon,*" she said. "Want me to repeat it?" Collins' wife asked.

"No," Jill answered. "I've got it. I'm off to find him in Richmond. Thanks, Melanie."

The huge front door of Deacon Malway's mansion swung open. The well-dressed man met Jill with a grim stare, asking curtly, "Yes, ma'am?"

"May I see Mr. Burt Collins, please," she asked, smiling. "I understand he's in a dinner meeting here."

The door attendant glanced at another who hurriedly joined him. When he saw Jill, a curious expression came over his face. He turned to consult still a third man. Jill noticed the slight bulge under the left armpit of his suit jacket.

"Mr. Collins can't see you now," the first man said. "If you like, you may leave a message for him." He was firm but polite and he also sported a bulge beneath his left armpit.

It all aroused Jill's curiosity. "I need to talk to Burt Collins immediately. It'll take only a few moments."

"Jim," the second man said, "let her into the foyer. I'll be right back."

Jill noticed the exquisite mahogany furnishings in the entrance hall. On the second floor another well-dressed man leaned over the banister and motioned that it was all right to oblige her. The man directed her up the stairs. Another man, smaller-framed compared to the others, asked her to wait in the hall. He went through the double doors and leaned over Burt Collins' chair.

He left the doors slightly ajar and Jill moved forward taking a quick peek. When she pushed the door and it opened slightly she saw part of a long table surrounded by distinguished looking men. Then she heard a solemn white-haired man at the end of the table sharply break the conversation, asking, "Who is that young woman?"

Heads turned. Collins answered quickly, "She's on our campaign staff. Excuse me, I'll be just a moment." The guard exited quickly and left the doors open for Collins.

Jill caught a glimpse of the other end of the table that jolted her. The sight of Eric, sitting there with all those men was the last thing she expected to see that evening. It startled her. Eric's eyes met hers briefly. He was subtle and only she could tell they were iced with anger. Quickly he looked away, as if he didn't recognize her. Suddenly she remembered what he had told her about seeing him if he were undercover. She swallowed hard and turned away, too.

"What are you doing here?" Collins' harsh question broke her train of thought when he came up on her. But as she spoke, she continued silently asking herself what Eric and Collins were doing in the same meeting.

"Bailor called. I'm sorry if I've disturbed you by coming here, Burt. But it's urgent. Look at this." She handed him the newspaper.

The campaign manager hurriedly scanned the article. "I'll bet he's jumping through his ass on this one." There was a smirk on his face and a high pitch in his voice.

"Bailor said he left some notes on his desk," Jill told him. "But you know if I use those, he'll only get in deeper."

Collins pulled out his pen and began jotting down a few notes in the paper's margin. "How did you find me here?" he asked, scratching out some ideas for a rebuttal.

When she did not respond, he tried again. "Jill, *how* did you find me here?" he repeated.

She tried to peek through to the library again but someone closed the double doors. "Melanie. She said you wrote down some-thing about fund-raising alongside this address in your date book." She turned to see he was taking in her every gesture. "Are all these people supporting Moorehead?"

He wrote a few lines. He looked up at her again and forced out with as much calm as he could collect, "Basically it's a business meeting, but some are considering donating to the campaign." He was still writing then he hesitated. "Okay, these are the points to cover. Don't repeat any of the attack words they used in the article. Just make it a general response and use these." He sounded like a nervous debate coach. "And whatever you do, don't let Moorehead see it before it goes to press or he'll change it and make an idiot of himself." Pointing the rolled newspaper at her, he suddenly slapped it into his palm, and added, "I know the wire services picked up this one."

The shock of seeing Eric and the tension of a long hard day left her emotionally drained. She fought against the fatigue and her fear.

Collins noticed the daze and touched her shoulder. "Are you okay?"

"I'm fine, Burt." Her voice was shaky. "Just tired. There's a lot going on. I've got to drive all the way back to D.C. tonight." Resolutely, she reached for the newspaper, descended the stairs, and then hurried to her car.

When Collins briskly returned to the library, Deacon looked up. "Is everything all right, Burt?"

Stopping behind his chair, Collins gave the men what he hoped would be an acceptable explanation. "She's our campaign press secretary. She has no clue. It's not a problem. Moorehead has his ass in a sling again, belonging to a club that excludes minorities. The press caught on to it."

Everyone laughed. Even Deacon smirked, despite his usual well-controlled presence.

Eric only half listened. He was wondering if anyone had seen the look that had passed between them. If anyone had noticed their expressions of recognition, what could he say? At Langley and the Farm where they trained, Chauncey taught them to have their cover stories ready long before the need arose. A prized former case officer, Chauncey turned instructor when his legs could not run so fast anymore. False starts and prolonged hesitations finger you as guilty Chauncey taught them. Eric's throat was becoming dry. *Had Jill made any verbal slips before she left? Would she be able to get home? Would she disappear like Kendall? he thought.*

Eric and Collins in the same meeting? Jill thought, but Eric is undercover, he's got to be. After a guard at the mansion's front door disappeared, Jill glanced around the yard. Then she crouched at the rear of her automobile. The last time she had let the air out of a tire was back in high school during a football game. A ballpoint pen still worked just fine. And there was just enough summer daylight left to see the valve stem. She unscrewed the tiny cap.

Across the street and deep in the woods, Patrick, a CIA case officer assigned to surveillance of the mansion, watched through the oncoming darkness with interest. He laid down the binoculars, adjusted a special long distance lens on the camera, and then snapped a few frames.

"You're not going to believe this," he said into his radio. "She's flattening her own tire." The call finished with orders to keep a watchful eye for anything else. They would watch the girl.

Five minutes after leaving, Jill again appeared at the mansion's front door. "I'm sorry about this," she said to the annoyed security guard. "I must have rolled over something just before I pulled into the driveway. My tire's flat."

The guard stood still, blocking her way.

"I would like to see Mr. Collins again," she asked, thinking it was not so great a command, as the guard seemed to think it was. "It will take only a moment."

"We can call a tow truck for you," the man suggested politely, "or a garage."

"That would be very kind of you," she said. "However, I'm going to be late with the work Mr. Collins assigned to me because of my flat. I really should see him."

After hesitating, the guard said, "I'll tell him."

"Thank you. Tell him I'll be waiting outside." This time she could feel the suspicion around her.

When Collins received the message, Deacon asked with some annoyance, "Now what?"

"I'm terribly sorry about this," Collins apologized. "It seems that now my staff member has a flat tire."

"I really need you here," Deacon said, his amusement gone, "to go over this political strategy. This is *your* baby, Burt."

It was the perfect moment for Eric to stand up and place his hand on the shoulder of an embarrassed Collins. "I'll stand in for you with the flat tire. This won't exactly be hardship duty, as good-looking as she is. Besides, you won't need me here until later."

"I'm warning you," Collins smiled his relief. "She has a secret lover stashed away somewhere, and none of us on the campaign staff knows who he is."

"I can handle that." Eric quickly strode out the door and down the stairs. She was waiting just outside the front door. "Hello," he said to her quickly in a loud voice. "I'm Eric Brent." Eric extended his hand. "I understand you're having some trouble. Mr. Collins can't leave just now. Can I help? Flat tire, is it?" He looked at her and grinned politely as if he were another person inside Eric's body.

Fearing that any verbal response would sound too familiar, Jill merely nodded, but her eyes were filled with questions.

"Well, let's take a look at it," Eric said.

The two walked to her red Mustang in the driveway, talking all the way about the inconvenience of flat tires on roads late at night. Before they were out of earshot of the guard at the door, he motioned to one of them that he had the tire situation under control.

"What the hell is going on in there?" Jill exclaimed in a low voice. "You and Collins and all those men? With all those armed guards? That's no fundraiser. I'm representing Moorehead and Collins to the public and the media. I'm in the middle of all this, Eric, and I want to know what's going on?"

"First things first," he said quietly, putting his fingers across her lips. "What's the matter with the tire?"

"I let the air out."

"Damn it, Jill." He looked back at the mansion. "Quick," he said, "open the trunk and I'll get the spare. Don't talk if anyone comes over to help."

One of the guards walked around the yard, but it was obvious he was more interested in security than in changing a tire. He helped Eric jack up the Mustang. Another, who came behind him, aided in lifting the spare tire and placing it on the lugs. Eric thanked them and the two reluctantly walked back to the mansion, turning around every few feet, scrutinizing them.

Jill leaned against the car watching his every move, her arms folded across her chest. When the last lug nut was on tight and he had returned the jack into the trunk, she refused to leave without an explanation. Placing his hand against her midriff, he quickly and firmly backed her against the car saying grimly, "You don't know what you've stepped into. Do what I say. *Understand?*"

"Yes," she answered in a worried whisper. She had never seen him so tightly wound.

"Drive straight to your apartment in Georgetown as fast as you can and *stay there.* I'll talk with you later."

He loosened his grip and she took in a long, deep breath. His eyes held only anger and alarm and she knew that she had blundered into something dangerous for him and perhaps for herself, too. "You'll come there?"

"Just *do* it." He practically shoved her into the car, then slipped back and raised his voice. "Well, Miss Warren, I hope the tire will hold long enough for you to drive home. You should have a garage check it out later. It was nice meeting you." He extended his hand.

"Thank you for your help," she responded with a forced smile. "You're such a *gentleman*."

CHAPTER 37

[Keyword: Valleybriefs, Fresno, California (UPI)—. . . Some of the equipment was actually mislocated and has since been found, authorities said. But three jeeps and four trailers reported stolen from the Chance Avenue armory and some communications, camping and camouflage equipment reported missing from another NG facility near the Fresno Air Terminal are still missing . . . .— **United Press International]** [37]*

August 15th Early Evening

She passed every truck on the road and made it to her apartment thirty minutes earlier than usual from Richmond. Throwing the day's mail on her bedside table she undressed quickly and put on her pale blue, silk robe. Carrying a cup of chamomile and ginger tea and Collins' notes under her arm, she propped herself up in bed.

No sooner than she relaxed, the doorbell rang suddenly and she lunged forward then decided to lean back against the pillows. It was too early for Eric if he were coming at all. She decided no campaign zealot was going to keep her up but there were more bell rings. Then the knocker clanged loudly enough to wake everyone on the quaint street. Maybe it's news about Eric, she thought happily, and hurried to the door. Squinting through the peephole, she called out, "Who is it?"

"Miss Warren," a strange man spoke to her in a low voice. "Open the door, please."

"What do you want? It's late."

"Miss Warren, Eric sent us. It's about the meeting you crashed tonight."

Jill cracked the door with the chain still fastened. Dressed in neat, conservative gray suits two men stood waiting to be admitted. "What *about* the meeting tonight?"

"We know it's late," one of the men said in a soft Southern accent, "but may we come in, please."

"How do I know who you are?"

The young man with a slight Southern drawl, blond hair, and tanned face held a Langley identification card through the narrow opening. She examined briefly the blue and gold embossed card with the agency eagle and shield and then handed it back to him. "This still doesn't tell me who you are."

Both men laughed quietly "Miss Warren," the other dark-haired man said very low, "Miss Warren, we're special police officers from Internal Security at Langley." This second man sounded more West Coast and so smooth. His voice, calm. "Miss Warren, we *do* need to speak with you. I think you know what I mean."

Reluctantly, she unlatched the door. "Come in, but please be brief. My head is really pounding." Little beads of perspiration had formed underneath her eyes, and she felt feverish. "Please sit down," she pointed to the sofa. "What's this about?"

The two men scanned the front steps, checking to make sure no one followed them, before closing the door and following Jill to the living room. "This evening," the blond-haired man said, "you stumbled into a very unusual meeting. Eric was there."

"Yes, I know. But I didn't upset anything. He did tell you that?"

"Miss Warren, our contact with Eric is limited at the moment. However, your adventure tonight makes you a serious security risk. Not that you can't be trusted, but having knowledge of that meeting may be very dangerous both to you and Eric," the man's calm voice responded.

She refused to believe that the men were concerned for her personal safety. Their demeanor was one of *I've got a secret* and what they were going to do about the secret seemed all part of the game. Of course, Eric knew where she drew the line, but obviously someone at Langley didn't.

Tossing her head to one side and pushing back a mass of dark hair, she said firmly, "I understand your concern, but no one at that mansion in Richmond suspects that I know Eric. I have a very legitimate reason for being there especially after an article appeared in the afternoon paper derogatory to Moorehead." She paused to clear her dry throat. "Then my tire went flat. You must know I'm in a campaign along with Burt Collins, and if my employer is a target of a political slur it's my job to track it down." Jill paused again. "What *was* going on there?"

The blond special police officer's expression reminded her of a cat with a mouthful of feathers. "Miss Warren, we need to explain a few things," he drawled, "this is much more serious than you can imagine. We would like you to come with us to Langley, *now.*"

"But why?" she exclaimed. Her head began to painfully throb and every bone in her body protested at the thought of going out anywhere. "I would never do anything to hurt Eric or put him in danger. Why must I go anywhere tonight?"

The dark-haired man spoke again. "We can't discuss this here, Miss Warren, we know only one small portion of this investigation. You stumbled into a serious situation that needs attention at a higher level."

"This is unbelievable!" she gasped, her hand brushing her burning forehead and the beads of sweat forming.

The two special security officers from Langley's internal security looked at each other. "Miss Warren," the Southern accent said, "let me say this again, we can't discuss it here. Come with us now—you'll be brought back soon."

Jill could feel the veins in her lower eyelids bulging like balloons full of water. Eric told her once that he would always call first if anything ever endangered her safety. She thought about it. She spoke calmly and deliberately, her voice starting to crack. "I have to get up at five o'clock and meet candidate Moorehead at the office by seven. I've been on the road all day and I'm nauseated. I'm sorry, gentlemen, but I'm not going *anywhere* tonight. If you want to come by my campaign headquarters tomorrow and discuss this, okay."

"No, Miss Warren. You'd run the risk of someone following you or seeing you meet with us," said the dark-haired man.

She cried out angrily, "This has gone far enough. Eric knows I'm not going to tell anything that could harm him, or this country. I'm sick and I have no intention of leaving this apartment tonight." She stood up, pulled at the ties on her robe, and rubbed a hand across her throbbing forehead.

Quickly glancing at each other, the two case officers got up. The blond man spoke bluntly. "We're really surprised you won't come. You're putting your personal feelings, and pleasing your candidate, before national security."

"Eric Brent knows what my stand was and is as a journalist and as a citizen. The way I feel you couldn't pry me from my bed with a crowbar."

"We're *concerned* with your safety," the dark-haired man added solemnly again.

Jill marched across the room and opened the door. "Sorry, gentlemen."

"*We're* sorry." They spoke almost in unison. The blond man continued, "We're *truly* sorry. But you *will* come with us. You can come quietly under your own power or we'll carry you. Take your choice. One way or the other you're going with us *tonight*." He pointed to the door, his tone completely changed, and the muscles in his cheeks taut.

"No!" she cried out.

A visual signal passed between the two security officers; both quickly rushed her. Suddenly a hand covered her mouth; one grabbed her around the legs and wrestled Jill to the floor. She struggled frantically. One man tied a handkerchief around her mouth and another across her eyes then cuffed her with plastic handcuffs while the other ran to the bedroom and grabbed a blanket. "I'm sorry it has to be this way," the dark-haired man holding her said. "I wish you'd understood—saved you the ordeal of having to go like this."

Jill tried to kick him in the groin but her strength was about gone. They wrapped her in the blanket, turned out the lights and carried her down the steps. She couldn't see and her struggling was useless with the two pairs of strong hands holding onto her. She tried to cry out, but the now moist handkerchief around her mouth felt tighter every time she cried out.

She was dumped into the back seat of a car and sped away. Jill bobbed around with the car's motion whenever it spun around a corner or stopped in traffic. In her struggle to uncover her face and breathe cool air, she fell off the seat and lay across the hump in the floor. Her head still throbbed and pounded, and her wrists felt sore from her frantic pulling at the handcuffs.

"If you behave yourself, I'll help you get more comfortable," obviously the calm voiced one was not driving.

Jill moaned in agreement. He leaned over the back and his strong hands pulled at the blanket. He was suddenly gentler with her as he rearranged her to lay down more comfortably across the car's back seat. She still could not see but she could hear less and less traffic around her outside. There also seemed to be less street lights as she did not have as many overhead light flashes against the handkerchief across her eyes. She could feel the car's movements as suddenly they turned off what seemed a long public road and made a turn then another circle. She couldn't hear public traffic anymore. The car slowed a little, then sped up as it quickly passed more lights and she heard radios and men's voices move past her window. They were not stopped or inspected at any checkpoint or security gate . . . she assumed they had been waved through some protected area. It seemed hours when the car finally stopped but it had only been 25 minutes.

She couldn't distinguish that the car now rested in some parking garage underneath a large building. They opened the door, helped her to her feet, and untied the white handkerchiefs from around her face. "I hope you'll cooperate and behave like a lady," the blond special officer drawled. "But if you don't, no one can hear you *now*." He slammed the door. "We're here."

She stared around her and realized the men were leading her to an elevator open and waiting at the lower basement car park. The night wind blew the loose dark strands of hair away from her face. Two large tears rolled down her cheeks. The blanket fell to the ground. The dark-haired special officer picked it up and carried it as they walked Jill to the garage elevator in the underground complex. The men escorted her to the second floor. They exited the elevator and turned a tight corner and then entered another private elevator, this one a little smaller. They exited on another higher level floor and this time their steps echoed on the polished floors of the long empty hallways.

There seemed to be many small conference rooms that she passed by on the floor. She guessed that the room where they ushered her was the office of some high-ranking person. The office led to a small conference area furnished with elegantly styled sofas and chairs. Large gold leaf-framed oil paintings of American Indians hung on the walls. The plush pale beige carpet was soothing and despite her agitation, Jill longed to stretch out on it and sleep. The dark-haired security officer pointed to a door. "There's a bathroom in there."

She ignored him.

"Would you like coffee?" the southern drawl asked.

She shook her head and rearranged the ties on her robe, still not believing where she was.

Soon another man entered the room, older than the other two. They whispered back and forth. He greeted her politely, eyed her nightclothes, and gave her a look that was a reproach for her refusal to come.

"We're sorry about the way you were brought in. I can assure you that what we're dealing with is well worth inconveniencing you for one night. I think you'll agree when you understand." He looked at the officers then back at Jill. "Let us know if we can make you more comfortable. When Eric arrives, we'll talk."

The older man left the room and the dark-haired security officer reached in his pocket and brought out a Swiss Army knife.

"I'm going to cut this off," the dark-haired one said, "but if you can't behave, you'll be restrained again." He cut the plastic handcuffs away and gently inspected the red rings on her wrists. "Please stop wasting your energy. When Eric arrives, it'll be okay." He walked away.

She sat on the edge of the desk, pushed her hair back and watched the young man leave. She walked to the window and looked out—nothing but darkness then a few lights flickering through trees and scattering a large parking area. From every pore of her body, frustration, loss of sleep, anger, and pain suddenly began to build to a fierce explosion. "Bastards!" she yelled. Grabbing a crystal vase from a table, she entered the adjoining conference room and threw it against a windowpane, shattering the glass. Small pieces scattered and slivers sprinkled across the pale beige carpet. It felt so good to release her rage; she ran back to the office, snatched a heavy, battery-powered pencil sharpener on the desk and then ran back to the conference room. Jill blasted away at another set of windows.

The two security officers and the older man came rushing in. The blond had drawn his pistol. When he saw what happened he placed the gun back beneath his jacket in disgust. The older man made a quick exit.

"Jill, damn it, you're being ridiculous. What the hell do you think *that* accomplished?" he shouted.

It was the first time either one had used her first name.

The older man returned with another special internal security officer who grabbed her and restrained her wrists, this time with metal handcuffs. The older man shut the conference room door, sealing it off from the office area. They quickly placed a comfortable chair dead center in the room, sat her in it, and then tied her down.

"Damn it, woman!" exclaimed the older man, his anger visible. "What the hell's the matter with you? I've never heard of anyone who had to be dragged in here like this. I suppose you think we tie people up all the time? Well, I'll tell you something, young woman, this is the first time in my service here that I've had to lock handcuffs on anyone!" He turned to the dark-haired officer. "One of you stays with her until Brent comes. I'm going to see Chief Ross."

CHAPTER 38

[Keyword: Valleybriefs, Fresno, California (UPI)—. . . Police Detective Ron Hopper working with military investigators said there is a possibility the equipment could have gone to some paramilitary organization or could have been sold to clandestine marijuana plantation operators. "We are pretty sure that the stolen equipment has not made its way to a Third World country," he said.—United Press International] [38]

August 15th Late Evening

Buried in statistics, reports and photographs, John Ross didn't look up when the older man stormed into his office. He shifted his position and pulled his pipe from his mouth. "Yeah?" Ross asked. He still didn't look up but continued scribbling.

"The girl's here."

"Good. Any problems?"

The older man didn't respond.

Ross looked up. "Problems?"

"A few." Then the older man shook his head and nodded toward an upper floor at Langley. He threw handcuff keys on top of Ross' desk.

The Chief slumped back in his chair. "Let's have it."

The man explained about Jill's abduction and her rampage. Ross threw his stubby pencil on the desk, jerked his pipe from his mouth and grabbed his suit jacket. "She what? She did what?" he shouted as he raged down the hall. "Damn it! Brent, that asshole! What does he see in these half-baked broads? Damned women! Whose window did she break?" he asked as he stomped down the hall; the older man hustling close behind him.

"Maxwell's."

"Maxwell's—Charlie Maxwell? Oh, lovely . . . fucking lovely!" Ross said sarcastically.

"You think we can get it fixed before morning?"

The older man answered, "Doubt it. Don't worry about it. Maxwell's got so many holes in there from throwing telephones against the wall—no one will notice the windows."

The office door burst open and Ross blew in with the older man still trailing. The tanned security officer sat in the chair opposite Jill. When Ross stormed in front of her chair, Jill looked at his polished leather boots then up into his face, taking in his fury. Quickly her flashing eyes darted to the carpet.

"Are you happy?" he yelled. "Are you happy now? Do you know how much that window cost? Twelve hundred dollars that window cost the taxpayers."

Jill hung her head.

"What the hell's the matter with you? Do you think we'd waste our time dragging you in here if it weren't critical? He bent over, lifted up her chin, waved his finger in front of her face. "I've got news for you, lady. You're going to find out how small you really are!" He let her chin drop from his hand and began to walk full circle around her chair. "You don't want to behave yourself and comfortably wait for Eric? Fine. You can stay trussed up like a Christmas turkey until he gets here." He passed in front of the chair and leaned over into her face. "I'll tell you right now, Miss Warren, you try any more temper tantrums and you'll find your butt in a cell until this is all over."

Opening the conference room door, Chief Ross surveyed the two broken windows. "Two? Damn, Herb, you didn't tell me she broke two windows!" He looked at Jill again. "That's twenty-four hundred dollars!" He looked back at the older man. "Get maintenance here tonight." The air conditioning was rapidly seeping out of the room. He slammed the door shut, saying "Shit!" under his breath. He turned to her. "There's a law in this country about the destruction of public property. You know you could be arrested for the damage you did to this building?"

"So arrest me!" Jill exclaimed angrily. "Bring in a stenographer and I'll make a statement if you like. I'm sure the police would be interested . . . ."

"Shut up," Ross said, and spun around on his heel toward the door. As he left, he said to the two special security officers, "You two stay here until Brent comes." He glanced at the older man with disgust. "Herb, let's get out of here. The next time Brent calls in to have spider-woman here picked up—pull in a pair of bad boys from the special ops group . . . let *them* go after her. *Damn women . . . .*"

The meeting in Richmond had been unusually long. It was nearly five in the morning before they drove Eric through the back gate at Langley. He had switched cars in Fredericksburg, per Ross' orders, and slept in the back seat the rest of the way to the complex.

"All we need now," Ross had told the case officer driving him in, "is for a Right Guardsman to even smell him coming in this direction and it'll all go to hell. Pete and Patrick will be your tail."

Papers, computer sheets and folders cluttered Ross' desk when Eric entered his office. Judging by the long numbered sheets and maps spread out on the floor and the empty cups of coffee and deserted sandwich wrappers, he suspected Ross had been at it all night.

"Where is she?" Eric exclaimed. "Is she okay?"

"Let's talk about this. Sit down, Eric. She's okay, but I thought we were going to have to call out most of internal security before her grand entrance was over." Ross took a sip of coffee from a brown mug. "Pete and Patrick were in a van across the street. Pete said it looked like she stumbled into the situation—she made no contacts or stops on the way home. And she made no phone calls from her apartment."

"Ross, I think it was just a coincidence."

"How many 'coincidences' have you ever seen that are real? Anyway, if it isn't, we'll know soon."

"What are you going to do with her?" asked Eric.

"That's something I hope you have an answer for. I don't know what the hell to do with her. If Oldfield finds out, he'll have her put in a cell somewhere until this is over to protect both of you. You know that, don't you?"

"Does he have to know?"

After placing his empty mug back on his desk, Ross rubbed his hand across his forehead. "Technically, Jason is heading up this one. He may not have her put away but he isn't going to like any of this. Don't you realize that you're our one source that hasn't dried up? You're the only lifeline we have open. Eric, I don't like this any better than you do but the minute that girl saw you there you knew what had to be done."

"Ross, she can be trusted. I know her."

"Trust is nice but control is better. She's also a journalist who almost blew open one of the biggest espionage cases at that nuclear plant spill. And you think she's going to sit still for this?"

"She'll sit on it if I ask her to." Eric took off his tie and hung it around his neck. He walked to a window watching daylight coming up over the complex . . . a familiar sight. Suddenly he turned and faced Ross. "I know her. I can handle her."

"Uh-huh—good luck. I was beginning to think no window was safe in this building."

"What?"

"Never mind. You'll see soon enough." Ross pushed his chair away from the desk then rested his boots on top of the drawer. "Eric, I know how you feel about her. That's okay. But don't go hanging your ass out because you think you're in love again." Ross paused to search for his pipe. "Now, I'm willing to go upstairs with this, but I've got to know before I walk into Jason's office what to expect from her. If that girl spills her guts and Oldfield finds out we had her and let her go, he'll make sure that we're all singing soprano." He stopped and sighed deeply. He lit the pipe's bowl and as he puffed he asked, "Have you got that, Eric? Can you fathom what that means?"

Eric nodded. "I can fathom. Where is she?"

"Come on, then," Ross said reluctantly, getting up. "I'll take you to the dragon's den."

That first blinding light of early morning was breaking through the curtains when Eric first saw Jill. She was still cuffed and tied to her chair, her head tilted backward in exhaustion. Her lips slightly parted, her breaths were deep and rhythmic.

"Was this really necessary?" he snapped. He started pulling at the metal cuffs and held out his hand for the key.

"Sorry, Eric, it was this time." Ross pulled the key from his pocket and tossed it then he opened the door to the adjoining room and Eric saw the workers at the broken windows. After excusing the other case officers, he closed the door again. "That girl's got a little temper, but she's okay, just a few ruffled feathers."

Eric bent down on one knee. His fingers worked quickly at removing the cuffs. He touched alongside her temple with the back of his hand. "She's burning up!" he exclaimed.

The dark-haired internal security man appeared again and whispered something to Ross.

Ross then walked close to Eric and bent down. "Our *Project Director* is on the phone," he said to Eric, lifting his eyebrows. "Let me handle this for now. I'll be in my office if you need me." Ross made a fast exit.

Jill flexed her wrists, rubbed her eyes, and looked up at Eric. Her voice was soft and lacked expression. "Why did you have me picked up?"

"Jill, I had no idea you would turn them down; and I never dreamed that you would resist when they insisted."

"National security or not, I'm not used to being hauled off in the middle of the night. And I wasn't sure of their intentions. You always told me if anyone tried to pick me up, you'd call first to let me know."

"I couldn't call you, Jill, not this time. I think you know that. I thought my telling you to go straight home would trip something in that stubborn brain of yours." He opened the conference room door, and looked again at the fractured mess that lay on the carpet and the jagged panes in the windows. He slammed the door. "The real reason they brought you here is because you were a reporter. I was afraid your curiosity would lead you to poke your nose into all this before I could explain."

"Eric, I don't believe you. As tired as I was, I wouldn't report the end of the world if it happened last night."

His voice dropped. "Jill, I thought you'd be sitting here comfortably waiting for me."

"What's going to happen?" she asked.

"I think they're going to let you come with me."

"You mean they kidnapped me here like this," her voice grew louder and he could tell she was getting a cold from the squeak at the end of her words, "and now after all these fun and games, they're going to let me go?"

"They only brought you in here because they didn't know if you'd blown my cover."

"Eric!"

"Jill, for all they knew, you could be working against me. They were protecting me." He bent down in front of her and cupped his hands over hers. "You don't realize what you stepped into. I can't say much more than that. But it's so serious they'll put you away if you don't cooperate."

"Eric," she gasped, "you can't mean that!"

"Jill, I've never been more serious in my life. If you saw or heard anything from that meeting and it's leaked, we'll be in for a real horror story in this country."

"What kind of cooperation do they want? I'm not up to selling my soul, at least not this week."

Eric smiled at her. She had still not lost her sense of humor. "It has to do with your talents as a writer. You can be of use to them later and that may save you from being put away now."

"Oh, I get it. Slave labor, right? A little free writing project to save my hide?"

"Jill, knock off the crap," Eric said.

"I was a journalist, Eric; I don't know what these people want."

Eric watched her massage her swollen wrists and try to clear her watery eyes. Her mouth was turned down, fighting its normal smile pattern. "Now isn't the time to explain," he said softly. Let's go back to your apartment. You need sleep . . . I need sleep. We'll talk later."

"I've got to meet Moorehead in two hours," she said glancing at her watch. "It's a press conference, an important one. I feel rotten and disgusted and . . . ."

Eric gently maneuvered his arm around her waist and guided her down the hall. "We'll take care of him," he promised. "Moorehead will get a reasonable explanation about your absence from a doctor, about some illness."

"What doctor? What illness?"

"Never mind. I'll let you know what you need to know, when you need to know it." It amused him to say it. "We're going home."

Lifting her in one smooth sweep, he carried her out, feeling her nestle her head against his chest, her eyes closed. He kissed her forehead as he walked her out the back entrance to a waiting car and driver. Pete was waiting there to drive her home.

Standing at the window Ross watched Eric putting Jill into the waiting car as though there was nothing unusual about carrying a robed young woman out of the intelligence fortress at sunup.

Sam Walsh, a night intel supervisor, and the only other Agency regular there in the room cupped his hand over the phone's receiver,

"Jason wants to know what we're going to tell Oldfield about those windows?"

"I'll come up with something." Ross walked about the office, stretching his arms to the ceiling. He returned to his window, watching Eric's car disappear. "Tell him we're going to have her tailed closely. If she even breathes heavy, *I want to know about it.*"

CHAPTER 39

August 16th

It was too late to be called breakfast, but with blueberry muffins, juice and coffee, it tasted like morning. The electric pot churned again re-heating the strong coffee for the third time. Jill pulled the English muffin halves out of the oven and set them on the table.

Eric reached for a muffin and gnawed at the crusty edge. "I hope Oldfield will tell me that you can be released in my custody if you're *manageable.*"

"But I won't be in *your* custody."

"No. But only Ross and I will know that. There'll be someone around to look after you, but you've got to promise not to screw this up. My butt is on the line for this, too."

Jill shook her head in disbelief still holding the large blue pottery-made coffee mug to her mouth with both hands. The hot brew slowly washed the remnants of sleep down her throat. "What type of cell would I get if I refuse to go along?"

"It wouldn't exactly be a cell," he said. "More like an apartment somewhere, guarded twenty-four hours a day. Or it would be a community where there were others whose lives were in danger, or who for some reason would be dangerous to themselves if released."

"Sounds cozy."

"It's not that bad."

"Could you visit me?" she asked.

"No. I wouldn't be allowed anywhere near there, now or later. Eventually, you would join *me*."

"Will I hear from you from now on?"

"I'll try to be in touch but it won't be easy. You'll have a shadow until the end of the campaign."

"A shadow? Why all this? You know I won't *betray* you."

"I'm not worried about that," Eric interrupted, "A lot is at stake, and others are not willing to take that chance. Jill, some of the men at that mansion saw you. *You* may be in danger now." He noticed her looking away from him, gazing out the kitchen window in deep thought. He paused, and then asked, "Are you sorry we got together again?"

"No. I'm not sorry about that. I just wish we didn't have to live like this—running, hiding, trying to remember my last conversation so that when I lie again, I can keep the same story." She looked away again.

Eric checked his military watch and stood away from the table. He added somberly, "I thought I made the right decision. In some countries around the world there are no choices. Ordinary people have to live hiding and running to survive."

"Aren't there enough men who thrive on the ragged edge? Is this worth it for you to do it?" she asked.

"It is when that choice exists," he answered her. "Jill, I like what I do. Though you may not see it now, there is great honor and skill in guarding the gate."

"But there is also great risk. What happens when your choices get so narrow and you're in so deep that it becomes your life all the time?"

"The campaign has become your life for now. Is there honor in pushing someone on the American public that you personally have no respect for?" he asked her. "You can accept that?"

Her pleading expression back at him made him sad. *Regroup.* He wondered if this was the assignment that would keep him forever *undercover.* Would this be the stretch from which he could never emerge? He couldn't help remember what Chauncey, one of his instructors at the Farm, told him. Chauncey had trained most of them. He told them if they were good and if they stayed, it could happen like the changing of the seasons, without their consciously realizing it. "Follow the course of least resistance," Chauncey used to tell them. "For some of you it will be easier to stay put and live out your cover."

CHAPTER 40

August 17th

The case officers and others met in the conference room at Langley Complex promptly at one o'clock. Former DCI Jason sat at one end of the table next to Ross and another supervisor.

Oldfield breezed into the room toting an armload of notes and extra yellow pads.

That morning, to keep the air conditioning from escaping, two workers hung panels of canvas across the broken windows at the end of the room and taped the rough, paint-splattered covering to the sides of the walls. It did little to keep the room cool. They hoped to install the replacement glass before one o'clock but someone postponed the job. Replacement windows were coming in from a special vendor on Maryland's Eastern Shore. Luckily, the office's real occupant was off briefing the President on national security matters. It was the only room available for the meeting.

"What the hell is this?" Oldfield asked Jason, pointing to the patchwork. Squinting his eyes, he surveyed the entire window breakage, scowling.

Ross had his answer ready: "Rumor is we had a scaffolding crew up to work on the air conditioning ducts. One guy got unbalanced and fell into the windows. No one was hurt."

"And it broke *two* windows?" Oldfield asked unbelievingly.

"I get paid by the rumor. It's not a perfect system," Ross said.

"I see. Some damn clumsy people work around here." Current DCI Oldfield sat down at the head of the table.

Jason grinned to himself, carefully avoiding Chief John Ross' glance. The explanation amused him. He sat straight in his chair with both hands clasped and his elbows comfortably resting on the armrests; his round, gold-rimmed wire glasses sat perfectly straight on his nose.

Oldfield called for reports and randomly wrote down notes on sheets of yellow paper. Occasionally he asked for clarification on minor points. When the reporting finished he pushed his chair back and looked around the table. "What about Deacon?"

No one spoke. Some of the men glanced in Jason's direction hoping that he would handle the question.

Jason was blunt. "We're sure now that he's in the upper ranks," he answered.

Oldfield frowned. "How involved is he, Stuart?"

Stuart Jason removed his glasses and pinched the bridge of his nose with his forefinger and thumb, squeezing the tension away. "He's either heading it up or, at least, one of the top three men involved."

"Personal opinion or is there proof?" Oldfield shot back.

"One of our men stationed in the southeast section of the investigation brought in firsthand knowledge, but I know Deacon. The whole operation is his signature.

I know of no other man who would have attempted such an undertaking—right under our noses."

No one was sure whether Jason's statement was an objective remark or a compliment.

"What's your next move?" Oldfield asked pointedly.

"We need to find out where some of their arms are stored. We already know which ones of ours are being drained, then re-supplied gradually. This is not difficult to track down. There are others we've only heard about, private warehouses full of stolen arms and they're not nearly so easy to find. The next step is to look at the East Coast section."

Oldfield called the meeting to an end with a blunt, "Thank you gentlemen. Carry on." His manner was more that of a royal commanding the servants to continue their cleanup jobs.

When everyone else had gone, Jason cornered Ross. "Did Brent say anything to you about Deacon's health?"

"No, sir." Ross looked puzzled. "I'm not sure what you mean?"

"Did he look well or worn down? That type of thing."

"No, he reported nothing like that. I could pass it on, though."

"It's probably not that important for the investigation. I just remembered his having a heart condition. Obviously he's worked through it."

Ross looked into Jason's worried face. "They still tell stories about him, you know?"

"I'm sure they do," Jason responded.

"Why is he doing this?" Ross questioned.

"Deacon completely believes that he's some great visionary. He thinks he's going to keep something he believes in from being destroyed."

"And?" Ross questioned.

"And . . . there is a dark side to the man. One I hope Eric won't put together until it's over."

Ross frowned. "It's the first time I've had trouble telling the good guys from the bad."

"It may not be long before we'll have to choose which side we're on. It's a tough 'row we're hoeing.'" Jason sighed and shook his head as they exchanged tired looks.

Jason spent the rest of the day with some of the "old heads" from within the inner intelligence circles. He was sifting between the cracks trying to find the rest of the picture from those who knew first hand but would never give it up to Oldfield.

Chauncey, the pre-eminent old-timer from the farm, a heavily muscular-framed, gray-haired man told Stuart Jason more of what he wanted. "Stu, there are some in the field who are not reporting all they're finding out. Apparently the plan looks too tempting to some of 'em to resist."

Jason waited patiently for the rest. He studied the round face before him. The man's jowls hung in a slight bulge but his body was still athletic and he often proved that he could still outmaneuver some of the younger men in training.

"I don't have any numbers," Chauncey spoke calmly, looking at Jason from underneath puffy eyelids, "but one is too many. Those Guard boys have a good line to lay on 'em. In four different areas some are not reporting information that I know damn well they have, 'cause the backup reported it. If this movement succeeds, there'll be big power shifts at the complex. There are a few cocky bastards who are counting on it and one has even shot his mouth off hinting about it. I happened to be within earshot and heard it all."

Jason leaned back in his chair and laid two fingers alongside his temple. "How much does Oldfield know?"

"He knows some of the figures aren't adding up and he obviously knows what the Reserves are up to. What he doesn't know is that two of his own top aides would love nothing better than to toss his ass out the window and take over when the Right Guard moves in. Stu, I wouldn't mind that so much but those little bastards are just like him. When are they going to stop jamming these political types down our throats?"

Jason looked intently at the man. "Does Right Guard look good to you too, Chauncey?"

"I don't need to explain myself to you," Chauncey snapped back. "You know what Deacon was and I certainly wouldn't follow him. My concern is whether they pull it off or not, we're going to see some serious blood in the streets. I sure as hell didn't expect it to look so good to some of *our* men that they'd withhold information from *you*. They're beginning to tie my hands, Stu. How can any of us give you an accurate analysis when some are trying to cover for the Guardsmen?"

Stuart Jason answered, "I know what you're up against. I don't think they're going to move just yet. Within a month we'll have a better picture and then we'll make our move."

"Stu, I know about your proposal. It would help us here if you could pull it off."

"Pull what off?" Jason asked.

"If we can put their operation down early and it never makes it to the press, then we won't have to arrest those Guardsmen. Right?" Chauncey's eyebrows lifted.

"Where did that come from?" Jason responded.

"Stu, even you can't keep down what I want to know." Chauncey maneuvered a subtle smile. "One suggestion, break in if you have to, or wiretap. Use it flagrantly so the evidence will be thrown out of court. Stu, you wouldn't be able to haul in everyone anyway. And, hell, maybe if our people knew those men wouldn't be punished and taken from their families, they'd stop playing games with the information."

"I'll think about it, Chauncey. But I'm not the only lead here."

"You know you can't tell Oldfield. He's looking for a blue ribbon for his first year in. He doesn't like Mike Halstead any more than the rest of us but I do think he'd turn those Guardsmen's names over to that FBI son-of-a-bitch to make the arrests."

Chauncey's words haunted him. Jason needed hard facts and they were not coming in. Twenty-four hours after meeting Chauncey he finally consented to the wiretapping sending an official message down the line to the case officers—"no arrests." However, Jason emphasized he was heading up the project and that any case officer caught tampering with the information would be answerable to *him* and no one else in the Agency.

That was all that needed to be said. Four days later the information began trickling in.

CHAPTER 41

August 25th

"It scares many of them that he's *so new*. Take him in slowly and watch him closely." Deacon told Rake who was in Virginia on a secure phone. "The process is about to begin any day."

Though optimistic in the meetings, in private the word from everyone was "caution."

"I think he'll be valuable to us," Deacon added, "but just because some of them are mesmerized with his H-PAR, let's not go overboard until we know him better." Rake covered every angle with Eric in Phase One of his orientation—their philosophy, how the Right Guard was built and their goals. Phase Two, plans and strategy, would now include how they would use the military without their knowing it and how to keep the "unknowing" in line. Deacon and General Randolph even allowed Rake to take Eric to a fort outside Richmond. However, whether it was by neglect or design, no one told Major William Adkins about Eric Brent's invitation to *his* fort.

Eric and Rake met just outside the gate of the military reservation's new barracks, forty miles from Richmond. One of the detainment centers, it was another former small base turned Right Guard installation.

"Where have you been lately?" Rake asked, with a disarming smile when they left their cars.

"H-PAR takes most of my time," Eric responded. "You know, checking it out with lawyers, patent research, writing letters."

"Come on, I've got something to show you." Rake said, "One aspect of the plan is here."

"Here? This is an Army base," Eric responded.

"It's a base used in the summer for training. I got permission this morning to show you around. You won't be anywhere near here when the plan goes into action, but you'll visit later. This is all General Randolph's stomping grounds."

"I thought he was in charge of the arsenal?" Eric was puzzled.

"He is, but everyone will be carrying out extra assignments. Some of the top men will do relatively menial tasks when we make our first move because their real stations won't be operative until later. They'll help those who need immediate support then they'll go to their permanent stations."

Eric walked with him through the grounds until the old white clapboard and green roofed barracks came into view.

"That's one station, there," Rake stopped to point to the fifteen barracks some of the guardsmen recently renovated.

"Station? You mean right here on a military base?"

Rake laughed. "It's the easiest to hide . . . right out in the open."

Eric asked, frowning, "How are you going to keep the men stationed here from knowing what's happening?"

Rake ignored his question preferring to concentrate on the recent progress they made on the buildings. "Those barracks will be detainment centers for rioters. The detainees will stay there until they learn a trade, or show that they can support themselves. Then they'll be released."

"Suppose they can't learn?"

"Medical and psychiatric teams will evaluate them and they'll be registered in therapy, medical or occupational help programs."

"I thought that's what the Right Guard was against?"

"Against?" Rake looked back at him.

"You know . . . government-sponsored programs."

"It's not *all* the programs, Eric; it's the way they are carried out." Glancing down at the columns of figures covering the pages in his hands, he looked up at Eric and winked. "We convinced a certain politician we needed to provide space for the Reserve soldiers at annual training. I don't know exactly what the other centers across the country did to get theirs okayed, but it worked for us."

"And the politicians believe it?"

"Eric, you know as well as I do, most politicians don't look much farther than their aides or secretaries for a way to get re-elected. This politician needed some publicity for his constituency and he rustled the funds around until he got what he wanted. Then he passed it over to our base." Rake waved his hand in the air toward the buildings. "Convincing the commander he needed this from an inside Right Guardsman, was a piece of cake."

"What will they do when they find out how you're going to use those barracks? I thought you didn't want to be anywhere near a military base." Eric was digging.

"Eric, go back to your Air Force days. Remember when an order was given? Did the ranks stand there and question why they were doing it? Hell, no! They fell in line and carried out orders or someone kicked them in the ass. It's no different here. Half of these guys won't know the real military is on the sidelines watching this plan happen until it's all over; then they'll have to fall in line with those really in command."

"Sounds like Nazis." Eric remembered stories from his father and threw it out to see what Rake would say.

"Eric, if this country continues on its socialist path, you'll have a real Nazi-type solution on your hands before you know it. When the economic picture gets bad they'll start looking for a scapegoat just like they did with the Jews." Rake paused and looked about him to make sure no one was within earshot. "No one is going to get hurt here. Their ticket out of this situation is to learn a trade or convince those in charge that they can support themselves. Even if some can find jobs, but still want to learn another trade, or improve themselves by training, they can live here until they finish it. They'll be allowed to do that."

"You know, Rake . . . some are bound to get hurt."

Rake looked at Eric out of the corner of his eye. "The only people who can possibly get hurt are those who take to the streets to steal and loot for the things that'll no longer be handed to them on a silver platter. They're the parasites who would steal from your home and kill your . . ." Rake's voice trailed away.

Eric stared at Rake in a strange way. "You have any moral problems with it?"

Rake knew the rest of the world would ask the same thing soon. He answered carefully. "Is it moral to let welfare state and bureaucratic extortionists exist and rob people who *work* for their paycheck and we have no real say about where it goes? Is it moral knowing that when there are more of them than us they'll descend on us like locusts to take even more than they're given now and still not produce a damn thing? Is it moral to take away self-esteem, pride, and cripple the minds of some people by teaching them that the government grows a money tree just for them? How about 'money doesn't need to be backed by a product or a service to make it valuable?' Is that moral, Eric?"

Eric didn't answer. They walked together in silence around the barracks. Eric studied the faces of the military engineers directing the workmen near the building and listened to their joking. He thought some of them were typical of other men in uniform throughout the world. Would they carry out orders without question and without being held personally responsible for their acts?

"Are you Benson?" a soldier called out to Rake from a nearby construction trailer. Rake yelled back then he hurried inside to a phone. He held the receiver tightly in his hand and responded quietly to the person on the other end. Eric joined him and when he was within hearing distance, Rake turned his back. When he finished, he said excitedly to Eric, "Let's go, Eric, we've got something to do."

"What's up?"

Rake waited until they were outside the gate before answering. "We've got to get back to Richmond and help Randolph."

"What about here?"

"This can wait until later. Like I said, you won't be near here when the plan is activated. What you'll be doing—well, you'll get a taste of it tonight."

"Randolph? I'll be with General Cyrus Randolph?"

"You'll see. Let's both take cars. You remember how to get to the arsenal, don't you?" Eric nodded his head. "Good. I'll see you there about seven. Wait for me in the driveway. Randolph gets a little nervous when someone new comes around without a familiar face alongside."

CHAPTER 42

August 28th

Rake pulled his car alongside Eric's sports car in the arsenal driveway at quarter to seven. On their way to Randolph's door he stopped Eric, his smile vanished. "Until now, all you've had is theory. What you see tonight is a point of no return for you."

This is it, thought Eric and the muscle alongside his jaw jumped.

"Remember Deacon's words about withdrawing in silence if you change your mind? If you want out after tonight and you talk—they won't let you live long enough to plead."

It was a familiar tune. This was the Rake he kept seeing flashes of: the man whose serious side and whose appealing humor, meshed like wild flowers around barbed wire. Eric could not define him. Was he a man of principles or did he rise on occasion to meet only those principles he wanted most to uphold? Whichever it was, Eric still liked him and he felt deeply troubled by that.

They were ushered to the top level of the old arsenal where Randolph was waiting for them. The summertime darkness would not descend until almost eight thirty. Streaks of red and gold still lingered in the western sky.

Rake's words came dry and authoritative. "We got Deacon's call," he said to General Randolph.

Randolph nodded. He seemed to be giving his best effort at being polite to Eric, but Eric felt the man definitely didn't approve of his being there.

Randolph led them to an elevator hidden behind a partition. Considering the age of the arsenal and its added new construction it amazed Eric that the elevator was so quiet as it carried them to the bottom level. The heavy doors opened and closed to the sound of solid steel strength muffled by the walls. The room they entered was dark but he could smell the damp walls and feel the cool stale air. He looked for alternate routes out of any area he entered, a habit taken from Chauncey's training, long ago. He spotted a pathway door leading through a long tunnel to the outside.

Randolph switched on the lights then began pointing out new boxes of equipment. Reaching for the clipboard on the wall, he carefully jotted down in pencil the figures on the boxes.

Eric followed the two men. They read the stencils on the sides of the large crates. He tried to etch in his memory the locales of origin. Most were from depots in Massachusetts, New York, Utah, New Mexico, and California. His heart beat furiously as he read the labels on each box. Most contained hand weapons—pistols, blackjacks, tear-gas guns, and others, "ammunition." Still others, containing replacement parts were stacked nearby.

"These recent boxes were unexpected," he heard the General tell Rake, "but when they said they had it, hell yes, I took it."

"How much lead time did you have?" Rake asked.

"I didn't know until today," Randolph answered. "That's why Deacon called you at the fort. It needs to be inventoried tonight because those boys out in Idaho want it by the end of the week. Their depot doesn't have any of this. We'll swap it out for window grills and wire mesh for the new barracks."

Randolph opened a desk drawer and took out a thick black ledger book. "Start with this," he growled. "I'll be back in a minute with the other one." The elevator whisked the General back upstairs.

Before getting down to work, Rake gave Eric a quick tour of the adjoining rooms. All were crammed with boxes and racks of arms and supplies, mostly small weapons and riot control supplies for soldiers to contain civil disorder. The tour was too brief for Eric to count boxes and to make intelligent guesses about numbers. Eric had time only to count the number of rooms and remember vaguely what kinds of items each of the eleven rooms held. The huge man-made hill where the old Civil War arsenal rested contained in its belly enough equipment to start a small war or prevent one, which-ever its owners proposed.

"This is just one of many distribution centers across the coun-try," Rake said. "This one will take care of Virginia, parts of West Virginia, and the Carolinas."

Eric swallowed his amazement and looked appropriately impressed. "How did you get all this stuff without the military missing it?"

"Sometimes we don't," Rake chuckled. "That's when I'm called out of the sack at two in the morning to help get it back to the original depot."

"And no one catches on?" Eric shook his head.

"I suppose those who got too close got the choice of disappear-ing or keeping their mouths shut. As Deacon says, everyone has a vulnerable spot. You just have to find it."

Eric pitched in and the two began checking off a list and stacking boxes. The Right Guard ability to organize and move this equipment with little or no notice stunned Eric. Deacon was the master planner Eric thought. It could only be Deacon's strategic and systematic touch that inspired Stuart Jason's recall.

Jason was the one man in the CIA who could match Deacon's ingenuity and Jason knew Deacon like a brother.

CHAPTER 43

September 1st

Secretary of Defense Kurt Hoffman cradled the red receiver back onto the phone then gathered the boxes of computer sheets and intelligence reports and headed for the Oval Office.

President Price Harkins Foster, Jr. had never been described as a handsome man, but his arched eyebrows, dark brown hair splashed with gray and chiseled chin, made him a striking figure. His speech and movements were precise and well rehearsed giving him an air of control and power. To the American public he looked exactly like a chief executive should and that's how they voted.

In fact, "Junior," as he had been called from childhood, possessed neither a powerful intellect nor strong moral courage. He was, however, the perfect politician—always acting with an eye to the mirror of public opinion. If it were not for the daily ministrations of his beautiful and highly intelligent wife, Marie, he would never have risen beyond a state legislator. He was not one who inspired great allegiance or confidence, particularly with those who worked closely with him but oddly enough, he was not a bad President. He knew how to appreciate talent and kept them close to his side.

After an abrupt arrival at the Oval office, Secretary Hoffman heaved his aching frame into a comfortable chair. The President then bombarded him with questions about the military and missing weapons. The stolid, rotund little man in front of him endured, unruffled. His thoughts turned abruptly away from his sore back and his lengthy scrutiny of reports to the President's jerky hand movements and the perspiration on his upper lip.

Secretary Hoffman opened a box he set on the floor and lifted out what seemed miles of attached computer sheets. He read aloud a few paragraphs from intelligence reports then offered the rest to the President. When President Foster rummaged through the number-lined, top secret-stamped papers, Hoffman settled down, his stubby fingers exploring a jacket pocket, his eyes fixed on the President. *Our leader*, he thought methodically, pulling off his glasses and cleaning the thick lenses with a handkerchief. He regarded him as a captain lost at sea and all the resources in the country blindly following.

"So," the President addressed him, "we're certain about the group?"

"Yes sir. The arms are definitely arriving and departing again after they've been counted."

"Is this contained within the Guard and the Reserves only?"

After pausing, Secretary Hoffman spoke carefully. "We're not sure. The possibility of much wider involvement is there but we have no proof."

Resting his chin on his hand, the President sighed deeply. "What are they planning? They should know damn well that anything they could muster in arms we could take care of from within the regular military. Is it a splinter group, or what?"

"Mr. President, it's our understanding that, at a minimum, they are well incorporated in the Reserves and the National Guard and the involvement may go quite high in rank."

The President shot off more questions in rapid succession. Hoffman tackled each one first with a thoughtful pause, then gave answers that were too controlled and factual.

"I think it's time everyone meets about this, Kurt." The President surveyed the papers again. "Tell CIA and their people I want a meeting. Get in touch with the FBI Director, too." The President rang for one of his long-time trusted assistants, Margie, a white-haired woman who joined him 18 years ago. He instructed her to set up a time and a date for the proposed meeting.

While Margie made notes in two date books, listing the names of all those to notify, Secretary Hoffman's mind worked furiously.

The President had recently signed a recommendation that would allow yet another invasive use of the Social Security number to come into being and gain another step closer to a national identification number and less privacy. That act bothered Secretary Hoffman.

As a young boy in Germany, Hoffman experienced the results of economic collapse and the search for a scapegoat. He knew the insanity that dealt a horrifying hand to the Jews and other minorities when their rights as free citizens were taken from them in the name of government. He had experienced citizens' disarmament in Germany and the inability of the people to defend themselves against internal oppression. Like those in his family who still wore the concentration camp numbers, those memories and experiences bore char marks into his soul.

The current state of the government reminded him of another all-too-powerful government, out of touch and out of control. If they were not stopped, his adopted country would go down the road to another people's revolution, strangling the words "freedom" and "republic" until they would lose any semblance to their definition.

Obviously, the President did not have the entire story and would not have it until the intelligence community decided which way they would move on their information. As Secretary of Defense, he didn't know what the intelligence services were doing but, as Kurt Hoffman, he understood well what was happening, not only in the secret circles, but even in the President's own cabinet and on the White House staff. He predicted the smoke long before there was any sign of fire but he preferred to remain his own man.

After the woman left, the President stood up and walked around his office. He was more than just concerned. "What are your thoughts on this? Are others in the Pentagon concerned over it?"

"There is a lot of concern, Mr. President, among other agencies, and Guard Bureau carried out an investigation of its own."

"Has the Guard been corrupted from within? You know I've had a bill introduced into Congress about safeguards on military equipment. If it passes, that would help the matter. They should know we're on to them, and whatever they're planning will be stopped."

Although Secretary Hoffman knew that the President still thought only a handful in the Guard had been involved, he refrained from passing on his personal interpretations. He preferred not to surrender his secret thoughts without bargaining for something in return. In his early years as a junior officer in the State Department, he learned never to show all his cards. He trusted the bureaucracy about as much as he trusted a card shark's stacked deck.

CHAPTER 44

September 5th

The appointment was arranged at Langley only after the current DCI Oldfield refused three invitations to FBI Director Mike Halstead's office claiming it was not possible for him to come at the times given. Halstead stormed into Oldfield's office for the third time in two days and was held up at the secretary's desk. "Where is he?"

The secretary looked up with a noncommittal expression. "I'm sorry, Director Halstead. He's in a meeting."

He gave her a look designed to remind her of his rank. "Didn't Director Oldfield know our meeting was scheduled for *this morning*?"

"It's on my calendar, sir. I'm sure the DCI must know."

With one hand stroking the back of his neck, the FBI Director stood for a moment staring away in silence, nursing his fury toward the CIA chief. Suddenly, he pushed by the secretary and threw open Oldfield's door. Oldfield seated at his desk, Halstead demanded an explanation.

Oldfield looked up. Before greeting the angry man, he calmly finished the sentence he was writing on a legal pad and added another. He said coolly, "Sit down, Mike, I'll be with you in a minute."

Halstead exclaimed angrily, "We've been working on those stolen arms cases for months! Just when we get set to prosecute, I find out that your renegades have been using wiretapping without court orders. The whole damn effort won't hold water once the judge gets wind of it!"

Oldfield stifled a smirk. "It never seemed to bother you over there before. If I had a dollar for every time you and your people stepped over others to get what you wanted, I'd be a rich man."

"Sometimes the circumstances call for it," Halstead retorted, his pitch raised. "We don't do it as a matter of course."

"True, Mike, but *we* don't push innocent people to the edge," Oldfield leaned forward, "and we don't harass for the sake of making a case."

Halstead felt the muscles in his face quiver. "You can't, you son-of-a-bitch! You don't have powers of arrest!"

Oldfield sat back and rolled his eyes, "Thank God for small favors. All we're interested in is just *knowing*."

Halstead began pacing back and forth.

"Sit down, Mike." Oldfield nodded to a large dark blue stuffed chair.

"This is no social call Oldfield." Clearing his throat, FBI Director Halstead stalked to the window and looked out over the complex's lawns to compose himself. "We know about one of your men who is *under* in Richmond. You people are up to your ears in the Right Guard investigation. We also know that you've been withholding information we need. Apparently you know who's been stealing the weapons, how much the military is involved, and other crimes that are outside your purview."

Oldfield remained composed in his chair with his arms calmly folded, but his eyes betrayed the intensity of a predator eyeing his prey, waiting. He smoldered listening to the FBI chief rave wildly about obstruction of justice. "Is that it, Mike?" he finally said.

"One last thing, Oldfield. I've set up an appointment with the Department of Justice and the Attorney General. I'm going to put a stop to these games you and your agency are playing."

Oldfield remained unimpressed. "Your being here tells me that you don't have much of a leg to stand on. If you did, you wouldn't be coming to me, you'd already be at the Attorney General's office." He stood up abruptly, adding, "Don't be such an ass! If we *had* the information you are claiming—*which we don't*—I'd be the last man here to lay it in your hands. You'd go out and arrest the first likely person you could find, just so you can play for the media."

Halstead's mouth opened with a strangled gasp at Oldfield's charge. He was stunned as he watched the CIA chief angrily toss an address book on the other side of his working area.

Oldfield pointed to the door. "Don't come around here pissing and moaning. You've got your job to do and we have ours!" Halstead stormed out of the office with nothing on his mind but vengeance.

CHAPTER 45

September 9th

"How are you, Eric, my friend?" Wolfgang Shumacher's voice was unmistakable. His English had not improved since the last time Eric remembered seeing him. He was a part of the homeland, that secret piece of Eric he never expressed to anyone. It was a rare person he allowed close to him. He was extended family.

Wolfgang Shumacher met Eric on his way to the National Aeronautics & Space Administration in Hampton, Virginia, from a high-level NASA conference in Washington. It involved a special seminar put on by the propulsion lab, he said, and they would be making use of the wind tunnels at NASA. He wanted to see Eric at the home of a mutual German friend of his late father. The host family was away on a trip and except for the help—they would be alone at the friend's horse farm.

The two men met outside the large estate house and strolled to where young thoroughbreds were being led out to pasture.

"You look well. Your stomach, they piece it back together?" Shumacher asked, slapping Eric on his back.

"I do okay," Eric answered. "I have a flare up once in a while when I don't eat right."

"Yes, I see. We old ones have that problem too," and when he laughed, creases formed from his cheeks to his sparkling eyes. What little hair that was left on his head was the color of steel and his blue eyes danced when he talked. He carried an air of a former high-ranking military officer and was still a striking figure of a man.

"And your shoulder?" Shumacher asked in his heavy accent.

"Practically healed," Eric answered.

"You hear from Anna?" Shumacher asked.

"We talk every few months on the phone. She seems very happy being married and a mother."

"Yes. Since the little ones, your sister writes me so seldom. You know, Eric, I feel she is mine sometimes. And Hans?"

"He's not so good about writing or calling, either. He travels a lot. After his second marriage, I hear from him about twice a year."

"Computers, is it not?" Shumacher asked.

"Yes. He's very good. We use some of the systems he's de-signed. Gifted, they say," Eric added.

Shumacher approached a wooden rail and he turned to watch the young horses graze. "Elegant, are they not?" he stated. "Your father was an exceptional dressage rider. You know, Eric, there was not much he was *not* good at doing . . . especially knowing how to sidestep political winds blowing him where he did not wish to go. You *know* what I am saying now?" Shumacher's eyes suddenly hooded with concern.

Eric nodded, still concentrating on the thoroughbreds.

"There are some of us who are interested in your weapon. Your idea for the firing mechanism, the liquid propellant idea—you're arousing a lot of interest at NASA. True, it's an old concept but leave it to a German to come up with a new technological twist. I think you might have it." Shumacher reached out his sturdy hand on Eric's good shoulder and squeezed it. "My God, Eric . . . you could *really* have it!"

"Wolfgang, Can you *help me*?" Eric asked. His manner sud-denly changed, his voice lowering.

Schumacher's excited tone suddenly vanished. "I think there is some financial help we can offer but we must wait." Shumacher turned and looked into his eyes then his timbre changed to a deathly quiet. He hesitated like an old experienced warrior counseling the young combatant. He lowered his voice too and waited for the right moment. "Are you in *this nonsense,* too?" he almost whispered.

"How much do you know?" Eric asked.

"Enough to know the agency is using you. They'll cut you to pieces and throw you to wolves if it pleases them."

"The investigation? You've heard?"

"You always hear something. We are everywhere, Eric. Those of us who survived the bowels of Satan, we know when the wind begins to blow foul. But, I say nothing." Shumacher paused and the more intense his voice became the more his German accent emerged. "Eric, this is not *your* fight, yet you risk all that you have worked on. This is worth it, yes?"

"I have reasons. They are worth it."

"I see." Shumacher paused a few seconds. He watched a young chestnut-colored thoroughbred led on a lunge line around the training ring. "Eric, you must know something now. I promised your father many things before he died. As your mother grieved and wasted away, I promised her too, to help all of you. I am an old man. There is not much for me now except to give advice and warn the young when hell is near."

"What do you *know*?" Eric asked.

"Eric, there is more involved than what you are doing there."

"I don't understand," Eric questioned.

"You *must* be careful. There is a man involved in this military *thing* that your father knew—an American. He tried to destroy Frederick after the war. This man, he will not stop at the grave if he knows who you are."

"Who is he?" Eric asked.

Shumacher hesitated then pronounced slowly, "When I knew him it was Deek Connors Malway. You know this man?"

Eric shook his head, no.

Shumacher's eyes drifted into an unfocused stare. "In Germany after the war, it was winter and your family was sent to our camp . . . settled in near our pathetic little hut. One night I heard your mother's screams . . . ."

"Please, Wolfgang," Eric stopped him before he could finish. "I remember, but why are you telling me this?"

"Captain Deek Connors Malway—Eric, they called him 'Deacon' in the detention camp. It was said he arranged your mother's rape and stood in the shadows. Watched while your mother struggled. We knew he had something to do with it though we could never prove it."

Eric's lower jaw opened and he swallowed hard. He was motionless except for his erratic breathing. His nostrils flared like the young unbroken thoroughbreds in the ring before him.

"When your father was in the camp they knew he had a wealth of knowledge about electronics, radar and Russian intelligence and technology. Your father, Eric, was a linguistics master in the technical and scientific languages and one of the first men the Americans wanted in the brain drain after the war. This man, Deacon Malway, was trying to force him into delivering his information into the hands of private industry. The American industrialists wanted to keep this information from their government and get rich off it. Frederick didn't want to do it. He feared if he helped Malway and the government found out, the Americans would turn him over to the Russians. Our own people, 'the German benefactors,' we negotiated and made a deal with the Pentagon and your father was granted an early opportunity to come to the U.S."

Shumacher remarked solemnly, "*We* have plans for this Deacon, now. His reign is over."

"I want him!" Eric demanded.

"**No!**" Shumacher answered sternly. "Let the *others* do it. This Deacon hurt more than just *your* family. You stay clear of this. You hear what I say now?"

With a defiant stare, Eric turned to Schumacher's familiar, hardened face: a face sculpted like his own. "No," Eric whispered. Then he added, "*He's mine.*"

CHAPTER 46

September 11th

Burt Collins, Moorehead's campaign manager, held a small box under his arm as though it were a secret prize. He arrived in Arkansas after a two-hour flight delay and on entering Major Adkins' office on the base, he turned it over to him.

"How long can you stay?" Adkins asked, carefully pulling open the sides. Every pleat of his uniform was in pressed and tucked and he looked much the commanding officer of the headquarters unit.

"Only until tonight. The campaign staff thinks I'm in Northern Virginia. I flew out under another name."

"Is this it?" asked Adkins.

"No. I have some others to deliver. One to Maryland, one to North Carolina, and one to be shipped out to California."

"Do they work well?" Adkins lifted the phone from its box, looked at the intricate dials and switch on its underside.

"Damn right. It's the best. Guaranteed to help us with communication during the operation. No calls can be monitored with that scrambler." Collins pointed to the bottom device. "All the phone company will know is that their lines are registering an extra load."

"What about the others?"

"Most of the other sets are already installed. Deacon had his put in first along with those on the West Coast. Except for Colorado

235

and their crew and the three I'm delivering, the rest are in. Sometime during the weekend one of our people from Richmond will help install yours."

Adkins reached in his pocket, retrieved a white envelope, and handed Collins his personal money for the scrambler. "I think that'll cover all the communications equipment, including the gadget and the radio. You wouldn't believe the money I've put out lately!"

"Tell me about it," Collins said, as he finished counting the bills. "What we've put in isn't half as much as in some states. In Virginia and up and down the East Coast, the higher-ups are drained financially. Some have gone in together to buy homes and estates abroad if something goes wrong."

Adkins turned the phone over to inspect the switch on the bottom. "What about you?"

"My father left me a small hunting lodge in the northern part of Canada. It's leased out now. If things get bad enough, I suppose I'll go there."

Adkins laid the phone in the box. "We're all paranoid, but it doesn't hurt to have an ace in the hole if things don't work out right."

Collins nodded. He thought of all the men who had emptied their personal investments, some at a great financial loss. They were willing to pay any price to save their country. Some gave private lands to the Right Guard to build special facilities. Laborers, hand selected to work in confidence for "the government," were patching up old buildings and constructing new ones all over the country.

Adkins picked up a large brown envelope and handed it to the campaign manager. "This was brought in here, sealed, early this morning. Deacon knew you were coming."

"There seems to be little Deacon doesn't know," Collins said. The sealed envelope displayed the courier's initials. Collins took the envelope. His and Adkins' names were printed on the outside. Adkins initialed his name as witness for Collins. The courier would return it to Deacon's office.

Printed on non-duplicate paper, the message was the one they were looking for. He read it twice then looked up slowly at Adkins, now seated on top of his desk. "So! Deacon has picked the hour. I knew it was close." With a quick series of rips, he tore the message up, dropped the pieces in a nearby ashtray, and set fire to them. "How many others know?"

"By tomorrow all locations will know." Without saying more, Adkins handed Collins a file containing announcements designed for television and radio. "Davenport came by three days ago. Since we will ultimately be headquarters after the takeover, he wanted to make sure I had these available. That's when I knew it wouldn't be far away."

Collins read the announcements, carefully worded so as not to alarm the public yet explain the motives of their new leaders and the reasons for recovering the arms and equipment. "Initially, most of the public won't know that anything out of the ordinary occurred," Deacon told them. "The sights of National Guardsmen and Reservists in military trucks or standing guard on street corners are what most Americans will see."

"What about emergency plans?" Collins asked.

"According to Deacon, most of us will know the recall strategy but the men in the White House that day won't know what the recall is until a few hours before Flight Hour. It's Deacon's way of keeping tight security until the last moment."

"He's thought of everything," Collins said.

Adkins bit his lower lip. "*I hope to God he has.*"

CHAPTER 47

September 14th

Deacon and Randolph finished a light lunch served on the mezzanine of the Jefferson, an elegant old Richmond hotel. Pausing for the waiter to return with coffee, Deacon relaxed with a cigar. He watched the General self-consciously hiding his gnarled arthritic hands in his lap. "What did the article say, Cyrus?"

The arsenal commander glanced around to make sure of their privacy. "The wire services picked it up and it was printed all across the country. Here." He handed Deacon the creased paper. "It's on the lower right hand side of page two."

Before Deacon finished reading about an arsenal break-in in New York State, his eyebrows lifted. The paper listed probable items stolen. A police chief in the area called it the work of some militaristic white supremacy group. Deacon hoped that other papers too, had also buried it deep in their back pages.

Randolph lowered his voice to a whisper, "It's the fifth time in the past eight months that break-in accounts have appeared in newspapers. This is not good. I don't like it."

In his reassuring fashion, Deacon neatly folded the paper and laid it beside his plate. Puffing on the pungent cigar, he pushed his chair away from the table. "Cyrus, isolated incidents don't make the front pages. It'll be a damn rare soul anywhere in this country who'll even remember that page two story tomorrow."

CHAPTER 48

September 16th

The Winston P. Wilson Matches at Camp Robinson attracted crack pistol shooters from across the country. Eric recognized some of the other top rated military shooters on the plane to Arkansas and when he arrived at the airport terminal.

Ross was standing stiff as a tin soldier near the baggage pick-up ramp. Motel mattresses never agreed with him. After making sure that Eric had seen him, he walked slowly away. Eric followed the supervisor and saw a waiting car with only Pete at the wheel. He entered the car and the two drove off.

A few blocks away in an alley, Ross left his own car and joined Pete and Eric. "Why didn't you come with the team?" Ross asked.

"I had some business in Richmond to finish up. It wasn't necessary for me to be with them when they arrived. The first day at these competitions is just check-in."

Eric's body ached from the crowded plane. The car's soft seat felt good and he slumped down. He'd scarcely slept the night before.

"How's the invention coming?" Ross seemed composed while asking about what he considered minutiae the way he always did before a dangerous assignment.

"You mean in the Right Guard or elsewhere?"

241

"Take your pick. If the Guard pulls through, you'll be their fair-haired boy."

"I may have an investor in Richmond," Eric said.

"One?"

"The men I need with the bucks I need, not a lot of 'em out here, John."

John Ross nodded his head in silent agreement.

Eric was following the usual pattern in those hours before an assignment. First he had sought the company of those who understood what that bottomless pit feels like in your guts. Then, there would be seclusion. Those final hours spent alone made it easier somehow to transform into his cover. He knew his solitude would come later. For now, John Ross skillfully kept the pace going.

"We have a room for you. Everything is taken at Camp Robinson—unless those guys are holding a bunk for you," Ross said.

"I was hoping the camp would fill up. I'd rather stay at another motel, anyway. I need some time alone." Eric felt a strange sensation and paused, studying his supervisor's face. "Anything wrong?"

"No. Maybe something good. We intercepted a message being sent to all the main sites from Deacon."

"How did you know it was from Deacon?"

"Was coded that way," Ross' voice lowered. "Do you have any idea when the Guard's plan is to go into action?" He looked at the younger man with one of his typical glances: one eye open, the other squinted closed. Ross knew the answer.

"Rake told me on the phone last night that he had something important to discuss but that's all. I *can* tell you where some of the arms are being stored."

Ross' attention perked up.

"Jason's hunch was right," Eric added. "Beloin Arsenal in Richmond is up to its rafters in small arms weapons. A shipment came in unexpectedly and Randolph needed some help. They sent Benson and me over. I counted eleven rooms, most of them stacked to the ceiling with arms and ammo in boxes and crates."

"Where are these rooms in the arsenal?"

"In the lower level."

Ross was pleased. "Jason thought the one supporting the Richmond area would be near the city. Have you made a diagram?"

"It's here in the report along with a list of cities that were shown on the boxes." Eric handed Ross some crumpled papers from an inside jacket pocket.

"Good," Ross said.

Pete drove toward Camp Robinson, following the motel-lined highway. Ross mulled over Eric's news, scribbled a few notes on a pad, and then suddenly indicated a large motel on the left side of the road. "How does that look to you?"

"Looks good as any. Why?"

"It's near us. We made your reservation in the Virginia team's name." The car passed the motel and stopped at a crowded shopping center. They parked far away from the stores. "Have you got everything?" Ross asked.

"Yes."

"What about transportation? I thought you were going to rent a car."

"I've got some plans of my own. If they fall through, I'll send you word."

"We could arrange for a Jeep from the post. No problem."

"No. I want to do it *my* way. If it doesn't work out, you'll know," Eric responded. Reaching in his pocket, Ross pulled out a small brown envelope and handed it to Eric. "When we intercepted Deacon's message, we also found this."

Eric opened the envelope and scanned the sheet.

"That's the new expediter code: 'Captain Brower.' "It's a security code for fast access and entry throughout the installation."

"For tomorrow?" Eric asked.

"Yeah. It changes every day. We were damn lucky to get that one. We learned that they pick the names only two days in advance—to give just enough time for everyone to get it."

"According to our information, it's used like any other expediter or emergency code system. They don't have time to tie up lines checking out security. So, for those who know the code, they can go just about anywhere with it. I guess they figure if you're in enough to know the code, you're in enough to be left alone."

Pete lifted his head and glanced at Eric from the rear view mirror while turning off the engine. His summer cold made his voice raspy, sounding like an old smoker's voice. "If you get yourself in trouble, your escape and evasion team will be about two miles away from the installation." He tossed a small object about the size of a matchbox at Eric. "If you can't get out or if anything looks like it's turning to shit before your eyes, use that. If we hear that signal, we'll be there to extract you in minutes."

The small radio signal beacon was the same Eric had used before; he shoved it in his pocket. "How come I got backup in the bushes?"

"No way to get any closer." Ross broke in and squinted one eye at Eric. "We can't risk you getting blown, not now. Besides," Ross said, touching Eric's shoulder as he was beginning to leave the car, "no sense in getting you drilled again if the cover goes bad."

Ross emerged from the car and entered another one waiting for him three parking spots over.

"Are you expecting anything big?" Eric asked as Pete drove him back to his motel.

"Nothing a .44 Mag can't fix." Pete opened his coat revealing a huge handgun strapped under his armpit. "We'll be in touch when you return to your room tomorrow. We don't want any logged phone calls coming out of your room."

Pete dropped him off short of the lobby and drove away. Eric became anxious and motionless for a fraction of a moment. He felt like an old buck smelling the hunter's scent and movement on an autumn day.

CHAPTER 49

September 17th

The motel filled up early with members of other military and civilian teams, all hauling gun boxes back and forth in the lobby. The civilian shooters exchanged state insignias and patches like baseball cards. The military shooters exchanged "challenge coins" some made especially for the match: a military custom.

After settling into his room, Eric hitched a ride with a young army officer going near the camp's motor pool.

Entering the faded building, he watched as members of other state teams converged on the two tech sergeants at the long counter. Both were trying to get vehicles assigned for the competitors' weeklong stay. The cars, Jeeps and small trucks were gathered from different units in the Arkansas area for the visiting rifle and pistol teams. The maintenance books, filled with hand receipts, lay in neat piles on the countertop.

Chauncey's lessons came through loud and clear to Eric; "A good con man can not only quickly assess the moment, he can size up the person he must con. He must know how to convincingly lie, get out of a lie or prevent the subject from looking further." Chauncey always added, "Never stray too far from the truth." Eric waited in line with the others, listening to the macho posturing.

"You couldn't hit a bull in the ass with a pole ax," one soldier in front of him yelled at another state's team member across the room.

"Connelly, I'm going to show you what it's all about this year," the other man shouted back. Some of the team's members laughed at the exchanges between the two.

When Vermont's team name was called out, Eric was standing close behind the sergeant. When the man flipped the sheets to the "V" section, Eric scanned the opposite page where he saw "Virginia Team." The Virginia pistol team, just as Rake had said, had only one listing: a vehicle checked out on the sheet. They assigned two vehicles for each team. When his turn came, Eric guessed from the way the tech sergeant's eyes were drooping that they were working an extra drill weekend. "Virginia," Eric said, looking away from the desk at the picture of a large busted young woman on an auto parts calendar which was hanging on an inside wall. With a callused finger, blackened in spots from auto grease, the tech sergeant looked at the list. The Virginia team was crossed off in one column under "pistol." The column under "rifle" was still blank.

Casually, Eric continued to look at the calendar.

The overweight tech sergeant, red-faced from the sun, looked again at another sheet to see if the cross out was reentered. He spoke in a friendly but authoritative tone. "Y'all have already peeked up yer vehicle."

"We've only picked up one." Eric faked a puzzled expression and waited, knowing that his luck on the mission depended on the sergeant not knowing that the Virginia rifle team was left at home for this match.

"Are yer from the rifle team?"

Eric nodded. He let the photo on the wall absorb him. If the sergeant challenged him, the young woman sprawled on the calendar would provide him with a believable excuse that he wasn't paying attention to what the sergeant was saying.

"Hell, ain't that just like 'em?" The sergeant smiled, revealing a dark gap between his two front teeth. "We're always the last to know anythin.'" He turned around, scratched his chin, and looked in another small binder. "Well," he said, "we've got a couple of spare vehicles. Let me see what I can do. How many members do yer have?"

Eric nodded his head, and then held up five fingers.

"Can yah get by with a Jeep?" he asked? "No more vans around, they are all assigned."

"Sure."

"Okay. I got a Jeep." The man scratched his chin again. "I got a big three-quarter ton out there but that's too big for yer. If yer can manage with a Jeep, I've got a spare one yer can barrah. It's not assigned yet." Obligingly he entered the serial number and scrawled that it was assigned to Virginia's Rifle Team. "Here, fill in this hand receipt for me."

Eric took the paper and haphazardly scrawled a name.

The tech sergeant tore off copies for his files and handed Eric the green maintenance book and the key to unlock the padlock holding down the steering wheel. "Here yer go. Y'all have a good time now." His red face beamed as he smiled, showing the space between his teeth again. Then the tech sergeant turned with a little jerk to help another in line. But suddenly he turned back, saying quickly, "Yer might check that thang for gas, I don't know how much is in it. Make sure the vehicle is clean when yer bring it back. We can't take back no dirty vehicles. We borrowed 'em from other units. Make sure it's clean and full of gas and oil, and fill out that log book ever' day."

"Will do." Eric walked out feeling a little bad about putting the man on. Walking to another building, he finished registering and picked up his scorecard and relay assignments. No matter the con, his guts reminded him it was he and not the good-natured tech sergeant who would be laying his life on the line tomorrow.

CHAPTER 50

September 17th Evening

"Hey, man, where have you been?" Rake's voice rang out through the receiver. Eric laid the plans he was reading on the floor.

"You knew I'd be arriving late. I sent you word," Eric said.

"I knew you had an appointment about the H-PAR. But I thought you'd arrive earlier in the day. The team got together this morning and went over strategy." He laughed—"typical bullshit."

"You can't tell me the Air Force didn't give you guys the same stuff when you were on their team."

"Yeah, but we had a dynamite rifle team to back us up on the other line."

"Hey, it's not my job to get those guys up to par. Too bad they couldn't make it. I have enough to do with these pistol team members, without worrying about someone else's team."

"Did you make it to motel headquarters in time to get checked in and pick up your score cards and relay assignments?" Rake asked.

"Yeah, I took care of it." Eric responded.

"You got some time on your hands?" Eric asked. Eric knew that Rake would hardly have time to eat when he was there as team coordinator.

"Jees, do I have time! I won't even answer that. Look, Eric, the reason I got in touch is to tell you that you don't have to attend the coaching clinics tomorrow. These new men I brought with me need it bad. You shoot well, though it kills me to admit it, you won't need any practice unless you want it."

"Ok," Eric laughed to keep Rake's mood up. "I wasn't planning to show up anyway."

"Look, competition begins Sunday. You should be on the last relay. That'll give us time to have breakfast together. I think it would be good for the whole team to eat together that morning."

"Where?"

"Mess hall. Just look for us there."

"Okay, Rake. Give 'em hell." Eric said.

"Yeah. I should live so long. See you Sunday."

He ate dinner alone at a restaurant near his motel, returning early to try for some much-needed sleep. His thoughts were on Jill as he went to bed. Three times he was wakened by loud laughter coming from a nearby room. He tossed and turned for another hour or so and finally fell into a fitful sleep.

CHAPTER 51

September 18th

Eric grimaced in front of his motel mirror staring at the new image of himself he just created. His hair was now brown and carefully pushed up into his olive cap. He wondered how Jill would react to a major's gold leaf and the strange name on his olive drab uniform.

Some of the pistol shooters were up early and he heard them slamming the doors, leaving for breakfast. He tilted the cap toward the bridge of his nose, shadowing his eyes, remembering every detail including switching his watch to the other wrist and wearing a wedding band. He changed the Jeep's license plates and serial number the night before.

Jason's words from Langley were, "We don't think much has changed inside. From the KH-11 overhead photos there may be a few new warehouses or plane hangars. You can see from the old maps that those structures were not there before."

Langley was closing in. Now they needed to know for sure what Installation Seventeen held. According to former DCI Stuart Jason, "All the satellites in space can't tell us that."

Eric's Jeep made a loud chugging sound, blocking out the noise of other traffic but not his deep concentration on the memorized routes into the compound, its layout and street names. As he drove along the highway he noticed a Volkswagen van carrying four longhaired young men. The van's driver didn't look back to check for a clear lane as he pulled in front of the Jeep, just inches away from a collision. Eric swerved and blew the horn. The van quickly slid back into its former lane. Two young men turned around and through the window Eric could see them giving him the finger.

Only thirty minutes away, Eric saw the insignificant exit marker reading "Pine Bluff." He followed the ramp. Two more turns and he swerved unexpectedly onto a wide sandy trail. The antennae on top of the installation's airport control tower were his first glimpse of Seventeen. The closer he drove the more he began to rely on training. He made himself breathe in deeply and slowly.

Buildings began to take shape behind trees and hills. A flight of U.S. Army Cobra gunship helicopters appeared in formation hovering above the installation—their angular shapes were stunning, floating in a perfect pattern. He slowed down to watch and to focus once more on his mission.

At the entrance gate a young guard stood at attention. Eric remembered "unremarkable entry"—words Jason had drilled home. He fingered again the small automatic underneath his armpit. No doubt the Jeep's number was already phoned in. He glanced at the green light flickering on a panel in the guard station.

"Can I help you, sir?"

"Major Frank Morrison," Eric said leaning over the steering wheel. Then he added in the expediter code Ross gave him. *"I'm here to see Captain Brower."*

The soldier's face perked up. He hurried back inside the newly painted gatehouse, opened a drawer and took out a small green speckled tin lapel button. "You'll need this, sir." He handed the pin to Eric and watched him clip it snugly on his left lapel. The guard lifted the driver's side windshield wiper and placed a red tag on the jeep's windshield. "Sir, do you need directions to the headquarters building?"

He remembered the triangular shape of the base and for an instant, the map he had studied came to visual memory. "No," Eric responded. "I'm going by the tank farm first."

"Yes, sir, sorry for the delay."

The base looked no different from a hundred other small busy compounds across the country. Men walked about in military uniforms hurrying from one building to another, carrying papers and clipboards, or moving supplies from trucks. On a small, slightly terraced area at Eric's first turn, a group of helmeted guardsmen were going through a tear gas drill.

The layout of the former secret testing ground had remained the same since the War when the best and brightest were brought in to work on top-secret projects. New electrified barbed wire fencing surrounded the installation and metal warning signs were posted every twenty feet around the restricted area.

Reaching the airfield, Eric's mouth gaped open at the sight of six U.S. Air Force four-engine C-130 Hercules assault transport planes and two army C-7 Caribou transport planes. He sat amazed, with his arms draped over the steering wheel. "Where the hell did they get their hands on those?" he muttered under his breath. How could any air unit commander overlook an inventory of three, two, even one huge cargo plane like the C-130? It was like having an elephant leave the zoo and no one noticing.

Quickly pulling a piece of paper from his shirt, he recorded what tail numbers he could see and noted the different states the aircraft hailed from. Two of the C-130s were from Mississippi, one from Georgia, and one from Ohio. One Caribou showed chipped paint around the riveting and its identification letters were painted over, for sure one of those missing from the inventories from way back.

Fascinated by the collection of various states' aircraft Eric marveled at how clever they had been. On drill weekends, the men filed flight plans to destinations that could include Installation Seventeen.

The map Jason gave him told Eric little about the locations or the buildings' contents. Eric chose a structure at the installation on which they had the least information. It was too big to be a barracks yet too small to be a hangar. The small black box on one corner of the building alerted him to alarm systems similar to ones he had broken into and disarmed before.

Exaggerating his swagger, he carried a small bag and strode to the two men guarding the entrance. "Good day, gentlemen, I'm Major Morrison. I am here to inspect the security system and alarms. If you'll show me the main switch and the wiring routes, I'll take a look and be on my way."

The two men glanced at each other. "I'm sorry, major," the taller one said. "I'll have to check with headquarters. We have no orders here to let anyone touch the alarm system."

"*Captain Brower* reported the problem yesterday and said it needed to be checked out immediately," Eric said. His heart rate soared. "I was told you had an alarm go off last night, and the maintenance crew couldn't duplicate the problem, so they asked me to check it out. I'm sure Major Adkins would not be too happy . . . ."

"It's fine, sir," the taller soldier said glancing at the green-speckled tab on Eric's collar. "The main switch is inside to the right of the door. You need help?" The soldier stepped aside.

"No. Since the technicians couldn't find the problem, I suspect you can't help much either. If I am going to get this done today, I'll need some uninterrupted time to check out the line work inside," he told them, hefting his bag with an air of superiority. "It may take me a while to run it all. I'll call you if I need something." Both men looked annoyed at his attitude but did not follow him in. It was almost too easy, but the thought of those two changing their minds and showing up help raised his blood pressure.

As the others throughout the base, the building was a large open warehouse. It was cool inside. Eric searched for a light, then reached up and pulled a chain from the ceiling. With its naked bulb swinging back and forth, the light's movement alternately revealed then shadowed boxes lined up in neat rows throughout the warehouse. Huge, heavy lumber crates, boarded securely on top, were piled in a separate group. They stacked the bulky containers so one could see the labels and their contents while walking up the aisles.

Eric carefully walked between them. His footsteps against the roughened concrete made a crisp, crackling sound.

The swinging overhead light did not provide the detailed view he wanted so he took a penlight from his shirt pocket. A closer look at the crates sent his pulse soaring. Pulling a miniature fast lens camera from his workbag, he snapped a few shots of the serial numbers on the boxes.

As he bent down, focusing through the camera's tiny reflex lens for another shot, he saw the insignia. The crossed-cannon field guns of the field artillery caused him to lower the apparatus and reach again for his penlight. He studied the contour of the crate. Hurriedly he read more numbers and letters in red and black. Sweat began to form underneath his armpits. He glanced at his shirt to see if it were showing through. Appearing out of a cooled building and passing in front of two guards with sweat beads on his face and a soaked shirt could be fatal. Carefully taking off his shirt, Eric hung it across the end of a large crate.

He bent over and searched for markings on another crate. When his penlight illuminated a second red insignia on one crate his heart began to pump still faster. The logo was two beakers with crossed stems and centered with a six-sided geometric figure—the army's Chemical Corps insignia. His fingers touched the stencil and followed its outline. There were eight serial numbers on the label along with lot numbers and point of origin. He counted eight boxes to each unit and all seemed to be the same. Biological or chemical warfare? He didn't know. The thought made his stomach feel like acid was slowly burning through its lining.

A small field mouse scampered across his shoe and he jumped up, knocking his workbag off a nearby crate—the fall making a metallic ring. Blood rushed to his head; his temples throbbed like an internal alarm. He stood motionless, listening for the two men outside the door. No footsteps. The guards did not hear the noise.

It can't be, he told himself. *There's been no mention of chemical warfare.* They must have switched the warheads. Could this be a disguise for something else? Uneasy thoughts raced through his mind and unsteady hands fumbled for his workbag. What else had Rake not told him? Or did Rake know himself? Was there a clique within the Right Guard that planned to use the rebel organization to reach yet another end?

Grabbing a large screwdriver out of the workbag, his eyes darted from the lid he was trying to pry off to the door behind him. He jimmied the top up a few inches then used the small light to examine the inside. "Damn," he said under his breath. He could see nothing. The top must come off. Another heave and the lid moved.

Pushing aside a burlap type covering, he could smell the musty sawdust. Poking his fingers into the grainy filling he felt a hard cool surface. Eric followed the object's circumference. He couldn't see it, but the touch was unmistakable. His heart pounded loudly against his chest wall.

The surprised sight and touch of handling the bio/chemical warheads were like curiously opening a familiar toy chest, but reaching in and fingering the cool, clammy body of a python curled up, sleeping inside the box.

"Sir?" a guard leaned against the door and yelled out. "You doin' all right in there?"

Eric's composure almost collapsed suppressing the urge to shout back. Eric managed to sound calm. "I'm just fine. It shouldn't be too much longer."

"Yes, sir."

More time: he needed just a few more minutes. Heaving the projectile from the sawdust bed, he thought of every convincing possibility for its presence. They could be filled with something else like tear gas, for large-scale crowd dispersal. No. Tear gas was never put in missile heads. These were not even conventional warheads.

He pushed his cap back on his head away from his face. Maybe the bio/chemical engineers have come up with something new and non-lethal. He knew he was only kidding himself.

Backing away from the box, he scanned the other crates. There was no more time to open another. He looked at their serials and found eight numbers on each one. The warehouse seemed half-filled with the weighty containers. As he again studied the Chemical Corps emblem pressed into the metal on the warhead's side, he curled in his bottom lip and shook his head. Moving fast, Eric grasped the cylinder and heaved the heavy object on top of another crate and out of the door's view. Although rusty, he still recalled the drill from his training days. Eric loosened the four locking screws that tightly bolted on the warhead. Sweat beaded on his lower lip and on his forehead as the last screw released its hold. His first turn of the warhead didn't budge. Two more tries left his hands red and swelling from strain until he noticed the rubber matting on the floor. Taking a small knife from the bag, he cut an eight-inch strip from the floor mat and wrapped the stripping around the cylinder.

"Sir, we'll be changing guard here in about five minutes."

Eric stopped to yell, "I'll be out before then, sergeant." He let go of the cylinder just long enough to allow blood recirculation in his hands and to wipe his brow. There was no more time. He gave the warhead one final twist, straining so hard the veins in his temples and throat bulged out. The cone slowly moved. He gripped it again. Gently, he rotated the warhead until it was separated from the cylinder. It was different from others he had seen. The Chemical Corps markings were also on its backside, and the numbers and color codings were different from those he remembered. He shoved the screws into his pockets and laid the end of the rocket cylinder back into place. A blank tag dangled from a nearby crate. Watching it slowly turn then spin around, it gave him an idea.

Unraveling the tiny wires, he freed the tag then searched for a marker pen in his bag. His hand-scrawled note read, "Warhead removed for bench check, possible damage." He scrawled in an old date. Placing the note with the cylinder inside the crate and covering it back with sawdust; he lowered the top of the crate quickly over the box and pushed the nails firmly back into the holes where he'd pried them. Eric pulled a handkerchief from his pocket and wiped away his perspiration. He reached for his shirt, put it on, and then quickly buttoned it. Cradling the warhead in his workbag, he toted it to the door.

"I found a hole in the wiring where the mice had chewed through," he told the men standing guard. "I fixed it and the alarms are reset and checked, along with some new relays. There should be no further problems as long as you get rid of the *mice*." He walked to his Jeep.

Torn between wanting to escape with the warhead and wanting to stay and search more, he climbed in the Jeep and drove on to where he saw five Ranger helicopters tied down on the airfield. Again the Cobras in formation hovered overhead getting ready to leave. Eric stopped the Jeep and wiped his soiled handkerchief across his brow. He pulled his cap low over his forehead.

"Sir?"

Eric counted to five slowly then turned.

A soldier stood facing him. "I'm sorry, sir." Two soldiers out of nowhere approached him. Their hands were close to their sides where their pistols hung.

Eric said nothing but held his arm close to his pocket where he had hidden the distress radio beacon.

"I'm sorry about this, major," one man said. "Could you please move your vehicle, sir?"

"We have a wide load coming through here shortly," the other added.

Eric's chest collapsed relieving his tension. "Of course, sergeant. I was just watching the Cobras."

"Yes, sir. I can never get used to it, either." The sergeant turned and squinted through the sun's glare at the hovering helicopters; the two men walked away flagging others to move their vehicles.

It crossed Eric's mind a second time that he should run with the information. However, headquarters building was crowded and could provide some cover while he looked inside. In investigative work safety in numbers often drives a case officer to take chances. He parked the Jeep and got out.

People moved in and out of the large headquarters building as on a normal drill weekend. He slowed down and assumed a purposeful expression similar to that of the men who were bustling around him going in and out of offices and up the stairs.

Instead of plaques, handwritten signs in neat block letters of blue ink on cardboard adorned the office doors. He walked up and down the halls with the look of a man on a mission.

Adkins' second floor office was empty. Furnished in typical military fashion, it reflected his opinion of the mission: serious, organized and frugal.

Eric felt a sudden stab of fear as he descended the stairs. The warhead in the Jeep! What if someone checked his vehicle's numbers more thoroughly? His stomach churned. He feared it was careless.

Through an open door to a planning room, he saw a group of men studying a map. He paused then walked in as if he belonged there. Their eyes remained focused on the large hanging map. Cutting his eyes downward on top of the room's lone desk, he spotted a folder someone had left: "Priority" written on its tab.

As a lieutenant was explaining to the men some point on the map, Eric edged closer to the folder and brushed his hand near its top. Quickly he flicked open the file and saw what appeared to be many copies of an organizational chart of some kind. He closed the folder and with his fingers underneath its edge, brushed one stapled copy out and onto the floor. Bending over to tie his shoelace, he stuffed the information up his pants leg and into the stretch garter that bloused his pants.

"Is everything all right, sir?"

He counted seconds again, and then Eric looked in the direction of the voice. A young clerk was looking at him curiously.

"Yes," he answered. "These new laces are worthless." The clerk picked up the "priority" folder on the desk and with a polite "Yes, sir," hurried away with it.

The sour rolls in his stomach told him that he just took the last big chance for the day. Now feet and stomach headed for an exit before his mind could disagree.

Although both wide gates to the entrance area were open, the stifled panic in his soul was still there: a reminder that more than once case officers could have the run of an area only to be picked up on their way out. Hiding his apprehension with his best forced casual smile, he approached the main gate.

There was definite interest over something coming down the road. The soldier at the guard post hardly looked at him as he slowed then drove on by. Others at the entrance were talking and pointing toward an entourage that was kicking up dust so badly most of the men began to triangle handkerchiefs and tie them across their faces.

Eric pulled out his and tied it across his nose. His cap pulled down, it camouflaged most of his face. Once out on the dusty road, a smile came across his lips. He couldn't have come up with a better cover if he had planned it himself when he saw them.

Dust filtered through the cloth, causing him to cough. He heard a roar of engines long before he could catch a glimpse of the massive tracked vehicles kicking up whirls of dust. They were not running at full speed but he recognized the powerful sounds before him. He pulled off to give them room.

Five dust-covered shadows crawled past him down the road. With his heart thumping and eyes straining to see, he counted five tanks on huge tank transports emerging from their mountain hideouts like dragons leaving a cave. He noted their types but was unsuccessful searching for their serial numbers.

"Damn," he muttered as the Jeep's tires rocked over stones and skirted potholes.

After climbing over two-thirds of the uneven road, he stopped, pulled the handkerchief off and looked back. All he could see was the antennae topping the control tower and puffs of dust blowing up over the trees. He closed his eyes and sucked in fresh air, forcing himself to cough hard, cleaning his lungs and easing his tension.

From a nearby mountaintop, two case officers from the agency's Special Ops Group were in deep camouflage watching Eric signal by taking off his cap and wiping his forehead with a broad gesture. They lingered a few minutes longer to make sure Eric was not followed then one radioed the leader of the non-combatant Escape and Evasion group nearby. The intelligence operation was nearly over and the five-man ops group may not be needed after all.

Eric turned again to look back. There was no one in sight. He reached in his pocket and disarmed the distress beacon. It was only a short way now to the highway and soon no more driving on wagon trails.

The 'helos' were tagged with the right name, Cobra. Swift and deadly and with a cloud bursting sound, they appeared over the ridge. One moment there had been silence, next, the two Cobra copters were overhead; so close to him, Eric felt sure he could read the expressions on the pilot's faces. The sound of their engines was deafening as they swooped low over him. He pulled off on the side of the road with a jerk of the wheel and fell to the metal grate floor, searching for the unarmed beacon. The noise of their engines reverberated against the atmosphere sounding like the sky was coming apart.

They circled, swooped again, even lower than the first time. Eric drew his gun and waited. Sweating again, he listened for their deafening sound, but the engine's noises were becoming weaker instead of stronger. Peering out over the Jeep's hood he saw the Cobras flying in formation nose down, as if lowered by a puppeteer's string. The trailing copter was rocking from side to side, giving the familiar and mischievous aviator's wave.

On his scan radio, Eric heard one pilot radio the other. "That'll send the good Major's pants to the cleaners!"

At first flushed with anger over their fun . . . then relief, Eric scrambled to the steering wheel and flung the Jeep in gear.

CHAPTER 52

September 19th

"What did you get?" Ross asked Eric as he walked in and looked about Ross' slightly seedy motel room. Ross turned up the air conditioning to compensate for the additional body in from the heat. Patrick and another supervisor waited patiently for him to start.

Eric handed him the organizational chart he stole from a folder. "This may interest you."

"Well, well. So we now have a hierarchy for our Number Seventeen." After carefully studying the list, Ross looked up. "Jason's going to be pleased to get his hands on this." Eric gave him the notepad he carried away from the installation.

After reading the scribbled notes, the Chief added, "Cobras, riot gear, light armor, transports and . . . tanks?"

"Five of them. The serials for the Cobras and the transports are on the next page. The tanks were too clouded in dust. I couldn't get close enough."

"What about headquarters?" Ross asked.

"Just as we thought. Organized and packed to the hilt with gear. It's a command post for other camps throughout the country."

"How did you find that out?"

"I overheard some conversation and it's also on the org charts," Eric told him.

"Did you see anybody you knew?"

"I tried to get myself out of there before that happened."

"We got a call from an undersecretary at the Defense Department," Ross said with a smile. "He wanted to know why we needed a "911 force" to stand by for one man and his escape and evasion team in a mission on U.S. soil."

"What did you tell them?" Eric asked in disbelief. He knew DOD would have played no part in the escape and evasion team. It was their Special Ops Group that spearheaded the effort.

"I told them *nothing*, but Jason told them it was none of their goddamn business. Oldfield's upset again over Jason's authority." Ross paused then added, "Nothing new."

Eric piled two pillows on Ross' neatly made bed and leaned back. He knew that many at CIA were using his investigation at the installation to make their own decision about which way they were going to go once the Right Guard made itself known to the American public. What amused him was the way it would be explained and rationalized to the Defense Department and to the White House. He, too, would remain noncommittal until he knew all the details. It was quite clear: everyone was playing this one close to the chest.

Ross lifted his eyes from the note pad. "What was the morale like?"

"Unbelievable!" Eric propped his arms behind his head. "Serious and high. It's been some time since I've seen military men move with such a sense of purpose."

Pursing his lips, Ross touched them with his forefinger. "What about arms? Anything interesting in the warehouses?"

"Boxes of rifles and ammunition, that type of thing." Eric said.

"I wonder what else they have." Ross looked up at Eric, then back at the notes. When he finished reading the pad he laid it on a nearby table. He folded his arms in front of him and stared at Eric, waiting. "There's more?"

"I had to do something unconventional," Eric said. "But do me one favor, please. I want you to hear me out before you set your hair on fire."

"Let's have it," Ross demanded.

"I found crates of surface-to-surface and air-to-surface missile warheads."

"*Jee-eesus H. . . .!*" Ross leaned forward.

"That's not the bad part. The warheads . . . ."

"What about them?" Ross asked.

"They're not conventional."

"What are you talking about?" the Chief asked him.

Eric met Ross' frozen stare. "I'm not sure if it's bio or chemical warfare."

"It better not have anything to do with what you did," Ross responded.

"Ross, whatever it is, good or bad, I don't want to hear it. Two hours from now, if you still think I strayed—give it to me then."

"You know, Eric, when you talk like that, I get this real ugly feeling right here," and Ross rubbed his gut.

"I came across the warheads; it didn't make any sense that they would have tactical, short-range high explosives. I knew there had to be something else—like maybe bugs!"

"How do you know?"

"They don't use high explosives or tear gas in missile heads with Chemical Corps insignia on them."

"And?" Ross seated himself, crossing and nervously recrossing his legs.

"Well, I knew if they were going to be used, we'd have to know what was inside for the antidote."

Chief John Ross put his head in his hand.

Carefully, Eric pulled a cone about the size of a small coffee can out of his workbag.

"*Goddamn it!*" Ross jammed his hands back in his pockets. "What are they going to do when they find it's gone?!!"

"I covered it. Even if they do go into the crate I opened, they'll find a tag that says the missing warhead was damaged and returned to the depot for repair. Besides, I don't think they'll look in that crate for some time. It was the last one in the back of the warehouse."

Ross stared blankly at the warhead. "Jason expects me back tomorrow. Hope you don't think I'm going to take it with me. Will this damn thing go off?" Ross asked. It wasn't clear whether Ross was pleased or thoroughly disgusted at the catch.

Eric smiled. "Beats me."

"Eric, goddamn it! Is this thing going to do anything before it gets turned in?"

"No. I've deactivated it. It's not a highly explosive item anyway. There're only enough explosives in it to rupture it and spread the bugs."

"*Christ.* Spare me the details."

Patrick was already on the portable radio. He glanced at the warhead, "We need a laundry pickup. Lots of dirty linen. How about a rush?"

CHAPTER 53

September 20th

They spoke little during their first two hours gliding on the Potomac River. Former Director of Central Intelligence, Stuart Jason scanned the horizon. His firm hands on the sail he felt the taut strength of the wind taking the boat out. It was unusual to get such a good wind near Washington that wasn't on the congressional floor. However, when the opportunity came for a warm September's day sail, he took advantage of it on the Potomac. The "Sea Phantom" was his pride and joy. Both he and his wife often indulged their love for sailing.

Ross was asked to join Jason and Secretary of Defense Hoffman for lunch and an afternoon on the sailboat.

By two o'clock, Jason's nose reddened and a thick spray coated his glasses. The September sun, still warm, tanned Jason's neck and bleached the hair on his forearms; at the helm he appeared younger than his years. Whether in a planning room or at the helm of his boat, he appeared as steady as a rock. His every movement was deliberate and he was constantly aware of flexed muscles or other body language around him. There never seemed to be a situation where he was out of his element or was not fully cognizant of what was going on around him.

The collar to Ross' yellow sailing jacket fluttered in the breeze. He sat with arms folded against his chest. Owing to Eric's discovery of the missiles there were late night meetings at Langley and sleepless nights at home. Although his eyes were red and tired he kept constant eye to eye contact with the other two men, occasionally glancing at Secretary Hoffman and then back at Jason.

The Secretary's pudgy fingers held on to the side of the boat as if he were clutching life itself. When the sailboat reached a smooth run, he quickly pulled off his glasses, wiped them carefully, and then replaced them across his broad nose.

"Kurt," Jason asked, chuckling and noticing Secretary Hoffman's blue jacket zipped to his neck. "Why is an old navy man like you acting like a landlubber out here?"

The rotund little man was amused. "We had real ships then, my friend. Not toys like this," the Secretary laughed.

"Do I make you nervous, Mr. Secretary?" Jason quipped back.

"No. It's not you, Stu, it's this filthy water. I'm not wearing a body condom and don't want to face a typhoid shot if I fall in."

They all laughed and then Jason abruptly changed the subject. He was ready to talk. "What's your analysis, Kurt?"

"You probably know more than I do right now," the Secretary said, suddenly serious. "Stu, I'd just repeat your intelligence reports and what you've already read."

Moving further into smoother water, Jason sat back and anchored his feet against the side of the boat, bracing himself. "Maybe so, but what *your* analysts have come up with could help us."

"As of yesterday's data there's no sign of a foreign connection. There would be plenty of interest, mind you, from various delegations in Eastern Europe. Even in the Orient, a few ugly heads have reared up to give warnings or pose questions. They're all just standing on the sidelines like the rest of us, wondering what's happening." Secretary Hoffman looked over the side of the boat, propped himself up higher then let go of its side.

"What about the embassies?" Stuart Jason asked him.

"Nothing much there, Stu. I think most of those in the know from overseas, right now, are mainly big industrialists who can be called on for supplies if the Right Guard is suddenly frozen here. And you?"

"Our case officers, the go-betweens, even a few top honchos into gun running, are keeping a lid on." Jason paused and looked directly at Secretary Hoffman. "No one wants to be on the losing side, do they?" He had thrown out the bait and struck a nerve; now he waited to hear the Secretary's reaction.

Ross waited too, holding himself silent.

Smiling and shaking his head, Kurt Hoffman gazed down at the deck of the boat. "Stu, don't play with me. I'm an old hand at these games." He pulled his glasses off again and wiped away another spot. "Battle lines are being drawn, aren't they? I knew you would get around to *me* sooner or later. I don't think Oldfield knows yet exactly what he's dealing with right under his own nose. What a time to have such a man at the Agency's helm." Looking out over the water he went on. "Yes, there are rumblings in the Defense Department. They've tried to hide them. Occasionally there are unexplained absences of top brass and every so often inventories of highly controlled weapons show up missing on our inventories. This year, the 'in' thing is to have summer homes out of the country. I'd be a fool not to realize what's going on."

"The President?"

"He doesn't know much but if he could read between the lines of the information he's been given, he'd be much more worried than he is now."

Ross continued listening in silence.

"I wonder what goes through people's minds when they pick a President," Secretary Hoffman mused. "It's too bad the qualifications don't have anything to do with a thorough knowledge of history and an understanding of the nature of man."

After a pause, Secretary Hoffman's eyes met Stuart Jason's full on. "No, Stu. I haven't yet decided what to do if they take over. I see both sides, and I think I see the same thing you see. For a lot of people those men represent nothing but the ideals and ideas of great past patriots. Ideals that most of the elected in Washington are incapable of understanding unless it has something like 'preliminary fact-finding committee' behind its title. But even if we do agree with their motives and even if they have the numbers to be successful, which I doubt, their method is all wrong." He began choosing his words carefully. "I would suspect, mind you, it's just a suspicion that you and your people would want to see it happen only if the Right Guard could succeed, and only if they do nothing to warrant being called traitors. You know as well as I do, the dangers we face if they are undermanned and underpowered. Violence and bloodshed could make this country come off like a Third World nation. If the people do not understand what these men want to do and try to crush them, we'd end up—mentally and physically spent.

"Do you really believe," Jason exclaimed, "there is any logical thinking going on now?"

"Only in the minds and hands of those men who can do something about it," Secretary Hoffman responded. "If the Right Guard fails, the rest of the country will point at us and them and start a witch hunt for anyone who dared dream that this country could become better than it is today."

Jason gazed at the horizon and at the other sailboats speckling his view. "Damn! We've barely caught on to them. Can you imagine how much *we don't know?*" He spoke as though talking to himself. "I wish to God we had more time." Jason shook his head and looked back at the horizon.

A sailboat passed them with two middle-aged couples on board. The man at the helm held a beer at his waist where a large stomach billowed out over his white sailing shorts. He talked loudly with another man who stood nearby smoking a large cigar. Two bikini-clad older women sunning themselves on the boat's deck sat up and waved like young girls on their first outing. Both were overweight and bulging out of their swimsuits. Secretary Hoffman observed them with amusement. The sight disgusted Ross and he looked away. Jason didn't notice them. He kept squinting his eyes at the sun and at the flapping sails.

Secretary Hoffman asked, "What do your correlation studies show about the missing arms?"

"They run pretty much along the same lines as yours." Jason responded. "The crimes involving large scale theft of weapons and arms have appeared around the same times and in the same areas that weapons have been moved in and out of the arsenals."

"But, Stu, that's been going on all along."

"It's stopped. No new movements now for a few weeks."

"Maybe they are just lying low." Secretary Hoffman said.

The wind began to kick up and carry the sails out. Jason steered the boat, then said in a lowered voice, "No, Kurt. They're ready to move."

Hoffman sat back down on the deck. "Why now? They've had chances to do it sooner."

"No. There were items they were waiting for. It's a guess, but I think it's their last insurance policy to allow them to get out of the country if things go wrong." Jason then signaled Ross.

"Mr. Secretary, one of our men found missile warheads in a warehouse on one of their key bases. Not just one or two but crates of them. No one knows if they'll really use them," explained Ross.

The startled Secretary of Defense exclaimed sharply, "What are they?"

Ross and Jason crossed glances. Jason nodded and Ross continued. "Bugs. But it seems that it is different from what we have seen before. From what the lab can tell us, the virus is newly developed, very fast acting and potentially lethal. There is an obscure but very cheap antidote that we have just found out has been mass produced this month by a firm closely connected to Deacon. There have been shipments from the company to all of the Right Guard bases.

Secretary Hoffman rolled his eyes and shut his lids tightly, then brought his hand to his broad forehead. "My God, do you think they're planning to use it?" he asked incredulously and turned to Jason.

"I don't know," Jason responded. "My guess is it will be just a deterrent but they have kept its existence a secret so there is no telling. The fact remains, *they do have them.*"

"What are you going to do?" Hoffman asked.

"We haven't decided, Kurt. Oldfield needs to know—at least some of this. Together we'll all make a decision. But I do need your help. I need you to get a backchannel message to the Attorney General that all our wiretapping for this investigation was unauthorized."

"How do you propose I do that?" Hoffman asked then sat back in the boat and crossed his arms over his chest.

"Don't play games with *me* now." Jason spoke sternly. "I know you can get damn near what you please out of him and the White House, too. Kurt, the FBI has come up with some sordid information. I want the Attorney General to know about the wiretapping to ensure that whatever is revealed will be thrown out of court as inadmissible evidence."

"Are you protecting the Right Guard?" Secretary Hoffman asked.

"It's not protection for them. The best end game is that this movement gets called off: no one knows except us and the Right Guard—no press, no big roundup and no purges. We just quietly move those involved out of the military and into obscurity."

Secretary Hoffman shook his head. "What about the bio warheads. Have you thought of the consequences if they use them or even have an accident with them? If they have as many of them stored away as Ross says they could immobilize the country in one day. *Stu, do you realize what you're asking me to do?*"

Stuart Jason glanced directly at Ross, and then quickly looked away.

Ross got the message. "If you'll excuse me, Mr. Secretary, I'm going below for a moment. Can I bring anyone anything from the galley?"

"Coffee would be fine for me," said Secretary Hoffman. "Stu?"

"The same," Jason said.

Not used to deck shoes, Ross carefully stepped across the deck and disappeared below. Jason waited until he was below.

"The Attorney General is going to want to know why I suddenly gave him this information," said Hoffman. "What do I tell him?"

"You'll think of something, Kurt."

Secretary Hoffman scratched his chin, then pulled off his glasses and rubbed one lens. "What makes you think I'm going to do it?"

Leaning back, Jason took in the glorious view of the sunlit sails against a blue sky, beating against the wind. "I think you'll do it," he said, "because you know the man Deacon *was*. You worked with him, too. You tell me. Would he, of all people, fire those missiles?"

Secretary Hoffman took in a labored breath and shook his head. "That was a long time ago," he answered. How do I know what Deacon has become now? His actions read like those of a madman. Stu, *he's dangerous.* We all *knew* it even back then," the Secretary added.

"He won't fire them off," Jason responded, "He's capable of *threatening* to do it to get what he wants—but *he won't fire them.*"

Secretary Hoffman said nothing.

"When did you know Deacon was involved?" Jason asked.

"When I heard what they were planning and the reasoning behind it—I knew he had to be involved. Oldfield thinks Deacon and his men are out to get the minorities, destroy them. What stupidity!" Moving closer to Jason, he added, "Do you remember the discussion we had that night you were sent out to meet us in Germany from the mission? You with a shoulder wound, Deacon's leg torn up—but he was still talking U.S. politics. 'The poor are still slaves of this country. They've been nursed by the government and weaned of their self-esteem. If they don't develop their own self-pride by making it on their own, once they do arrive, no one will respect them for it!'" Secretary Hoffman spoke Deacon's words forcefully, imitating him and pounding his fist on the side of the boat.

"It's not the poor he's after, Kurt. It's the stupid masses whether white, yellow, black, brown, who think they have the right to take another man's wealth because they want it; the parasites with the philosophy, 'I want yours. You owe it to me.'"

Secretary Hoffman sighed. "I know. I can hear Deacon now. I thought he was crazier than hell then."

"I'll get an appointment with the Attorney General tomorrow," Secretary Hoffman said.

"Better make it tonight, Kurt. Those men are going to move soon. I don't know how much time we have left. Weeks, days—I just don't know."

"You *feel it*?" Hoffman's eyes were suddenly fixed on Ross returning with two cups of steaming coffee.

"No," said Jason. "I *know* it. I know it as surely as if I were sitting inside Deacon's head, looking out through his eyes."

CHAPTER 54

September 21st

On the last day of the pistol match there was much cleaning and wiping down the guns and rifles. Men hurriedly toted gun boxes in all directions. The contestants were heading home with their trophies, most leaving Arkansas on Friday. Like a high school coach, Rake made his team stay behind until the end. He was holding a private clinic for his pistol shooters and giving critiques on their performances at a far end of the range. With all the seriousness of a Boy Scout leader explaining the technicalities of manhood he went over each target and pointed to their sighting mistakes.

Eric dropped his suitcase, leaned against a back wall, and watched Rake working with the team.

Noticing Eric, Rake stopped and quickly stepped toward him. "You leaving?"

"I just turned my Jeep in. A lieutenant is going to give me a lift back to the airport," Eric said.

"I never figured out how you got your hands on a Jeep down here."

"Magic. Does it every time."

Rake shook his head. "You're an egotistical bastard. You did all right here, despite being an old Air Force puke."

"The Air Force Pistol Team would have whipped all these scores, if they *still had a team*," Eric told him.

"Yeah. Our precious Congress says it's not the Air Force's primary mission to be good shooters, so it's wasteful to spend good money on a team we don't need."

"Need I tell you where Congress can cram it?" Eric said.

Rake laughed and rested his arm on Eric's shoulder. The two walked to the other side of the range, away from where the team was putting up new targets. "I've got some news for you. We're moving soon."

"How soon?" Eric asked.

"About two weeks. They held a meeting yesterday. Deacon says the timing is right. People and supplies have fallen into position just as they expected. I don't think they'll make a fuss over your H-PAR before the takeover, but they're going to be interested in it over the next few months.

"What's the date?" Eric asked him.

After a moment's hesitation, Rake checked to make sure no one was within earshot then said, "The second week in October. The Saturday before Columbus Day."

"Why then?"

"Want it near a federal holiday on a Monday. Some of us thought at first it would be the Labor Day weekend, but Kendall's accident and a few other problems delayed it until October."

"Why is it so important for it to go down before a federal holiday?"

"Eric, on a Friday before a holiday, almost all federal and state employees will be chomping at the bit to get away. Most of them won't be reachable until Tuesday. We'll have plenty of time to move in and take over before they have a chance even to hear what happened."

Eric took in a deep breath.

Rake slapped him on the shoulder. "Don't worry, my friend, you'll be with some pretty competent men. It sounds a little scary now, but we can't miss."

"Will I be with you when this goes down?" Eric asked.

"I'm not even sure yet where I'll be. Talk is that you'll be with Randolph at the arsenal. I may be there, too," Rake said.

"Will I be stationed with him permanently?" Eric asked.

"No. We'll all be doing 'war duty' on Wings Day. After the first mission is done, we'll be reassigned where we are needed." Rake looked back at the team. They were getting ready to fire again. "Look," he added, "I've got to tend to those guys. I'll see you in Richmond."

"Rake," Eric exclaimed, "What's Randolph going to be doing that he'll need me?"

"Distribution. He'll explain when we see him this week. Important stuff."

CHAPTER 55

September 22nd

"What does he mean by distribution?" Ross asked Eric later from a secure phone line near Richmond's airport.

"I think getting the arms out to the right people on time."

"At the arsenal?"

"Yeah and I am sure timed with all of the other distribution points." Tired from his twice-delayed flight from the pistol match in Arkansas, Eric was dragging.

"Are Rake and Randolph going to be there, too?" Ross asked him.

"I'm pretty sure Randolph will be there. Rake says he may or may not. It's to begin the Saturday before Columbus Day. They call it Wings Day."

"Good. We'll be watching a little closer from now on. If anything changes let me know by the phone code. There's no use risking your being seen up here in Washington."

"What's the bottom line on Wings Day?" Eric asked.

"We will use as little force as possible," Ross answered, "but as much as necessary to keep them from getting away."

"How's Jill?"

"She's okay. Protection was keeping tabs on her."

"What do you mean, *was?*" Eric was concerned remembering the last time the Marshall's Office had helped to protect a key witness in a case involving the federal government. The witness was killed on his second day of "protection."

"No problems. But she spots them every time. It makes them nervous."

"You know, Ross," Eric exclaimed, breathing hard. "I really wish you'd . . . ."

"I know," Ross cut in quickly. "I've already had it done. I didn't like the way it was playing out either. One of ours has been assigned to shadow her until it's over."

"But she's all right?"

"She's fine," Ross told him. "Her father's ill, though. I was told today that she's going home to Norfolk."

"How bad is it?"

"Kidney trouble, maybe some failure." Ross waited. "You've got enough to worry about now. If anything comes up you need to know, I'll be in touch." Ross' voice was almost understanding until he added, "Play it close, Eric, we've got more riding on you than just your butt."

CHAPTER 56

October 6th

Word was that Jill gave Scott Barren a "thanks, but no thanks" to any present or future plans. Throughout the week, there was a score of scorching hot phone calls from his apartment to hers. There were a few emotional and distraught scenes between them outside her Georgetown apartment but none of the operators wanted to interfere unless things got out of hand.

"He's giving it up hard," Pete told Eric one afternoon on a secure line. "Could be regrouping for a final try."

"I'm not giving him that chance," Eric responded. "She needs a reminder of what she's missed."

"You comin' up?" Pete asked.

"Can you help me get in without *God'n'everybody knowing about it?*" Eric asked.

Pete laughed then reminded Eric, "You'll *owe* me big."

"Do it, Pete," Eric ordered. "I'm not losing her again."

IT WAS DARK when Eric walked through the Watson's woods in Bel Air outside Richmond, and entered an upper middle-class development a quarter mile from his carriage house apartment. He climbed into the big delivery service van temporarily parked in the development on Garden Hill Road.

Pete smiled when Eric entered the brown van, picked up a box that was lying in the adjoining seat and carried it in the back. Eric opened it and put on a brown deliveryman's loose uniform that was obviously meant for someone fifteen pounds heavier. "Losing a little weight?" Pete grinned at Eric when he came back to the front of the van.

"Working too damn hard," Eric quipped back. His brown and yellow package delivery uniform was bagging at his knees but it didn't matter. It was night and no one would really notice him. They were on their way to Washington, D.C.

Ten minutes before he slid in through the unlocked rear door of Jill's Georgetown apartment, he phoned her. He told her, "No lights." Jill's apartment was designed with Palladian windows, a classic Jeffersonian and Italian architectural touch. They were elegant, tall and wide windows stretching from ceiling to floor-too easy for passersby on the street to see movement and inside of the rooms at night. Now in the darkness he moved carefully from the kitchen then down the hall feeling his way around a table and chair and following the faint shadowy patterns that a period Georgetown street lamp was throwing on the walls.

"Eric?" she whispered from the living room where he found her propped up against pillows on the comfortable sofa, waiting. The street lamp gave just enough light to see her silhouette stand up, the contours of her face and that mass of cascading dark hair blending into the shadows.

They said nothing. He unzipped his jacket and threw it on a nearby chair. Jill stood up, . . . untied an elegant, white silk robe and gently laid it over his jacket. Slowly she began unbuttoning his shirt and spreading it apart. She pulled at his belt and firmly stroked him with her right hand and fingertips then closed her eyes when she felt him responding to her.

Her pale beige silk nightgown fell from her shoulders to her waist then dropped to her ankles and she stood naked gazing at him in the darkness. Jill's dark eyes glistened, reflecting the lamppost's light and she looked surreal with the soft shadows throughout the apartment defining her curves and lithe movements. The faint fragrance of citrus and roses was now musky and emerging was a woman's scent—nature's chemistry instead of a poor over-the-counter replicate which, to Eric, needed no improvement. When he pulled her close to him, she kissed the muscular ridge on his chest then guided his left hand upward and placed it on her breast. Lifting her chin ever so gently he could not stop kissing and tasting her as he slowly slid her backward to the bedroom.

When delicate caressing became impassioned enthusiasm, she raised her head from the large mahogany carved framed bed and playfully bit him on his lower lip. Tender sighs quickly turned to breathy gasps as gentle and agile beginnings of exploring each other's body gave way to sudden unrestrained sounds of surprise and pleasure—quickly followed by swift and deep lunges.

Passion played out in two acts. The first—an urgent sexual charge that ignited lovers who were struggling to recapture a lost union. The second, just before dawn, was unhurried and skillful: more a soothing celebration and familiar acceptance of who they were and why they wanted to be together again.

Though they still had not used the "L word," there was no need for promises, explanations, or unveiling of lies. It was physical power and grace in motion—the soul's life dance—without words, without clichés. It was the way they originally began on some lost Saturday afternoon.

CHAPTER 57

Thursday of Columbus Day Weekend

Secretary Hoffman and former DCI Stuart Jason entered a side door of the White House only minutes before their appointment with President Foster. Current DCI, James Oldfield, was late.

Secretary Hoffman nervously said, "Stu, I took care of *that item* you asked about." The two walked slowly toward the Oval Office, glancing up at each person who passed by, expecting to see Oldfield at every turn.

"What happened?" Jason asked Secretary Hoffman.

Hoffman lowered his voice. "When I saw the Attorney General on the illegal wiretapping, he agreed. He had to. This morning I got back a fireball reply when he *understood everything.*"

"Strong?" Jason asked, the corners of his mouth betraying his satisfaction.

"Oh, yes. The wording reflected his mood and his rather zealous use of the word 'fuck' in an official memo," said the Secretary. "The Attorney General is upset that no one told him what the Agency was up to and that you're covered under the National Security Act. Technically, what you did *was* illegal. But after he sparred with us and the attorneys, he's decided not to take it any farther. You're not to do it again. Consider your hands slapped."

"At least Halstead can't throw everybody in sight in jail if we can't contain it," Jason said.

"So, you saved them from prosecution?" the Secretary added.

"I hope I have. No one wants a public spectacle. What's more important we have the rest of the country to worry about including the public's attitude toward their military." Both men stopped just outside the Oval Office.

"The President is waiting for you, gentlemen," the middle-aged secretary, Margie, greeted them. "Please go right in. Is Director Oldfield coming?"

"He'll be a few minutes late," Jason answered.

At that moment the current DCI, James Oldfield, blustered through the door. There was no sweat on his temples; he had apparently not been rushing—just fashionably late.

President Foster shook hands with the three men and ushered them toward chairs. Jason sat so close he could clearly see the semi-famous rings of green and blue around the black pupils in the President's eyes. *Funny the things you notice when the stress is sky-high* thought Jason.

"Thank you, Mr. President, for seeing us on such short notice." Oldfield waited for his chief to sit down, and then he drew his chair closest to his desk.

"All right, gentlemen," Foster spoke slowly in a serious tone. "I limited this meeting to you three as Stuart asked. I want you to know I did it only because your agencies or departments are directly involved with this situation at hand."

No one spoke. Oldfield, his legal pad at an angle on his lap, waited for the others to spill their information.

"We think they're going to move soon, Mr. President," Secretary Hoffman said, the words sounding ominous. "We have a date, it looks like Columbus Day weekend but, of course all that could change."

The President leaned forward, "And they'll do what?"

"We believe it to be a well-planned, surgically precise takeover of the government, led by the Guard but made up of military and civilians with military background. They are calling for a strict interpretation of the Constitution and opposing what they say is illegal government taxation, unsanctioned spending, and repetitive giveaway programs that are destroying the country." Secretary Hoffman glanced at Jason just long enough to make eye contact then looked back at President Foster.

"How many are involved, Mr. Secretary?"

The Secretary of Defense cleared his throat. "We think there could be thousands. The leadership is centered on the East Coast but the movement appears to be nationwide."

What Secretary Hoffman was telling the President made Jason's skin crawl. According to the reports on his desk it was more than just thousands. Reservists and Guardsmen all across the United States were involved, north, south, east and west. Hoffman did not mention the potential threat of chemical or germ use.

"You have a plan for me?"

"Yes, Mr. President," Director Oldfield answered. "Secretary Hoffman, former Director Jason and I have a plan designed to temporarily halt any further movement."

Foster was fidgeting, fingering his tie. He left his chair and walked nervously around the men.

"It's a temporary measure," Jason repeated, "but it's designed to keep them off balance until we know exactly what they're up to. We recommend that you initiate an Alert—a President's Readiness Evaluation across the country. It would serve two purposes: first, to move every one of the Guardsmen and Reserves back to their home bases to be accounted for and second, an alert for the regular military if we need them. As far as the media is concerned, you can say that you are concerned with the state of readiness of the military and decided to call an alert to ensure identifying any problems."

Hoffman's face became a little flushed. "There are two other things we recommend, sir," he added, looking back at Jason.

"Yes?"

"That we continue to be solely in charge of this operation."

"And?" President Foster asked.

"That no arrests be made once their operation is put down."

The President's mouth gaped opened, as did Oldfield's, but Secretary Hoffman continued. "If these men are arrested, it will destroy public trust in the National Guard and Reserve force. Mr. President, by the Constitution, we cannot dismantle the Guard, and besides they're much too valuable a force to break up."

From the pallor in his face, the President was stunned returning to his chair.

"Hopefully," Secretary Hoffman inserted, "we uncovered the conspiracy in time. It would be very counterproductive to arrest any of them. If you make one arrest, the entire event will become public."

"The blow to our military capabilities and this country would be catastrophic," Jason added. "It is simply not worth it. In a case where hysteria and mass panic are possibilities, the truth should be withheld indefinitely if possible, or at least until we know *what* and *who* are involved."

"I fear the American public initially would react badly to this," Secretary Hoffman exclaimed. "I predict they would be unrealistic, uninformed and over-reactive at this time. The press would have a holiday. We're just getting over Vietnam. Too many civilians are already suspicious of the government over military expansion/reduction issues. Exposing the plotters would shatter what public confidence that's left." The Secretary paused.

Despite his position as head of U.S. Intelligence, Oldfield had uncharacteristically said little. Jason knew why. Oldfield did not want to confirm how little he knew in front of the man who had appointed him.

As Secretary Hoffman picked up and continued to argue his points, the President's demeanor and opposition made it obvious that the meeting was going nowhere.

Hoffman then reluctantly added in his bombshell, "The Attorney General's office knows about the illegal wiretaps. Nothing that has been gathered so far can be used in court."

The chief executive slammed his hands on the desk as if to crush that last statement back to its source. "Now I see what this is all about. No wonder you didn't want the Justice Department and the FBI here! They're not going to be able to convict anyone, anyway. You've apparently already *fixed* that. So, what the hell are you doing here?" In disgust the President got up and paced the room again. "You think you are really running the show, don't you? I'm just sitting in that chair, and you're manipulating the findings of the investigation without my authority or *anyone else's.*"

Even DCI Oldfield refused to take the bait. The President's comment held some truth but no one dared say so.

Secretary Hoffman, with a calm finality added, "Mr. President, if either the FBI or Justice took control of this, you would have had no options. Their arrests would not solve the problem and the media would immediately be right in the middle of it. You would have a circus on your hands that would make Watergate pale in comparison. In fact, what <u>has</u> happened here is *we have given you a chance to do something positive for the safety and longevity of this country and some options that you would never have had, had we not made these choices.* As much as you don't like it right now, our options are few."

Stuart Jason sat staring at the door to the Oval Office. As Hoffman talked, his mind turned over the scenario that could be Wings Day: he could see the door bursting open, a small squad of men quickly entering and apprehending a surprised, then frightened Chief Executive. There would be a struggle, panic and gunfire. Another American President shot, this time bleeding his life away on the dark blue and gold carpet, his blood, and the blood of many others in the chaos to come.

Secretary Hoffman's words took the wind out of President Foster's bluster, and the nation's chief dropped into his seat. He rubbed his forehead and turned to the window open to the White House lawn and gardens. He pondered in silence. No one wanted to interrupt it.

"Do the ends justify such means?" The President asked turning back to the men in his office and obviously still angered.

Jason answered before Secretary Hoffman could say more. "No, Mr. President. The ends *dictate* the means on this one."

Silence again in the room. The ultimate question of whose power was absolute, lay in a delicate balance though no one there would have admitted it. It was pure poker: Texas hold 'em—Washington style. Knowledge, insight and placement are power in the nation's capital and they were the chips in front of them all. The hand was in play and dressed in business suits, sitting in the most powerful office in the free world, they waited for someone to fold.

Finally, it happened. President Foster reluctantly agreed. *No arrests.* He granted a readiness call to come from his office, one they hoped would postpone disaster and isolate the instigators of the Right Guard movement.

Former DCI Jason was still troubled. Would the President's readiness call come too late? If he correctly plotted Deacon's strategy, it followed that Deacon might anticipate *his* every move. What now? Jason worried. Supposed Deacon learned of his counters in time? Was his leadership strong and fast enough to thwart Deacon in his hour of glory? Jason was keenly aware: both of them knew the games so well and to each seasoned player the moves were fairly predictable.

CHAPTER 58

Thursday of Columbus Day Weekend, Evening

Eric sipped a beer and looked out the window of the carriage house apartment. After a run in the woods, Jager plopped down at his feet. The last fiery rays of the sunset reminded him of Jill's apartment in Georgetown and the way the calming hues of the bedroom mixed with sunlight and glowed throughout the room and on her body.

After returning from the pistol match Rake and General Randolph requested that Eric attend many all night meetings going over plans. Randolph was beginning to like him and talk to him, instead of grunting at him with his crooked finger where the inventory was to go, or which record book he wanted used.

Sipping his beer with his feet propped up on a coffee table, he rested. His eyes were heavy with fatigue. He wanted a few quiet hours away from Rake and the others, and the close surveillance by Ross and the Agency. If the plans changed and the Guardsmen moved sooner, there would be no time to tell Ross, hence his shadow was in place.

His thoughts turned to the others across the country that also infiltrated and were "standing by" for the last instruction they would receive before the Right Guard moved. He wondered if some were feeling as uneasy as he was.

Eric's attention suddenly switched to the lights flickering out in the Watson home across from the carriage house. Watson's wife and a visiting nephew were standing by the front door, as he seemed to be locking up the old home. They were taking advantage of the upcoming holiday, Columbus Day, to drive her nephew home to Fredericksburg.

Watson saw Eric in the window and waved. Eric waved back. They left a light on a timer near the living room window and in Watson's attic workshop. Another of Watson's safeguards, he told Eric once, so that the house didn't look empty. Watching them go made Eric feel lonelier. They did not socialize much but it was comforting knowing that someone friendly was nearby. Watching the Watson family leave the driveway he slumped into a comfortable chair and drifted back to what was before him.

Would the Right Guard abide by the President's order or go ahead with their plans? Who in Virginia would find out first? Would he be able to escape in time? What was Ross working on? Suppose Ross couldn't reach him? Escape and evasion plans mulled over and over in his already clouded thoughts.

The machine pistol Ross sent him lay inside a box on the table. He stared at it and thought about what was coming. Finally, the pressure of the worries became too much and he reached for the unsecured line. He knew it was neither smart nor Agency practice to break cover even if it were a phone call, but he felt he had to talk to Jill. He needed to hear the sound of her voice and to salve his rattled nerves.

"Eric!" she screamed with delight.

"Hi there," he said.

"Is anything wrong?"

"Do I *sound* strange?" he asked her.

"Well, yes. Have you been sleeping?"

"Somewhat," he lied. "They said your dad was ill. How is he?"

"He's going on a kidney dialysis machine soon."

"Is it temporary?"

"No. I don't think so. It sounds pretty permanent. They put a shunt in his arm and closed it back up," she explained."

She sounded exhausted. She faded out at the ends of her sentences and there was a crack in her otherwise melodious style of talking.

"How's he taking it?" Eric asked.

"Well, he's been active all his life, rearing a daughter and four sons and holding down a large business. How would you take it?"

"Not too well," he said.

"He's depressed, but we're all supporting him, and I think it's helping. Look," Jill added, "I don't want my family to know about my run-in at the complex, or come to think of it, any of this. You promise me that?"

"I promise," he answered.

"Good. They've got enough to worry about without all this on their minds too."

"By the way, what are you going to be doing tomorrow?" he asked her.

"I've taken the day off from the campaign and going to Norfolk to see Dad in the hospital. Why?"

"I just want to know what you're doing these days, that's all." She'll be safe, he thought. At least she would be away from Washington and Richmond if things broke bad. "I may be in Norfolk myself. I thought I might be able to visit your dad."

"Great," she perked up.

"It's only a maybe. Things are picking up here," he said.

"If you can make it, give me a call here at my apartment. I'm not leaving until around eight o'clock."

"Will do." He paused again. "Jill, I want us to be together." There was such a long pause on the line, Eric thought she had not heard, but then—"Yes, me too. Eric. Remember that—*wherever you are tomorrow.*"

She knew. Not from what he said but from what he hadn't said. It would be soon and it could be bad. His voice betrayed him. "Please watch yourself."

"Okay," she answered. "*You do the same.*"

"Jill, when you see your father, tell him I think he reared a rare beauty."

"Why—I think he already knows that."

"Jill, we'll spend some serious time together very soon."

"Threat or promise?" she asked.

"It's a promise. Bye."

He found it hard to hang up the phone. More than anything, he wanted her with him now just to hold her warm body close to him, to feel her chest rise and fall slowly against his to reach out and stroke her soft, bare back. But the thought kept returning to him: in two days, the readiness call would come from the President.

"No one is to know the alert status until afterward," the President demanded in a final message to Secretary Hoffman.

Through channels, Ross relayed that information to Eric. "It must seem real enough so they won't know we are on to them. Once the President's alert begins, the men involved in this conspiracy should scramble back to their home units"—they all hoped.

At dusk, Eric had set one of Fran Watson's classical records on the stereo, turned the volume up, and raised the window facing the trees. He left the carriage house with Jager and walked down a path leading to Watson's target practicing area. The crisp October air carried the thundering 1812 Overture deep into the dense woods with him. The reds and oranges of autumn had exploded into colors so vibrant they seemed to be burning. Early autumn rains were still in the soil and the fallen leaves over the moss felt like a plush carpet underfoot.

He remembered similar walks like this high in the Virginia mountains years ago. As he and his father walked through the woods Eric listened to him talk about a devastated Germany and why he came to America. Though Eric was too young to remember details, his father described the grand estate home and land that was left behind and the great hunts with visiting aristocracy. He had also talked about war, its deceit, horror and its entrapments. Eric was thirteen then and it was the last autumn that the two had shared together. The ravages of war finally claimed his father's heart—in body *and* spirit.

The walk behind the carriage house was too brief. Eric wanted to go on and on as if it would lead to some peace but it was not going to happen this day. The sun set, the path back darkened, and the music ringing through the crisp golden leaves eventually faded away as Eric trudged back to reality with Jager, man's best friend, close behind.

CHAPTER 59

Friday of Columbus Day Weekend

All day Randolph stalked behind Eric throughout the old Civil War arsenal like a weathered coach sizing up a walk-on. By late afternoon as the General continued shadowing Eric's steps, he rechecked every inventory mark Eric put to paper.

Soldiers had been arriving for two days. The morale and sense of purpose of the numbers of men moving items into groups and rechecking equipment in the belly of the huge hill seemed to breathe life into a fortress that once stood only as a remnant of Civil War history.

Despite the number of new faces to Randolph, he still seemed more interested in Eric and occasionally picked up Eric's stock inventory lists and checked them against the contents in the heavily stocked cement storage rooms. Even Rake noticed Randolph's close scrutiny of Eric while Rake was keeping busy with his own assignment at the arsenal. When the phone rang after dinnertime in the main underground hall leading to the huge storage rooms, no one paid much attention. Eric had just returned from the arsenal's kitchen and the last dinner shift. Another group arriving, he thought, watching Randolph holding the phone to his ear and facing the wall. It was only when Randolph yelled, "No!" and punched one of the hold buttons that Eric became suspicious. "Rake?" Randolph yelled out. "Rake!"

Immediately, Rake charged around the corner.

"To the office. There's a problem." Randolph then turned to Eric in disgust. "Have you finished with that last batch of riot headgear?"

"Yes sir," Eric responded.

"Work with Tobias over there. I may need you soon," old Randolph snarled at him. Rake and the retired General left the storage area. Behind Randolph's back, Rake shrugged his shoulders and lifted his eyebrows at Eric. He, too, seemed puzzled at the old man's behavior.

After Randolph and Rake entered the elevator, Eric left one of the storage rooms long enough to watch the numbers over the elevator doors. The elevator stopped at the top floor near Randolph's office and the rear of the building.

It was too soon for the recall, Eric thought. Jill? Did someone find out about Jill in the meeting? His palms sweated and he wiped them against his fatigues. Thoughts of escape came to mind. He wondered if now he should follow the escape route he planned. His first move was to jam the elevator. Should he do it now or wait? Hesitation, he thought, was dangerous. The last time he hesitated it cost him a wounded shoulder and almost his life. His inner voice was telling him, "Run, goddamn it. Don't wait." But his head was reminding him, "If they don't know about the recall, stay put. You're one of a handful on the inside. Hang in there."

Eric left the elevator and checked the 9 mm machine pistol he hid behind one of the large wooden crates marked "bullet-proof vests." He again checked that a round was chambered and a full magazine in place. No sense in playing around if the game is up he thought. He laid the machine pistol back in its hiding place and picked up his inventory list again. At half past midnight, most of the others left the storage areas for their tents pitched in the woods behind the arsenal near the riverbank.

Suddenly a hand grabbed his healing shoulder and spun him around. The shoulder was still sensitive and his arm went up to defend it. He grimaced at the unexpected intruder. Rake wasn't looking for clues. He was beaming at Eric.

"Deacon wants you to go to the White House," he said.

"What!" Eric asked incredulously.

"They've had some problems in Washington."

"What kind of problems?" Eric came back, not believing what he heard.

"You haven't been told this, but they need you to be a part of the action. Eric, the President is going to be taken by two congressmen and some inside people."

"When?"

"In a few hours," Rake answered. "The two congressmen are from the Armed Forces Committee. They scheduled a Saturday meeting with the President—this morning. The President canceled it. They needed a blockbuster to reopen that meeting. Deacon said to use you and your H-PAR."

"Why?" Eric asked.

"Panic move, probably."

"What did the congressmen say?" Eric asked him . . . his heart pounding.

"They told the President that you went before their committee seeking research and development funds on a liquid propellant firing mechanism, you'd gotten the usual run-around and were discouraged."

"So?" Eric asked.

"They said there was some very dangerous, covert, foreign interest now and it would be very damaging to national security and Foster's Presidency if H-PAR gets into the wrong hands. The White House bought it."

Eric looked away from Rake in disbelief. "Where was Ross?" he wondered. He had noticed the "utility trucks" in the area all week. The agency had instigated some "overload blackouts" in the area for a few weeks. There had even been some well placed stories of power sharing and electricity purchases from another nearby community in the papers and on television. Case officers, dressed like linemen, climbed up and down utility poles with cable and line repair equipment hanging from leatherwork belts. Every two days they seemed to enter a different neighborhood near the arsenal. At one intersection Eric had noticed someone he thought was his buddy Patrick scurrying up a pole with a cable and a phone receiver over his shoulder, but he wasn't sure.

Back at Langley, everyone knew he was still considered a new recruit by Right Guard standards. *Ross won't be ready for this*, Eric thought. How could he ever get through to him now?

Rake slapped him on the back. "*You are taking the President!*" he stated, "My friend you are going to be somebody around here!" Rake nodded toward the elevator. "Randolph wants to see you. He's a little upset about the change in plans but don't let it get to you. This was Deacon's order."

Eric swallowed hard and forced a nervous smile on his face.

CHAPTER 60

Friday of Columbus Day Weekend, Early Evening

Rake and Eric entered retired General Randolph's top floor office. Randolph solemnly stared out of his window and into the darkness over the James River. Occasionally his arthritic fingers rescued the ash-laden cigarette in his mouth and he flicked it into a World War II cannon brass casing. "I don't like this one goddamn bit," he threw out at Eric. "As far as I'm concerned you're too green to let out of my sight, but this is Deacon's decision." Randolph crossed his arms over his chest and glared at the two then back at Eric alone. "You're only a door opener. You hear me? You stand back and stay out of the damn way. You'll take your orders from *our* people *in* there." Randolph blew smoke in Eric's direction. "You understand that?"

Eric nodded. He then uttered a low, "I understand. But will I be armed?"

Randolph was exasperated. "Arms will be supplied there, you idiot! You won't be able to take arms into the White House." Randolph took in a deep breath and blew smoke out again in a wide path. "Two of our men are taking you up to D.C. Go home first and change into a suit and pick up any papers or drawings you need to show that gun concept." Randolph nodded in the direction of the driveway outside the arsenal. "They're waiting for you now," he said to Eric. "It's late but you can sleep on the way. Go downstairs and turn over all of your inventory sheets to Tobias. Give him your book with the computer printout sheets and the rest of the files. *You* won't need them tomorrow."

Eric welcomed the chance to return to the storage bin and retrieve the machine pistol he hid earlier. He left a jacket in the storage area two days ago and it would be just what he needed to carry out the machine pistol.

Randolph turned. "Rake, I'll need you here." Then Randolph added sarcastically under his breath, ". . . if Deacon doesn't have any other *emergency* plans for you."

CHAPTER 61

Columbus Day Weekend, Friday ... After Midnight

They were only one team investigating one arsenal. They knew at that same moment Agency case officers and agents from the FBI, National Security Agency, Army Central Intelligence Division, other military intelligence groups and special investigators around the country at other designated Right Guard hot spots, men like themselves—were watching and waiting.

With their night scopes aimed at the old arsenal, Ross' case officers watched from the woods. From across the street, the men saw cars and mini vans hauling small groups of men dressed in battle fatigues entering the long arsenal driveway, disappear around a hedge and then re-emerge empty. It had been going on all night.

Right Guard activity around the U.S. was steadily increasing for three days, now it was slowing dramatically. Two of the handful who penetrated the Right Guard network said the takeover would be on a holiday. Only Eric's report seemed certain that Columbus Day weekend would be the target date. Current DCI Oldfield, of course, wasn't sure, saying he needed more information. Regardless, former DCI Jason told them to brace themselves and those working in the field who had been in "the company" during Jason's tenure, followed his orders without question.

It surprised the alerted case officers when Eric and two men left the arsenal, close to 2 a.m. Someone excitedly whispered into a radio, "It's Eric, he's leaving with two of 'em."

Pete reached for his night scope and watched intently as Eric, dressed in his fatigues and carrying what seemed to be a rolled up jacket, entered the sedan's back seat and the men sped out the driveway.

"They're moving. It's a dark gray Mercedes sedan," someone said.

"Is it marked? Is it marked?" Pete frantically called into the radio. At that moment, an Agency helicopter silently sitting in a school's playground surrounded by woods, rotated its blades, and prepared to lift off. It had been freshly painted with St. Agnes Hospital Emergency on its side. Two white power utility trucks started up and inched within two blocks of the arsenal. They waited in a dark stretch of the road where there were no street lamps. Another case officer in blue jeans, a black silver-studded jacket and red and yellow flames on his helmet, started his motorcycle. The pilot waited in the lot of a nearby shopping center for the next message through the radiophone in his helmet.

Armed case officers in five chase cars left their various parking spots at the same all-night shopping center at staggered times. They hurried to cover the only three exits where the sedan could emerge.

"I can't see any markings," Patrick urgently shouted into the helicopter's radio as he held his night scope.

The first white marker truck designed as a Virginia Electric Power Company utility van followed directions from the air but could not reach the Mercedes in time before it turned.

The motorcycle followed a respectable distance and when the Mercedes turned away from the highway and back toward Bel Air, the case officer on the cycle radioed they were probably going to Eric's apartment. When he confirmed it, he passed the sedan and continued down the winding road.

"Pat, we're moving near the apartment. Shut down until you hear from me," Pete radioed back to the helicopter.

"Got it," Patrick came back. He motioned to the pilot to go down to a clearing near a school's sports field. Quickly the helicopter throttled back and then set down, hidden again by dense woods.

The sedan turned into the driveway near the Watson home and stopped beside Eric's carriage house apartment.

The three men entered through the ground door and quickly disappeared up the carriage house stairs.

When everyone heard the location, case officers scrambled to new positions.

"You want me to move to the other yard?" one case officer asked.

"No. Too risky," Pete whispered back. "Dogs. See if you can get up in that tree," he pointed. They were deep in Watson's woods and feared getting too close to neighbors' homes. One case officer climbed a tree with his binoculars and gave moment by moment descriptions of what appeared in the upstairs windows of the little carriage house. Eric was alone in his bedroom. He was putting on a suit, and then seemed to be searching for something. Pete saw Eric shove a small gun under his belt behind him, then put something wrapped in a piece of clothing inside a bureau drawer.

On the line with Ross, Pete reported, "Eric seems okay. He's got a heater." They waited.

At a quarter past four, Eric and the two men left the carriage house. Pete grabbed the radiophone. "Pat, they're out. Get it up!" Immediately the chopper lifted again and made a wide circle over the area. The power utility trucks started driving toward the highway as the chase cars and the motorcyclist were alerted. The case officer on the motorcycle turned his black silver-studded jacket inside out and emerged with a blue one and switched helmets with the one that was on his passenger's seat. He peeled temporary colored decals off the motorcycle and put them in a side bag. When the Mercedes was out of sight, Pete dashed from the woods to a waiting station wagon and sped away.

"Where are they, Pat?" Pete asked from his new position in the wagon.

"They're going toward the highway," Patrick reported from the air.

"You've got two chances to get it marked. There are two stoplights before they cross over the bridge into the downtown area."

"Mark it *now*!" Pete urgently hollered back into the phone.

The trucks took off and followed behind the Mercedes in the right lane. At the first stoplight two cars in the left lane kept them from pulling alongside. At the second stoplight one truck veered off at an exit for downtown while the second utility truck pulled alongside the Mercedes. Seconds before the light turned green, an isotope in a needle-fine mist sprayed out above the car from an overhanging arm of the truck.

From the air Patrick was holding a special scope to his eyes. "I see it, I see it! Good job." The helicopter changed direction and the motorcycle followed the car across the bridge. The utility truck lumbered off onto an exit.

"Pat, when you come down, stay close. I may need you if we have problems," Pete said. "Kirby, you and Jordan get up to D.C. we'll need you there."

"Roger that," Patrick's answer came back from the helicopter.

When the Mercedes exited the downtown ramp, the motorcycle fell back a few blocks. "He's in the back seat. I pulled beside them once. Eric saw me but I couldn't see any signal. It's still too dark inside the car," the case officer said low into his helmet microphone. "He looks okay, though."

Pete heard the message sitting beside a case officer driver in the station wagon.

"Good," he said. "Break-off the bike, Kirby. The chase cars have him now."

"You think they're going *to do him*?" one of the case officers in a chase car radioed Pete on the scrambled radio band.

"Ross and I don't think so," Pete responded. "They wouldn't take him out like this to end it. They have something else in mind."

"Should we extract or follow?" another case officer radioed in.

"Langley says stay on 'em," Pete said. "They're heading north, looks like to Washington. If that's their destination, we have about two hours to try to figure this out."

The others radioed in and agreed.

For the next half-hour the five chase cars followed the Mercedes sedan, hop-scotching and moving up and back. When it was clear to Pete that they were going to stay on Interstate 95 in the direction of Washington, he radioed out. "Jordan, you and I stay with him. The rest of you head home." One by one they fell back on the interstate route then vanished.

The closer they moved to Northern Virginia and Washington, D.C. another plan now would pick up and be activated.

CHAPTER 62

Columbus Day Weekend, Saturday Early Morning

The Mercedes stopped in Doswell, a small town along the route to Washington, D.C. At a large truck stop, the sedan driver went to the bathroom. In Fredericksburg, the sedan pulled over again, for coffee. Once in Northern Virginia, another group of chase cars Ross alerted from Langley would follow the Mercedes.

The strange entourage arrived in Washington about 6:00 a.m. The sedan seemed to wander aimlessly from one street to another then back again, until it picked a spot at a restaurant that opened early.

One of the chase cars pulled up at the same restaurant. Another parked nearby at a service station. The others hid on side streets. The new helicopter overhead now *appeared* to be a local Washington, D.C. television traffic control broadcaster.

It was a popular Saturday breakfast café. Other cars kept turning in, too, waiting until 6:30 a.m. for the restaurant to open its doors. A few casually dressed locals ambled up from the street and sat on the curb by the entrance. Some turned to notice the Mercedes, an uncommon car in this neighborhood.

No one had seen Eric since he left Fredericksburg, and they could not see anything at all through the back window.

"I don't like it," Pete said in the radio from across the street. "Send someone in to take a look."

Five minutes later a young man dressed in faded jeans and a worn tee shirt walked up to the curbing of the restaurant. Everyone was suddenly crowding around the door waiting for a man in a soiled white chef's coat and hat to open the restaurant door.

The young case officer held an unlit cigarette, slapped his right shirt pocket and asked the other people standing at the door, "Are they letting anyone in yet?" No, they all answered, shaking their heads. From a distance, *he appeared* to be asking for a light and no one had one. He slapped his jean pockets as he approached the Mercedes and tapped the driver's window. The driver just looked at him and rolled the window down a few inches.

"Got a light?" the young man asked.

The driver shook his head, no, and then the other man reached on the dash and handed the driver a paper matchbook. The driver pushed it through the crack in the window.

The young man stood there and lit the end of his cigarette, cupping his hands over the end to help the flame. He threw the match down then went inside the open restaurant and ordered. When the case officer left the restaurant with a Styrofoam cup in his hand, he walked down a side street and got into a beat-up yellow van. "He's back there," the young man's voice suddenly came over the radio.

"Does he look all right?" Pete asked.

"Seems to be okay. He's lying down on the back seat. As I was leaving, he stirred. His jacket was off and he's not restrained. I think he's just sleeping."

The driver of the Mercedes finally entered the restaurant and returned to the sedan with a white bag and a cardboard box holding three cups.

"Breakfast," Pete mouthed silently as they watched the man enter the car.

Suddenly Eric's head and shoulders appeared in the back window.

"Well, look who's up," someone said over the radio. Pete heard it and he nodded with relief at the case officer in the back of the wagon.

Again they waited. Two hours and one well-guarded pee break passed then the Mercedes pulled out. When it drove within three blocks of the White House, Pete phoned Ross again and alerted him of their location.

Ross told him, "I'm on my way."

Twenty minutes after Ross arrived and joined Pete in the wagon, Eric was let out of the Mercedes a block from the White House.

When he slipped on a suit jacket, one of the case officers radioed, "Pete, where's his pistol? He doesn't have it."

"I don't know. He must have stuffed it in the back seat. I think he took it off 'cause he's going in the *Big House*," Pete answered.

The White House? It doesn't figure; no reason for it, Ross thought. He held a pair of binoculars to his eyes.

They watched as Eric greeted two new faces.

"What the hell are they doing *in this* area?" Ross asked. "Nothing around here but government buildings and they're all closed."

Pete solemnly answered, "The only action in this part of town *is* the White House."

"Oh, g*od*!" Ross said watching the three men pass through the White House gate.

"Aren't they congressmen?" Ross asked Pete.

"I recognize one," Pete answered. "The taller one is Joseph Calliman. I don't know the other one."

A voice came over the radio, "Two big ones: Joe Calliman and George Bailey."

"You know them?" Ross asked turning to Pete.

". . . Armed Services Committee," Pete answered.

Ross picked up the radio and asked for Jason. "When's the recall?"

Jason responded, "Any time now."

"We should get on the inside now," Ross said to Jason. "I'm concerned about *Galileo*," Ross stated emphatically, using the code name for the President.

"You know anyone in there?" Jason asked over the radio.

"I have an old college crony who's in protocol. We see each other occasionally."

"Who is he?" Jason persisted.

"Ed Becker."

"Is that all you've got?" Jason asked him.

"That's it on short notice," Ross told him. "He's got the run of the place but if he works Saturdays it'll be a miracle."

"What's the number?" Jason asked.

Ross flipped through a small brown leather address book then gave Jason the phone number.

Jason was silent on his end of the radio for a few moments then came back. "His wife says he's working in the 'Big House' today. You think he's clean?" Jason asked.

"He's the only chance we have. I'm banking on it. What else is left?" Ross asked him.

"Go for it!" Jason told him emphatically. "Just go for it!"

Ross hustled away from the station wagon. In a phone booth two blocks away he called Ed Becker. The call was friendly and Ross asked him about having coffee.

"Sure," Becker said. "You on the outside?"

"Yeah," Ross replied.

"Come on up. I'll tell security. But John, you know you can't bring *anything* in with you," Becker warned the Chief.

"I'm not *carrying*, Ed."

"Good. A guard will bring you in."

A White House security guard accompanied Ross to Becker's office and pointed to the door. Secret Service agents seemed curious and followed a respectful distance. When Ross knocked and the office door opened, Becker saw the agents and waved his hand that Chief Ross was known and okay.

Ed Becker walked toward him and extended his hand. The two settled back in his office.

"Ed, I'm not here for coffee," Ross said as soon as they sat down. His posture suddenly stiffened and his friendly manner became serious.

Ed Becker didn't seem surprised. He leaned back in his chair and put his hands behind his head. "What's up?" he asked.

"I need your help," Ross began. "We're into an investigation. We think someone in White House security might try to compromise the President. Ed, I need to be physically close to the President. He's in that meeting now. We have to move fast."

Ed Becker's face froze. "Why are you involved in this? Wouldn't this be a Secret Service issue?"

"You want to talk to Stuart Jason?" Ross asked nodding toward the phone.

"He's in on this?"

"He's heading it up," Ross replied. Then he leaned forward. "Ed, I need to be close in case things go wrong. Those of us on this case didn't expect this. We were caught off guard."

Ross could tell Ed Becker was mulling over in his mind the seriousness of the situation. Becker's face froze into a stare. Friend or not, using your influence so a member of the intelligence service could get near a President in the White House was not something to pass on lightly. Protocol dictated Secret Service notification immediately.

"Are they after the President?" Becker asked calmly, focusing his eyes back on Ross.

"Yes," Ross answered. "And one of ours is in there too. I called you, Ed, because I knew you were the only one to get me in quickly and quietly."

"Man, I can't do this," Becker responded.

"Ed, there is no time. For what it will take for me to explain this to the Secret Service, the President may die in the next few moments. We go back far. You have my word on Stuart Jason giving you high cover. Are you in or out?—*There is no more time!*"

"Let's go," Becker suddenly said, and they left his office hurriedly. "What's going to happen?" he asked Ross as they turned a corner.

"I'm not sure, but when I see it, I'll know. Our inside man will give the cue."

Just then, another White House security guard passed them. "I'll explain later," Ross whispered.

Ed Becker led the CIA Chief Ross to another office that adjoined the President's secretary's office. As they entered, a gray-haired, middle aged secretary looked up from her typing and removed the audio plugs from her ears.

"We need to look at next month's dignitary list," Ed Becker asked her.

"Yes, sir," she answered politely, searched through a lower desk file drawer, and pulled out a manila folder.

Ed Becker nodded toward a small leather sofa in a reception area that served all three offices. He and Ross sat quietly and pretended to review the list. They also could see the secretary, Margie, writing at her desk. Both men listened and glanced out into the hall whenever someone passed by. Ed Becker still had no idea what they were looking for.

CHAPTER 63

Columbus Day Weekend, Saturday Mid Morning

Eric and the two congressional representatives shook hands with the President of the United States. The two congressmen plunged into a discussion about the concept and its ramifications to its defense.

Eric watched as Calliman's forehead began to sweat profusely. No one had confided in Eric the detailed Right Guard game plan. But from the profound and overactive responses the two men gave to President Foster's questions, the young case officer suspected the President would know soon their reason for being there.

"Oh, hello, Robin." Eric could hear Margie greeting a young man. They were talking just outside the cracked door. "I'm sorry," she said, "he's meeting . . ."

"Calliman, Bailey and Brent. I know. Isn't it just like him to forget? He asked me to bring these in." He held out a folder with some hurriedly photocopied papers. "Background material. I suppose I'm a little late," Robin said.

"I could take them in for you." She stood and straightened the skirt of a blue knit suit.

"No. I have to explain a few things about the order of these reports. He didn't tell you?"

"He didn't. But if the President is expecting you, I guess it's all right. Things have been hectic with him lately."

After knocking, the young senior aide entered. Eric watched as Congressman George Bailey looked up at the newcomer and nodded complacently. Joe Calliman stared at him. Eric forced himself to slow his breathing. *Where was Ross?*

"Come in, Robin," the President said. "Gentlemen, this is Robin Hensley." He turned to Robin. "What did you find?"

Robin handed the folder to the President. "It's pretty much the same information the congressmen here will have, sir. But if you'll notice, the problems of past liquid propellant systems are outlined on page forty-two. You'll find it interesting reading."

The President reached for the folder. He nodded at Eric and sat back down to scan the outline. Excusing himself, the President became engrossed in the information, scrutinizing each line and even following some of the sentences with a pointed finger.

Eric caught Calliman glancing at Robin Hensley. Hensley nodded his head. Bailey stood up, and walked around a chair to one side of the President's desk.

Eric took a deep breath as he watched Hensley's right hand slide deep into his pocket. He knew the young aide was searching for the grip of his weapon. The President was still reading. Calliman dabbed his beading forehead with a handkerchief.

The President finished the report and finally looked up.

"Yes, Robin?" said the President, glancing up at him.

Eric frantically thought *where was the Secret Service?* Was there an inside man on their team or had they temporarily been distracted?

Eric sensed the moment had come. 'Case officer's instinct,' Chauncey would have called it. *What am I supposed to do now?* he asked himself, and got ready to jump Robin if he pulled out a weapon. Maybe he could knock it out of his hands before he pointed it at the President. He wondered if Bailey and Calliman had their own weapons. He began maneuvering to a more favorable position if he had to try to take them off balance as well. It all seemed to be happening in slow motion. He was silently orchestrating a symphony of movements to protect the President. *Where the hell was Ross and backup?*

CHAPTER 64

Saturday, Late Morning

Deacon pounded the desk repeatedly. "Damn! Damn! Damn!" He exploded from the chair in his office at the bustling installation near Pine Bluff, Arkansas. He threw the phone receiver down, scattering papers everywhere. "You finish it," Deacon said to Adkins. "I need time to think."

Adkins remained outwardly calm. But, there could be only one thing that could upset Deacon like this on Wings Day. He picked up the black receiver and heard "Phoenix" then an explanation.

"Sir," a voice from Ohio said excitedly, "this morning the President ordered an emergency surprise readiness call. No one knows why, but he's called for an accounting of Guardsmen and Reservists at their assigned units. Our men here in Ohio are rushing back to their home units. What do we do?"

Major Adkins shuddered. His words failed him.

"Sir, are you there?" the voice asked again.

"I'm here. We're in a meeting about this now. I'll get back to you. Stand by until you hear from us."

The door to his office burst open. Pilots and logistics officers and support personnel from downstairs rushed in.

"We've just heard," Deacon grimly said to them between deep breaths. The men stood motionless waiting for his next command.

"Major Adkins," a pilot asked in a tense voice, "the switchboard and the expediter code phones are jammed. It's a readiness call for the entire country. What's happened?"

Every eye fixed upon Deacon. The only sound was the far ringing of the newly installed phones on a lower floor. Deacon looked down then his eyes moved from side to side, as if he was reading something invisible.

"Put Phoenix into action," he said referring to the code for shutdown. We're going to have to pull it back," he said. "Phoenix is active. We'll regroup later when we know more. To go ahead now, is far too dangerous."

The men rushed back to their phones. Calls went out to every unit in the country. "Phoenix. Regroup later," was heard over and over through the receivers.

"What do you think?" Adkins asked Deacon, his face masked with tension.

"We were *compromised*," Deacon said. "If we shut down now and submerge, they won't be able to do us much damage. We may still have a chance to come back."

"What about the facilities?" Adkins asked beginning to panic.

"We can keep a small group here masquerading for a few more weeks then slip away, or we can disband now. The real bulk of the equipment is at other installations and bases and we can still realign the inventories," Deacon quickly responded.

Adkins got up and stared out the window. Men were scrambling in and out of vehicles and he could hear the commotion and the word "Phoenix" as they began to pack up and shut down.

Deacon set a steady hand on the major's shoulder. "Billy, we all knew the risks. It's only a postponement. But now, we need to give those men some direction."

Halfway down the hall Deacon suddenly stopped Adkins, "Oh my God! The President!" The words came in a hoarse whisper. In his dismay over the news he had nearly forgotten that the two congressmen were in the White House, about to take President Foster *into custody.*

Adkins' face suddenly grew pale.

"Billy, for God's sake, go try to get through to Robin. *He must be stopped.*"

Adkins crashed down the stairs, flung himself into the planning room, and grabbed a trunk line.

He was saying frantically, "White House? Extension 1247. Robin Hensley, please."

After an eternity a female voice responded, "Mr. Hensley's office."

"Is Robin in?"

"No, sir. He's in a meeting with the President. May I take a message?"

"No. I must speak to him. It's *urgent.*"

"Hold on, sir." The woman spoke calmly despite the anxiety in Adkins' voice. She left the line to answer another call. After a few tortured seconds for Adkins, she said, "Sir, I can't reach him until late this afternoon."

"Look, Miss. This is an emergency. I must reach him immediately. Can you call or connect me through to the Oval Office lines?"

"No, sir. There is no way I can do that. The President's phone is on a different line. But if you can hold for the operator, she could reconnect you. I'll try."

Adkins burst out, "God Damn it, woman, it is vital to this country that I get through now!!"

"Sir, I'm still trying to get you through to the operator, but for some reason I'm having difficulty making the connection. Excuse me. I'll try again."

Deacon pulled his wallet from a back pocket, then held a piece of paper before Adkins' eyes. "Timson," he said, his voice a mere whisper, "the Secret Service agent who's helping them there. This is his phone number near the containment room. Try him. Maybe

you can get him to make tracks for the Oval Office and stop Robin!"
Deacon handed Adkins the piece of paper and then scurried from
the headquarters to the airfield. He quickly boarded the small jet to
take him to Virginia. He had to talk to Randolph who had sent him
a coded message that read, "Hurry, need special help here. Phoenix
in action. Submerge before revelation."

CHAPTER 65

Columbus Day Weekend, Saturday Early Afternoon

The Oval Office door burst open. Robin Hensley froze in position. His Walther pistol was half out of his pocket underneath his jacket, his sweaty fingers in a death hold around the gun's grip. Calliman swallowed as if trying to digest rocks in his stomach. Bailey put a nervous hand across his opened mouth. Eric flinched, almost ducking as the door flew open, then exhaled in relief.

The President frowned and seemed frustrated at the interruption. Secret Service Agent Timson held out a folder to Robin Hensley, saying, "Mr. Hensley, a committeeman said this was urgent—to give it to you right away. No one else was available to bring it to you."

"What?" Robin Hensley reacted. He was actually shaking. His hand released the pistol grip and the gun fell back into his pocket. His hand slowly emerged from his pocket and he reached for the folder.

The expression on Hensley's face was that of stark disbelief as he faced the man who was supposed to be in the containment room at that moment waiting for *him*.

"He also said you needed to be in Washington this afternoon. Your *Phoenix flight has also been canceled.*"

They knew that Timson's accent on the word Phoenix meant Deacon's "Hour of Flight." Something had gone wrong, terribly wrong and it caused Calliman to twitch his eyes uncontrollably. He coughed.

Hensley finally responded, "Thank you, Timson." The Secret Service agent nodded and hurried away.

Calliman brought hot coffee to his lips, suddenly jerking it away as it burned his mouth, spilling some on his tie. Bailey backed away from the President's desk and nervously reached behind him searching for the arms of his chair. He slowly slid back into its seat.

Eric thought he understood. *It must be the alert. Thank God!* he said to himself; the *alert must be stopping them*. He penciled on one edge of his concept papers, "Timson," then "Hensley." Ross would have two of the White House inside men.

Robin Hensley fumbled with the folder, vainly searching for more information.

"Robin?" The President asked, standing up. "Is everything okay?"

"I'm sorry, sir—this, uh, is a highly personal problem I have to take care of immediately. Nothing life threatening. Would you excuse me, sir?"

"Yes. Thank you for the file, Robin."

"Gentlemen, I'll see you later," Robin said to the two congressmen. Calliman and Bailey gawked wide-eyed at Robin Hensley, anticipating some cryptic signal or body language before he left the room. None came other than exasperated facial winces of bewilderment from both congressmen. As Hensley opened the door to leave, Eric saw Ross in a reception area seated on a small sofa with another man.

Ross, with Ed Becker sitting beside him, lifted his eyebrows in an inquisitive gesture and nodded in the direction of Hensley who had just hurried by.

Eric thought he knew what he was asking and he nodded his head, yes, ever so slightly. The door shut.

Calliman sat back, tending his suffering burned mouth from the hot coffee. Bailey glanced sharply at Calliman. The two congressmen tried to continue the meeting as if nothing out of the ordinary had happened—*or almost happened.* Conversations became stilted and awkward and full of pregnant pauses.

Both men diverted the sudden clumsiness by asking Eric to give the President a technical explanation of his concept. President Foster gave him his full attention having no idea of the danger he had so narrowly escaped.

Adkins lifted the receiver in the plans room and Hensley blurted out excitedly through the receiver, "Your message got to me just in time. Phoenix is going down."

The President's Oval Office door opened again quickly without warning. Whether by habit or reflex, Ed Becker came to his feet in a flash. Ross remained seated on the reception area sofa but looked up. Only Eric would know that the pulsating knot below Ross' left temple was his nerves in high gear.

Ross could see Eric emerging first. The two congressmen were standing in front of the President. Calliman was shaking his hand. Eric waited for the two men to pass him. He followed them out and down a hallway.

"My God!" Ed Becker whispered leaning over to Ross. "That's Congressmen Bailey and Calliman. What are *they* up to?"

Ross said nothing but monitored Eric's expression. When he saw Eric look back over his shoulder at him and go down the hall, Ross followed.

Eric turned again and when he did, Ross raised his eyebrows and tilted his head slightly sideways, silently asking, *What's going on?*

Eric slowly tore the edge from his concept paper where he scratched the names "Timson and Hensley," and dropped the torn scrap of paper beside him on the floor. He kept walking.

Ross retrieved the scrap and slipped it into his pants pocket. He turned back, walked a few steps, and then pulled it out again reading as he walked. He hurried back to the reception room to find Ed Becker. "Where can I find these two men?" he asked his friend, holding out the paper.

Becker led him into an empty secretary's office and closed the door. He scrutinized the wrinkled paper. "Timson is a Secret Service agent and Hensley is Protocol in internal White House security," Becker just gaped at Ross.

Ross lifted a phone receiver and dialed a number. "Apparently it was called off at the last minute. Nothing happened here," he said into the phone, "but I have two more on the inside."

Absorbed in the phone conversation Ross suddenly paused. He answered, "Yes, he's still with them and is okay," referring to Eric. "Is he talking to them now? Got it."

"What's happening?" Ed Becker mouthed the words silently like he couldn't believe what he just saw and was now hearing.

"You'd better stay with me," Ross told Becker. "You'll be safer for now, and I may need you to help me move through the White House."

"What about the Secret Service? We need to get to them!" Becker said in a panic.

"Stuart Jason is working with them now," Ross told his friend. "Ed, it's okay. The Secret Service will be like bats swarming out of hell in a few seconds."

Becker was shaking so he couldn't speak. He only nodded his head, yes.

Ross' attention went back to the phone receiver. "Let the two congressmen pass through. Once they are out follow them and then pick 'em up. Also get those two couriers who brought Eric up here replaced with ours."

Pete and another case officer, Jordan, dressed in dark conservative business suits and tan rain overcoats were accompanied by two CIA security officers. Though none of them had powers of arrest, where Agency personnel are involved, they can detain. The four men, separated by a few meters, walked down two blocks where the Mercedes sedan waited for Eric. They approached from the rear of the block behind the sedan and walked toward the car at a casual but deliberate pace.

The sedan's windows were halfway down. The two Right Guard couriers were smoking and intently watching for Eric to appear from his White House meeting.

Pete and Jordan assisted as the two CIA security officers jumped the two couriers at the same time with such speed that neither one saw the foursome coming. One moment the couriers' concentration centered on the Washington traffic, the next—they both had guns at their heads from outside the car's lowered windows.

"One at a time, get out and put your hands on the roof. You first," one of the security officers yelled at the driver of the Mercedes.

Slowly the men opened the door and stepped out. When their hands rested on the car's roof, the agency security officers slapped handcuffs around their wrists and clamped them shut.

A white van left its parking space halfway down the block and sped toward them. The two Right Guard couriers were thrown inside the van and it rushed away. Pete and Jordan slid into the Mercedes' front seat and parked beside Lafayette Park across from the White House. As soon as they pulled up and stopped, Eric and the two congressmen passed the guard shack and left the White House grounds. Once on the public street, four of the agency's case officers approached the two congressmen. They spoke briefly to the two congressmen. Secret Service agents suddenly materialized out of nowhere and then grasped the congressmen's elbows and ushered them into another sedan and sped away.

Eric saw Pete's hand signal and recognized him and Jordan in the Mercedes across the street.

Eric didn't respond to the slight smirk at the corners of Pete's mouth when the Mercedes slowly pulled up to the curbing. He merely entered the rear and immediately reached for his gun he had shoved deep in the crevice of the car's back seat. He pulled it out and hid it under his waistband near the small of his back.

Pete handed him a field radiophone. "Jason wants to talk to you right away," he said.

"What's Ross going to do?" Eric asked.

"They're going to round up all the Right Guard conspirators they can find and interrogate them."

"What are they telling them?"

"What we've heard so far is, 'leave your weapons in your offices and exit the East Wing.' They were told no prosecution if they don't play any games," Pete responded.

Stuart Jason's voice suddenly came across the radio. "*What happened?*" he asked Eric.

"The President's readiness recall must have gotten to them in time," Eric answered.

"How close was it?"

"Hensley was going for it. We were seconds away from hell breaking loose."

"Did Galileo pick up that anything strange was going on?" Former DCI Jason asked referring to the President.

"No, but I think he felt that the information wasn't very substantive. The rest of the meeting was awkward and ad-libbed."

"I guess so," Jason responded. "They had to go forward with a meeting they had no plans for." Jason then chuckled. "Did Galileo make you promise not to sell your gun invention to the foreign natives?"

Eric laughed. "I damn near promised him anything he wanted."

Jason responded, "Eric, another time, another place—your invention will breathe life again. Good work." Then he added, "The President is being informed now about what almost happened. You have to get back to Richmond fast. You're the only inside man we have in the arsenal. We need you to help identify and interrogate the men there. We also picked up Deacon at the Richmond airport. Tell Ross he's being taken to the arsenal first."

Eric's heart pounded on hearing Deacon's name, and his free hand formed a sudden fist.

"Drive back?" Eric asked.

"No," Jason told him. "You and Ross will be picked up at the Pentagon's helipad."

Eric released his tight fist. "Yes, sir. We're on our way."

CHAPTER 66

Columbus Day Weekend, Saturday Mid Afternoon

The October Virginia sky was becoming cloudy when Ross, Eric, and two other case officers boarded the helicopter on the West Side of the Pentagon leaving for Richmond. Despite the noisiness of the flight, Eric listened closely to the information one of the case officers on board the flight gave them about the rush on Beloin Arsenal in Richmond.

"Patrick, George, Sam and Talmadge led the squads in," the case officer recounted with excitement. "Everything went smooth as silk. They were in fatigues, driving trucks like they were there to load up. No problems. Not a shot fired."

When their helicopter finally lowered at the arsenal, they found a few men huddled outside in a group. Eric searched for Rake, then Deacon.

"Pat," Ross shouted, motioning toward the arsenal. "Get everyone inside the building and out of the road's view."

Inside, the slow process of checking identifications and segregating the officers from the enlisted men began. When they finished, Ross turned to Eric's colorless face.

"You feel all right?"

"I'm okay," Eric responded.

"I may need you to identify some of 'em," Ross said. "A few won't give their names."

All three men entered the arsenal and into the interrogation room. The huge arsenal living room chosen for the interrogation looked different in the late afternoon's crimson shadows. Eric's attention went to the double sliding doors facing the James River. On entering the room, he and General Randolph saw each other immediately.

Randolph sprang from his chair and lunged toward him, his grotesquely misshapen hands knotted into fists. Before the furious General could follow through, two case officers nearby restrained him. "You son-of-a-bitch," he yelled at Eric. "You traitor! Goddamn trash! I knew you were no good." He was so torn with anger that his face flushed a dark red. Two case officers led him off to a separate room.

"Eric," Chief Ross said, "Go to the other room. You aren't going to be popular around here and we'd like their cooperation, at least for now." Eric moved into the next room and remained half-hidden but angled himself so he could hear the interrogations going on.

"Name?" a case officer asked the man sitting across the living room table facing him.

"Rake Giles Benson." Rake stared blankly toward the river. "Rank?"

"Captain, Virginia Army National Guard."

From his position near the door, Eric studied Rake and his interrogator. Eric felt an unreachable pain gnawing at his innards, choking his breath. Rake never saw him. He looked only at his interrogator then at the river. In a low, quiet voice, he answered the questions carefully.

Eric could almost feel the convulsions going through Rake's body and the anguish in his soul. This was the part he hated. The friendship he had felt for and from Rake was real and Eric knew his principles were in earnest.

Another interrogator fired his questions over and over. When Patrick saw Eric staring intently at Benson, he came over and said, "Look, man I know this is difficult. Why don't you just take it easy? We'll call you in if we need some help. You should leave here."

"Thanks, Patrick. I'm okay. They're having a pretty hard time with this."

Soon, more back-up case officers arrived in a civilian car and a van. Within minutes they were helping the others haul up weapons from the basement storage area, as Eric watched.

A half-hour later, Patrick returned to check on Eric. "You okay?" Patrick asked.

"Yeah. Tired, but okay."

Patrick had a faint smile at the corners of his mouth. "You did a good job, Eric. It was the right thing to do."

"I hope it'll be good enough," Eric answered.

"We've all been there, Eric. Nobody likes the bad aftertaste, but it had to be done."

Without answering, Eric shuffled among the boxes and crates being stacked outside the arsenal. They opened some to confirm the contents. Eric looked inside two of them but every few minutes he glanced back at the arsenal door.

"Pat, where are they holding Deacon?" Eric asked casually, still pretending to read the ends of the crates.

"He's on the second floor. Ross has him in some office up there. He's not saying much."

Eric reached behind his pants waistband and felt the gun he hid there when he arrived at the arsenal. He left Patrick reading and sorting in the crate area then slipped on to the elevator to the arsenal's second floor.

Another agency case officer stood outside Cyrus Randolph's office door. He recognized Eric.

"Ross in there?" Eric questioned him.

"Yeah. He's with the rest of 'em. The white-haired guy is not doing so well. Could be having a heart attack."

"He sent for me," Eric stated with authority. The case officer just opened the office door and let him enter. When he closed the door behind him, Eric pulled out his gun.

John Ross suddenly stopped interrogating the white-haired man and sprang to his feet. "Eric, no!"

Another case officer tried to move closer to him but Eric kept the gun pointed at Deacon. Seated at Randolph's desk, Deacon was breathing hard and started to cough but still appeared to be in command. His arrogance kept him from admitting what or who was before him.

"Does the name vonErhenrich mean anything to you?" Eric asked.

Deacon's face grew pale. ". . . vonErhenrich?"

"After the war . . . retention camps . . . a captain with a vengeance for blood, greed and cruelty," Eric spoke to help the man remember.

Eric quietly watched the man's expression transform from questioning to defiance.

"It was only a scare," Deacon said, "I would never . . ."

"You would have never what?" Eric shouted. "Had my mother raped, my father beaten?" Eric turned slightly, "Ross, don't move, god damn it. It doesn't matter now."

Ross nodded to the two other case officers not to get any closer.

"We didn't kill her. It was meant to keep them under control. We all used scare tactics. We still do! They withheld information the government needed."

"Information *you* needed," Eric shouted.

Deacon coughed again.

"My mother was four months pregnant," Eric spoke slowly. "My unborn brother died that night."

"Eric," Ross blurted. "His death isn't worth what they'll do to you. Not here, not now," Ross shouted. The office door opened and two other case officers pulled their guns when they saw what was happening.

"Get the hell out!" Ross yelled at them. "Leave us alone."

Horrified, the men paused and looked at each other then backed out the door.

Ross slowly moved toward Eric skillfully attempting to shift his body between the gun and Deacon. "Eric," he almost whispered as he came closer. "Not now. We need to debrief him. Jason *needs* this information. We've got an entire insurrection to dismantle."

Eric said nothing. His gun still pointed at Deacon.

"We'll take care of it later," Ross said, inching closer. Ross stopped when he was very close to Eric. "Look at him, he may not make it anyway," he added referring to Deacon's coughing and grasping his chest. Gently, and ever so carefully, Ross lowered his hand on top of the gun. Then with a sly smile he whispered, "Vengeance is mine, saith the *Director*." With Ross' hand still over the gun, Eric very slowly lowered it to his side.

"You owe me," Eric snapped back under his breath.

"Give it time, my friend. Give it time." The Chief immediately sprang into action shouting at the case officers nearby, "Get this man out of here *now*." They quickly slapped cuffs on Deacon's wrists.

Pete and another operator couldn't rush Deacon fast enough to a waiting emergency van outside.

CHAPTER 67

Columbus Day Weekend, Saturday Late Afternoon

The interrogations lasted longer than anyone wanted to remember. When all the processing ended, the officers and the enlisted men were brought together again on the top floor of the old arsenal building. Eric and Patrick stood together near a side door and stopped anyone who tried to enter. Ross waited until everyone was in the room. He faced a sea of worried, frustrated faces.

"Give it up," Ross began sternly. "It **is** over. We have now, or will soon have, the rest of the Right Guard units across the country, just as we have you. So far no news of this has leaked. If the American public realizes what happened here, they'd come after your asses and the whole lot of you would go to jail or be shot. So listen up and shut up. I am about to tell you what we're going to do about this, and I guarantee you if the slightest word of this leaks it would be viewed as a *cover-up*."

The word "cover-up" brought up a few chins. Curiosity suddenly glistened in the rows of worried eyes.

Ross paused to draw a deep breath; a muscle in his back twitched and tense fatigue gripped his insides. He needed coffee but he dared not drink it for fear he would throw it up.

"You are not going to be arrested," Ross told them. A few men sat up and some stretched to see him. "You're not going to be charged with conspiracy to overthrow the American government. You are going to be released, but a free future is up to you. The National Guard and the Reserves are too damn important to destroy, and we are going to put our asses on the line to protect it. This country desperately needs to keep its military strength high. If the reserve component is destroyed there will have to be a full-time standing army and the reserves will be cut back or eliminated. Defense appropriations will skyrocket and it'll cost us all billions."

"Gentlemen," he continued, "*I am offering you a deal.* This deal is totally contingent upon your total cooperation. Somebody screws it up and everyone goes down. I take it you all understand."

The room was silent. No one dared move.

"Here is the deal," Ross began. "Go home. Keep your mouths shut. I want you to understand that your conspiracy failed and there is no second chance. You will continue as members of the Guard and the Reserves but, when your next re-up period comes, you will get out. Rest assured we have all your names. None of the members of this conspiracy will ever again get a promotion or any other consideration. Some of you who are near retirement will be allowed to retire. If you haven't completed your hitch for retirement you will still have to get out. If we are going to keep this from the media, we can't stop you from rejoining, and we are not going to try. But if you do, you'll be frozen in your present ranks. If you sign up for a correspondence course, the paperwork will be lost. If you sign up for a school, you won't be sent. If you're on flying status, you're grounded. Your paychecks will never be right. If you go on two weeks summer camp to any military installation, your orders will be screwed up so you won't get paid or be able to use any base privileges. If you're an enlisted man, you'll catch every 'rat' duty there is."

The tension among the men, like one big muscle twisting and cramping under stress, was almost too much to bear. Some of them began to stare away in disbelief, as they were mulling shattered dreams.

"We suggest you finish the commitments you've made so as not to arouse suspicions. We don't want whole groups of Guardsmen suddenly resigning. Although we may not catch every man guilty of treason, we have enough of you. If you decide to go public, you will all be convicted of the felony of treason and even if you never spend a day in jail you'll be marked for the rest of your life as being a felon and a traitor to your country. You'll be lucky to get jobs in a car wash." Again, Ross stopped for a moment and leaned against a table. "Gentlemen, if none of this grabs you, there are lots of other ways. The Internal Revenue Service will make your life goddamn miserable. There isn't a man here who can account for every penny and we will ruin you. IRS has been used before and will be used again."

His voice changed and became less commanding. "True, if we prosecuted you later it's probable that everyone involved in this investigation would be charged with covering up the biggest conspiracy ever organized against the American government. I hope you're intelligent enough to realize that, we will have each other over a barrel. We know how you were able to get as far as you did, and why, and we know how to keep that from happening again. We don't see this offer as betraying the American public, but we know how the public reacts. We are sticking our necks in a noose for the good of this country and if you are ultimately the patriots that you claim to be, you will cooperate. Do I make myself clear?"

There was a deathly silence in the vast room, nothing but solemn nods to acknowledge his speech.

Ross saw the color revive in some of the faces.

Patrick came inside the room. He signaled to Ross meaning that something was going on outside.

The Chief walked to the glass doors opening to the river and looked out. "Gentlemen," he continued briskly, "here come the super cops. The FBI has only one thing in mind: to prosecute you for whatever they can get. First, they'll advise you of your rights. Heed their every word. Then, they'll tell you that you will be indicted for a crime. They'll go through all the motions and say all the things you might expect. As you know, before any arrests can be made, a Grand Jury would have to hold a hearing. In collecting evidence, we technically violated rules of evidence and, in some cases, your Constitutional rights. We did it to protect you. The FBI agents are just finding that fact out, and they are not happy. If they talk you into cooperating, you'll do nothing but burn everyone. If they come back later to offer you amnesty or any other deal and you cooperate, you'll take everyone down with you. As far as you know, you were here on regular orders. It's now up to you how you handle it." Ross' throat became dry and he coughed. "When the FBI releases you, don't forget we're in the midst of a President's Readiness Alert. Go back to your original units and check in. Dismissed!" The men scrambled in every direction to break up the appearance of an assemblage.

Patrick went outside again, then turned back to Ross and nodded. The FBI agents were arriving in their cars and vans and hustling up the hill.

Ross announced with a grimace, "He-ee-ee-re they come!"

CHAPTER 68

Columbus Day Weekend, Saturday Early Evening

It was late afternoon before the FBI's interrogations concluded. The soldiers went through the second ordeal stoically and without a hitch. They refused to offer any more than their names, rank and serial numbers. When finally released, they rushed to their cars and trucks and sped away to get back to their units for the President's readiness call.

Eric walked back among the rows of crates to take a last look at the arms and the stenciled decals.

He was unaware of Rake standing at the top of the driveway near the brick wall watching him, until he felt a chill, and turned. When their eyes met, Rake said without rancor, but with a tremor in his voice, "I can't believe you were *with them*. Why, Eric?" His words had no force and were spoken in almost a whisper.

Eric's throat tightened, and for the first time he noticed the age lines that were beginning to show in Rake's face.

"You've won for now," Rake said. "But Right Guard will go underground, and some day . . . ." He blinked to rid the water now collecting under his eyelids.

"We had to do what we knew was right, Rake. You could have destroyed this country and there are lots of other foreign wolves waiting, standing in line to help take us apart," Eric said.

"We have common beliefs about many of the things we spoke about, Rake, and we obviously weren't out to do you all in." Eric pointed to the FBI agents leaving the arsenal, "they're after your blood, not us."

"They'll never get a thing," said Rake. "They won't be able to touch the real patriots." There was no hint of malice, only a pale, sickly expression on his face.

"There may be another time and another place," Eric answered, straining to maintain his composure. He looked toward the car waiting for him at the end of the arsenal drive. "I've got to go."

Rake walked along with him part of the way. "You're going to have to go on ice."

"Don't know," Eric lied. At the end of the drive they stopped. A case officer, waiting by the car, had nervously opened the car door and stood waiting for Eric, his shotgun in view—watching Rake's every move. Eric felt an uncontrollable urge to reach out, touch Rake's hand.

"You and me," Rake choked, "we're the same man. We both know what's happening out here. When the day comes that those who won't work outnumber honest, hard working people, they'll vote their own kind into office to take more and more. Then whose side will you be on, Eric?"

Eric said nothing.

Rake already knew his answer.

"It would have *worked*," Rake said low.

"Many didn't knock the idea or even your motives. It was your *method*," Eric responded. "It would have ripped us all apart."

Cold rain began to drizzle down through the trees around the old arsenal. The gnarled dark limbs of the towering naked oaks resembled weary sentinels who had lost their cloaks.

"It's an idea whose time has come," Rake told him, glancing at another case officer anxiously approaching them with a shotgun. Rake added with a twisted smile, "I'll see you next time around—*on our side*."

Eric was silent. He knew he did not want to see a "next time." A sick stillness had grabbed his insides and wouldn't let go; he felt hot and his muscles ached from tension. He looked up and felt the cool drops of rain touching his warm face and mixing with the salty moisture seeping from the corners of his eyes.

At least Rake was free, Eric thought. He would not die like his brother Beau, a strong life in a helpless situation. Though Rake would not believe it yet, he would walk a free man's path.

Eric never said good-bye. He couldn't. He hurried to join other case officers from the company, standing at the foot of the hill, holding their own weapons in full sight and nervously waiting for him.

CHAPTER 69

Columbus Day Weekend, Sunday Morning

Eric heard later on Columbus Day Sunday, that Ross, Oldfield and Jason had studied each bit of the vast amount of information that was pouring in from the banks of telephone lines from the Guard Bureau to the intelligence complex. Aside from the update on figures, other information about the Guardsmen and Reservists now returning to their units was meticulously noted: their attitudes, their inventories of weapons, everything possible to ensure they would keep their end of the bargain.

In the end it all came together like a rehearsed stage play and when the final curtain went down and the various actors left, the entire movement took on an eerie and unsettling silence.

When the third coffee run came around Sunday morning, Jason denied himself another cup. It was his turn to monitor the strategic command conference room while Oldfield and Ross slept and stretched out on cots in a nearby room.

Jason watched as Agency staff manned the lines. When something unusual was reported, he plugged in his own headset and listened.

"Sir," a young man began, walking up to the former DCI with a new figure to report. "As of five minutes ago, about seventy percent of the men have returned or reported in."

Jason nodded and noted it on the pad as he composed the first draft of the report to Oldfield.

"I can take over, sir," Ross said, standing over him. Former DCI Jason looked up. Ross' wrinkled shirtsleeves were rolled up and his tie hung in a loose knot around a widely opened collar. A day's beard growth lightly shadowed the Chief's face.

"What are you doing up?" Jason asked the Chief. "You've got a few more hours yet before you come on."

"I'm fine, sir. I had plenty of rest on my first shift off. This time I needed only a couple of hours."

Jason handed him his latest figures from his lap pad. Ross studied the scribbled marks on the blue-lined yellow paper.

"They're returning to their bases, John," Jason said. "Seventy percent have returned to their home units and more are trickling in."

"Any troubles, sir?" Ross covered a yawn and stretched his arms behind his head.

"There were a few incidents in the Midwest, but that's mild compared to what they were capable of doing." With a smile, Jason added, "Everything's been very smooth. Not a shot had to be fired." He looked up at Ross then back at his papers and said low, as if talking to himself, "For once we came home with the best of what we could hope for."

Ross wanted to tell the former Director that it was *he*, Stuart Jason, who was responsible for the non-violent status and that his strategy had brought them their success, but he knew that the man wouldn't allow him to say so.

"It was the best because we *had the best* leading it," Ross responded. He walked away to go over the figures.

"Sir," an aide handed the phone to an exhausted Jason. He pushed his glasses on top of his head, his thumb and forefinger rubbed the bridge of his nose.

"Stu?" The familiar voice of Vincent Johnston, an old friend, high in the Guard Bureau called out.

"Yes, Vincent, I'm here."

"How's it going from your end?"

"I think it's probably the same thing you people are getting. It's shutting down," Jason said.

"Yeah. Stu, I've got some interesting data for you. Canadian sources have reported an unusual number of military-age men crossing the borders. They want to know what the hell's going on."

"They'll know in good time, Vincent. Not now, but in good time."

"Do you want me to do anything about it?

"No. Anything overt would only draw attention. The first rush will be over soon and they'll realize soon enough about no prosecutions. Once word passes, they'll quietly come home. Just keep a watchful eye on the numbers, ranks, and the rest and don't let on to the Canadians anything more than that until they're officially informed by the seventh floor."

"Okay, Stu. Also, our special unit is in Installation Seventeen guarding those warheads. Can we start removing them?"

"I think it's okay now. Our last reports showed that most of the Right Guardsmen have already gone. You should have no trouble there."

"Fine. We're moving in right away."

Oldfield entered the room with a disgruntled expression on his face. Loss of sleep did not agree with him and made him even more insufferable. He rudely grabbed the report a case officer was holding and walked off to take his first cup of coffee in several hours. A few other men in the room caught the incident and they rolled their eyes and went back to their work.

When he finished reading the report, Oldfield threw it on the conference table and walked toward Jason, rolling up his sleeves on the way. "What's happening out there?" he asked, sounding like he was asking for a half-time score.

"The readiness call sent them home," Jason said in a precise, unassuming voice without looking up.

"And the defense posture?" Oldfield gulped more coffee.

"Everything's fine. They're all returning to their units."

"The case officers out there okay?" Oldfield asked.

"We have a handful out there who will stay with their units in the hot spots until it's all over. They will keep their fingers on the pulse for a while."

"The White House called. The President wants to know more about the defense posture and what happened yesterday." Jason suddenly felt almost smothered with doubt. Slowly he looked up at the man chosen to fill his position. His words came softly yet deliberately. "I'm not sure *whom we delivered from whom yesterday.*"

"Divided loyalties, Stuart?" Oldfield snapped back.

"No," the former DCI responded. "I understand both sides. Our destiny was to follow the one we chose."

There was a momentary pause. Oldfield ignored his comment and took in more coffee. "Once this is all over," Oldfield began, "they'll have a little more ahead of them than just retreating in silence."

Jason looked up, a little surprised. "No arrests, no convictions—**that was the deal, James!**"

"It still stands," Oldfield agreed. "But, I've suggested to Defense that they go through a long debriefing period to clean house and reorient their thinking. Defense wants all of them suspended without pay during that period then reinstated only to the end of their hitch."

"You'll only get a handful if you do that," Jason responded. "That kind of action will only reach a few, and we risk the chance of detailed disclosure," he was angry at Oldfield. Jason knew Kurt Hoffman would never have offered that. What rock was Oldfield digging behind and what idiot would make such a deal? Now was not the time to fight Oldfield. If it could be done at all, it would be soon and on Jason's turf. Jason would work it behind the scenes with those who knew him and trusted him; the current DCI, James Oldfield would never see it coming. No prosecution was what they promised. No prosecution was what they were going to stand by.

Jason quietly left the conference room and settled a weary mind and body on a nearby sofa. *When will the struggle be over, he thought.*

CHAPTER 70

November 5th Early Evening

Packing the dog's yellow feeding bowl, Eric missed the dog's cold nose pressing against his arms in the morning, trying to get his master out of bed for breakfast. The case officers picked up Jager late the night before. The Springador was already en route to a temporary kennel in Maine where a safe house in a highly secured neighborhood awaited Eric and Jill.

Eric had been at Langley for a few days and the last of the packing was delayed. Earlier in the day other case officers helped him frantically pack most of the remaining cardboard boxes. Ross' orders were, "Throw everything in a bag and get the hell out of there." To the case officers, Ross sounded like an old C-130 pilot, "*Throw it in the back and let's go.*"

It was early evening and he was alone and labeling the last of the boxes, when the knock at the door startled him. He almost stumbled over his packed brown suitcases waiting just outside the kitchen where Pete parked them before leaving. Swiftly he reached for his service Walther and stood behind the door. "Who is it?"

Jill's voice sounded sad. "I'm a press secretary out of a job. Know anyone who's going to run for anything?"

"Hi there!" He pulled her across the threshold and closed his arms around her with his gun still in his hand. He held her

347

closely, his lips pressed hard against her mouth. He crushed the length of her hair in his hand then slowly he let her go. "I heard about Moorehead losing. I'm not sorry for him but I know how *you* must feel."

"I like the reception," she smiled and whispered. Then Jill added, "It wasn't the campaign that lost. The man lost. I don't think he really wanted it. Not this time. He's actually been civil to everyone. The pressure's off him now."

"I've got a few more things to separate here. Did you come straight from D.C.? Keep talking," Eric left the room.

"No. I've been in Norfolk. Dad's coming home soon and I wanted to see him again before we left for New England." She surveyed the living room and its oriental decor. "So this is where you've been hiding! When they gave me your address, the men told me it would be simple for me to find. Simple, heck."

"What did you do with your apartment?" he yelled out.

"One of my friends from the campaign, Julie, is going to stay there for six months. After that . . . well, I just don't know."

"What did you tell your parents?"

"About what?" He heard her rummaging through a cardboard box.

"About your going to Maine," he shouted.

"Everyone thinks I'm going on an extended vacation. Campaign exhaustion."

Eric returned to the living room with two more boxes. Jill peeked out a side window of the carriage house. "I see my shadow is there."

Eric assumed it was Patrick sitting in a dark car across the road. "Does it bother you?" He began dragging in another box.

"If I had a choice in the matter, it might. I think this is all crazy. But if there's any real danger to whatever you're doing, I guess I'm glad he's out there." She paused and picked up a magazine on the kitchenette table. "When will I know what's going on? Why can't you tell me any of the details?"

"You know too much already."

"Maybe by your standards I know a lot. But I'm in the dark about what you're doing, and . . . ."

He cut her off, his voice stern but playful. "I'll let you know, what you need to know, when you need to know it."

"Eric, I really don't want to hear that phrase again." She peeked out the window again at the man across the street. "How long will we be in Maine?"

He stopped suddenly; his heart skipped a beat when he heard her.

"Eric? I said . . . ."

"I don't know." He responded to her. "Probably until they are satisfied you're not going to spill your guts."

"Hm-mm-mm. Pleasant group of guys you work for."

He didn't know how long she would be in Maine, but he knew for a fact that it would be longer than a vacation. Soon she would discover that the man in the dark car was waiting for the *two* of them, driving them yet to another location to switch cars. Langley was waiting for their final debriefing and this time it would be at a safe house.

Jill accidentally bumped into a box sitting on the edge of a table and it fell to the floor with a loud crash. Eric ran in with his gun in his hand. He took a deep breath and laid the gun down on the sofa, then pulled her nearer. "I'm sorry. Please just bear with me. I'm jumpy, too—and stay out of the boxes!"

"You really have something to fear don't you?"

"We *both* do. You didn't do yourself any favors when you crashed that meeting and saw me there."

"That bad?"

"Right now, yes." He pushed more boxes toward the living room. "Where are your things?"

"In my trunk."

"Go downstairs. Get everything out and put it beside the Watson's mailbox. Lock your car up and put your keys inside the box.

Then come back here. It's getting late and we have to be in Washington before eight tonight."

She was gone only a minute when Eric heard the door open. It was a faint sound, but Jill was usually quiet as she moved about. "You back already?" he called from the bathroom where he was checking the medicine cabinet. The silence brought him out.

Major William Adkins stood motionless in the living room, his sweaty hand gripping the .45 automatic. "You traitor," he said through clenched teeth, his lips barely moving. Eric could smell the strong odor of liquor on his breath and in his clothes. "You fucking stool pigeon! I came back to make sure you paid. You screwed us just like you did my old man of his dreams. Military spies, industrial spies, you're all alike. You're rotten. I should have killed you when I first laid eyes on you."

Eric's heart was in his throat. All he could think of was where was Jill? Was she okay? She and Adkins must have missed each other. Or else . . . .

"You don't get it, do you, Adkins. We did what we *had* to do. You would all have been shot or in prison once the public found out."

Off balance from alcohol, his red eyes watering down his unshaven face, Adkins held the gun with an unsteady hand. "You son-of-a-bitch. My stepfather knew the gun had been tampered with at Aberdeen that day."

"This isn't about Right Guard, is it? Well, I didn't know Halsey, if that's what's bothering you. That was long before my time." *Where was Jill?!*

Adkins didn't want to hear it. He waved his gun at Eric to stop talking.

In desperation Eric scanned the room for anything he could use to put the man off balance so he could disarm him. Nothing. Everything was packed. His gun was on the sofa and out of reach.

"We'd already decided no last-minute members. Then you came along. I knew something was wrong, but you even got next to Deacon. You're a traitor and you don't deserve to live." Adkins steadied his aim.

A shot fired out and Eric dived for the floor, miraculously not hit this time. The shot sounded too muffled to be from Adkins' gun. Eric quickly rolled over behind the sofa then back again when he heard Adkins slump to the floor. The shot apparently came from outside the carriage house window. He crawled over to where Adkins lay bleeding from his shoulder. Glass and blood lay everywhere.

Eric looked up and followed where the trajectory *had* to come from—the third story workshop of the large Watson home where Eric had seen the glow of light from his carriage house.

Tools for working on pistols, rifles, and reloading ammunitions were meticulously hung on wall pegs in the workshop. Matt Watson peered through his night scope at the man who lay like a limp dishrag on the carriage house floor. He took off his glasses, wiped his forehead and glasses with a handkerchief then casually peered again and saw Eric bending over the man.

His attic night-light threw a glare on a small glass-framed box containing the third Intelligence Medal for Valor, a rare CIA award generally only given for acts of exceptional bravery. The same award granted Stuart Jason and Eric Brent. Next to his award, a yellowed black and white picture in a gold-toned frame revealed a handful of men standing together in black, unadorned paramilitary uniforms next to an Asian rice paddy. Watson's face was thinner and younger then, standing among the men. At one edge of the picture someone had autographed the group photo in blue ink: *"To my honored friend, Matt, whose eagle eye and steady hand saved me more than once from the Grim Reaper."* The signature underneath read, "Stuart J."

CHAPTER 71

November 5th, Late Evening

Jill's high-pitched scream alerted Patrick, sitting in the dark car. He scrambled to the carriage house. She was close behind him as he stormed in then froze with his gun held out in front of him. Somehow, she and Adkins had missed each other when he approached Eric's apartment.

"I'm okay, Pat," Eric responded. "Where is she? *Where's Jill?* She okay?"

"I'm here," and she peeked over Patrick's shoulder at the man who lay bleeding on the floor.

Calmly Watson walked into the living room. "Get her down to the car and get those," he ordered and pointed to Eric's suitcases. Patrick hurried Jill down the stairs.

Watson bent down on one knee and examined Adkins' shoulder wound. "He'll live," he said, "but he's going to have one hell of a hangover."

"How did you know he was coming?" Eric asked.

"I didn't. I was called back from my vacation to keep an eye on the carriage house until you were picked up. They thought you might bear a little watching."

There was no light throughout the Watson house for the past couple of nights. Only a cat or *a sniper*, Eric reflected, could have

353

lived like that in the dark. Suddenly Eric remembered. "It was Quantico, wasn't it?"

Watson only smiled. He remained silent.

"You guest-lectured that class on night sniping at the Marine base. You were the best, they told us. Still in the company?"

Watson gently set one hand on Eric's shoulder. "I work with computers. I'm on vacation right now," he said deliberately. Eric heard Adkins' sudden groan.

"He'll make it," Watson assured him. "There's an ambulance on the way."

Eric grasped Watson's arm and squeezed it conveying his thanks and all the other things he wanted to say but would have sounded trite trying.

"You'd better go, Eric," Watson warned. "If more of them look for you tonight you may not be so lucky next time." Eric hastily descended the stairs and jumped into the car where Jill and Patrick waited.

By the time the car reached the highway, Jill was grilling both men. Finally, Eric held up his hand and said firmly, "Stop this. The debriefing from the guys at *the house* will cover most of it," that was all the answer Eric would give her.

During the first half-hour on the road she continued to pelt him with questions, one after another until she was exhausted from the effort. Patrick looked at Eric in the rear view mirror, raised his eyebrows and cocked his head slightly at Eric. Eric saw him and closed his eyes, and slightly shook his head from side to side. He decided to let her persist, feeling she needed to purge it out of her system. She finally fell asleep and went limp like a worn out child, leaning on his shoulder, her arms reaching around his middle. Her delicate face surrounded by dark masses of sable brown hair almost looked angelic when she slept.

Once she was asleep, he whispered very low, "I love you," holding her close with one arm. He knew she wouldn't hear him and he gently kissed her forehead. He understood she still did not know what she had stepped into by seeking him out at the Right Guard meeting at the mansion. He wondered how he was going to explain her future secure custody to her. One protective arm around Jill, his other hand rested on his service pistol beside him on the back seat, his eyes moving from side to side across the highway. He breathed in citrus and roses and nervously fingered the pistol's grip every time a car passed them.

CHAPTER 72

[National Guardsmen Focus of Federal Probe into Stolen Weapons Parts, New York, (UPI)—Several upstate New York National Guardsmen are the focus of an ongoing federal criminal probe into weapons parts stolen from armories in Rochester and Buffalo, officials confirmed Thursday . . . . Stolen parts were sold to other guard personnel, as well as civilians and in some cases were used to convert semi-automatic weapons into fully automatic weapons, officials said . . . . "There is evidence indicating a scheme and conspiracy exists to steal a substantial number of weapons parts. Our report suggests a basis for grand jury action, said Lt. Col. Peter Kutschera, a spokesman at New York National Guard headquarters in Albany. Kutschera said evidence gathered by the National Guard Criminal Investigative Directorate indicated the ring has operated for at least seven years . . . .] [39]

November 10th Penobscot Bay, Coast of Maine

The sun rose like a lighthouse beacon in the autumn mornings in Maine. Muted and fading reds and oranges emerged into a crisp fall day. The wind blew cold and Jill adjusted the bulky collar of her black woolen sweater. She stood motionless looking across the bay, clutching the dark outer greatcoat closer around her neck. She began walking alone along the rocky shore in front of the old renovated sea captain's house in Belfast, a small Maine coastal town.

A fine mist was rising off the bay making the view a little eerie. The sun would burn it off by mid morning. Peering through the damp misty veil, she remembered Ross' words about being rescued by boat should there be *trouble*. Jill still didn't know exactly what trouble could come or from who but she believed Ross and she trusted Eric. All she knew for the moment was that freedom and safety would come from the water's edge.

Jill paused soberly at the shoreline watching a lobsterman glide to his trap line on the still, frigid water. The damp chill seeped through her heavy sweater and corduroy slacks and even the long over coat flapping in the strong breeze—making her shiver and cold. She was a striking and somewhat mysterious looking figure dressed in black against the grey rocks and water landscape with the last colors of autumn fading in the trees on shore. Strands of her long, dark hair blew around her delicate, porcelain-colored face as she scrutinized the lobsterman's every move.

Twenty feet away from her, Patrick sat on a seawall with binoculars. He scanned the shoreline with particular interest in the approaching boat. She could see Pete watching out the window on the second floor of the old house.

The same view evoked Eric's interest. He scanned the landscape from his bedroom window then hurried down the narrow stairs. "She okay?" he asked, walking from the kitchen to the glass enclosed front porch. He leaned close to a fireplace built into the old home's wall facing the windows and the water. His chilled skin soaked in the warmth from the fiery grate as he rubbed his hands. His puffy eyes evidenced his restless sleep and he searched for another green-checkered mug and the coffeepot.

"*She's* okay. Just scouting out the area," Ross said. He lifted his cup and took another swallow. "I'll be leaving in a day or so. Pete and Patrick will be here for a few weeks. Then the other guys in the community will take over." Ross watched Eric sip the steaming black coffee and then turned his gaze out the large double-paned window facing the bay.

"Eric, we're setting up a doctor's appointment for you in Boston, a specialist."

"Ross, my shoulder is fine. It's not necessary."

"It's your guts I'm concerned about. I don't want to fight you on this."

Eric was remembering his last two meals of red meat on the fly/drive up to the safe house in Maine. The bouts of upset stomach had left him weak with an acid feeling throughout his body.

Ross had noticed.

"I'll go. No problem," Eric told him.

"Good," Ross answered. "You need rest and tending to," Ross added and he almost sounded compassionate. He then nodded toward Jill outside. "Does *she* understand what *all of this means?*"

"Most of it." Eric set his cup on the table. "It's unfair to throw everything on her at once. I want to take it easy, pace it out. We'll have the time now."

John Ross kept studying Jill outside the picture window. He saw a beautiful young woman—untrained, uninitiated and independent—suddenly transplanted to a protected community and loved by someone he personally had responsibility for. It would make any Chief nervous and occasionally set his hair on fire. He scrutinized her walking and pausing at the huge dark craggy rocks along the shore. "Eric, if she stays, for her own safety, you need to get some ID on her and she must know how to protect herself—verbally—*until she can learn the rest.*"

Eric whistled for Jager and pushed open the wind-tattered screen door. "She will, Ross. She will." He closed the porch door behind him. The black Springador jumped to the seawall, sprang over the side, and ran to Jill, still exploring the shoreline. Barking at the lobsterman, Jager danced around her then ran along the water's edge.

"Well?" Eric said walking briskly toward her, his chilled hands in his pockets and his hair tousled by a sharp wind off the bay.

"I'm getting acquainted with Maine," she answered.

"Do you like it?"

"I don't know yet. Ask me again when I've been locked inside for the winter." The serious tone in her voice was begging him for answers.

When his arms caressed her shoulders, she held on tight. "Jill," he whispered, holding her close. "If you *decide* to stay, you're going to be busy up here; you won't have time to be homesick."

"Decisions, more decisions," she said quietly. "At least for the moment, it won't be *my* decision, will it?"

Eric said nothing.

Then, she turned toward him. "I can't talk to you about any of this?" she asked.

"Not now," he answered. "Maybe sometime in the future. There'll be plenty of evenings for *you* to discuss it," and he smiled at her. "You can create an otherwise pretty normal life, get back into education or writing projects. You always said you wanted to publish children's stories and write magazine features. You're interested in anthropology, maybe you can go back to university. You can do that. It's going to be tight up here for six months but we can do some shopping in New York and maybe take off for Canada. There's a lot around to see."

"*Education*, yes. Maybe I could teach here. I always thought I could be a good teacher. I think I'd like that." She stopped and glanced back at the shore line. "New adventures," she responded without looking at him.

"Jill, it's more important now that you be safe and with me. I can't protect you if we are apart. I want you with me." He paused. "Is that so bad?" he asked her gently.

"It's just the sudden change and that man shot in the carriage house, and . . ." her voice trailed off, "It is all pretty surreal. Guess I'm a small town girl after all." Then she somberly looked up into his face. "Is this your life? *Really?*"

"No, Jill. Most of it is waiting, working with analytics, solitary, little action, training . . . lonely. Guarding some formless gate and unsure that your sacrifice will ever be appreciated, pride in skilled teamwork that you were part of something that helped a bigger, worthwhile cause—a cause that only a handful of grateful people will ever know or care about but ultimately could affect an entire nation or the world." He smiled back at her quietly knowing that it also included a skillfully developed and uncanny trained ability to understand in-depth, any multi-leveled world around you and how it *really* worked and *didn't, and how you move in and out of it.* But for now, that would go unsaid. All he could offer up was, "I know. *I* signed up for it. *You didn't.*" He paused and sighed. "Put all that on a shelf for a while. We'll soon create our own normalcy. I'm not running anywhere *this time.*" He nodded at the sea captain's house, "When these men leave, we'll be alone again . . . *another beginning for us*; a better one this time and a new world will open up for you soon."

"For how long?"

Eric didn't know. He glanced across the Penobscot Bay and shook his head. He knew he loved her and he couldn't lie to her anymore about what would affect their future together: she could read his backbone. He also didn't know if this was his last stint. If they stayed together and he remained in, she would be a part of it now. As a girlfriend or wife she would be a sort of unsolicited soldier. He knew it was time to think about it and, unlike Chauncey back at the 'farm,' he wanted to leave before he *couldn't* walk away from it.

The lobsterman pulled his trap and released it again to the dark, cold water. No catch. After checking his buoy he moved away from the line toward his other traps.

Jill sighed and then smiled as she accepted Eric's arm around her waist. They moved quietly together along the water's edge.

Walking among the dark craggy rocks, Eric and Jill walked farther and farther away from the safe house with Jager scampering behind them.

"Will there ever be a time," she asked watching the ripples of the lobsterman's receding boat, "when we won't have to keep looking back over our shoulders?"

"Yes, it'll come," Eric said confidently but he really didn't know *when* it would come. He drew her closer to him and she accepted his reach without hesitation, placing her head on his shoulder as they walked. He knew that soon they would have to contend with her family and friends about being in Maine. *How would she deal with it? How would her family react to her extended vacation?* He didn't know but he would be beside her now, guiding her, discovering for himself if his was a lifestyle where she could find her place and rhythm and call it a home.

An unmarked patrol boat quietly glided in front of them, and the water gently rippled in its path. For Jill it was a fresh reminder of where they were and why. From its deck, an occasional binoculared glance raked the shoreline of the quaint Maine community along the Bay. A couple of the "boaters" wore blue baseball caps, the others wore red. The men aboard with their sculptured hair cuts had an un-Maine-like way of dressing casually with far too much taste.

Chief John Ross observed all this from his seat at the large round oak table near the Bay window. Eric and Jill had wandered far enough from their secure area for his liking. He set his coffee mug down, threw his half-finished, hand-scrawled field report on a chair and poked his head out the front door—letting out one of those sharp, crisp whistles boys achieve when they are ten.

Patrick turned instantly from the Bay.

"Pat!" Ross yelled, nodding toward Eric and Jill, "Go bring 'em back to reality."

REFERENCES

1. "Rip-offs from U.S. Arms Stockpiles: Will it be an A-Bomb next?" *US News and World Report.* 1 March 1976, p. 22.

2. "Big Cache Of Guns, Ammo Stolen From Guard Armory" *Charleston Daily Mail* (Charleston, West Virginia), 5 July 1974.

3. "Gigantic Theft Of Weapons From Armory" *Oakland Tribune* (Oakland, California), 5 July 1974.

4. "Missing rifle truck just lagging behind" *Syracuse Herald Journal* (Syracuse, New York), 7 July 1978.

5. Horowitz, Sari. "District Police Chase Down Stolen Weapons Carrier" *Washington Post* (Washington, DC), 15 July 1988, p. B1.

6. "Mass armory secured" *Kennebec Journal* (Augusta, Maine), 18 August 1976.

7. "Armory burglars had inside data?" *Chronicle-Telegram* (Elyria, Ohio), 6 July 1974, p. 2.

8. "Dateline: Boston" Body: "…theft of Small Arms…" *Reuters, Ltd.* 15 May 1979, AM cycle.

9. "Dateline: Fresno California" Body: "…theft of military vehicles and equipment…" *United Press International.* 31 August 1987, BC cycle.

10. Newark Police Report: "Fence, trucks damaged" *The Advocate* (Newark, New Jersey), 25 October 1975, p. 6.

11. Riesel, Victor. "Combat units roam nation" *Herald Times Reporter* (Manitowoc, Wisconsin), 2 February 1977, p. 4.

12. "The State" Body: "Thieves cut through..." *Los Angeles Times* (Los Angeles, California), 11 March 1986, p. 2.

13. "Armory burglars steal firearms" *Kennebec Journal* (Augusta, Maine), 17 August 1976, p. 15.

14. "Ohio Armory Safe by Electronics," *Coshocton Tribune* (Coshocton, Ohio), 5 July 1974.

15. Hackworth, David H. "Last Taps for Fort Ord" *Newsweek,* 9 March 1992, p. 38.

16. "Thefts of U.S. Weapons Said to Benefit Terrorists" *New York Times* (New York, New York), 22 June 1981, p. 3.

17. "NYC police probe possibility that M-16 rifles..." *New York Times* (New York, New York), 1 December, 1971, p. 1.

18. "Security Devices Hinder Thefts At Many Armories" *Lincoln Star* (Lincoln, Nebraska), 8 July 1974.

19. "No Ties Suspected In Weapons Thefts" *Charleston Daily Mail* (Charleston, West Virginia), 6 September 1974.

20. Cook, Louise. "Most Armories Unguarded, Some Have Security Alarms" *Warren Times Observer* (Warren, Pennsylvania), 8 July 1974.

21. "Arms stolen at Armory" *Newport Daily News* (Newport, Rhode Island), 5 July 1974, p. 10.

22. "Rip-offs from U.S. Arms Stockpiles: Will it be an A-Bomb next?" *US News and World Report.* 1 March 1976, p. 22.

23. Tatro, Nick. "Patrols too costly, Alarm systems protect armories" *Syracuse Herald Journal* (Syracuse, New York), 8 July 1974, p. 17.

24. "Large Arms Supply Stolen From Guard" *Charleston Gazette* (Charleston, West Virginia), 6 September 1974.

25. Tatro, Nick. "Security Standards Vary At National Guard Armories" *Lima News* (Lima, Ohio), 9 July 1974.

26. "F-14 Brake Parts Stolen In Norfolk" *Richmond News Leader* (Richmond, Virginia), 13 February 1986, p. 19.

27. Abstract "Govt. witness scheduled to testify..." *New York Times* (New York, New York), 1 October 1972, p. 41.

28. Abstract "...National Guard spokesman says..." *New York Times* (New York, New York), 6 July 1974, p. 46.

29. Abstract "4 gunmen dressed in..." *New York Times* (New York, New York), 30 Nov 1971, p. 47.

30. "The State" Body: "Thieves cut through..." *Los Angeles Times* (Los Angeles, California), 11 March 1986, p. 2.

31. "Dateline: Boston." Body: "...theft of Small Arms..." *Reuters, Ltd* 15 May 1979, AM cycle.

32. "Dateline: Boston." Body: "...theft of Small Arms..." *Reuters, Ltd* 15 May 1979, AM cycle.

33. Abstract "Newburyport, Mass, armory heavily damaged by..." *New York Times* (New York, New York), 21 September 1970, p. 35.

34. Abstract "Natl Guard units in Ill..." *New York Times* (New York, New York), 9 September 1974, p. 32.

35. "Dateline: Honolulu" Body: "Machine guns, .45 caliber pistols..." *United Press International* 21 November 1981, PM cycle.

36. "Dateline: Fresno California". Body: "...Investigators looking into..." *United Press International* 31 August 1987, BC cycle.

37. "Dateline: Fresno California". Body: "...Investigators looking into..." *United Press International* 31 August 1987, BC cycle.

38. "Dateline: Fresno California". Body: "...Investigators looking into..." *United Press International* 31 August 1987, BC cycle.

39. Procari, Charles F. "National Guardsmen focus of federal probe into stolen weapons parts". *United Press International* 27 July 1989, BC cycle.